Vengeance Is Mine

A Novel

Pamela King Cable

In a world where over two billion people profess Christianity, I lost my religion before my twenty-eighth birthday. I had lived with fire and brimstone until it scorched and burned any spiritual covenant I had. The church destroyed my faith, deceived those I loved, and delivered me to the brink of destruction with no lifeline. Meeting my sin-sick soul head-on, I left the church in its entirety to find God. To this day, I cannot enter a house of worship without experiencing symptoms of PTSD. Though I found a new personal relationship with Jesus Christ, I don't belong in the evangelical community. I doubt I ever will.

— Pamela Cable

Televenge Trilogy:
TELEVENGE
AVENGE US ALL
VENGEANCE IS MINE

Other books by this author:

SOUTHERN FRIED WOMEN
A collection of short stories

THE SANCTUM
*A coming-of-age Southern tale dusted with magic
and set in a volatile time in America
when the winds of change begin to blow.*

Lynn Andreozzi ~ Many thanks for your incredible attention to detail and professionalism in designing the re-release covers of this trilogy. We are truly grateful.

Julie Murkette ~ Thank you, friend and mentor, for your tireless work in book design, and for your counsel. This trilogy would not have been possible without you.

For Michael, as always

Names of God

Adonai-Jehovah: The Lord Our Sovereign

El-Elyon: The Lord Most High

El-Olam: The Everlasting God

El-Shaddai:
The God Who Is Sufficient for the Needs of His People

Jehovah-Elohim: The Eternal Creator

Jehovah-Jireh: The Lord Our Provider

Jehovah-Nissi: The Lord Our Banner

Jehovah-Ropheka: The Lord Our Healer

Jehovah-Shalom: The Lord Our Peace

Jehovah-Tsidkenu: The Lord Our Righteousness

Jehova-Mekaddishkem: The Lord Our Sanctifer

Jehovah-Sabaoth: The Lord of Hosts

Jehovah-Shammah: The Lord is Present

Jehovah-Rohi: The Lord Our Shepherd

Jehovah-Hoseenu: The Lord Our Maker

Jehovah-Eloheenu: The Lord Our God

Beware of false prophets,
which come to you in sheep's clothing,
but inwardly they are ravening wolves.
Ye shall know them by their fruits…
Not everyone that saith unto me
Lord, Lord,
shall enter into the kingdom of heaven;
But he that doeth the will of my father
which is in heaven.
Many will say to me in that day,
Lord, Lord,
have we not prophesied
in thy name?
And in thy name have cast out devils?
And in thy name done many wonderful works?
And then will I profess unto them,
I never knew you.
Depart from me,
ye that work iniquity.
—Matthew 7:15-23 KJV

Dearly beloved, avenge not yourselves,
but rather give place unto wrath:
For it is written,
Vengeance is Mine;
I will repay, saith the Lord.
—Romans 12:19 KJV

We are each of us responsible
for the evil
we may have prevented.
—James Martineau

Out of suffering have emerged the strongest souls;
the most massive characters are seared with scars.
—Kahlil Gibran (1883-1931)

Someone rolled my injured, pregnant body into a room with bright lights suspended over me. Brilliant illumination that warmed and soothed my skin. I shook my head, remembering it was too soon; I had to wait for Mavis.

The surrounding glare and sounds of an emergency room faded as I fell into deep darkness, suddenly aware of hands motioning to me. Strong hands, large with square palms. They weren't Joe's, Daddy's, Coot's, or anyone's hands I recognized. Jesus? No. There were no scars on the palms. All I knew was that I needed those hands leading me deeper into unconsciousness, and as he reached for me, I saw he was missing the top of his left ring finger. Unafraid, I felt his hands touch my own, calming and gentle—the hands of a man I could not place.

But every dream must end, and every slumber has an awakening.

Chapter 1

BEHOLD, I STAND AT THE DOOR AND KNOCK
March 1993

ANDIE

Another night. The same old dream. The comforting hands that came as I gave birth to a baby I would never know, a child I would never raise. And then there were the nightmares: the sorrowful sound of the wind, the deafening roar of big city traffic, dense gray rain, a black car on shimmering pavement, the fear in Mavis's voice, a never-ending scream, children torn from their mother, men who preyed upon loneliness and stupidity, and endless phone calls from collection agencies.

Night terrors.

I awoke in tangled sheets, sweaty and alone. I should've known my dreams and nightmares would follow me to that place. In the daunting silence, I listened to every breath echo in the room, reminding me—I had a mission. And to stay alive a little while longer.

Still made of blood, muscle, and bone, I gathered my wits long enough to pull myself up and reach for my cup of warm Dr. Pepper, yearning for someone who loved me to empathize with my aging body. Exhausted after a fitful sleep, I thought how nice it would be to talk to another person—a steady, quiet, reassuring loved one—to share a recipe, discuss the weather, and chat about the latest styles. Conversations I once took for granted.

I sat in the muted morning sun and missed Dixie and Aunt Wy, longed for the swish of their clothes, the touch of their fingers on my forehead, in my hair. The faint scents of their perfume, the sheen of their clean skin, starkly contrasting my own. I closed my eyes and pictured their child-like grins, felt their sense of fun and play, and the comfort of their presence. Their existence remained only in my memory as I rested my head against the wall.

Shoving back the blue afghan that once belonged to Mavis, thankful the unfamiliar apartment had fallen silent, I didn't make a sound as I pulled on my wrinkled clothes. A bottle of shampoo, a bar of soap, toilet paper, a toothbrush, and a hairbrush sat in the bathroom. But makeup and clean clothes were a forgotten luxury.

I dispensed with a shower that morning, brushing my teeth, or looking at my hair. *Good enough.* I crawled off the mattress and walked through fly-plagued puddles of sunlight streaming through filthy windows and an ocean of dust.

The quiet morning diverged from the nighttime sounds of neighboring apartments. At night, I left the window air conditioner running for relief from the shouting, slamming doors, screaming kids, drunken adults, loud stereos, and TVs. Only early in the morning did the place fall into a silent stupor.

Pausing by the window, I strained my eyes to search for my car. I had parked behind the apartments next to a few mangled grocery carts stolen from a nearby Food Lion. The car would soon succumb to an ancient carburetor; I had no spare repair funds. The mechanic shook his head. "About a week, probably. It's hard to find anyone who still rebuilds these things. And a rebuild—it'll cost you."

I remembered my daddy working on his carburetor. "Runs like a champ," he'd say after he finished. I missed him. He'd fix my carburetor. He could fix anything except maybe my life. *Not that he didn't try.*

The same day I moved into the Magnolia Monarch apartment, I sold my Honda for next to nothing to a sixteen-year-old boy with a new driver's license. I knew the Reverend's goons would scour the city for my car. They would kill me if they found me. I'd given a false name to the landlord. When he asked for identification, I told him I'd lost my driver's license. He winked and said, "Okay. Whatever." Time to hide. Just a month. No more calls to Dixie and Aunt Wy.

In the end, an old Pontiac provided limited transportation. A mangled trunk lid, a half-dozen crimps here and there, and patches of rust on the doors. The beater car had started; one hundred dollars cash for the 1980 Bonneville with two hundred thousand miles. No title, no license plate. I didn't want one. Wouldn't need one. I'd go out and start it occasionally—take my chances and drive it once more to my rendezvous with *Reverend* Calvin Artury at Tanglewood Park on April sixth.

After brushing away dead flies and live spiders on the windowsill, I rested my chin on my arms and gazed at the forlorn car. My dreams had wholly unraveled and vanished. *Truth, Andie. Tell the truth.* Pushing past the panic in my throat, the truth came out, choking me. *The dream never began.*

My new residence sat unceremoniously in a field of weeds, where the sharps of thorn thickets and scrawny pines snagged plastic bags and wet newspaper. The low-income housing consisted of over fifty wood-clad apartments. The ones underneath, like mine, being the cheaper basement efficiencies. Weathered and neglected, the length of the two-story building was a faded relic of unfulfilled dreams. Its exterior had fallen in chunks, its doors gouged and stained from years of abuse. Laundry and plastic chairs bedecked the railings and balconies. Someone had forgotten to mow the lawns that had worn to a few stretches of weeds and dirt. In the front by the office, strewn with dead leaves, an in-ground pool had cracked and dried up, with somebody's old shoe thrown into the deep end.

I peered into the distance for the interstate truck stop. I'd surprised myself how easily I quit my job. Working afternoons and nights at The Pit Stop was no rewarding career, although it had fed me and kept me going. I didn't miss its searing whitewash of fluorescent lights and wary travelers with bloodshot eyes seeking gasoline, a restroom, and coffee. Like ghosts in the night, their origins and destinations were unknown. Some nights, it was as though the truck stop and I existed on an unmapped highway to immortality. At least until the sun rose.

Three more weeks of waiting. Waiting for my life's mission to begin and, thankfully, end. April sixth—a day of liberation. Every ounce of hope had faded to black. Hope for what? For Calvin Artury's plane to crash? For him to die of a heart attack? For another miserable soul to pull the trigger instead of me? I wouldn't last that long. My patience, along with everything else, had worn to a frazzle. I stared into the morning light. *Prison will be worth it to see him dead. The madness will stop.* "And my children will be safe," I said aloud.

I thought maybe I'd take a taxi to Tanglewood Park. The landlord could sell the old Pontiac with the busted carburetor to cover my electric bill. I'd leave Mavis's old blue afghan on the mattress for the next poor tenant and mail my photo albums to my attorney. I wouldn't need the memories anymore, or an attorney for that matter. I'd plead guilty with pleasure.

I opened my purse to check my cash. A twenty, two tens, a five, three ones, and some change—forty-nine dollars to last until

April sixth. I shoved the money back into the zippered pocket and collapsed to the mattress to nibble at a dry deli-case cheese sandwich for breakfast. My stomach was in no mood for it. I had lost my appetite. When—last week? Last year, maybe? I couldn't remember good food as I tossed the half-eaten sandwich into a cardboard box I used for garbage. Food sat like a rock inside me.

I'd quit smoking. There was no extra money for cigarettes, even cheap ones.

My photo albums lay open. A picture of Dillon in a football uniform stared at me, and I rubbed my thumb over it. An unknown donor from the school had paid the fees for his uniform. My heart ached so badly that I had to stand and catch my breath as if someone had dropped me into the deepest end of a lake and I needed to paddle quickly to the top. It was hard to believe God had blessed me with two beautiful children and then allowed them to be whisked away and put into Joe and Selma's care. Joe, a father who was never home, and Selma, of all people. Not much older than Dillon and Gracie. A woman who never bore children and didn't want mine.

I closed the drapes and took another deep breath. Glancing down at the albums again, I saw the old photo of Mavis and me when I was pregnant with the baby I never knew. Standing in the Baptist Church parking lot, our arms wrapped tight around each other, I'd been silly to think we'd grow old together. Another snapshot of the twins playing along a path at some playground I'd taken them to when they were little. *I had a family once.* Every picture was a loathsome reminder of my life and all that had happened. A reminder of how far Calvin Artury pushed a perfectly normal person to commit a totally irrational act. I sighed. My tears had abandoned me.

The sun had risen above the treetops behind the parking lot. I dreamed of stretching out in one of Maudy's redwood lounges, lifting my face to the sun, and making up the sleep I'd lost for the past fifteen years. Of course, my ex-mother-in-law had probably buried me by now. At least in her mind. Someone knocked on the door as I reached for my purse to gather change for vending machine coffee at the nearby gas station.

I glanced down at my wrinkled knit shorts and tank top, then up at the clock on the wall. Later than I thought. Already noon.

Insistent, whoever it was knocked again.

Confident I could defend myself, I pulled my loaded .380 automatic out of my purse and laid it on the bed. If I recognized anyone from the House of Praise, I'd not hesitate to use it. I'd also watched too many movies about drug addicts breaking into ghetto apartments in the middle of the day, or maybe it was a tenant who had watched me come and go, constantly alone. But fear had become as senseless as hope. *Might as well answer the door and let my attacker know I'm fully armed.* But I wasn't trigger-happy, either. I didn't want to shoot an innocent door-knocker, so I purposely left the gun on the mattress in plain sight and within easy reach.

"It's probably a Jehovah's Witness. Or the ghetto Avon lady," I mumbled. Leaning over the kitchenette sink, I peeked through dusty curtains covering the small window. I spotted a large, rusting, distant cousin to my own car. A relic from the era when mechanics knew how to fix carburetors. A nameless color, hubcaps lost in roadside history, and tires as slick as a baby's butt. Someone had parked parallel to the apartments; I couldn't see the license plate.

Moving to the door, I looked through the peephole. It gave me a mottled glimpse of a man with a well-trimmed beard hovering on the other side of the threshold. Few men at the House of Praise wore beards because Calvin didn't like them and had said so from the pulpit. In that respect, it was comforting to know he probably wasn't from the church. His image was blurred, and he seemed to be alone. Sucking in a deep breath, I refused to allow my past to infect my courage. I clicked open the deadbolt, cracking the door open slightly. A face emerged above the heavy chain lock secure in its holder, and I found myself speechless.

Tall with broad shoulders, he wore khaki shorts, a black polo shirt open at the throat, and held his sunglasses in his hand. His brown eyes with thick lashes stared directly into mine. His brow was wrinkled, but a trimmed mustache matched his close-cropped beard over a firm jaw. Hair as thick and wavy as mine appeared wind-mussed, but salt and pepper in color. He had dimples on both sides of his face you could fall into. Screwed in as firmly as bolts into a washer. His ruddy complexion shouted early forties, and he was trim but not skinny.

I'd never seen him before, but he smiled as if he knew me. Mind-numbingly handsome, my mind went blank. I opened my mouth to ask what he wanted, but all I managed was a squeaky, embarrassing, "Um, c-can I help you?"

"Yes," he said. Impossible as it seemed, his little off-kilter smile grew in intensity. "Marguerite Valdez?"

I tried to focus and not stare at his chest. I cleared my throat. "Who wants to know?"

"Sorry. I'm Matthew Callahan. A social worker for the county."

"So?"

"I'm looking for the Valdez family."

"They're not here, and I'm not her." I practically spat.

He nodded, his stare moving past me, over my head, and into the room behind me. I turned my head to follow his gaze. "I'm sorry, they gave me this apartment number," he said. "Do you know her or anyone who might know her?"

He'd seen the gun. I was sure of it.

"No. Try Mr. Gibbs, the landlord."

"I did. He told me she lived here. Obviously, he doesn't know who he's renting to."

"I think he's drunk half the time." Silence. "Is that all?"

He hesitated.

More silence.

As I stared at the man who called himself Matthew Callahan, I figured he probably had a wife who cheated on him, which meant either his wife was a looney tune or he was a rotten husband, like all the rest. Why would I think that? Not everyone cheats. At least I was still naïve enough to think so. *He's probably cheating on his wife with this Valdez woman.*

Strange, though. Although well-groomed, relaxed, and well-spoken with a hint of a southern accent, he didn't fit the car he drove. Of course, who would drive a nice car into a neighborhood where folks drank beer for breakfast? But didn't social workers travel in packs to the seedy side of town? The wolves who took my babies did.

"Sorry," I said. "I don't know this Valdez woman. You'll have to ask someone else. I hope you find her." The pitch in my voice could've chipped ice. He didn't look discouraged. In fact, he didn't look put off in the least.

He sighed instead and said, "Well. Since I can't find the Valdez family and I am a social worker, a traveling psychologist of sorts, do you want to talk about anything?"

Now I was positive he'd seen my gun. I stood there, waiting for him to leave, not knowing what to say.

"Can I show you my identification and credentials? It won't take long." Charming and undoubtedly friendly enough, he looked perfectly harmless. But then again, so had Jeffrey Dahmer.

"No. No thanks."

His disappointment showed across his face, but he didn't budge. He obviously didn't give up easily, and I admired that in a person.

"Look, ma'am," he said in a slow drawl, the steadiness in his voice some kind of anchor. "What's your name? At least tell me your name. I'm trying desperately here. You look like you have a lot on your mind. I see you've got a gun. Your apartment appears empty. What's it all about? I really don't want to call the police." He shoved his hands into his pockets.

My eyes turned to fire. "You have no right to come in here. None. No warrant, no reason. Mind your own damn business. There's no need to call the police. It's my gun. I have every right to own it. I have a permit. Go away!" I slammed the door in his face.

He yelled through the door. "Just talk to me!"

My back against the door, I heard him standing outside, shuffling his feet. Surely, he didn't think I would open my door to a total stranger, let alone a serial killer who eats his victims.

I watched him through the slit in the dusty curtains over the sink. When I didn't answer, his gaze drifted slowly to meet my eyes. "If you're planning a suicide," he yelled, "you'll do it with me banging on your door! Please," he said, "please talk to me."

Suicide? He thinks I'm suicidal? Lord knows I've fought a good fight to stay alive! How dare he! Yet the bleak hopelessness I'd felt at three a.m. had become a mood I couldn't shake.

I bolted to the bathroom. Wiping my forehead with a less-than-clean towel, I stopped to stare in the mirror at a stranger beneath wild-woman hair and sunken features. Gaunt eyes with dark circles stared back at me. I had been dying slowly, and it showed on my face like a lifetime of hard drinking.

I smoothed my hair behind my ears again, appalled at the lines on my forehead and the dirt under my nails. I'd not washed myself since—I couldn't remember. Looking down again at my torn and dirty clothes, I realized I hadn't eaten a balanced meal in what? Over a year? My skin was pulled tight, and I could count my ribs and see the hard curve of my hip bones. My belly caved in, and for the first time, my collarbone protruded.

What would it hurt to spend a few minutes listening to him make a fool of himself? Someone to talk to, at least. Something to do other than roam through photo albums, wondering how to stay sane while the past suffocated me. What would it hurt to talk?

I recalled the week after Joe finally left, trying to make an appointment with a professional Christian counselor. One whose advertisement in the phone book professed to *focus on your family*. His fee was one thousand dollars upfront. Neither family wanted to deal with my mistakes and problems or, God forbid, help me expose Calvin. Then, the local Assembly of God church heard of my struggles and brought a nice offering to the house. I was grateful, but all it did was pay a month's mortgage. Band-Aids covering wounds. That's all any well-meaning congregation, family member, or neighbor offered.

Nobody other than John Rossi wanted to sit down and really listen to me. Help me uncover Calvin for the demon he was. Everyone was afraid of him like I once was. The world had enough problems to care about mine. *So, why does this man on my doorstep want to talk to me out of the blue?*

I opened the door again to shoo him away like an annoying cat. "Git! Go on, go! And mind your own business!"

I watched him leave. *Good.*

A minute later, a tapping on the large window on the other side of the room startled me. He had walked to the parking lot on the east side of the building. *This guy doesn't give up!* I opened the drapes a little and shouted, "Go away! I swear I'll shoot you, drag you in here, and say you broke in!"

His eyes widened as I pointed my gun at his chest. I yelled louder. "Don't worry! I've shot no one who didn't deserve it!" He shook his head and silently walked away.

But in another moment, he was at my door again with a heavy dose of frustration. "I'm not leaving, ma'am. At least give me your name so I can tell the police who you are when you're dead!"

Again, I opened the door a crack, keeping it chained. "You don't give up, do you!?"

"You kidding? I'm an old mountain boy. I've been around guns all my life, but not a pretty lady wanting to use one on herself."

"What makes you think I'm suicidal? And don't call me pretty. You're wasting fancy words. For the love of God, go away! Leave me alone!" I leaned against the door and attempted to close it one more time.

But Matthew Callahan thrust his hands through the opening, holding the door ajar the four inches allowed by the chain, his fingers on the inside of the apartment. "Ma'am, I *do* love God, and I have a sixth sense when it comes to death," he said. "I see it all over your face."

I stepped back, my mouth wide open, staring at his hands. Where had I seen them? *Please, God, tell me where.* My mind moved at the speed of light to a bright hospital room, doctors and nurses whirling around me, a baby quiet inside my womb, my foot and head wounded, something placed on my face. I fell down a long, dark tunnel of sleep, reaching out to the strange hands. Hands that pulled me from the grip of death. Whose hands they belonged to and what the vision meant had not crossed my mind but a few times since losing my infant son. And yet, I never forgot them. Beautiful hands with a missing left ring finger. Missing down to the first knuckle—just like—the hands holding my door open at that moment.

Unconsciously, I touched the small scar on my forehead and stepped forward within inches of him. "My name is Andie Rose Oliver," I said softly. "May I see your identification?"

Shock showed on his face at my sudden change of heart. He reached for his wallet and patted his body. "Wait, wait right there. Don't close the door, please. It's in the car. I'll be right back."

In seconds, he returned and shoved his driver's license and business card through the opening. I glanced at them and unlatched the chain as if I'd lost all fear, unlike moments before. All trepidation was gone. I had no thoughts of leaving the door open for my safety, and I promptly closed it behind us as he stepped into the apartment.

His gaze sweep the length of my bare legs before it traveled slowly up to meet my eyes again. I motioned for him to have a seat. "I'd offer you coffee and Danish, but the maid took the day off. So, Mr. Callahan, why must you talk to me since you can't find your Valdez woman?"

He sat on the metal folding chair, the only chair in the apartment, leaned forward, and rested his elbows on his knees. "Please, call me Matthew. May I call you Andie?"

I nodded. Underneath Mavis's afghan, my gun lay on the sheet, loaded and ready.

He smiled his beautifully crooked smile again. "You might as well sit, too. Let's talk."

Chapter 2

A PLAN IN MOTION
March 1993

MATTHEW

I gave her my most charming smile. I had not expected this petite, ragged woman to open the door. Instead, I fully imagined she would tell me to buzz off, and I'd have to call for support on this unexpected fresh case. The top of her head barely came to my chin. But she was undeniably sensual and beautiful under the pain of her life. I plainly saw her distress. A woman in a wafer-thin white tank top and plaid shorts that were long overdue for the trash bin; she didn't seem to mind her appearance. Younger than me by maybe two or three years; it was hard to tell. My training and experience told me she was close to exhaustion and possibly a mental breakdown.

I took in the room and the odor of poverty. I had smelled it before. The tiny apartment, if you could call it that, was as bare as I suspected. Swatting flies away from my face and arms, I heaved a deep sigh at her living conditions. They moved me. And then I waited as she gave me another slow once-over, deciding I wasn't out to harm her.

I saw a metal chair and sat. She slid down the wall a few seconds later, landing on a filthy mattress opposite me. Her stringy shoulder-length hair moved every time she did. A slight smattering of golden freckles dusted the bridge of her nose. But her piercing pale blue eyes cut me to the quick. They sparkled with an unspoken challenge, daring me not to think about moving toward her.

She had positioned her gun under a blanket, close enough to grab if needed. Swiftly, I realized I'd broken all the rules, ignored my training, and lost control of my common sense. I'd never approached a person like her in possession of a gun. So why her? Why now?

I could not look away as she crossed her shapely legs and rested her small hands on her lap. Her hands. I stared at her hands and her ring. From the moment she opened the door, her expression remained guarded. There was an edge to her. But a glimpse of curiosity and a sudden flash of warmth in her eyes broke her definite distance.

I had honed my people skills until I thought I read most adults like a book. But Andie Oliver wasn't giving anything away. I wondered if she was naturally wary or if the harrowing life experiences I suspected she had made her that way.

She remained silent, patiently waiting for me to begin. I shifted and waited through her silence, glancing toward the parking lot, deciding how to launch into something that made sense to her. I wasn't exactly sure where to start or how to convince her I was there to help. She blinked, her eyes watery. I had to say something. I supposed the beginning was best.

"Until a couple years ago, I lived day to day. I lost my daughter, Jessie, to a childhood disease in 1987. She was ten. I live in the mountains northwest of here, and after Jessie died, I didn't leave my house much. But—after counseling and my mother kicking my ass out the door one day, I returned to work."

I cleared my throat and continued. "I'm a grief counselor. Do you know what that is, Andie?"

She shook her head and said nothing.

"I help people. Destitute and hurting people. Those who need someone to talk to when there's no one left. It's what I do. You could say it's my calling. I've made a good living and now pass on what the good Lord gave me. My ability to make a difference. If even for a moment."

I felt the pain of Jessie's death again, and it surprised me. The cold reality of my mother's words still lingered inside my head. My mother, Bobbie Sue. How I loved her. Assertive. A born leader. Larger-than-life.

New tears filled Andie's flashing eyes. "Tell me more," she said.

I smiled warmly at her and shifted again on the uncomfortable metal chair. "The last time I took Jessie to Baptist Hospital, her prognosis was six months. She lasted three weeks, which, in many ways, was a blessing." I looked away from her. Why was I telling her this? "My wife and I had divorced months before her death." I sighed and smiled again. "But Jessie—she was a fighter until the end."

It took me by surprise when she jumped into the conversation.

"I know what it feels like to lose a child." Andie began her life story, and as she talked, I realized she could not stop. A dam had burst, and from it flowed a flood of words that must have been stored for years in the reservoirs of her mind and heart. From front to back, cover to cover, unfolding the lies, deception, and horrors. Her ex-husband, Joe, and his cheating heart. Reverend Calvin Artury, whom I certainly knew of. She called his church a cult, and an organized crime ring, all in the name of the Lord. Artury the Godfather, Artury the control freak, Artury the pedophile. And she spoke about the murder of her childhood friend, Mavis.

"Artury gave the order. I can't prove it. But I'm sure of it. I just don't know who raped her, slit her throat," she said. Artury's men were looking for her. She mentioned that, too.

Andie rubbed her arms. She appeared hopeless and scared. But she wasn't crazy. I'd seen crazy, and Andie wasn't it. I believed her. The truth was in her eyes and voice.

"For a while, I thought I arrived at the bottom of my barrel because I fell from grace," she said. Her gaze went to the ceiling, away from me. "It wasn't that at all. It happened gradually. I've been numb with grief for years. Brian, that was my baby, Mavis, Rupert, then Daddy. My children. They took important people from me. It altered the course of my life. Before I knew it, an ocean of grief lapped at my feet. My existence became a blur of funerals, vegetable trays, condolence cards, and the stench of separation and death. I guess I'm not normal. When they took Dillon and Gracie, my belief in God and everything good toppled over in a gust of wind, like that fairytale house made of straw."

My heart went out to her. I looked around at the dark couple of rooms that smelled like decaying apples. I had to get her out of there. She didn't deserve this. The situation had emotionally drained the poor woman. I leaned back against the wall and slowly put my plan into motion.

ANDIE

He planted a seed of an unspoken alliance between us. In the few moments I knew him, I believed he was a man of feeling. One who had loved and had been loved. A man who had loved his child. I let down my guard a little but kept a few things to myself, especially John's murder. I was not ready to talk about every atrocity of my life. Especially with somebody I'd just met. I sensed he was intentionally kind and deliberately calm.

Telling my story had been painful and further exhausted me. I pressed my back against the wall and followed the line of his shoulders, the way his polo shirt clung to his veiny upper arms like a second skin. I imagined him as the outdoors type from his rugged appearance, deep tan, and the tiny creases at the corners of his eyes—probably from squinting in the sunlight. He filled the chair and made it seem small, like a child's chair. His gaze slid past me as he compassionately focused on the apartment's interior and my meager possessions. I had a feeling about how he looked at me, too, with unreserved and utter sympathy. To the point, I turned away from the raw emotion on his face.

Matthew Callahan wasn't like anyone I'd met. Yet, I had no precognition that a stranger—someone of his height, build, and good looks—would appear out of thin air and rescue me on a white horse. Joe had been handsome, too—way too handsome. I would never go down that road again.

Matthew

I stood, walked over, and leaned against the battered countertop in the kitchen area. It took only an instant to realize the place was truly empty.

"Is this everything you own?"

"You're looking at it. I gave away the rest. There was no reason to keep anything but what meant the most to me. I doubt they'll let me keep my photo albums in prison."

I stared at her, astonished by her remark.

She shot back. "Why do you think I have this gun? To go on a damn turkey shoot?" She bit at her tongue. I was sure she hadn't meant to give away her plans.

I sat in the chair again and planted my elbows on my knees. I threaded my fingers together and stared into her eyes. Amazed at myself, I believed every word she spoke. I'd heard wild and off-the-wall stories before. Many from women like her. But she was different. Because of the certain danger she was in, should anyone discover her whereabouts—I immediately made Andie my private concern. I would not report her to my department, which went against more rules, but I didn't trust everyone downtown. Andie needed protection, not exposure.

"I can help you."

"Help me how? Help me kill him?"

"No. Of course not. Help you put your life back together."

"Hmm. You feel that sorry for me? You a white knight or something?"

"No," I grinned at her quick wit. "It's like I said. God's been rather good to me. In return, I assist those who are truly in need."

"And I'm the neediest thing you've got going today, right? I mean, since you can't find your Valdez lady person, whoever she is. Your damsel in distress."

"Marguerite Valdez is an illegal alien. My department helped her get a green card to protect her five children from an abusive and alcoholic husband. She's thirty years old, but they say she looks sixty. I never met her. I heard she learned to speak English in a few months. I'm filling in for a friend who works in Forsyth County. The department head requested I look in on her on my way home. I am concerned she's not here. I'll have to call the county office and let them know. They'll start a search. With any luck, they'll find her alive and well and working at one of the local restaurants where she interviewed."

"Sorry." Andie lowered her head. "I forget there are others as miserable as me."

"Actually, few have lost it all. Marguerite still has her children. You're one of the few women I've met who found your 'barrel's bottom,' as you say."

"Thanks for pointing that out."

"It doesn't mean there's no hope."

I watched her tap her bare foot on the carpet. "I was full of hope once. Passed it out like candy from my pocket, Mavis used to say." She stiffened. "You're not looking at an innocent child on a cereal commercial. A missing person on a milk carton. You're dealing with a middle-aged woman with baggage. Lots of it." She shook her head. "Wait a minute. You don't even know me. Few have offered help unless there were strings attached and sex was involved."

"I'm here as a professional, Andie. I'm not here to solicit anything from you."

ANDIE

As he raised his brow at my comment, I almost laughed. "I'm sorry for my bluntness, but you need to know you'll usher in Armageddon if you go face-to-face with Calvin Artury."

"I've thought of it," he admitted.

"All of it?" I knew he did not know who he was dealing with. "He's dangerous and powerful. Most people wouldn't believe it."

He nodded. "I believe you. I've heard things." Matthew gave me a stern look and a heavy sigh. "I knew someone who attended service there."

"Yeah? Who?"

He shrugged. "A friend." He looked down at a picture of the twins I had forgotten to put back in the album. "Are those your children?"

"Yes. They're twins."

"They're beautiful."

"Yes. They are. Thank you."

"I've been fortunate. My children were loved and well cared for. My son, Conner, grew up happy and healthy. I hate to think of Artury molesting any child, a child I can rescue."

Our eyes met. "You have a son? How many children do you have?"

He leaned back and crossed his legs. Relaxed. It was as if we'd met in a hotel lobby and were simply chatting. "Only Conner. He's sixteen."

I sighed. *The same age as Dillon and Gracie.*

I saw his mind working. I doubted a man like Matthew Callahan had been celibate since his divorce. "How does your ex-wife feel about what you do? Where is your son?"

"My marriage lasted ten years. She got sick of living in the middle of God's half-acre and of me devoting tons of time to social work and other people's marriages. Too bad I couldn't save my own," he chuckled. "My son is a wonderful young man. He attends school in Boston. Brenda, who was my wife, moved back to her hometown and joined a golf league and a country club. Home for her was the ocean and tennis courts—Boston. She's a good mother; we wanted different things. When Jessie died, she'd had all the mountain air she could stand. Brenda took Conner and moved away. After Jessie and Conner were gone, I lost myself. But that's been said. My son visits me in the summer and on holidays. I've rebuilt my life to a degree of contentment. Now, like I said, I want to help others rebuild theirs. Someday, I'll start a camp for underprivileged kids."

There was something strangely refreshing in the voice of a man who loved his children. I reveled in it until it stirred up the thick, raw emotion in my heart I didn't want him to see.

MATTHEW

Concerned about how much I had revealed of myself to a stranger, I continued, nonetheless. "I listen to my gut. I want to make you an offer." Feeling myself blush again, I realized the sexual overtones of my statement. I shook my head. "No. Not that kind of offer. An honest and non-sexual job offer." And yet, despite my meaning, I felt a spark of sensuality. "I'm also a philanthropist, as my colleagues would say."

She scrunched her brows. "A what?"

I laughed. "Never mind. I anonymously seek out charities or deserving individuals. People who feed the homeless, foster children, and provide after-school care—those types of people. Individuals with a servant's heart or organizations whose sole purpose is to support their community. I've started a couple of foundations, and because I work from home, I need office help. Do you have any clerical skills? Can you type?"

She appeared shocked, but nodded.

"Good. I have an overburdened secretary, Ivy; she's been with me now; well, let's see, I guess since God was a boy. Poor thing. I work her hard, and she's pestering me for help. She's also my housekeeper and manages things when I'm gone. A sweetie, though. She and her husband, Tobias, own a house on the property. Tobias manages our few employees, the vineyard, the gardens, and the animals. I love dogs. Do you like dogs? Anyway, Ivy and my mother were roommates in college. I can't imagine life without them."

I stopped to take a breath. "Andie. Come and stay in one of the guest rooms in my house in West Jefferson. The house and property have been in my father's family for over a hundred years. I'll protect you. Artury will never know you're there. And here is something else to consider. I've got connections. I can't promise, but there's a chance I can make arrangements for you to see your children secretly until we can straighten this whole thing out." Rubbing the back of my neck, I watched her eyes, hoping I had assured her I'd do my best.

She stared back and stroked her throat. Concern flickered across her face, and her round eyes blinked. Tears filled the corners until they slid down her cheeks. She shivered but remained quiet.

I saw they had stressed her to the point of collapse. Only from careful observation of her countenance did I sense a cheated youth. An accumulation of endured hardships intended for a woman far surpassing her age. Her body and mind needed rest and someone to care about her. She needed a way out and a way back in if it made her feel more secure. I wanted to reach out to her, but stayed seated to avoid scaring her.

"Tell you what," I said. "If I can't help you, and you aren't healthy and on your way to wholeness after six months, I'll bring you back here, and you can finish your plan. I won't stop you." I said it, knowing I could make a difference. Bring back some of the happiness so many had robbed her of.

Until the day I met Andie, I'd made it my policy to steer clear of anything to do with a beautiful woman. It wasn't because I didn't possess self-control, but it had been ages since a woman landed on my romantic radar to any significant degree, and I didn't want my attention diverted from my work. Illegal aliens, parental abductions, domestic abuse and violence, custody battles—those were the cases I handled. Give me drunken parents to deal with, and I was in my element. But a woman like Andie? She didn't need to witness my heartache on top of her own. It all hit too close to home.

But I couldn't stop myself.

Her face reminded me of a porcelain doll, albeit a sad doll with a dirty face and neglected hair. She wouldn't have much to bring with her, which was good because I was sure it smelled like the inside of her apartment, the sour odor of unwashed clothes and overripe fruit. Smells she undoubtedly was used to.

"So, Andie. Will you help me? You can call the county, not give your name. They'll tell you all about me. I come with references," I said and smiled.

ANDIE

He has a vineyard and a housekeeper? Say no thanks and get him the hell out of here.

We sat in silence for some time while I processed his proposal and white-knuckled the mattress beneath me. And then, after a deep breath, I took another run at him. "I've seen things go bad with opposing Calvin on any level," I warned. Compelled to be honest, I had to ensure he knew what he was in for. "This isn't the movies. Not everyone ends up happy." I also hated getting caught up in anything I'd regret. Falling victim to an abusive lifestyle with someone I foolishly trusted would end me.

But then I looked at his hands again, and an incredible amount of peace flooded my heart.

Still. Did he really need my typing skills? Countless qualified typists would happily take his money—and stay in his guest room. He could probably nail Calvin all by himself if he knew where to look, who to talk to, and had the patience—and the balls. Nobody ever had the balls to go up against the illustrious *Reverend*.

"You can do this yourself," I suggested. "You can track down the people who know all about him. I'll even give you the evidence in my bank lockbox."

Matthew shook his head. "It's not that easy. These things take time. It's taken him years to drive you to this point. I can't devote *round-the-clock* effort to this in the immediate future. However, by working together steadily, we could put him behind bars. In the meantime, we will work on getting your children back."

I smiled when he mentioned my children again. "Where did you say you live?"

"On a farm in the Blue Ridge, near West Jefferson. I, uh, own property all over the state." He coughed. "My, uh, my work keeps Ivy and me busy. Believe it or not, it can be overwhelming. The paperwork is endless. So," he shrugged again, "I'm eager to get started. You help me, I'll work for you. What do you say?"

"If you end up slitting my throat, I'll come back and haunt you. But—I believe you. I—I've seen your hands before."

"My hands?" He smiled with candor, but I didn't return the smile.

"Yes. It's the only reason I let you in here."

He smiled again, anyway. A slow smile that stirred my emotions. Emotions, I forgot I had. Matthew Callahan, my knight in shining armor. Possibly.

Oh, I was quite aware of his handsome face as I tried to ignore the warnings, and yet my heart let me know I was still a woman despite my rotten life.

I felt myself grinding my teeth, vacillating, hesitant, and searching for words to discourage him from taking my case. He needed to look elsewhere if he wanted something besides my typing skills.

"And another thing, it's been a while since I've typed anything," I said.

His eye-crinkling smile deepened. A smile that turned men like *Clint Eastwood* and *Sean Connery* into Hollywood legends. "No problem. I'll give you a refresher course," he said.

I rubbed at the scar on my foot, reminding myself of the night I first saw his hands. Only his professed desire to help me get my kids back finally moved me to take him up on his offer. That and the sun beating bright in the sky like a fiery-hot heart. Or perhaps it was because I heard birds sing for the first time in a long while. Then again, maybe it was simply the thought of the mountains. A place Daddy loved. Or possibly the echo of Mavis's words suddenly ringing in my ears: *That's your answer, Andie. Unconditional love.* In the end, I'm not sure why, exactly, I went with him. I wasn't used to anyone wanting to help me. Not like that. And I wished his eyes weren't shining with as much unrelenting hope as they were warmth.

"You ever type on a computer?" he asked.

I shook my head. "Nope. But I can learn. And please don't worry; if we uncover that ministry for what it truly is, it won't even take a month to turn my life around. I'll be out of your hair in no time, and Calvin will eat his last meal on death row. Hopefully." Standing to brush off my clothes, I felt the embarrassment of my appearance. "I must look awful."

"You're fine," he said. "A little worn around the edges, but fine." He was being kind.

I rolled my eyes at him. "No one has ever cared enough to listen to me. I've trusted no one with everything I know. It is dangerous. I wasn't kidding when I said they were looking for me. You're absolutely positive you want to tackle this?" Silently, I asked myself the same question.

"I've never been more sure of anything in my life," he said.

I wished I could've said the same.

"Let's gather your things," he said.

"Did I say I'd go with you?"

"You didn't say you wouldn't."

I laughed. "I need a shower first. And a cup of coffee in the worst way."

"But will you take my offer and stay in my guest room? I'm not asking for a lifetime commitment."

I saw him wince. "Against my better judgment, yes, I'll go with you. A commitment? I'll never give you one."

"Fair enough."

I looked at his left hand with the missing finger, my hoped-for confirmation that God had sent him. I didn't want to get wrapped up in his needs and wants. No doubt, few women turned him down. I'd learned my lessons about men. When protecting my heart, I was tough as a rump roast from an old cow.

"I call all the shots when it comes to Calvin."

"Right. You're the boss," he said. "You know him best."

"Unfortunately, I do. But before we go, I'd like to talk about wages. I didn't give Mr. Gibbs a deposit for my electricity with my first week's rent. And next week, I've got to pay the bank for my lockbox."

"How does a thousand a week sound?" His somber look told me he had no second thoughts about his offer.

I nearly swallowed my tongue. "You serious?"

"Of course. Are you thinking more?"

"Now, I'm not complaining, but damn, that's a lot of money. Joe and I didn't make that kind of money together in the seventeen years we were married. I'm not afraid of hard work, but is this a sixty-hour-a-week job?"

Matthew piled my photograph albums together. "You drive a hard bargain. Listen, you've had the weight of the world on your shoulders. How about you get rested first and take a few days off from all that worry? We'll talk about wages later." He winked. "And as for sending money to pay for your lockbox, I will ensure it's paid in advance. I don't want any ties back to you."

I nodded in slow agreement.

To be safe, I shuffled into the bathroom with my gun and purse, then gathered my few toiletries before stepping into a hot shower. *Am I dreaming? Will he be gone when I come out?*

"I'm going after coffee," Matthew hollered. "How do you like it?"

"With cream," I yelled back. I stuck my head out of the shower to see his reflection in the mirror over the sink and caught him smiling.

"I think I can handle that. From now on, I'll remember how you like your coffee."

That's what I'm afraid of.

∞

True to his word, Matthew had two Styrofoam cups of coffee waiting after I showered and changed into a semi-clean blue denim skirt and a white T-shirt. He'd dug up a donut somewhere, too. Flicking a fly off my cup, I took a sip, then picked up a plastic grocery bag while staring at the donut like I'd never seen one before.

"Let me." Matthew reached across me and took the bag to finish gathering my things. The soft scratch of his beard brushed against my temple, and his warm breath passed by my cheek.

With both hands, I grabbed the donut as if grabbing a lifeline. I think my desperation shocked him. "Mmm. Tastes good. Thanks for this." I stared into my cup. *Get a grip, Andie.*

"You're welcome. I stopped by the office, paid your electric bill, and told the manager that the woman in apartment 12 was vacating today. I assumed you used another name. You're supposed to drop off your key." He folded the blue afghan and held it under his left arm, then lifted my stack of photo albums and Daddy's old Bible with his right. "Take your bag of clothes and toiletries there, and let's go."

Matthew's generosity astounded me. I looked around the stark room, collected my gun and purse, and left the sheets and mattress on the floor for the next poor tenant. This was my last chance, or I was a lamb being led to the slaughter. But I was too tired to care. Any way I sliced it, my decision to go with him was one last risk I would take.

"Oh, wait. What about my car?" I walked to the window and pointed it out to him.

"Do you care?"

I giggled. "No. I'll leave the key in it."

"Is it titled to you?"

"No, I bought it off an old geezer who couldn't find the title. He said if I fixed the flat, gave him a hundred dollars, and got it off his property, he'd give it to me. So I did."

Matthew laughed. "You're quite resourceful. Leave it here. They won't be able to trace it back to you since there was no title transfer."

With my hair still wet from my shower, I took a deep breath and picked up my plastic bag full of stuff I should've left behind. "I'm ready." I inhaled his clean, masculine scent. It had been too long since I'd been near a nice man, let alone smelled one. If he noticed my discomfort, he didn't let on.

Matthew opened the door. "Two hours ago, I thought I would lose you to that gun in your purse. Don't worry, Andie. This is a straightforward decision you're making. You need time, patience, rest, and access to the right people. You've never had the right people to help you nail this guy."

Intending to walk out the door behind him, I gasped as he held the door wide to let me go first. He followed me into the light. I stood blinking momentarily, staring through bright sunlight like someone had trapped me in a cave for months.

After I placed my meager belongings in the back seat, Matthew opened the passenger door for me. He then reached for my hand, gently squeezed it, and said, "Today, Andie Oliver. Today, your life has turned around. I promise."

Chapter 3

SHILOH

March 1993

ANDIE

Beneath his hand, I felt his strength and heartbeat. I kept telling myself it had to be real. Traveling to Matthew's home was the emotional experience of an unexpected blessing of profound significance. A premonition of good things to come. A dream. God had been silent for so long. "Please let this be real," I whispered.

The wipers waged a losing battle against a sudden spring rain as Matthew drove the Blue Ridge Parkway and then turned onto Route 16. To my left, the reflection of storm clouds on a gray-blue lake held me captive. Other than my experience at Mavis's grave, I hadn't bothered to look at the sky the past few months, and I watched the rain as if it were the first time I'd seen it. Well-kept farms, soaring trees, and lush landscapes dotted the hills and valleys. A few people had built their log homes high on mountain ledges to enjoy the full effect of the surrounding panorama.

"My farm is special, and we're almost there," said Matthew.

"How many acres is it?" I asked, recalling the beauty of Byron Stewart's fifty-acre horse farm.

Matthew cleared his throat. "I think the last surveyor said it was around a thousand."

I swallowed hard. "Oh."

We rode the rest of the way in silence.

Finally, Matthew grinned and patted the dashboard, as if thanking his old car for the ride. "It's over the next ridge. You can see they recently widened this road. Road crews cut out some of the mountain. It needs to heal before it looks good again."

I compared myself to the wounded road. I'd been scraped and cut, parts of my soul dug out and hauled away. I'd never be the same, like the road. And it'd take some time to heal before I looked good again. Just like the road.

Matthew turned the car onto a narrow two-lane drive. Winding up a steep mountain slope, the road ended at wrought-iron gates with a prominent C scrolled on the front. I looked at him.

"For Callahan," he said and smiled. Above the C, someone had attached the word *Shiloh* to an arch between stone pillars marking the entrance to a gravel road. As Matthew drove, the tires picked up tiny stones and pitted them against the underside of the ancient car, sounding like popcorn in a hot skillet.

Relief washed over me as I gazed out my window in awe. We entered an avenue of immense trees, tall pine, and oak, great straight trunks thrusting up through a shadowy canopy of green into the sky. The trees gave way to a meadow far to the right, where a stout white house stood in the middle. A picket fence surrounded the house like a sash on a dress. The two stories sparkled in a sudden burst of sunshine. I blinked, imagining great southern ladies and gentlemen calling it home in the years before the War of Northern Aggression, as Joe had called that war.

"Your home—it's beautiful! Quite the house! It's familiar to me, somehow."

"Yeah?" Matthew laughed. "That's not my house. That's where Ivy and Tobias live. My ancestors built that house in 1803."

"Oh, my. It's lovely. But it couldn't be familiar, could it? I've never been here before."

"Déjà vu," Matthew said with a chuckle. That's what Ivy would say. It's certainly not the sort of house you would mistake for another."

I pointed ahead. "You've got a barn. A nice one."

"You know about barns?"

"My sister-in-law, Libby. She lived on her uncle's horse farm for a while. I loved the barn."

"I built that one. Well, I helped. It was Tobias's design; he built it. Tobias and Ivy have lived in that house we passed since we moved to this place. Both houses share access to the property, including the barn and outbuildings." Matthew's voice, peaceful and calming, affected me like a drug.

My eyes grew heavy, and I longed for sleep. "Is this a road or a driveway? It seems to go on forever."

"It's a private drive. I have a crew that maintains it in the winter."

We rode to the meadow's farthest point and into a clearing, ending at a parking area designated by several neatly placed boulders between the gravel drive and pale-green piney woods. Debris and fallen leaves from the storm covered the area. I studied the parked cars through the rain-streaked windshield. In front of an extended garage with several doors sat a dented Jeep, a large pickup truck in decent condition, and a tiny red sports car that appeared new.

"I could've driven us straight to the front porch, but I want to leave this junker car here. I use it when traveling to rough neighborhoods. We'll walk up to the house. In case you're wondering, the Jeep is mine. It's great to drive around the farm. The truck belongs to Tobias, and I bought Ivy the red car last year for her sixty-fifth birthday."

"She drives a car like that?"

"When you meet her, you'll understand."

"Let me get your door for you." Matthew swung open the driver's door and unfolded his muscular frame from the car. He ran around to my side, opening my door wide again. I grabbed my purse and climbed out, stunned by his manners. We strolled up the wide flagstone walkway, breathing the cool air blowing down from the mountains. It was so clean and exhilarating, layered with the spice of a freshly washed forest and its sweet decaying soil.

"Damn, it's quiet here," I said.

"Yes, isn't it peaceful? This farm is the craziest place you've ever seen. Folks in Ashe County still call it the Christmas Tree Ranch; you'll see the trees in the back. It was once part of an even larger estate. The house was not in the best condition when I took it over. My dad leased out the farm until the renters passed on. I've spent the better part of the past fifteen years restoring it. I named this land Shiloh."

"I noticed the name on the gate. Does it mean something?"

"Shiloh is Hebrew for *a place of peace*. My great-great-grandfather fought and died for the Confederates at the Battle of Shiloh on April 6, 1862. He's buried here on the property. He fought against a brother in that same battle, who they also buried here. I'm a Civil War enthusiast. There's a good-sized cemetery on the property. I'll rest there someday," he said and smiled.

The word Shiloh and its meaning surged through me like an electric current, along with the date of April sixth. The day I had planned to murder Calvin. There were too many coincidences.

The flagstone turned into a short brick path as we passed through an arch of twisted wisteria cascading over a white trellis. I saw a clearing ahead and held my breath as the house came into view.

"Magnificent." The word bubbled from my lips as the enormity of the structure sent chills to my hairline. Though it sat half-hidden in its cloak of woods, I felt my knees weaken. A turn-of-the-century rural manor mansion, mixing various styles that somehow flattered one another. White clapboard siding, iconic columns, gingerbread gables, quaint dormer windows, a wide wraparound porch, and enormous stained-glass windows lovingly placed in carved oak front doors—I could have stared at the doors for the rest of the afternoon, admiring the tiny bits of glass sparkling in the sunlight.

Various trees leaned in and around the house, which someone painted a soft, almost buttery white. The shutters, a glossy black, contrasted nicely. Dark green ivy shrouded parts of the front, giving it a rich antebellum appearance. One giant black oak curled up from the ground, arching over a corner window while clematis tangled around the front porch posts. It reminded me of Gracie hiding beneath her messy Saturday morning hair. Though not yet in bloom, rose bushes and azaleas gracefully accented the flower beds and a stone fountain on the front lawn. The surrounding grounds stretched out like a five-star golf course.

"Tobias is particular about the grounds. I couldn't do this without him," Matthew said.

Climbing the front porch steps, I turned around to drink in the beauty of the rolling farm. Words, I—I had none. Every adjective I ever knew escaped me.

The covered entrance was partially screened, breezy, and wide. Someone had tucked plush accent pillows in garnets and blues against the back of a wicker porch swing and nearby similar white chairs. I walked to the far end of the porch and leaned over the railing until I saw the cottage we had passed by only moments before. I had thought it enormous when I first saw it, but it seemed like a child's playhouse compared to Matthew's mansion.

Suddenly, four barking dogs bounded up the steps to greet their master.

"Andie, come meet the Hounds of the Baskervilles," Matthew shouted, pointing to each dog. "Cookie, Max, Buddy, and Sissy." Their relentless barking and tail-wagging made me giggle. "They'll settle in a minute," he said.

Matthew whistled and shouted, "And last but not least, there's my special dog. The only dog allowed in the house. She's been with me for years. This is Sadie, my Golden. She was my daughter's dog as a pup. She's the queen of dogs. Say hello, Sadie."

"They're all great. Where do they stay if not in the house?"

"We built a large kennel behind the barn. The dogs are free to roam the farm most of the time. They're actually well-behaved unless they meet someone for the first time. From now on, they'll just nod and say hello."

After I gave each a quick rub behind their ears, I followed Matthew through the front doors. I stood in an immense foyer of polished floors, gleaming walls, and a perfect marble-topped table with an ornate gilded mirror hanging above it. Warm and dimly lit, someone had papered the foyer walls in a delicate rose and vine pattern. Large antique frames with oil landscapes hung on the walls. Fresh flowers accented tiger oak sideboards. Deep crown moldings separated the walls from the creamy-white ceilings, and a gentle wind blew in through the screen doors behind us, along with the scent of warm rain and the sound of barking dogs in the yard.

Scents of freshly baked apple pie and a rich, aromatic coffee suddenly swirled around our heads as we walked farther inside, the hardwood creaking beneath my feet like an old familiar song. The house oozed with history like old houses do; a grandfather clock chimed the hour in a nearby room. Large double doors trimmed with wider moldings led to rooms on either side of the entryway. Far beyond the staircase on the ground floor, the hall extended to what I assumed to be the dining and kitchen areas.

The foyer was grand pand imposing, with a high ceiling and a chandelier that sparkled like a thousand stars. I admired the generous staircase, its steps wide and inviting, curving gracefully up to the second floor. It was like something out of *Gone with the*

Wind, with a banister intricately carved, and elegant spindles that seemed to whisper tales of the past.

If Matthew had listened closely, he would've heard my jaw dropping.

"I thought Daddy's house was big," I said. "But this—this is something people would pay good money to see." I tried not to call attention to the excitement inside me, but I wasn't doing a good job of it.

It was an impressive piece of history, but as I looked around again, the feeling I had made a mistake fell on me like a cannonball. Until that morning, my life had spiraled slowly to Hell. It was too drastic a change in such a short time. Skepticism reared its ugly head again, and I started imagining the real reasons behind Matthew's kindness. The deep emotional sensuality of meeting him earlier that day gave way to concerns calling me from a place more familiar.

But then we walked into the kitchen. A kitchen like none I had ever seen. The recognizable aroma of cinnamon and butter greeted me like old friends. I would've been as proud as a blue-ribbon pie winner to have had a kitchen like that.

Pies and what looked like biscuits cooled on the counter; a fire burned under a large pot that smelled like chicken soup. As I tiptoed around the fairytale kitchen, Matthew's assistant, Ivy, floated in from a nearby pantry like *Glinda, the Good Witch of the North*, drifting into Munchkin land. I wasn't in Kansas anymore. Or rather, my tattered black-and-white life.

PAMELA KING CABLE

Chapter 4

Ivy and Tobias
March 1993

Andie

Ivy's high, exotic cheekbones emphasized her pleasant smile and slightly crooked teeth. A lovely Black woman with toffee-brown skin and few lines, Ivy emitted a richness born to few women. The sunlight through the windows caught the sparkle of diamonds on her fingers and around her neck. Her dark sapphire eyes flickered like her jewelry; I had never seen eyes like Ivy's. I had also never seen a pierced nose on a woman her age. A tiny diamond in her right nostril twinkled, and I had to stop myself from staring at it.

Her delicate, friendly face conveyed kindness and warmth. But her eyelids were enormous: great coffee-colored canopies fringed with dense, dark lashes, nearly as long as Tammy Faye Bakker's, only more natural-looking.

"Andie Oliver," said Matthew. "I'd like you to meet my dear friend, Ivy Dumass."

I froze. My feet had glued themselves to the floor. My mouth went dry, and my tongue was numb as Ivy extended her hand.

"I'm so pleased to meet you," she said. "Matthew phoned ahead, a consideration he rarely bestows on me. Told me you were on your way." Ivy shook my hand and then lightly kissed my cheek. "Please excuse the mess; I'm baking today."

"I—I'm sorry. I'm not sure I heard your last name correctly. D-u-m-a-s-s, Dumass?"

"Dumass is my married name. My maiden name was Boudreaux. *My* people are from Louisiana. You know the Dumass name, Andie?"

"Yes." I looked at Matthew. "Mavis. Her last name was Dumass."

Matthew turned to Ivy. "Any relation to a Dumass family in Winston-Salem?"

"Could be. Ask Tobias. He's the one from North Carolina."

From her mannerisms and speech, I presumed she was an educated woman. And then I remembered Matthew had said she was his mother's roommate in college. Ivy's constant and intoxicating smile switched off my panic button. I became unusually calm, as if watching our conversation from a distance.

She wasn't the typically dressed Black woman in North Carolina. An orange swirl of beaded earrings dangled two inches from the bottom of each earlobe, gracing the length of her neck. Adorned in Egyptian hieroglyphic print, Ivy's silk dress was more like a loose shift. A rainbow of colors. The dress reminded me of the Peter Max psychedelic posters I pinned on my bedroom wall as a teenager. Mavis would've loved her. A matching turban covered her head. Little tufts of Brillo-pad-gray poked out at the back and at her forehead. She was a song in motion.

"Oh! I love your earrings," she said. Then she stretched out her arm like a child and softly fingered my earlobes. "They're so pretty! Where did you get them?" Ivy's accent was a mixture of many, it seemed, and the whiteness of her teeth dazzled under full lips that broke into yet another leisurely smile.

I reached up with my right hand to feel my small gold hoops and noticed Ivy's expression change, staring at the mother/child ring on my finger. "I forgot I had these on. They were my mother's; she gave them to me years ago. I'm afraid they're the only earrings I own now."

But there went Ivy's smile again, more significant than before. She motioned for Matthew and me to follow her. "Come, let's get comfortable." She led us through the arched doorway into a large room with tall windows, lavish moldings, exquisite light fixtures, and high-coved ceilings of smooth white plaster. Beautiful wool area rugs sprawled beneath my feet.

"You've got a parlor!" I declared.

With a gesture of graciousness, Matthew laughed softly. "Kind of. It's my office. I spend most of my time in here."

To rest in such a room, in front of a snapping fire with vibrant colors of reds and golds, suddenly was all I wanted to do. On the wall, a series of small paintings drew my eye.

Ivy noticed. "Matthew showcased his collection of the Civil War artist *John Adams Elder* in here. Better light, you know. Much better light. Glorious battle scenes. Matthew says, and I agree, they're too controversial for other rooms in the house."

Cherrywood bookcases ran the room's length, filled with old and new books, potted plants in blue and white vases, gardening catalogs, and a collection of antique glassware. The parlor simply reached out and hugged me. Two leather sofas faced each other. An old traveling chest sat between them as a coffee table. Staring at the tobacco-brown sofas draped with soft plaid throws, I again imagined myself napping there, warmed in winter by a blazing fire. Or reading a novel on one of the high-back chairs with delicately embroidered fabric.

I gazed upward at an elaborately carved plaque hanging over the stone fireplace: *The Pioneer's Creed: The Cowards Never Started. The Weak Died Along the Way. Only the Strong Survived.* I had to be dreaming all of this.

Covered in white plantation shutters, the large windows appeared new. I walked to a window and moved the shutter aside. "Please forgive me; I'd love to see everything in the evening light."

"As long as you don't look at the dust. Matthew doesn't like me to clean around him when he works," Ivy said, raising her eyebrows.

Immediately, the light purpled and softened the room, growing warm and rich in hues of earth and fire as the sun set over the mountain.

I can always tell when Ivy's been in here," Matthew replied. "She arranges all my work in neat little piles, and I can't find zilch. I'm the guy who keeps things forever. I have problems getting rid of my shit."

"Matthew!" Ivy said in mock disgust.

And then, without a speck of warning, I wept. Overcome with fear and missing my children, I whirled around to face Matthew. "I shouldn't have come; I don't want to endanger any of you. I don't belong here."

Softly, he placed his hand on my shoulder. "And you don't belong in jail or dead, which is exactly where you'd end up if you weren't here with us. Please, Andie. You're safe here. Think about my offer." He stuck his hand in his back pocket and pulled out a cotton monogrammed handkerchief. Handing it to me, I touched the fingers of his left hand. Composing myself, I felt the strange peace I'd felt hours before, and I sighed deeply, hoping to calm the fear that followed me there.

"Pie and coffee?" Ivy suggested, attempting to brighten the mood.

While we waited for Ivy's pie, Matthew sat at his desk to attend to a few matters. He told me to wander through the house and holler if I got lost.

Awed by the old mansion's magnificence, I meandered from room to room, following its woodsy aroma. Everywhere I looked, grand and stately antiques stood in corners or sat on shelves.

Antiques like Dixie never had. The upstairs hallway, decorated with more exquisite paintings and Persian runners, stretched the length of the house.

The first bedroom I came to surprised me with a large white wicker birdcage and two yellow canaries that matched the lemon and white magnolia wallpaper, coordinated bedspread, and window treatments. *Laura Ashley*. I'd seen the print in magazines and remembered drooling over it. Finials carved in pinecone shapes adorned the ends of the curtain rods. Someone had placed a lovely antique four-poster bed opposite a working fireplace. Rolled quilts filled a nearby basket like a pile of logs. Someone had laid embroidered blankets with a freshly laundered scent at the end of the bed. A primitive table on four straight legs stood in the curved bay window. I peeked out the window at shades of purple, yellow, and coral pansies surrounding the neck of Matthew's property like a tropical lei. Ivy's white house appeared in the meadow through the branches of the black oak.

"This is your room."

I jumped. It was Ivy, wearing another gracious smile. "Sorry, Andie. I must remember to let you know when I'm behind you. Matthew gets so upset when I sneak up on him."

"It's okay. I'm a bit jumpy these days." I ran my hand across the side of the bed, feeling the softness of the down comforter. "This room is lovely. I'm not sure I'll be able to sleep in here after what I've been sleeping in."

"Don't be silly. It's just a room. May I be so bold to say Matthew is a knight in shining armor? You'll be fine now. Leave the rest to him. He'll work it out, whatever you've been through."

How did she know that's what I called him? "He's done this for other women? Bring them here, I mean."

"No. Never. He surprised me when he telephoned to say he was coming home with a visitor. And I was worried." Ivy smiled and looked away. "He invites few people to Shiloh. Matthew keeps his distance from the public unless he's working on a case. I say the man is too busy taking care of everybody else. He forgets he has needs, too." Ivy prepared the room for my stay. "It's been all business for him," she said, her smile unceasing. "I've never quite seen him like this, though. You are a mystery, Andie. A mystery for sure." Ivy cupped the side of my face with her soft hand. "But my spirit is at peace. I'm glad he brought you to this place."

I returned her smile. "Are you a woman of faith, Ivy?"

Ivy turned down my bed and took two plush yellow towels out of an armoire, placing them in the adjoining bathroom. "Many faiths. My mother raised me in the bayou. Born in Tammany Parish, I was. My grandmother practiced voodoo, but my father, now there, was a beautiful man. Father was of the Baptist faith. You can imagine the turmoil in our family. After my mother died, my father, a white man, mixed actually but looked white—a college professor, a fine, muscular man of character fit for presidents and kings—took me with him. Schooled in Paris and London until his death, I lived in both cities."

Ivy pulled a basket of bath soaps and shampoos from a small closet. "Then I returned to the States to finish my doctorate at Harvard, where I met Matthew's mother, Bobbie. She was at seminary. We became the closest of friends. And, of course, at Harvard, I met Tobias. We fell in love and worked hard for Doctor King during The Movement. Later, we moved south because I wanted to live near my friend Bobbie. My Tobias, he was fine with that. He would have followed me to the Amazon if he had to. He's from here, anyway. As a registered midwife, I delivered Matthew and his siblings."

"How wonderful," I said. In two brief minutes, she had offered me her entire life story.

Ivy sighed, though still smiling. "One day, over fifteen years ago, Matthew asked us to help him with a benefit for cancer research. The three of us have been together since."

"You said something about Matthew's mother in seminary?"

"Yes, she's a pastor. Hasn't he told you?"

I laughed. "I'm sure he was afraid to. I probably wouldn't have come with him."

"Not to worry, Andie. Pastor Bobbie is a precious woman. She's a country lady who preaches in a little holiness church in Valle Crucis, with a white steeple and everything. You'll never see her on TV."

"Good," I answered quickly, then shook my head. *Why would she tell me that?*

Ivy moved gracefully about the room as if her feet hovered above the floor. *Had Matthew told her about Calvin?* She seemed to know everything about me.

"My, I've been rattling on so. Coffee's ready; want some?"

Staring at her, I saw Mavis. She was Mavis at sixty-five. The physical resemblance was strong. Maybe because I wanted it to be. But their personalities were so similar I suddenly knew why I felt instantly at home with people I'd met only hours before.

❧

"This is way beyond what I envisioned," I told Matthew, walking into his office.

"It takes a staff to clean it, too," said Ivy. "I don't have the time. I'm afraid that assisting Matthew and his charities consumes most of my day."

"I can't imagine why," Matthew murmured.

"How can I help?" I asked.

"What do you think, Ivy? Andie can type and file for you. I'd like to give her a job while she's here."

"I've only been after you to get me some help for the past two years. She can start tomorrow. We have the Governor's Ball coming up. I need help with the menu."

"I'm a decent cook," I said. "I used to own a restaurant. Well. A little cafeteria, really." I lowered my eyes, humble and somewhat embarrassed about my homespun culinary skills. I figured pinto beans and cornbread were far beneath what these people were used to.

"You don't have to cook for this ball, Andie. But I would love your help in planning it. And praise be to Jesus," Ivy said. "If you can cook, I'd love you to do some of that around here. Wouldn't we, Matthew? I'd love a big pot of pinto beans!" Ivy cocked an eyebrow and grinned.

Matthew's eyes lit up. "Ah, Tobias. There you are."

"Mattie, we have a guest, no?"

"Yes, come meet Andie Oliver, my friend. Andie, don't let him fool you. When talking with me, Tobias reverts to his North Carolina farm-boy dialect. He was only educated in the North, where he says he lost his southern twang."

Tobias shot him a smile and an expression of devotion. "Nice to meet you, Andie. Such a pleasure. Whatever we can do to make your stay with us pleasant, please speak up."

I nodded and smiled. I thought only high-class hotels said stuff like that. As I noticed his pants that didn't fit, he spoke to me like talking to a small child, soft with a touch of sweetness. His hair glistened in the light, the color of table salt, cut so short his scalp showed at the crown, and his steel-rimmed eyeglasses slipped down his nose. A khaki shirt and scuffed brown boots made him appear free of the cares most live by. His disheveled style was endearing, another sign he didn't give two hoots for refinement. And yet, the glint of a diamond shone in his right earlobe, and I suspected he cleaned up well. A compact man, not quite six feet tall, who by midsummer probably turned so black he looked blue.

Handsome to a degree, Tobias's nose lay flat against his face, and his lips all but faded into the blackness of his skin. Gray-green eyes peered out from beneath narrow upper lids, coming close enough that I saw the length of his lashes, the deep lines in his forehead, and the pores in his skin. But what pulled me in were his gleaming white teeth that flashed when he smiled.

They drew me, the three of them, like bees to honeysuckle. Like a baby to a breast full of milk. They opened their hearts, as well as their arms. If not for the deep slashes wounding my heart, I would've thought I had died in that hellhole room at the Magnolia Monarch and landed in Heaven.

"Toby, you related to any Dumass family in the Winston-Salem area?" Ivy asked.

"Yes, why? You know a Dumass, Andie?"

I giggled and then let out a laugh, surprising all of them by the looks on their faces. "Yes, yes, I do. Do you know Rupert Dumass? He was my daddy's closest friend. Rupert married Loretta Pudrow, a Black woman, and loved her his entire life. Their daughter, Mavis, was my best friend."

"Rupert? Rupert Dumass? A White man who owned a large farm north of the city, correct? All tobacco?"

"Yes," I laughed again. "That's him."

They smiled at my contagious laughter.

"My daddy's name was Bud Parks."

"Parks rings a bell, 'tis true. But Rupert, I surely know. He is a cousin. We lost touch many years ago. A regrettable thing. How is Rupert?"

"He passed away some time ago, as did his wife—and Mavis."

"I am so sorry to hear that. What a shame. Rupert's father was Bertram Dumass. Bertram's brother, Denton, was *my* father—a white man who met my mother, Phoebe, a woman of deep color from the islands. My mother's skin was ebony. As you know, they could not marry in this state back then. My father never loved another; they were together until death parted them. Mixed-race marriages run in our family, it seems. It was not the popular thing to do in the South for the last few decades. My parents kept to themselves, stayed out of towns, and away from people. Rupert and his father brought supplies often; remember Mattie? I told you about those bad times. But let's remember good times tonight, shall we? By the way, my siblings are shades lighter than me."

"Ah," said Ivy. "That's true. Why didn't I think of it?"

"Because, woman, your beautiful head is busy filling itself with love for me," Tobias cooed and leaned over to kiss his wife.

"True again," Ivy chuckled after his kiss. "But I remember now the old pictures of you and your cousin Rupert. Pretty boys, both of you. One very White, one very Black."

"Nah," said Matthew. "I've seen pictures of you as a kid, Tobias," he teased, turning to me. "Andie, he was so ugly his mama put a ham hock in his back pocket to get the dogs to play with him."

Laughter lit up the room. "You bad, Mattie, oooh, such a bad boy." Tobias's chuckle filled my mind with memories of Rupert. I talked into the evening about Rupert's family and of his death, about my love for Mavis, and a little about *my* family.

Ivy's deep-dish apple pie melted on my tongue and along the sides of my mouth. The coffee was rich with cinnamon and pale with cream. Kona coffee, Ivy mentioned. I recognized the Royal Doulton cup and saucer. My mother once owned the entire set before she sold it at her pre-move massive garage sale.

The food, fire, and friendship were like being rocked to sleep as a child. Several times during the evening, my eyes met Matthew's, eyes that held a warm brown brilliance, making me shiver.

Ivy poured more coffee into my cup. "Would you like more pie, Andie?"

"If it's not too much trouble." I held my dish out with both hands like a homeless, hungry child in a soup line. "It's absolutely wonderful. I'd love the recipe."

We avoided discussing why I was there, and Matthew focused our conversation on the lighter side. I was grateful. As I finished my second piece of pie, my eyelids kept wanting to close. I saw

Matthew looking at me. His voice invaded my thoughts. "Andie, you are welcome to go to bed anytime you want. Did Ivy show you the deep cast-iron tub in your bathroom? Why don't you go up and enjoy it and then turn in for the night? We'll talk in the morning. By the way, Ivy agreed to take you to a few dress shops in town this week. You need clothes. It'll be an advance on your pay, okay?" He winked.

I smiled. "Fine, Matthew, that's fine. Thank you all so much for your kindness. I—I'm overwhelmed."

"It's our pleasure," said Tobias.

I said my goodnights to Matthew and Tobias, lingering a moment on Matthew's smile, and then followed Ivy out of the room and up the antebellum staircase.

"This house is big enough to get lost in," I said.

"You'll learn your way around," she said. "But don't forget to cover the bird cage tonight; otherwise, they'll wake you early."

In tears, I turned at the door to say goodnight. "I'm sorry. I'm simply overcome by your generosity. I'm not used to anyone caring about me except my parents. But Daddy's gone now, and Dixie, that's my mother, is living with my aunt in Charleston, and I—"

"—I'm happy you're with us," Ivy said, pulling me into a warm hug. "God remembers your tears as well as your prayers. Sleep well."

At her comment, all I could do was smile and nod. After a long tub soak, I covered the canaries' cage as Ivy instructed and climbed into bed. Fatigue rolled over me like a giant ocean wave. I slept at once, a deep, luxurious sleep. The first such sleep in over a decade.

Chapter 5

Something Special
March 1993

Matthew

I gave Andie a smile before she followed Ivy up to bed. A smile I hoped she'd interpret as a sincere apology from the world's idiot male population. I decided to send her roses while she worked for me; after all, wasn't Rose her middle name? I couldn't take my eyes off her. She was terribly needy, and I suspected I had only scratched the surface of what lay beneath her distress. I swallowed—twice—and reminded myself I had brought her to Shiloh for purely honorable intentions.

But she was easily the most beautiful female I'd ever met. Yet, her loveliness, though it lay beneath an unkempt and weary exterior, wasn't the only thing about her that impressed me. She was direct, which captivated my attention from the get-go. She was also natural and free-spirited, non-judgmental, speaking her thoughts without an agenda, as if she had no notion of the exquisite grace she wielded or the subtlety hidden under her destitution.

I watched her follow Ivy upstairs, noting the delicate curve of her waist. Although she wasn't tall, she carried herself as if she stood a clear distance above every woman in the Carolinas. Someone in her life had taught her the art of femininity. I also knew I had not sent a woman flowers for quite some time.

She liked me. I'd seen it in her eyes, although she pretended to have a not-on-your-life attitude when I flirted with her in my office earlier. Actually, it was her cold-day-in-Hell stance that caught me off guard. Again, I told myself that under normal circumstances, I would never involve myself with someone from a case who needed my help. My counsel. But these weren't normal circumstances. There was something incredibly special about her. I wanted to know more. And more of what she knew about Reverend Calvin Artury.

Chapter 6

A New Day
March 1993

Andie

The following morning, my eyes slowly drifted open with a dazed *where-am-I* expression to the sudden chirps of the canaries. Someone had taken the cover off the cage. *It must be late.*

Against the far wall stood an old-fashioned dry skink with a small mirror. My bare feet felt for the cool hardwood floor. The extra-large T-shirt I'd borrowed from Matthew hung almost to my knees. I crossed the room, my legs wobbly, feeling like I'd slept for a week. With pulse-pounding certainty, I knew I would not recognize my reflection. I'd taken over another body; there was no other way to describe the feeling.

My eyes flashed back at me and seemed larger and bluer than usual. They held an expression of words in a fairytale, an unnatural happiness as if dusted with magic or like I'd had too much wine. My tangled hair set off an unfamiliar pale face like a frame around a cameo, glowing vague and ghostly in the old, silvered glass. The wildness of my image was poles apart from how I usually pictured myself—plain, okay for thirty-eight—it shocked me. For a moment, I wondered if it was really me.

And then I let out a yelp. Matthew. His handsome face appeared next to mine in the mirror. Sadie, his dog, had followed him and softly wagged her tail against his leg. "I didn't hear you knock."

"I didn't. Sorry. I forgot my manners," he said and grinned. "How'd you sleep?"

"Like a rock." I smiled, rubbed my eyes, and allowed myself some pleasure in our shared moment.

"This house will do it to you." Pulling me away from my reflection, he linked his arm through mine. "There's more to see around here. But Ivy has breakfast ready. She told me she placed a robe on the back of your bathroom door; will that do for you?"

"I'm such a mess. Give me five minutes."

"Just five; I'm hungry."

I watched him leave, then padded into the bathroom. Ivy had also laid a pair of blue jeans and a soft flannel shirt on a dresser near the tub, and she had washed, mended, and folded all of my stinky clothes, including the afghan. *The woman is amazing.* A word I didn't say much. But each time I turned around, amazing Ivy was saying or doing something that sent me reeling. The jeans fit. I rolled up my shirtsleeves and slipped on a pair of house shoes she had set near the sink. Amazing.

A hand-painted landscape on the wall near my unmade bed captivated my attention. I stepped closer to observe the embroidered sampler beneath it. Dixie had loved old samplers and once had a collection of several on her bedroom wall. Displayed behind glass in an antique frame, it read, *Stitched by Emmie Callahan ~ 1887 ~ Great is Thy Faithfulness.* The miracle touched me to tears, and I touched it back with my fingertips.

❧

Ivy lifted orange French toast and maple-smoked bacon onto plates. It was a simple breakfast served with strawberry jam, sliced pineapple, and coffee, but to me, it was manna from Heaven. My hands trembled while I ate and Matthew read the newspaper. Neither of us spoke. I took in the quietness and enjoyed the view of the gardens. Sipping my coffee, I wrapped myself in the serenity. Not even my best daydreams compared to it. My body breathed—finally.

I offered to tidy up, but Ivy said I could help at supper. "Enjoy your first morning at Shiloh and explore the surrounding beauty," she said and smiled.

Matthew agreed and guided me on another tour downstairs. A paneled library at the far end of the house took my breath away. It boasted an opulent marble fireplace, floor-to-ceiling bookcases of mellow aged walnut, an antique pool table, a gun cabinet, and more exquisite, handcrafted cabinetry filled with hundreds of books. A black-and-white marble tile floor, set in a classic pattern of enormous diamonds, shone like glass.

On the opposite end of the house, in the large living room where Matthew entertained guests, whisper-soft colors, sentimental keepsakes, and a refined rustic charm set off the room. Two carved busts of Civil War heroes I didn't recognize sat on the mantel over a mammoth fireplace made of river rock. More arched windows topped two sets of double French doors leading to a stone terrace.

Matthew pointed and cleared his throat, his words almost apologetic. "There's a swimming pool, weight room, and decks that overlook the gardens out that way." But his following statement sent waves of sweetness to my tongue, and I savored his kindness. "I hope you have time to enjoy it all while you're here."

"Tell me," I said. "Did you renovate the entire house?"

"Pretty much. I was determined to restore this property in '79, while others laughed and said sinking money into it was the sort of foolish notion that would eat up my investments. But my mother had always loved this place, and Ivy and Tobias were on board. They bought into living here and helping me with my work. To me, the house and grounds were full of potential. I believed I could make it shine again and keep my mind and hands busy. It was my ex-wife who hated every minute of renovating. She was all too happy to leave it for her minimalistic, glass and chrome life in Boston."

An older woman appeared at the door. "Mr. Callahan, phone for you, sir."

"Excuse me, Andie: my work never stops. By the way, Kate, this is Andie. Kate and Ivy are good friends, and they clean this place together. Kate is here three days a week." As Matthew walked away, he smiled and said, "I'm always glad when Kate is here. She pays no attention to Ivy and leaves my shit alone."

Kate and I smiled at each other and exchanged pleasantries until she excused herself, listing the rooms she had to finish before noon. I thought of my little house on Turner Street. I put as much love into that house as Matthew did into his. I'd been proud to afford a simple gallon of paint. Then I stopped and counted. I'd moved into my house in 1979; *how could this be happening to me?* I almost skipped to the French doors. Opening them wide, I stepped out to the terrace and drank in the air, delicious, fragrant, and touched with a chill of early spring.

I descended a stone staircase to a carpet-like lawn and followed a pathway lined with berry bushes. The vast grounds rambled up to the thick forest in the distance, which rose into the horizon. I found the place intriguing. Wandering across the front lawn, I looked back at the house. A house of dreams. A castle. Beulah Land.

I passed the fountain and found a different path leading through a small wooden gate and down another stone stairway. The house disappeared from view at the bottom of the steps. But there, I discovered a secluded bluestone patio ringed with giant trees and a covered picnic area hosted by a massive stone fireplace. I stood in the center, absolutely awed. Southern white pine, black oak, and hickory, an occasional yellow poplar and hemlock—the ring of trees surrounded me like the walls of a shimmering canyon.

Nearby, a narrow creek trickled down the slope. Beyond it, the land dipped, then ascended among acres of Christmas trees that blended into the mountain. I saw nothing of civilization: no roads, power lines, or buildings. I turned to go back, but the cliffs and peaks around me halted my steps. As a child, I had listened to hours of Daddy telling me stories of tradition and lore filling these mountains—of the magic attained here. I lifted my face to the sky, offering a spur-of-the-moment prayer of thanks, soaking up the untold, undisturbed stillness of the surrounding history.

I breathed in the beauty of it and then stopped.

Did the enchantment of the place mean to overtake me? *Oh, God. What if my children are living in horror? How can I endure even the possibility of it?*

My emotions roller-coasted downward at a fast clip, slamming into a wall of guilt. I knew my daydreams and desires had often gotten the best of me in the past. After years of fighting for my sanity, I knew myself well. And I also knew my best chance of rescuing my children and bringing a sense of family back into our lives lay in Matthew Callahan's hands.

The snap of a twig and the rustle of leaves drew my attention. There were soft sounds of feet stepping on thick boughs of pine needles, flashes of motion and color flickering between the trees, and suddenly, he stood high on the hill. My breath caught in my throat. Ivy had called him my knight. His growing smile was as intimate as a mattress in an attic long ago.

Dressed like a lumberjack in a blue and white plaid flannel shirt rolled up to his forearms, faded jeans, and work boots, Matthew took the stairs two at a time. Walking toward me, he smiled again.

Gentleness emanated from him like a great glowing orb. A virtue I assumed he was born with. It radiated from his eyes down to his muscular legs.

The delight over his face and the scent of pure pleasure he gave off was like a wild animal encountering a mate. I wanted to run from it but froze in my tracks. Matthew could've bounded off into the woods and slipped into the camouflage of the trees like a twelve-point buck; it wouldn't have surprised me.

"Whatchoo doing out here, Miss Andie Rose?" His deep voice cut through the quiet, and the sweetness in him was almost childlike. And yet, his elegant ruggedness reminded me of the Cedars of Lebanon. Trees, some say, that were planted by God Himself.

Stopping before me, he stood tall and straight, his gaze searching for mine and finding it. That split-second connection was of such enormous intimacy that I had to walk backward in circles to catch my balance, hoping the extra space would soften the wild beat of my heart.

Never having feelings for anyone other than Joe, a new me emerged. My heart changed its beat, and I walked out of the darkness of my life into something else. Something so intense that it resurrected my hope. I decided to stay. *I'll stay with him until Dillon and Gracie are safe with me again and Calvin is behind bars.*

"Ready to go to work?" he asked.

I smiled, tilted my head slightly, and nodded, attempting to return his kindness.

With each step toward the house, my joy was made full. Justice would result from my joy. The dread dissipated, and I watched as God replaced ashes with beauty. I was no longer alone, no longer watched, stalked, or hunted. The familiar fretful strain evaporated. In its place, new emotions surfaced. In my wild and primitive state of mind, a mixture of the unknown and uncrushable enthusiasm was born.

For the first time, I felt I had a chance at life. I was still exhausted, every muscle ached, and my spirit remained broken. But with every passing minute, the peace that filled my soul when I met Matthew seeped into even the darkest corners of my being. A peace I didn't fully understand. My head said I should be afraid or, at the very least, uneasy, and yet my heart wanted to sing.

For, lo, the winter is past; the rain is over and gone . . . .

Chapter 7

The Gift of a Rose
March 1993

Andie

Matthew led me to his desk, offering me his soft leather chair. He pulled a straight chair next to mine, allowing himself access to his computer. A nerve above his dimple twittered in his cheek when he smiled. As I sat, my knee lightly touched his. Even through our jeans, such closeness, however innocent, unsettled me.

I forced myself to concentrate on the work ahead of us. He then handed me a yellow legal pad with letters he said he had composed in the early morning hours: letters directed to department heads in various social service agencies and one to a family court judge—all acquaintances of the Callahan family.

The letters gave nothing away as to my whereabouts or that Matthew was searching for information regarding my children. He only asked questions any social worker might ask about a judge taking teenage twins from their mother and how it might set a precedent for further custody cases. "A back door approach to getting any slip of information," he said.

Unrelated to our quest, he asked me to retype a contract about a land purchase he had bugged Ivy to type for the past week. He said he would have Ivy show me the filing system and passwords to access his computer files. Matthew took a few minutes to explain basic word processing, and I caught on quickly, finding I rather enjoyed it. I also found it interesting how well he typed with a missing finger.

And then, at the first opportune moment, I reached into my front pocket, pulled out a folded piece of stationery, and laid it in front of him: a picture of my children and an address. "That's Joe's address. I drove through the security gate once and got a threatening phone call from him the next day. They supervised my visits but canceled most of them for some stupid reason. I phoned my attorney a few hours after the judge took them from me to ask for help. He declined when I requested to make payments for legal fees. I guess attorneys don't work on credit."

Matthew scowled. He poured us both coffee from a carafe on a nearby table. "I'll bet they threatened your attorney by the time you called him." His expression hardened.

"Be careful, Matthew. Calvin's persuasive. He buys everybody off."

"I can't be bought. I know what he's worth, as much as I can find out on the surface. I never believed his slick TV message. Some gullible people, however, don't have the sense God gave a goat. How did you sit through that all those years? I mean, you don't seem the type." He sighed. "I don't mean to insult you. I'm sorry. It's hard for me to understand why thousands follow him and would seemingly die for him."

I sipped my coffee, hesitated, and then answered his question. "People are looking for God. When they see the miracles, they think they've found Him. They sit in Calvin's service with eyes like a deer in headlights, sucking it up with a puppet mentality. For many of them, their lives are a mess, or they have a sick child, or they're suffering from an ailment and believe he can heal them. Or they buy into the prosperity message. They want to believe it. He does their thinking for them in his revelation of Heaven and Hell. There's no freedom of religion in Artury's church. He tells them what to say, read, sing, wear, watch on TV, how to act. His followers attach themselves to every word he preaches and follow it to the letter. It's their pass into Heaven."

I gave Matthew a small, weary smile. "On the other hand, they don't know the evil behind the scenes within his inner circle. Calvin is a strong-willed, domineering man who rules with an iron fist. You don't dare doubt him; otherwise, it's blasphemy. He is the voice of God. There's much pressure through fear to believe him and public humiliation if you don't. They shun those who leave the church, stripping them of family until they return and confess their sins publicly. I've seen it played out many times. I've experienced it."

Matthew shook his head in disgust. "That's what happened to you."

"Worse than that." I sat for a second, hesitant to tell him more. "Most who disagree; Calvin delights in making them feel stupid. Or backslid from God. He brainwashes the majority, telling them they have no spiritual knowledge or experience to question him. It's scary watching him go into the vision, as he calls it. He claims to see Jesus, angels, Satan, and demons. People fall out under *the power*, roll in the aisles, rush to the altar, and go crazy. Because of his *visions*, he gets people saved or re-saved, fills them with fear and trembling, and then takes over their lives. Especially if he thinks you can contribute something, like a talent or money, to his cause."

I hesitated again, allowing my words to sink into Matthew, realizing he had never heard this from someone who had experienced it.

"It's a real shame because the youth are particularly vulnerable to his gift of persuasion and feigned expertise. The members will not criticize him outwardly, no matter how radical he is in his decisions or actions. Even with mild disagreement, few have the guts to open their mouth. Usually, when a person breaks away, they are so disillusioned and confused that they become alcoholics or addicts and lose it all. Which gives Calvin even more ammunition to prove he is of God. The congregation reasons that although their *Reverend* may be mistaken in some areas, the overall good he accomplishes outweighs any minor flaws. After all, he preaches from the Bible. And the miracles, they're real. So who is going to argue with that?"

Grim-faced, Matthew stood and walked to the windows. "I hear he gives thousands to charities all over the world. Food banks and such. I have to believe some good people blindly attend his church, brainwashed or not."

"Certainly. If you're not employed there or part of his team, you don't have a clue what goes on. And sure, his charitable notions look good, don't they? The fact is that Clavin's worldwide fan club includes rich and educated people. He's more than a spiritual celebrity. Not realizing it, people worship him. He's the ultimate authority. Nobody does anything but what he says. There's no board of deacons to challenge him."

I moved to the sofa. "I swear, he can make the sweetest granny look like a demon if he wants to. Every week, he serves up God on a golden platter. He's gotten away with lies and corruption for years while the police and the government look the other way. Separation of church and state, you know. Whatever he wants, he takes. And good people or not, nobody contests a blasted thing he says or does. Last but not least, he can get your last nickel before you know you've dropped it in the bucket."

I raised my coffee mug. "Someday, God has to stop the madness. As for me, I went through the motions to survive. I thought I had no choice. Which was stupid as I look back; I lost it all anyway."

Matthew walked over and inserted a stack of paper into what he had said was a printer. "To be quite honest, your incredible insight and assessment of Calvin astounds me. It's obvious you speak from experience. You've lived through hell because of this man. Perhaps God will use us to expose him for the world to see," he said, handing me a manila folder to file copies of the letters I had typed.

"I hope so," I said.

Until I arrived at Shiloh, the constant abrasion of living had left me void of hope. When I accidentally touched the back of Matthew's hand, another dose of contentment ribboned through me. I contemplated telling him about John Rossi but couldn't. There would come a time to talk about the murder I witnessed, but God would have to write that moment on the wall. In the meantime, I kept it hidden.

Matthew left me alone for the rest of the day. After reciting the long list of farm chores needing his attention, he said he planned to spend the day with Tobias and mentioned that we could have supper in town that evening if I would like.

"I'd love to, but I have nothing fitting to wear."

"Not to worry. Ivy is already working on it."

Of course she is. I could only nod and smile as he left the room.

Though I busied myself typing and filing most of the afternoon, my nerves got the best of me at the thought of dinner alone with Matthew. Several times, I'd barely made it to the toilet. Until Ivy walked in with a box of Imodium AD and a smart little black dress, which she thought *just might fit.*

"I bought it at the mall in Asheville last week. Way too small for me; my wide hips, you know. Been too busy to return it. Matthew said you might drive to town for supper. I thought you could use a new dress and there's no time to shop. So. Try on?"

"Oh yes, thank you. It's beautiful. But I'm afraid I've—"

"—No shoes? Size seven? Black shiny pumps hung from Ivy's other hand.

"Are you psychic?"

Ivy laughed. Her accent turned as thick as Cajun gumbo. "No, Andie, I swan, just very observant. Tobias and I have made it our life work to care for da Callahans. Salt of the earth. 'Specially, Matthew. He's like my own. Dat man has smiled more in the last twenty-four hours than I've seen in years. Now, please, go try on." Ivy kissed my cheek, leaving a bright red tattoo of her lips. I took in her scent and smiled—perfume and pot roast.

The dress fit. Perfectly. Matthew phoned to say we should be ready to leave by six o'clock. I picked the remains of *Really Red* toenail polish off my two middle toes and asked Ivy for remover and any extra polish she might have. I felt eighteen again.

After a long bath, an attempt to fix my hair, and a fight to cover the dark circles that still invaded the space around my eyes, I was ready to call the whole thing off and hide in my room.

"Andie?" It was Ivy again. "Some makeup and lipstick. I thought you might like it. And you should wear these." A pair of diamond earrings dangled from her fingertips. She handed them to me, and I let them roll around in the palm of my hand. "Ivy, I honestly shouldn't. I mean, are they real?"

"They're just earrings. Put them on. Enjoy."

"Thank you. Thank you so much. I'm so pale. I need the lipstick. But these, I'm not sure I can wear your earrings." I pulled out my gold hoops and slipped Ivy's diamonds into my earlobes at her insistence.

"You're beautiful, see?" Ivy lightly touched my face, looking at my reflection in the mirror.

I smiled. "The earrings are beautiful, not me."

"Silly girl. Learn to take a compliment. I bought them last year, on sale. Five thousand. Good price."

I choked. My eyes filled with tears as my hand covered my mouth.

"Simple jewelry. I say again, enjoy. And this is from Matthew. He asked me to give it to you."

My cheeks burning, I opened the shiny silver box. It was a bracelet. Pink pearls held together with a diamond clasp. "Oh," I whispered, running my finger over it. Biting my lip, I blinked. *A gift? From a man I hardly know?* The last gift I received from a man had been years before, and at that moment, I couldn't remember what Joe had bought me. Something made of olive wood from the Holy Land. It didn't matter because he took it when he left me.

Ivy lifted the bracelet from the box and placed it on my wrist. "Matthew hopes you like it. He thought you might accept it better if I gave it to you. He's happy you're here. Come down when you're ready."

Laughing as she left the room, Ivy looked back and said, "He said he'll take his shower and then meet you in his study."

That's when it struck me like an arrow from a cupid named Ivy. Matthew wasn't the one pushing.

Once again, my pot of guilt stirred within me. *This has to stop. I'm here to find my children, maybe learn a few computer skills, and start uncovering Calvin. Nothing more.*

It was all lovely, and maybe I deserved a little of it, but it was not my way of life. I had to get a firm grip and wake up and stop the ridiculous daydreams that had plagued me since I was a stupid girl. I clenched my jaw. Our relationship wasn't going anywhere. I would tell Matthew precisely that before the night was over.

Matthew

When I walked into the room where Andie waited, the tender spot I had in my head for her dropped to my heart. From across the room, she was pretty. But as I drew closer, she was beautiful. I suddenly realized that *pretty* was a fact about Andie, but beauty was her force.

She brushed her hair away from her face. Ivy's earrings looked stunning on her. Her lipstick, some shade of '50s red she had probably borrowed from Ivy, too, but was certainly appealing. I noticed her arms were bare. The little pink pearls I gave her followed each other around her dainty wrist. She tilted her head to one side a few degrees, a look she'd given me before that was meant to be friendly but better than a smile as she touched her earlobe. Her skin and face were full of light. Andie was as perfect in that light, at least that night, as the diamonds dangling from her ears.

"You're breathtaking," I said without hesitation as my heart pounded for mercy.

Desire. An emotion I once thought I'd never feel again burned inside my chest like an old Packard that someone hadn't driven in years. My glance swept over her, appreciating her attractiveness and the femininity of her black and elegant dress.

Earlier, working in my office, she had tied her hair back with a rubber band. Up close, her freshly washed hair floated down like molasses from a jar in glossy gold waves and bounced lightly around her shoulders. Her eyes, more sky-colored than bright blue, rose to me and held their warmth. The sight of her and the faster beat of my heart were as welcome as a ray of sunshine on a prison wall.

Andie

Surprised at his remark, I lingered on how he said it, with sincerity, and not overblown flattery. "Thanks. You clean up well, too." The way he stood there told me he had made it in life. A man of significant physical presence, he had dressed in the uniform of a man who knew how. He was all class: dark blue blazer, blue oxford shirt, and khaki pants, all perfectly pressed and creased, unlike the redneck or cowboy attire I typically encountered in my world.

"Thank you for the bracelet; it's lovely. You're too kind. Since I'm your employee, does this constitute sexual harassment?" Quickly, I regretted my question.

But he opened his mouth and laughed, showing flashes of perfectly white teeth in his tanned face. "Sure. I do it for all the women I bring to Shiloh." He winked.

I punched him playfully on the arm.

"I'm glad you like it, but damn, doesn't that beat all?" he teased.

"What?"

"I forgot to give you this." He held out a single rose. Deep, velvety red, and fragrant. "I figured you might like it since it was your middle name."

I winced. "I don't deserve these gifts."

"Not so. You are a gift."

Our eyes met, and in that unguarded moment, I mulled over his flattery, sniffed the rose, and searched for a rebuttal to his compliment to no avail. The air hummed between us. "It's my favorite. Daddy called me Rosebud. They were his favorite flowers, too. I should thank you for the compliment. Ivy said I should learn to accept them."

"She's always right, in case you haven't noticed."

I raised my eyebrows and nodded vigorously.

Matthew offered me his arm. "Shall we?"

"I'm starved. Where are we going?

"A little out-of-the-way place near Blowing Rock. I know the chef."

I took his arm and shivered. "Tonight, I'll stop being terrified. I'll sink into a few wonderful memories, not those I've tried to forget."

"Then let's make more good ones for you tonight."

"Alright."

He opened the door, and we stepped out onto the porch. "Your chariot awaits," he said and grinned, offering his arm again. A fairy godmother had transformed my old, rusted Pontiac into a BMW convertible. Royal blue and regal.

"Might be a little chilly." Matthew picked up a coat and a pair of gloves off a wicker rocker. "Ivy gave me these for you to wear, in case. Ah, here's a scarf so your hair doesn't fly around."

Touched by their simple thoughtfulness, I caressed the coat, gloves, and scarf like an orphan child opening her first Christmas gift. I gripped his arm as delicately as possible and we walked to the car.

Occasionally, Matthew looked over at me as we drove the Blue Ridge Parkway in comfortable silence, slowing down at the curves in the road and then speeding up. In the dim light, the hills once more took on the cloak of a well-told fairytale. The sun played like a strobe light through the trees until we ducked into the full shade of the mountains surrounding us. I pulled on the gloves, pushing down on the woolly spaces between each finger. The coat wrapped around me as if to say, *don't worry, these people will take care of you now.*

The groaning sounds of the BMW, the drafts of nightfall's sweet air—they wove a subtle, unfailing spell. The night air was alive on my face, like a young child's breath. It was good he didn't hear me singing over the noise, but I couldn't get the song out of my head that day. *He's like the wind...* My heart sang all the way to Blowing Rock. Over and over, that Patrick Swayze song, substituting he for she until the golden glow of evening faded into a blaze of stars spanning a moonless sky.

The drive to supper that night would've been enough if nothing else happened. The mood called for a new daydream. A fantasy. If only once. And all the things I wanted to say to remind him of why I was there—I had left at the house.

Chapter 8

A Forfeited Game
April 6, 1993

Reverend Calvin Artury

Disguised as an ordinary suburbanite in tennis shoes, sweat pants, a tennis racket slung over my shoulder, sunglasses, and a sweatband tight around my forehead, I showed up at Tanglewood Park on time, eager to play a rousing game of tennis with Andie Oliver.

DeSanto's crew had surrounded the perimeter strategically while I remained close to the courts. Their eyes fixed on me, ready to defend the Man of God—they had their instructions. Abduct the dark angel. Make sure some innocent soul discovers her body the following day with her wrists slit in a pool of unforgiving red.

But she never showed. I waited fifteen minutes, then stormed to a waiting car, infuriated by her blatant lies forcing me to play some twisted game of cat and mouse! Evan had waited in the car, ready to give me his typical *I told you so* glare.

"She stood me up! That foul harlot!"

Until then, no one dared touch me. No soul alive had challenged my authority or possessed evidence to destroy my ministry. No one until Andie. And the worst thing was, I believed her. She wasn't bluffing, and we all knew it. But I knew it best because I had come to the knowledge she was exactly like me. The question was, *could I find her before she got what she wanted?*

Andie Oliver was my one wayward sheep. I had left the ninety-and-nine and searched for her, but would never get her back into the fold. Never.

All we, like sheep, have gone astray! We have turned everyone to his own way, and the Lord hath laid on him the iniquity of us all!

Chapter 9

A Matter of Trust
April 1993

Andie

I felt we'd made little progress where Dillon and Gracie were concerned. My chance to murder Calvin had come and gone, and I became increasingly alarmed about my relationship with Matthew. For crying out loud, we weren't kids anymore. We were middle-aged and old enough to know better.

Long ago, I learned that guilt and elation were like oil and water. They didn't mix well. And yet, suppers with Matthew had been memorable. Ivy had undoubtedly seen to that. I even cooked a meal or two in his unbelievably modern kitchen, remorseful that I enjoyed that, too. The rave reviews from my new friends surprised me, and I caught myself daydreaming that I belonged at Shiloh.

Matthew spent a few days in the fields with Tobias, telling Ivy the farm had more immediate problems than the Governor's Ball. I resigned to printing invitations, filing stacks of paperwork, and typing letters—senseless and tedious work.

I'd finally had enough. I stood, stretched, and stepped outside. Accompanied by one or more of Matthew's dogs, I explored the grounds close to the house and found the old cemetery, the swimming pool, and the vegetable gardens. Matthew requested I not go to the winery or any public place without him. I understood he was concerned for my safety. It was quite a change from the life I had left behind and a welcome one, but it still filled me with a guilt-ridden conscience. I could not go one more day without hearing something about my children, or I would go mad. Farm work and Governor's Ball be damned. My children were my priority.

After breakfast the following morning, I tiptoed into Matthew's office with the mail. Soft guitar music played through a hidden sound system.

"Hi, Matthew. Mail call." I raised the stack in my hand. "Ivy said it's your turn."

He smiled. "Come in."

I walked to his desk, my shoulders back in modest confidence. He took the mail from me and dropped it on his desk without even so much as a glance. "Thank you."

"You're welcome. Sorry to disturb you."

I turned to leave, but he stopped me with an abrupt but courteous, "Please. Sit."

I sat directly across from him and crossed my legs at the ankles. My eyebrows rose with my posture, and I asked, "What's up?" Not the question I wanted to ask.

MATTHEW

"A few things," I said. "Give me a minute to review this report."

A warm breeze ruffled the mound of papers on my desk, but Andie's eyes lingered over the stacks of files that had slid to the floor; my paperwork sometimes buried me alive. Like Ivy, she was freakish about neatness. I'd already learned that about her. *Could I get used to it? Do I care?*

Yet her eyes alone brought fresh air into my mundane life. The way she smiled, the way, despite her circumstances, she never seemed to tire. Her intelligence and wit filled me with the energy I often lacked. I shuffled through the report I needed to discuss with her. The information she needed to know.

ANDIE

While he fumbled through his file, I looked around his office. He had wedged a stocked bar with a tiny sink and refrigerator into a corner. He kept a coffee pot or tea kettle running. His mahogany desk was nicked and dulled, what I saw of it. Stacks of papers and files covered the top, along with an array of pens, pencils, and a Civil War cannon paperweight made of iron the size of his fist. His business cards rested in a handmade decanter, probably painted by one of his children years before. Diplomas from some college called Villanova hung on the wall behind him, along with certificates that read Family Psychology at the top. Citations, thank-you letters, and photographs of what looked like an island vacation filled the rest of the wall. *Maybe he likes to travel.*

He liked to read; that was obvious. Besides reference material on various psychiatric disorders and books on grief, a small collection of old leather-bound books lined the shelves. *Probably first editions.* He displayed framed photos of his son and daughter on his large desk. Matthew loved his children; that wasn't hard to figure out.

I felt warm around him, safe for the first time since the day I left the security of my daddy's cocoon to marry Joe. *If I could only get over feeling guilty about feeling guilty.*

"Sleep well?" he asked.

I nodded. "Yes. Like I have every night since I've been here."

I counted Mississippi's. Ten of them. But he finally opened his mouth and said, "Anything on your mind?"

"Gracie and Dillon." My answer was quick and sharp.

He picked up a pen and shoved himself away from his desk. "Andie, I need to tell you something." He rolled his pen between his palms. "I've done some investigating."

I shot to my feet and fisted my hands on my hips. "Without telling me? Why?" My question hung in the air, unanswered.

"Sit, Andie. Please?"

I sat, but not happily.

"Trust me. I know what I'm doing. My goal here is to return your children to you and keep you and them safe in the process. You're right, however. You're a wanted woman within the House of Praise. I have an informant who has spent the past two weeks attending church services and talking to people at the Praise Buffet. If you go to Dillon and Gracie now, they'll find you. Do you want that? They are looking for you, Andie. Everywhere. No more shopping in town with Ivy or suppers out."

Matthew's serious look concerned me. "But I can't hold you here," he said. "You're not a prisoner. You can leave if you want, but let me stress how dangerous that would be. Please, Andie, consider yourself in hiding until we break this open and nail Artury to the wall and everyone involved."

I narrowed my eyes like a mother might do to a rambunctious toddler. Then I softened. "Matthew, I've got to know about my kids."

"And I'll tell you. I care about you, Andie. I don't want you going off half-cocked and ending up with a bullet in your head. But you definitely have keen insight. You're right about that church. I don't know why no one has fully investigated it, but I'm pushing now. I've been in touch with the Attorney General. I'm putting pressure on and calling in favors. Promise you'll let me handle this."

"I have so far, haven't I? I mean, I came here, trusted you, did as you asked, worked the past few weeks for you, waiting and hoping we'd make some headway, and you've done everything behind my back. You've got to trust me, too, Matthew. Now, how are they?"

"Okay, okay." He took a deep breath and opened a file. "When they were first taken from you, they refused to go to church, for counseling, for anything. Within two days, they ran away but didn't get far. From what my informant told me, Artury recruited someone from the church to watch them every moment."

"Oh, Matt!" My heart dropped to the vicinity of my feet. I stood again and ran my hands through my hair, wanting to pull it out.

"Don't worry, relax. They're fine. They're smart, those two. Instead of trying to find you, they ran to their Guardian ad Litem on their third attempt. They spilled their guts, and afterward, the court transferred them to where they are now."

Matthew referred to his file again. "They're with a Mr. and Mrs. Henry Darwood in Winston-Salem. It's highly unusual, but they live with an African-American family who evidently requested to take them in. The Darwoods went through the foster parent program several months before, and when they heard about your twins, they contacted the court. Seems your twins knew the Darwoods? The Guardian ad Litem petitioned that Dillon and Gracie move to their home temporarily. The Darwoods live in your children's old school district, but thank God, the kids aren't attending the House of Praise for now. They're old enough to refuse. It's been a blow for the church. Artury has everyone praying."

I had fallen back into the chair, wiping tears from my eyes. "Thank you," I said. "I can rest easy. Yes, the twins have known the Darwoods for a long time. They're good people. Gracie and Dillon will be fine. For now."

"My informant reported your ex-husband's attorney is fighting this. But I've got someone looking into how the court handled the custody case. Currently, Joe has four hours on Sunday to take them to church. That is, *if* he can get them to go. It seems your kids are extremely resistant to it."

I grinned. "I'm sure they are. They'll put up a stink about going anywhere with Joe. And if I know my ex-husband, he's not pushing it. It's not Joe who wants them; it's Calvin. We can't stop, Matthew. We have to expose it all. I'm surprised, in a way, because Dillon and Gracie have such kind spirits. Confrontation isn't something they enjoy. But I'm glad to hear they're resistant. And for now, they're safe. Velda and Henry love them. Can we get a message to the Darwoods, at least?"

"Can we really trust them?"

"Absolutely."

"Then I'll get word to the Darwoods to watch what they say to your children. I suspect their home is bugged. And I'll make sure Dillon and Gracie know you are safe. That will ease their minds."

Chapter 10

Steep Slopes

April 1993

MATTHEW

I sensed a significant load lifting from her shoulders. Andie smiled, which made me smile back at her. "How about a walk?" I asked.

"Don't I need to get to work?"

I rubbed my eyes. "I've been up since four this morning. I need a break, and it's Friday. Ivy's gone grocery shopping. She won't need you today. Let's take a picnic lunch up to a nice lookout spot on the mountain. Do you like to hike?"

"I do. When the air blew through the window this morning, I thought about camping along the New River with Daddy, hiking up Stone Mountain or Hanging Rock, finding the waterfalls at South Mountain State Park, or walking across the swinging bridge at Grandfather Mountain in the blistering heat, sunburned, and covered in bug bites."

"Those are great memories of your father. You loved him."

"I adored him. He was my world. He protected me as much as he could. I believe Joe would've done far more damage if not for Daddy putting the fear of God in him a couple of times. He'd like it here. We should talk about *your* family sometime."

"We will." I didn't mean to avoid the subject of my family, and I knew I'd have to soon, but I needed to wait. There was only so much she could handle at once.

But more and more, I loved the sound of her voice and the hint of Appalachia tucked in every syllable. Suppers with Andie had been light and easy, avoiding the trappings of family and heartbreak. I treated her warily for the first few days as if she might be hot to the touch or shatter like glass. Day after day, as I got to know her, I looked forward to seeing her. Even mending the fence with Tobias, I yearned to be near her. Listening to her talk so lovingly about her father made me feel closer to her somehow.

"I'll put together a food basket," I said. "You might want to change into a different pair of shoes."

Andie smiled. "Okay. I'll meet you on the back porch in ten minutes."

I laughed. "Back porch? Huh. And all this time, I thought it was a charming veranda."

ANDIE

With the dogs trailing behind us, Matthew handed me a walking stick. "It's great for fending snakes off the trail," he said. I raised my eyebrows, and he laughed.

We strolled past the barn and took a quick side trip to meet the horses. "I don't know if you like to ride, but we've got some wonderful trails. Here's my herd." Matthew pointed to every stall. "Smokey, Levi, Dan, and Judah. It was Tobias's idea to name them after the twelve tribes of Israel. Looks like we're on our way, except for old Smokey here. She's my mare."

"They're as magnificent as this farm," I said, rubbing Smokey between her enormous eyes. I spied a large, fenced area near the dog kennel. "What do you keep in there?"

"Look for yourself. Ivy's goats. Ivy loves goat cheese. You need to take a walk over to her house someday soon. She's a woman of many talents. That's why I latched onto her so many years ago. This farm belongs to Ivy and Tobias Dumass as much as it does to me."

Hearing the name *Dumass*, my abiding love for Mavis stirred within me. It struck me that my life's strange turn of events might be Mavis's doing after all.

MATTHEW

I heard her breaths become shorter and faster. "This trail is steep," she said. "I couldn't have made this climb when I weighed 200 pounds."

"You weighed that much once?"

"Yep, more than once. You might as well know I wasn't always *beautiful*, as you warmly call me."

"It's not healthy," I said.

"It's not pretty either," she replied with a snip.

I stopped to look at her, knowing exactly what she alluded to. Men are pigs because they only love you if you look like a James Bond girl. "Right, it's not pretty. I know all about weight. Once upon a time, I weighed fifty pounds more than I do now."

Andie grew winded as she increased her pace to keep up with my long legs. "But it's not the same for a man."

"How so?"

"For a woman to disappear from her husband's sight, all she needs to do is to become obese."

"Sad, isn't it?" I said. "Some men are definitely like that."

She didn't answer me. But I wasn't about to hike another foot until I said what was in my heart. We needed a pit stop. She needed to catch her breath. I put my foot on a fallen log beside the trail. Staring at my feet, I kicked a patch of moss off the log and tried not to mumble. I raised my eyes. "Andie, do you know what unconditional love is?"

"You mean like I have for my children?"

"Yes. But I'm talking about between a man and a woman."

"I think so. My parents had it, I believe. Mavis spoke about it. I can't say I've experienced it."

I nodded, my heart aching for her. "It's a shame, because when two people truly love each other, it's not about physical appearances or age or health. Unconditional love is steadfast, unwavering, and it grows with each passing day. I don't mean to lecture; it's just something I've come to believe. Anyway," I tried to lighten the mood, "skinny people are just hangers for their clothes." But my attempt at humor fell flat. She didn't respond, just wiped the sweat from her brow and took a swig of water from my canteen. "Listen, I didn't mean—"

"—I know what you meant. Joe made fun of my weight all my young life. He hated it. It made me worse, I think. I'm not sure if men can actually possess unconditional love. Maybe. A few. Very few."

I saw the pain in her eyes as she spoke, and it broke my heart. I had no way to convince her, no argument to sway her. And yet, a part of me wondered, was it even necessary to try?

Yes.

My heart finally convinced me. It was more than a rescue. I had a sudden, indisputable feeling of rightness. I stepped back, feeling an overwhelming urge to clutch her hair and pull her against my chest. I fought against it, breathing deeply and slowly until the craving passed. She was not only a needy woman whom I wanted to help out of a dangerous situation. It was more than that. Oh, yes—so much more.

Andie

We continued up the steep slopes of Shiloh's mountain. His giant boyish stride was challenging to keep up with. When we arrived at the top, the view from the cluster of rocks where we stood took away what little breath I had left. A bashful sun lingered in the sky, but the spring air did not lend one breeze in the day's heat. The unusual warmth filled the trees with hundreds of birds.

I sat on a warm rock as Matthew spread a blanket on the ground. He pulled out a simple lunch of bread, goat cheese, two apples, and a bottle of Shiloh wine. "A fruity Riesling," he said. After filling two empty plastic cups with wine, he set them in the sun, sliced the apples, and placed paper napkins beside our drinks. A light wind stirred the air. I ran my fingers through my hair and pushed wayward strands from my eyes. In four months, I'd have yet another birthday.

"And now, the *pièce de résistance*. Ivy's goat cheese." Matthew sliced the soft cheese into chunks while I watched quietly.

We were alone in the clearing. It had been a five-mile trek from the trailhead. Soon, the foliage would turn entirely green, and summer hikers and tourists were sure to infiltrate the Blue Ridge. But the Shiloh farm was Matthew's private piece of wilderness, the mountain and the sunlit countryside beneath us and beyond. Suddenly, I made the mistake of allowing my mind to revisit the past as I gazed at a turkey vulture gliding on a current above us.

"I'm sorry I didn't bring a white tablecloth or silver candlestick," Matthew said and grinned. "Too much to carry on a hike."

I didn't respond to his attempt to make me smile. Images from years gone by had returned. Scenes more familiar than the trail was to Matthew. Scars on my soul, rivaling the depth of the gorge below us.

"Okay," he said. "I've waited out the silence. Let's talk. What do you want to toast?"

I looked past him, at the sky and the vulture circling us. "The death of monsters."

Matthew gave me a puzzled look. "A strange toast."

Holding back my anger, I responded with, "It fits."

He held up his cup. "I suspect your meaning, and I agree. To the death of monsters. Religious and otherwise."

We touched cups and took a sip. The bread was soft, and the cheese was tart and delicious, but I only managed a few bites. Matthew downed a cup of wine and poured another. I nibbled my bread but wasn't interested in more food or drink. I stared at the sky. In my mind, events from the past demanded my attention like a circling flock of vultures.

"Neither of us has led a normal life, Andie." He said the wrong thing in his inept attempt to break the silence or lighten the mood.

"Normal? What's normal? Normal for me is waking from a nightmare and realizing you're still in one. Depression was normal for me. Having my heart broken every day. That was my *normal* life," I said, using air quotes with my fingers. "I've heard repressed anger and frustration results in depression. I can certainly believe it. Eating everything I got my hands on, I couldn't stop. It was all I had. It's how I coped. I spent every extra dime and money I didn't have on food. And then, when things got worse, I exchanged food for cigarettes. I bludgeoned my body to get through the day."

Matthew shook his head, obviously upset. "I did the same thing when Jessie died. All I did was eat, watch old movies, and sleep the days away. Except I never ran out of money."

I turned away. "Lucky you."

He grabbed my arm. "Hey, let's talk about this. Money doesn't buy happiness—"

"—Stop! I'm so sick of that overused and stupid cliché I want to puke. It buys a hell of a lot of happiness if you ask me! Do you know what it's like to have nothing? To live in poverty? Most of the time,

I worked sixty hours a week to keep a roof over my head and food on the table because Joe's paycheck was never enough. All those hours took me away from my children. Joe didn't care. He was never there! Do you know what it's like to want a child so bad you almost die to have one? And then, when you do have kids, they're stripped away! Do you know what it's like to have everything you hoped for and dreamed of yanked out from under you because some damn preacher said you were a dark angel?" I jerked my arm from his grasp.

Matthew's eyes filled with tears. A look I knew Joe was incapable of. He reached for my hand, but before he touched me, I said, "Let's go."

"What is it?"

"You don't know me or the world I live in. How could you possibly?"

"Your folks weren't poor," he said.

"No, but I *was!* I couldn't afford to feed my kids, Matt! Not on my own. My parents helped me, sure, and thank God they did, but they were nowhere close to having what you have here at Shiloh. And they had my needy sister to care for and deal with, and now my mother and aunt *still have* Caroline and her five kids to care for. How can you possibly understand what it was like for me, losing everyone I loved, being beaten and attacked in my home, first by my ex-husband, then by Calvin's thugs? Having evidence I can't use. They threatened to kill my kids, Matt! I lived in my car, for Christ's sake. Do you have any idea what that can do to a person? What is it actually like to live in your car? The hopelessness of driving around hour after hour, sleeping in a Honda—I cried until my head about split open. How could I possibly expect you to know what I've been through?"

I had to stand. Move. Get away from the vultures.

MATTHEW

I helped her stand, but I refused to move away from her. It caused Andie to look up at me. Her light blue eyes pierced me like nothing had before. Once again, my heart broke for her. "I'm sorry. I can't imagine the horror you've experienced. And yes, I'm blessed I've never had to worry about money, but circumstances can take it all away tomorrow. Life has to mean more than your bank account. We both know the pain of losing our children and someone we love to a monster."

She paid no attention to me. Her hands remained in fists. "Calvin, he put a curse on me," she said. "I've gone back and forth, over and over that muddy road for years, trying to understand: what sin did I commit to make God wash His hands of me? I'm angry, Matthew. I'm really, really angry! I've asked God why? Why! Why does He hear me only when I'm screaming at Him!?"

Her fury was no surprise. She'd earned it. I longed to hold her. Reassure her. Treading the ground in circles, her eyes ablaze, Andie swung her fists in the air until I grabbed her shoulders. "Stop, Andie. Look at me. Please look at me! You have a right to your anger. I'm not here to hurt you. I—I'm falling in love with you." Suddenly, I was so in love my mouth refused to work, and I was positive she thought me a babbling idiot. She had caught me off-guard, and I may have spoken the words far too soon, but I had to distill the anger in her, and the only way I knew was to pour out my heart at her feet.

She froze and stared at me, breathing rapidly, not uttering a sound or even twitching. Her face had disbelief written across it. Finally, she shot me a slight smile with her eyes.

"Is that okay with you?" I asked.

"Matthew—I don't want my bad luck to rub off on you. You know what I'm dealing with here; how—why would you fall in love with a woman like me?"

"I'm not afraid of what you've brought to me, Andie. The hell you've gone through is not because you deserved it! I see who you are underneath all of this, making you one tough, brave woman. I admire that you've made it this far! And as for your *bad luck*, let me worry about that. How about we turn your luck around? Together."

I pulled her to me in a friendly hug, not a romantic one. I was not about to force myself on her. Andie had experienced enough male dominance, sexual and otherwise, I was sure of it. I didn't expect her to love me back, but I would be honest with her every day for the rest of her life, hoping I would be in it. Even with all the fancy furniture, rugs, and crown molding, my home had become only a farmhouse to me. I'd been lonely for a long time and had not realized it until she came to Shiloh.

"I am angry, but you've made my life bearable," she said. "Thank you. And thank you for your kindness. I know your heart still hurts from losing your little girl. I can't imagine going through that. And it was rude of me not to acknowledge it. That was a horrible time for you. I'm sorry."

"Talking about Jessie has helped me more than you know. Maybe I shouldn't have told you about the love part. It seemed like the right thing to do. The right time to tell you. You needed a diversion."

"It's okay. Really. It's all crazy, I know. This place and you within such a short time, but," she hesitated, "I—I love you too. I'm certain of it."

My hand cupped the small of her back and drew her closer. Absorbing the magnitude of her grief and past horrors, I dared to touch her face with my fingers. Surprised, she pulled back, so I bent forward and simply kissed her tear-stained cheek. Her skin smelled sweet, like the wine we had drank only moments before. I kissed her again on the forehead. Her skin's softness only made me want to linger longer. But the longer I stood close to her, the stronger my need to kiss her lips. "Andie, suddenly, you are all my thoughts and hopes."

ANDIE

Let him kiss me with the kisses of his mouth, for thy love is better than wine. That Song of Solomon scripture rang in my head as his lips moved across my skin, tasting my salty tears. My breath caught on his cheek, and I turned slightly until my mouth was close to his. He accepted my invitation, his hands warm and strong, yet gentle, at the back of my neck. His third kiss was unlike any I ever had in my life. A kiss that began to chisel away at my anger.

Chapter 11

NIGERIA FOR JESUS
April 1993

REVEREND CALVIN ARTURY

The sight of my shadow startled me. Not since my ministry began had I worried about my casual indiscretions. Not until Andie Oliver didn't show up at Tanglewood Park. Furiously, I ordered Evan to get the truth from Joe by any means necessary.

After Evan put a gun to Joe's head, he pissed his pants but stuck to his story. He had no notion where his ex-wife had gone into hiding. I felt her threats to expose me to the press might have been bogus, as there was no sign of a police investigation, and not one reporter showed up asking questions. And so, possibly, she *was* bluffing.

Satan had taken her over. She didn't stand a chance at proving her lies and probably realized that fact right before she took a gun and blew off the top of her pretty head.

Still. I ordered Tony DeSanto to dispatch five men daily to search for her. He posted additional men to watch Andie's few friends, family members, and her children, hoping to see her surface.

Then, Tony discovered she had sold her car and quit her job, sending her last paycheck to an attorney who, after several visits from Percy Turlo, swore he hadn't seen her. Checking every flophouse, shelter, and low-rent apartment building in the city, someone found a beat-up Pontiac with four flat tires in the parking lot of the Magnolia Monarch apartment complex. A few of Andie's belongings littered the backseat. An old sweatshirt, a magazine, water bottles, and a receipt with her name on it from Space Savers Storage Units. The facility's owner had given away or sold all her possessions.

We received a small break when Percy shoved her picture in the superintendent's face at the Magnolia Monarch. For one hundred dollars, the super blubbered that a man from Social Services had paid her electric bill in cash and vacated with her shortly after she'd moved in. But the super was too drunk to remember names or faces. Even after Percy beat him like a dirty rug, he still couldn't remember.

But when I received Percy's report that Andie was indeed alive, I fell into a chair and massaged my chest. Within the hour, I offered a sizeable bonus to any of Tony's men who brought her to justice. My connections within the county offices, the police department, and the legal system had produced nothing. Nobody knew who had taken her from the apartment. Or they weren't talking. It seemed someone in Social Services had more pull and influence than I did.

Evan sent Percy to Florida to find Peter Collins since the traitor undoubtedly gave Andie ammunition to use at her disposal. But mercifully, Peter and his mother had died in their sleep. On the same night. Poor things. My beautiful Peter. I can tell you that the thought of him in Hell cost me a night's rest.

At my next Monday morning staff meeting, I pounded my fist on the conference table and declared, "As long as her children are in the area, she will be, too. I want her found!"

Of course, the congregation and my staff assumed I wanted to lead her back to salvation. Only Evan, Silas, and Tony's crew knew her days were numbered.

I felt an enormous pull of the Holy Spirit to protect the ministry. I no longer tolerated *any* derogatory remarks and swiftly eliminated all blasphemy that made it to my ear. I was, after all, a five-fold ministry rolled into one man of God. Apostle, prophet, evangelist, pastor, and teacher. *The Lord is my light and my salvation—whom shall I be afraid?... I will lie down and sleep in peace, for you alone, Oh Lord, make me dwell in safety.*

The people had packed the House of Praise to overflowing. Near completion, the newly remodeled ten-thousand-seat auditorium rumbled and vibrated from the beat of the drums, guitars, and a full orchestra accompanying the Men of Praise quartet. With Joe Oliver at the helm of our latest advanced audio system, the singers cast their voices over the great sanctuary. The team lifted their hands, leading my church audience in praise and worship, and singing my new favorite, *Our God is an awesome God.* The song raised service anticipation to new heights, and I reveled in it.

After Evan announced me, I bounded out during the congregation's standing ovation, my boots barely hitting the platform. Without delay, I omitted all preaching and entered into full-blown prophecy. The Holy Spirit blazed white-hot inside me, shooting outward into my arms and burning my fingertips. My eyes rolled back, and I stood straight with my feet together, lifting my arms out by my sides, palms forward, creating a cross for the people to witness. "The cross! The cross appears in a vision!"

Wild in their worship, the people cried out, their voices rising to a pinnacle of praise for a chance encounter with The Almighty. But that night, I had determined, because of Andie's threats, they were about to experience something else. The most forceful admonishment the Lord God had ever sent through me. For weeks, I had felt myself reeling from the torment of my dark angel and other recent vile and vicious rumors. And in the past several days, a few investigative journalists had been poking around the church and television complex, asking questions and possibly sitting among the faithful as I spoke.

"Thus saith the Lord!"

The shouting quieted.

"I have sent you my Holy Prophet, Calvin Artury." Methodically, like a dog on a chain, I paced back and forth over the carpeted platform. "For some, this is your last warning! I will cut you off because you lie!"

The dramatic and passionate delivery of God's message became His voice, not mine. "You speak untruths about the Prophet of God, my son, Calvin Artury. There will be no Calvary for you. I will *not* forgive you in this world nor in My Heaven. The kiss of death is yours this night, saith Jehovah-Shalom. I called you unto holiness, but Satan is leading you straight to eternal damnation. I will destroy your body *and* your soul. You will open your eyes in the fires of Hell and scream the scream of the damned!"

As the piano and organ music swelled, I shot my hands into electrically charged air and twirled, flinging sweat and spit across the altar. Suddenly, I stopped mid-twirl to face my audience.

"But! Tonight! I will serve you your last drop of mercy if you harken to *My* words!"

Dripping wet, I refused to stop the momentum. "Oh, people, cry out to Jehovah! Oh God, show mercy to your congregation! One more drop, one more drop of mercy! People, did you hear what He said to you tonight?"

I paced the altar again, weeping into my handkerchief. "How many sealed their doom here tonight? Wait, Lord; don't tell me; I don't want to know. Those whom I have loved and nurtured in God's plan, I implore you, *please*—you *must* listen to me! If you fight God's church, He will bring death and destruction to your door. Remember, Jehovah-Rohi has killed before, and He *will* kill again. Be assured, dear people, He will kill again!"

As the people wailed, it was time to bring my nemesis into the prophetic message.

"We must battle against dark angels who threaten Jehovah, threaten us! We must trample demons underfoot! These are the last days, and it will get worse. Saints of God, it will get worse! But remember, signs and wonders follow them who believe!"

Opposing the darkness attacking my ministry, I prayed loud and long, bringing the congregation to an elevated alarm and fear for my safety. They cried out for God to uncover dark angels who waged war against the House of Praise, their voices ascending to a feverish pitch I'd never heard from my church members before that night.

Travailing on the altar of God as more sweat poured from my face, I openly struggled under the magnitude of my predicament, which caused my knees to buckle. Pleading for my beloved members to understand the urgency of the hour, I fought to stand as several ushers rushed to assist me. Grabbing hold of my new golden pulpit to steady myself, I quickly wiped my face and stared directly at my audience, unable to stop my tears.

"When you blaspheme the Holy Ghost, you become like a demon from Hell. God has bestowed upon me the fruits and the gifts of the Spirit. I speak the oracles of God; I am Jehovah-Nissi's mouthpiece. He communicates through me!"

I silenced the music and bowed my head, feeling the Holy Spirit's sudden soft breeze move across the room's vastness, quieting the people.

After an unusual amount of time, I lifted my head to address my church. Though I dared not speak her name, I brought her sin into the light and set it before the congregation: "I am here to tell you this night—the ex-wife of one of my team members is this ministry's darkest angel." I allowed my message to permeate throughout the great auditorium. Turning silent once more for what felt like another eternity, I studied the people's faces. It pleased me as murmurs and whispered words of shock and outrage rolled over the massive congregation.

Then suddenly, although I resisted, my body yielded, and I began to dance in the Spirit, jumping and twirling as the music escalated. The people shouted, praising God again until, at last, I raised my hands and declared the prophecy's end. At that incredible moment, God's omnipotent force passed through me like a lightning bolt, and I jumped the altar railing, rushing up and down the aisles, laying hands on those I could reach.

"Oh, yes! It's true! But she has threatened this ministry for the final time!"

Pentecostal fire fell, encompassing my entire body. God's power flew from my lips into the air and spread among the people, their arms raised to the ceiling. As I walked past them, entire sections of the shouting audience fell where they stood. Stretched across their seats or lying on the floor, they wept in great agony, begging God for justice on my behalf. With many eyes closed, they reached as high as their faith took them to uncover the atrocities facing the House of Praise.

For over an hour, the lamentations continued.

But I wasn't foolish enough to believe everyone agreed with my methods, no matter how much God I brought before them. And yet, this was one risk I was willing to take. A risk to plant in the minds of every soul in that mammoth sanctuary. "Some of you may know this woman. If you see her, you must immediately report her whereabouts to a staff member so that we can inform the police."

Once more, I kept a close eye on my congregation as they sought the face of God. I suspected most knew of whom I spoke without naming her, what she looked like, and where she might be. Someone in that audience had to know where she was hiding. But I had made it clear she was God's number one enemy, and when Andie Oliver turned up as another victim of suicide, the faithful would rejoice and celebrate the Lord's battle and victory over my dark angel.

Within the week, preparations were underway for the largest televised miracle Crusade in the history of my worldwide ministry. *Africa*. Port Harcourt and then Lagos, both cities on the southern coast of Nigeria at the mouth of the Gulf of Guinea. We booked the first two weeks of August for these giant campaigns for souls and for the Nigerian people to receive their miracles and the gift of tongues to ensure their place in the rapture.

Mammoth platforms were underway. Constructed by the free labor of Nigerian men and women, these vast altars would elevate my entire team several feet above the crowds. I prepared my sermons for the people, making new lists of medical conditions, diseases, and infirmities to memorize and practice in front of a full-length mirror to deliver the full effect. "Healings for five thousand people with AIDS will take place tonight in this grand arena!"

I made mental notes to exclaim it with extra exhilaration and authority. Mentioning AIDS lifted any African crowd to pinnacles of excitement. That and witchcraft. "Witchcraft devils, oh sweet people, if you only opened your eyes to see what I see!" I looked into the mirror. I loved the way my body moved when I said the words. I felt on fire as I spoke the word *witchcraft* out loud, even in the privacy of my office.

"There are one thousand souls here tonight afflicted with a disease the doctors cannot diagnose, but God knows every affliction, and He will heal what medical science can't cure! This is the miracle power, people. Take it! Be thou every whit whole!"

I had fine-tuned my healing messages over the years, adding powerful new messages of rewritten prophecy. I would be ready by the Fourth of July annual revival at the House of Praise with additional new material to practice on *my* people first. If I received the response I wanted, I'd take it to Africa.

No one sold religion better than me. If given the opportunity, I'd go toe-to-toe with *Madalyn Murray O'Hair* and force prayer back into schools, overturning that damnable Supreme Court decision. I'd show her. I'd talk to Evan about it. If I pulled that off, I'd rule the Christian world.

But as it stood, it thrilled me that CNN agreed to send a team of reporters to cover the Nigerian Crusade. Evan said to expect prime-time press coverage on that tour and an immeasurable outpouring of love offerings. I instructed all three weekly House of Praise church services, the radio broadcasts, and the daily TV shows to devote time to taking up special offerings for the campaign.

We expected record crowds of a million or more to cram into the outdoor arenas, and it would take millions of dollars to pull it off. Massive audio and video equipment crates, blessed cloths, and translated tracts were in preparation for shipment. It was the American invasion of *Onward Christian Soldiers* on African soil.

Chapter 12

Sleepless In Shiloh
April 1993

ANDIE

The day ended with the first words of love spoken, holding hands, and trekking down the mountain. I didn't want to talk about the turn in our relationship. Not yet. I wasn't ready for long conversations and all the gooey stuff that went with it. My mind was too burdened to chase the dream of a life with Matthew, and I suspected he knew it. A vision of having my every need met and then some. As sweet as it sounded, it was too much to contemplate, and I appreciated he didn't push it.

Ivy returned to her house around six o'clock, and Tobias stepped inside the back door to say he'd finished mending the south pasture fence. He chatted with Matthew as I dished up Ivy's chicken and dumplings for supper. I handed Tobias containers to carry home, then Matthew and I picked up our plates and strolled to the sun porch.

Dark wood beams, stucco walls, terra cotta floor tiles, a fire, and arrangements of fresh flowers—another talent of Ivy's—surrounded us. Sitting at a small table, enjoying dinner but lost in thought, the quiet stifled all conversation.

"This was delicious," I said.

Matthew nodded, then yawned, stretching his arms over his head. "I'm heading to bed early. It's been a long day."

My voice cracked, and I cleared my throat, avoiding his eyes. "You deserve a good night's sleep. I plan to curl up in front of the TV for a while." I wasn't ready to see the inside of his bedroom. I wasn't sure I ever would be.

In further silence, we cleared the table and tidied up. Matthew's help amused me. I wasn't used to a man's help in the kitchen. He sensed my uneasiness because he flipped the dish towel over his shoulder, turned me gently to face him, and said, "Please read nothing into what I said to you today. Honesty is important to me, and letting you know how I feel is part of that. It'll only go as far as you want it to. I'm committed to bringing Artury down, but I'm more committed to ensuring you find happiness again, whether with me or somewhere else. It's entirely up to you."

"Thanks, Matt. Thanks for that." I gave him a weary shrug. "I guess I'm a scarred woman. Damaged goods. I usually accept what I'm offered, but no man has ever offered me much. It's a new experience. Please forgive me for not knowing where my head is right now."

"Understandable. Nothing to forgive. Good night," he said, planting a kiss on my forehead. "And you're not damaged goods, Andie. A bit dented and banged up, but a restorable piece of beauty. Like this farm. Have a good sleep," he said and smiled before walking away.

Listening to him trudging up the staircase, I felt like I was dying from emotional malnutrition. I wanted him to come back down and dispel my loneliness. At supper, I had the uncanny feeling I was looking through him toward some unspoken private sadness of his own. Possibly, we belonged together. When I thought about it, our meeting was more than a coincidence.

"Mavis? You listening? Did you have a hand in this?"

⁀

I tossed and turned, then reached across the king-sized bed. The sheets were cold. Pushing myself up on my elbows, I read the muted red glow of the digital clock—3:25 a.m. "I can't stand this."

I slid out of bed and into the jeans and shirt I'd hiked in the day before, pulled up my hair, and twisted it unevenly into a ponytail. Creeping out of my room and down the long staircase, I slipped into a pair of boots and somebody's old Carhartt coat hanging in the utility room. Quietly, I turned off the alarm, unlocked the back door, and headed to the barn.

I had to find something mindless to do. Something to occupy my time until I could sleep. Lying wide awake all night, I had examined the impossibility of it all and the improbability of living at Shiloh. And yet, knowing Dillon and Gracie resided with the Darwoods gave me a blessed sense of peace. Once Velda knew I was in safe hands, she would find a way to console the twins.

Overhead, the sleepy blue sky flickered dimly through the night's haze. I switched on the barn lights. The horses stirred. Judah and Dan poked their heads out of their stalls. The dogs woke, but once they saw me, they stopped barking. I gave each a good scratch behind their ears before they found a place to flop in the hay. I removed my coat, threw it into a corner, picked up a shovel and pitchfork, and got to work cleaning stalls.

Losing all track of time, I didn't notice the pink sky in the east. The morning air was cool and dry but full of promises of good things to come.

After singing the first few lines of *Aretha Franklin's RESPECT*, the rustling of feet caused me to almost jump out of my boots. I whirled around, hand to my throat. "Damn! You scared me to death!" I swallowed back the tightening in my chest.

"G'mornin' to you, too," he said. His thick morning voice reminded me of peanut butter fudge. Smooth, rich, and sweet, with a touch of salt. "Tobias told me you were out here. I didn't mean to spook you. Keep singing. I love it." With his shoulder resting against the planked barn wall, Matthew's presence was like a hard punch to my gut, which rumbled at seeing him. Six foot two inches of southern gentleman, his handsomely bearded face appeared healthy-looking in the cold air, his silvery hair tousled by the wind. Dressed for working outdoors, he jammed one hand into the pocket of his denim jacket over a gray wool sweater and the other into a pair of soft, well-worn jeans molded to his long legs. Scuffed boots crossed at the ankles—*whew*. No Ralph Lauren runway model ever looked better.

"No, sorry," I said. "My concert is over."

Matthew ran his hand over his mustache and grinned. I liked his air of confidence and calm, and suddenly I felt sleepy. But his deep-dimpled smile was most reassuring, and I also felt strangely comforted standing near him.

"Don't you need a break? This is hard work."

His silky words added heat to my blush, and I reined in a swoon. I'd never swooned in my life. I'd seen it done once or twice, but no man had ever given me a reason to swoon. Conscious of my gunked-up jeans, shit-covered boots, and sweat-soaked face, I forced my hands not to mess with my hair. God only knew what was in it. "Maybe you should wear a cowbell around your neck when you skulk. Whistle or holler or something."

"Was I skulking?"

"You certainly surprised me." *You surprise me, sure enough.* "Actually, you scared the shit out of me," I told him honestly.

"Speaking of shit. I see you don't mind putting your hands in it," he said.

I smiled and pointed to the clean stalls. "I got the floors as clean as I could." Not able to stand motionless around him, I looked for my coat.

"Stalls look good. I didn't realize you like to work with horses. It's a wonder they let you guide them out. They appear relaxed enough." Matthew walked over to Levi and patted his large, black rump. "They seem fine."

I lifted one shoulder and refrained from rolling my eyes, feigning indifference with the exact determination I used around the few men I scorned after the Jasper fiasco. It wasn't easy. Like a beetle tugging at a bud, I felt his tug on my closed heart. He made me squirm with thoughts, feelings, and vibrations I never had with Joe or experienced in my life. Suddenly, my magnolia heart opened. Had I not been a stinky mess, I might've kissed him.

Instead, I shot him a grin and chuckled. "I know little about horses, really. But I can clean their stalls. Yesiree, I've shoveled plenty of shit before. I'm not afraid of hard work or horse shit." *Oh my God, I'm rambling.*

He laughed, and I smiled as I bent over to tie my boot. But I felt my head spin when I straightened and tucked my shirt into my jeans. I leaned against the wall, forcing myself to breathe slowly. Sweat ran hot down my neck, my chest, and over my galloping heart.

"I still think you're beautiful," he said, guiding Levi back into his stall.

Plain tuckered out and sore, I bit back a sigh and gave him the glare of a mother with teenagers. "Eau de Equine. It's my signature fragrance. You like it?" I shook my head and snorted.

Matthew shot back. "I do. We should bottle and sell it. Put your picture on it." Unlike Joe, Matthew possessed a profound sense of humor and a clever mind behind his fine-looking face.

"What a bunch of hooey!" Rolling my eyes, I felt a brief, vicious satisfaction, having done something productive on my own and someone noticing.

"Why are you out here?" he asked. "Tobias will have to find something else for his helper to do this morning."

"Sorry. I couldn't sleep. I think I can now."

"Then why don't you? I'll let Ivy know. She won't mind."

Our eyes met. "Wonderful. I'll soak in the tub, then get some sleep. I had to think."

"Did you think about me?"

"Mostly."

"Good thoughts?"

"Wicked good thoughts," I teased. "But we need to talk."

"About?"

"Each other. Our families. I know only what you've told me, and that's not much. For instance, Ivy told me your mother was a preacher. Why didn't you mention that to me? And how did you lose the top of your finger? All we ever talk about is your work. I'd love to know more about your children, and you've told me nothing about your siblings—"

"—Whoa!" Matthew placed his hand on my shoulder and grinned. "We will talk, I promise. Later. You need to rest."

"Okay." I blew out a breath. Stopping along the flagstone path, I bent forward to poke my nose into a dogwood flower hanging from a tree. Taking in the place's splendor, I strolled to the house with Matthew following me. Spring perennials lined the walks while green buds sat ready to burst on every tree limb. Early morning sunlight percolated through the dense tangle of red maple and pine; the grounds of Shiloh were a peaceful, idyllic scene from a Currier and Ives postcard.

"Better leave your boots and coat outside. Ivy will pitch a fit if you take them in."

Tired, I managed a laugh. "Her fits are milk toast compared to my mother's."

Matthew opened the door, and I tiptoed inside. "When you get up this afternoon," he said, "I'll be at work in my office. We need to make plans to retrieve the items in your lockbox. We'll go after hours. No one will see you."

"You can do that?"

His smile of amusement embarrassed me.

"Never mind."

I barely held my eyes open as I slid my tired body up the stairs, my socks making muted padding sounds on the steps. My wintery heart had warmed again, and I felt myself plunging into something far more entangling than a casual liaison. I was grateful to live in the same universe with such a man. A man so sure of himself and his rightful place in the world. A man like Matthew Callahan.

Chapter 13

ICE-COLD INDIGNATION
May 1993

REVEREND CALVIN ARTURY

In my office, pouring through the scriptures, I spent time in the presence of The Most High, steeped in memories of my childhood. I had laid myself on the altar as a young seminary student, and Jehovah-Jireh rewarded me with many gifts, blessings, and lambs to sacrifice. I had given all. All to Jesus, I surrendered. My cleansings occurred monthly back then.

Every time I touched a man.

A great peace occurred, however, in my earliest childhood, when I was seven, during tent meeting week. It was a special time for Mama and me. I was a dutiful son, never leaving my mother alone—even though my father did. After a long, hot service under a canvas tent filled with wooden benches, straw floors, and the smell of sweat-soaked bodies, Mama and I enjoyed the swimming hole.

"Baptize me, Calvin!" Her spirited laughter, her soprano voice encouraging me to swim into the deep, Mama's playfulness rang in my memories as loud and pure as if it were yesterday. The ice-

cold creek water frightened me as a child. *"Go on, Calvin, no time like the present! Jump in!"* Her words surfaced at the top of my memory. *"Gotta bale hay when the sun shines, baby."*

I jumped in. I sure did. More than anything, I wanted to make Mama proud. Suddenly, a cesspool gurgled and seeped into the middle of my precious memories. *Get thee behind me, Satan. I refuse to think about my father's sisters!* Vile women who had attached leeches to my soul as a young boy.

At thirteen, I had escaped my oppressors, discovered church camp and kissing men. And except for the cherished memory of my mother, women were the barbed wire of my life. Keeping me from the Kingdom of God, women were an inscrutable force to be reckoned with. They never left me alone when I walked out of covenant with God. Prissy females with painted faces and pointy breasts. Loose women who threw themselves at me and not only in a bar. They followed me around the church, and I hated it.

Mama had told me the sure way to Heaven was to preach God's word. I also started preaching to keep women at arm's length.

In a new suit and shoes, my hair cut high and tight and neatly combed back with dashes of greasy kid stuff, I took pleasure in my look as a dapper young preacher. That's when I noticed Vivian.

She was seventeen and unreservedly happy. The prettiest girl I'd ever met that summer. Her coffee-brown eyes made me jittery watching her sing. Claiming salvation, Vivi did not befriend girls who swayed their hips like belly dancers down the aisle between rows of wooden benches packed hip-to-hip with the saints of God. Girls in thin cotton dusters who had fixed their eyes on any good-looking evangelist in town for the week. Girls who pranced straight to the altars in sweltering tent meetings and summer revivals to be noticed.

I directed the flock of primarily women in the sinner's prayer but was never sure if it was Jesus they sought or me. Flinging their unsaved arms into the air for deliverance from all sin, they shook their breasts and jiggled their behinds in front of every red-necked boy in town.

Aside from her sex, Vivian was different. She played the piano for her church and lived holy, like my mother. To my surprise, she said yes to receiving the baptism in the Spirit and to my marriage proposal. I went through with the marriage, figuring I was only in it for appearance's sake. Godly congregations in the '50s wanted their young pastors married off to a church member. I assumed Vivi would split once she opened my Pandora's box. And as I matured, I discovered not only men, but suddenly some women appealed to me. Monogamy was not my strong suit. Besides, what did Vivi know about becoming a preacher's wife?

But what *I* didn't know was the clout Vivi's daddy wielded. Ultimately, I praised God for Vivi: my blessing, my opportunity to enter the circles of the politically rich and famous. It was my big break, and I took it. It resulted in sanctuaries filled with wealthy members, sinners to save, and a chance to travel the world for Jesus.

Of course, I struggled with the scripture. My followers expected a family man. I'd married Vivi and tried hard. Sometimes it was good. But most times, sex with Vivi was like trying to put penny loafers on a pig. To her credit, she never gave up on me. She loved me until the end. I couldn't love her back. Not the way she deserved.

Fannie's voice interrupted my thoughts. "Reverend Artury, Pat Robertson's secretary, is on the line; she needs your response."

"Yes," I sighed. "Tell him I'll be there."

For months, The Christian Coalition had pushed for my participation. Political nonsense in my mind. My kingdom was not of this world, although I had publicly agreed with Billy Graham that evangelical Christians should organize corporately to gain control of Congress, the judiciary, and the executive branch of the American government. But Pat Robertson's Coalition sought to gain control of the Republican party. I wasn't entirely interested. I had enough on my plate.

My plan to amass millions of dollars and take the nation by storm wasn't for political gain, as were my colleagues. My desire to take the world for the cause of Christ, however, burned like an eternal flame in my soul.

Like my marriage to Vivi, I would attend the Road to Victory Conference for appearances' sake. In truth, I despised them all—Falwell, Robertson, Oliver North, all of them. Bloodsuckers on the mind of Christ. Their stealth tactics, however, were another matter. I had every intention of learning more about those maneuvers.

And yet, the irritation of too many meetings besieged me, grated on my nerves, and I was late for the next one. Only recently had I yearned for the country-boy preacher I once was. Leave the business side of things to Evan and everybody else. Except God had entrusted His kingdom into my hands. It was my cross to bear alone.

My legal team had called a meeting. More accusations of illegal dealings. False accusers never ceased to persecute the church, which suddenly included mine. From early Christianity, endless harassment and scandal followed the children of God, and as much as I wanted immunity from it, persecution, and not just from Andie Oliver, had found me, taking its toll on me mentally.

In the past months, I'd forgotten too many appointments. Community board meetings, my dentist, my stylist, my masseuse, and my dinner engagement with PTL network executives, arriving in time for coffee and dessert. How embarrassing. I'd even forgotten to schedule my annual trip to New York to meet with my tailor.

All I wanted was to prepare for my next sermon, spend time in prayer, and have a soft chest to lie on. The battles of the mind escalated with every legal inquest.

"Your car is here, Reverend."

Time for war.

I walked to my waiting car in a torrent of rain. The liquid needles bruised my flesh and soaked my hair. I had forgotten to open my umbrella.

Chapter 14

Strong Coffee and Intuition
May 1993

Andie

Ivy's presence filled a room and overtook it. Most people liked her, despite or perhaps because of her habit of telling you precisely what she thought. Her boisterous laugh was contagious. It was easy to see why Matthew loved her. Her protective glance followed me to the coffee pot. "How are you feeling? You slept in."

I checked my new watch, another gift from Ivy. "My goodness, it's ten o'clock. I guess I have. Easy to do here. You wanted help in the garden this morning. I'm sorry."

"No worries. I got Tobias out there now, planting tomatoes and beans. We'll have lots of canning to do come August."

I poured myself a mug of Ivy's coffee, rich and robust, with a kick like a Clydesdale. I recalled Matthew saying he valued Ivy for her unfailing courtesy, forty-five years of friendship, and her coffee.

"I know this is none of my business, Andie, and you've only been here a month. But time has no meaning when the stars, planets, and moon line up—and when all indications point the way."

"What are you talking about?"

"Did Matthew ask you to marry him yet?" Ivy beat three eggs into a bowl of coffee cake batter. "Have you thought of moving here?"

"Ivy. It's only been a month!" It did not surprise me that Ivy knew. I couldn't help but smile at her inquisitiveness. "If you must know, he's not asked. I've got nothing to move, anyway." I sat at the kitchen table by the window, drinking my coffee and folding towels from the dryer. The window rattled, and I glanced outside to see rain clouds moving across the sky.

"Huh. Tobias asked me to marry him the week after we met. At your age, a month is plenty of time. You best be thinking about your answer because I know Matthew, and he'll be asking. The man is in love. He wants you here. You need to think about it—about commitment—about marrying again. You know it was God who brought you to Shiloh."

"Other than my children, I've been thinking of little else. I don't know if I want to marry again. I've paid a steep price for my freedom." Fingering the baked warmth of the towels, I felt uncomfortable having that conversation with Ivy. My mind had become as weary as my body, and I wanted to crawl back into bed. "And I don't think God brought me here only to marry again."

"You sure your enthusiasm to remain single isn't just to mask your fear of another unfortunate marriage?"

I shot her a look of surprise. "Do you realize I was married one month out of high school? Married for almost seventeen years with never a moment's peace. Continually fearful of what would piss him off, what I was doing wrong. I no longer walk on eggshells or answer to anybody. Besides, Matthew doesn't need my baggage."

"I'm not trying to sell you on Matthew's virtues; I think you know a little of what they are. He's good and forthright; nothing shakes him. I've known him since I delivered him into this world."

Ivy greased her cake pan. "He'll not give you a moment's sorrow. Not if he can help it. Haven't you been at peace here?"

"Yes, of course." I pushed aside the towels, folded, stacked, and ready for the linen closet, and walked to the counter. "But doesn't everybody expect the wife to toe the line after the honeymoon? I tell you, Ivy, other than my daddy, all the men I've known wanted a maid or a sex kitten, not a wife."

"I don't know as I'd go that far," she said as she poured out the batter. "I only go by my marriage, not other folks'. I met Tobias, married him, and we've been in the same bed ever since. We take turns toeing the line, as you say." She leaned over the counter, smiled, and touched my face with her finger, leaving flour on my cheek. "I've prayed every day for fifteen years; God bless Matthew for bringing Tobias and me here to this place. And now He has, with you. Matthew needs you. And you need him."

"Oh, Ivy," I said, done in by the past few months' events. "My mind is tired." I rested my head on my hand. "It's more than I want to deal with right now." My thoughts bit into my logic and reasoning. "This is definitely a beautiful place to live." I chewed at my lip, remembering Shady Acres.

Ivy's toffee-brown arms shimmered with the flush of the oven's heat. "A slice of Heaven, for sure. I can hardly wait to return to the mountain when I'm gone," she said. Ivy sprinkled cinnamon and walnuts on the cake, then moved the pan onto the rack. "All you have to do is decide what *you* want. But Matthew will see this through—the mission you're on. And no matter your decision, he will abide by it."

That was the problem. I didn't know whether to give my heart away again and risk another terrible marriage or stay single and run my life the way I wanted. I finally learned to look for life's lessons, not miracles. I even thought I might enjoy a normal single life. The key word being—*normal.*

But becoming Matthew's wife, with what it entailed, made my heart leap. And then there was his ability to make me laugh on a whim, his soft touch, cool head, and voice—calm as a morning sunrise—I'd fallen in love with him. That much was true. I reasoned he wasn't like Joe, not by a long shot. Joe never made me laugh during our entire marriage. He made me frown a lot, cry frequently, and nurse a sorrowful heart nearly every day. I sighed. "Once you've suffered from a horrific marriage, you're not eager to get back into another one."

Ivy didn't answer. She raised her penciled-in eyebrows instead and loaded the dishwasher.

"Please don't mention all of this to Matt," I said.

"Not to worry. I'm bad to listen, but pass little on. It sounds to me, though—all that baggage you say you got needs dropping off at the nearest Goodwill box. Then, once your children are here with you, you throw the rest out."

Chapter 15

News From Home
May 1993

MATTHEW

Mug in hand, Andie closed the door to my office and sat in front of my desk. Although her eyes sparkled like the blue light of dawn in the cool shimmer of the morning, she looked tired. Extremely tired, if the shadows beneath her eyes were any indication. I'd worried most of the night, contemplating how to tell her that another person she loved had died.

"What's wrong, Matt?"

"I received word from my informant this morning. It's—"

"—*Who* is your informant, exactly? I think it's time you told me."

"Nobody you know. Not yet, anyway. It's my mother."

"Your preacher mama?" Andie giggled like a little girl.

"You bet. My mother, adorable as she is, has begged to play detective for me on several of my cases. The woman has read every Ellery Queen ever published. She was perfect for the job. Nobody suspected her. At first, I balked. My mother's safety was my chief concern. But she has done some great legwork on your behalf.

She's a smart cookie and coming to supper Saturday evening. I can't hold her back any longer. Mother's determined to meet you. She wants to see this dark angel I have hidden in my house. A dark angel she suspects I'm attached to."

"Oh, Matthew, no! I'm sure they've filled her head with lies about me!"

I smiled at her agonized expression. "Mother is a woman of extraordinary faith and reasoning. She doesn't believe a word of it. Or much of anything Artury preaches. But—"

"—What? Are my kids okay?"

"They're fine. In fact, Mother met them when she delivered the message to Mrs. Darwood. Your children are worried about you, but they're good. Mother said you must be beautiful if you look anything like your twins." I watched her blush. Andie did not know her true loveliness.

"There you go again—that word. But please thank your mother for me. I'm so grateful."

"Mrs. Darwood told Mother to tell you not to worry. She'll take good care of the twins. Mother liked Mrs. and Mrs. Darwood. They're quite aware of the gravity of the situation. They talked outside at the picnic table. We know someone definitely bugged their house by the questions your ex has asked the twins. Dillon and Gracie never knew why Mother was there. She plays a great Avon lady." Andie giggled again. I loved the sound of her voice. "But Andie, I need to tell you about your father-in-law."

"Al." Her eyes immediately teared up.

I nodded. "Mother said they announced in church that he passed away last week. Heart attack. He died peacefully in his sleep. They're burying him today in Lexington. In a cemetery near his boyhood church. Near his son, they said."

"Yes, of course. They would bury him next to Ted."

My heart ached watching her tears fall. "Were you close to him?"

"Yes. I was." Her hands wrapped tightly around her coffee mug. "I'm positive God took him. Al couldn't stand the hypocrisy. He was the only person on my side. Although he was powerless to do anything for me, he loved me. He did." She pulled a tissue from the box on my desk. "What hurts most is I can't go to the funeral or even send a card. Selma will be there instead of me. Selma. He didn't even like Selma. It's not fair."

She wiped her eyes. "I'm sure Joe will take Dillon and Gracie to the funeral. Maudy must be a wreck. I feel so helpless." Andie reached across the desk and touched my arm. "You stayed awake thinking about how to tell me this, didn't you?"

My eyes grew blurry with tears. "Yes," I said.

Her mouth opened slightly, and I saw the slightest hint of fear. A protective impulse surged inside me, a compulsion to shield and protect her. I walked around my desk and took her to the couch in front of the fireplace. Pulling her against my chest, I tucked her head under my chin and laced my fingers into her hair. It possessed only the slightest hint of silver. Most of its rich honey color shone gold and red. I sensed her thoughts were of Al, an old man she once knew and loved. She sat back to wipe tears from her eyes, and I felt her shiver.

"Are you okay?" I asked.

She shrugged, falling forward to bury herself in my chest again. Grasping my shirt, she reminded me of a sad little girl.

"Why?" she asked.

"Why what?"

"Just why," she whispered to my heart. On that cool June morning, the room glowed warm from the fire. The wind picked up, and the first drops of rain hit the windows. I had made it a habit to open the shutters every morning, knowing she liked them open. Holding her as tightly as possible wasn't much of an answer, but it was all I had.

Chapter 16

Graveyard Wisdom
June 1993

Andie

Matthew had gone to Boone for a meeting at the university. I sat for a light supper next to Tobias while Ivy announced we would avoid any more talk about my *inevitable marriage* to Matthew. "I'm not pushy," Ivy said. "But I feel you and Mattie have much to discuss. In the meantime, we shall leave this romance to blossom in God's time, hey Toby?"

"Whatever you say, woman. You know best." He winked at me, and I winked back. Ivy and Tobias had become dear friends, and in watching their playfulness, I yearned for a marriage like theirs.

After supper, I carried a glass of wine and sat by the fire in Matthew's office. I felt closer to him in that room and missed him. I smiled, realizing it.

"Mind if I join you?" Tobias held his usual coffee cup and piece of pie in his hands. More and more, I saw his resemblance to Rupert in his soft mannerisms and simple needs.

I motioned for him to sit. "Please. Join me. Put your feet up. The fire feels good."

"Ah," he said. "The smell and sound of hot embers. I love the songs only a fire can sing, don't you?"

"I do. My daddy did, too. He made a fire every day in the winter. We often huddled around it when the electricity was out."

Tobias chuckled. "I find it strange how cool the mountains can be in June."

Together, we watched it burn down to bright orange coals, pulsing like the glow of hundreds of fireflies. The room grew quiet until he turned to me, his smile broad and flashing. "How do you feel about Shiloh? Do you like it here?"

"Yes. I feel safe. Maybe for the first time since I left my parents' home. But I miss my children. I worry we will never find the right time to expose Calvin Artury to someone who will prosecute him and make it stick."

Tobias straightened and sipped his coffee. "I understand why you did not go to the police. Men like the Reverend pay powerful lawyers to explain away the evidence. Or they pay evil men to destroy it. You were alone. It must've been frightening."

"Terrified, is more the word. It's been quite a journey. I all but lost my mind, keeping it hidden inside me. I have evidence, but I've done nothing with it as of today. But I hope Calvin has prepared his explanation for his fall from grace because, at some point, I plan to use that evidence."

"Hmmm," Tobias groaned. "The man is an enigma." He rose to stoke the fire. "Do you think you've lost your ability to love again?"

I sighed. "I don't mean to be elusive as a wet fish. Truly. Matthew deserves better."

Tobias slumped back in his chair, his legs sprawled out. "I know Matthew well. He doesn't think about you giving him what he deserves. His life's purpose is giving to others, especially those he loves. His capacity for love is an amazing virtue not seen in most men. Matthew's love for God, well, it's a childlike thing. Yet strong and unbending. Here is something you must remember: often God will put us where we don't think we belong, which makes the miracle of our redemption and His vengeance against our enemies that much sweeter."

As I mulled over his wise words, I suspected Tobias was wise beyond his sixty-five years. Godly. A trustworthy man, as much as my daddy and Rupert. I felt something special about him deep in my heart.

I stood and wandered to the window, loving the exquisite house Matthew restored—a calm, green sanctuary in the middle of a mountain meadow. I treasured the view of the old cemetery from his office window, fenced in with granite posts and iron chains bordered by ancient oaks. The gravestones laid low, some worn nearly smooth, dating back to the Civil War and the Battle of Shiloh—I'd read most of them.

Blessed are those who mourn, for they will receive comfort. Someone had carved the beatitude into a massive piece of granite at the cemetery entrance. I thought about that scripture, sharing the fire with Tobias. In the window, the reflection of the flames lit up the more lonely and hurtful moments of my life.

I felt Tobias watching me, and I wanted to explain myself further. "When Joe and I were first married, I loved God in a way I doubt I ever will again."

"Ah, the inexperienced adoration of a new bride. Unfettered and blind as a newborn kitten," he said.

"But I can't find my faith, Tobias. I'm trying, but—" Choked by tears, I struggled to catch my breath. "I can't find God anywhere."

Tobias rose from his chair, walked over, and stood beside me at the window. "When you can't find your faith, when you can't find God, there's only one thing you can do."

"And what's that?"

"Trust Him. Be patient. Let Him find *you.*"

Chapter 17

C.S.K.
June 1993

ANDIE

I'd fallen asleep sitting in a chair in Matthew's office when I felt his lips brush a gentle kiss across my forehead like a whisper. I stirred, smiling at him.

"I missed you," he said. "I raced home. I feel sixteen. Couldn't concentrate on the meeting. Not a lick."

Heavy and half-open, my eyes glanced at the clock. "You're home early."

"Right, but I see you're ready for bed."

I yawned. "I guess I am."

"Then off with you. I'll see you in the morning."

"Leftovers are in the fridge. Ivy told me to tell you."

"Good. I'm hungry."

"Goodnight, then." I wanted to stay up and talk, but I wanted to sleep more. He kissed me again, pulled me into a brief hug, smiled, and turned me around, pointing me to the stairs. I dragged my sleepy body upstairs to my room, closed the door, and crawled into bed.

Two hours into a restless sleep, my eyes snapped open. Something new and inevitable rose in me, like a fin above water. It circled my heart, drawing a line between the past and present. At two a.m. I needed to see him.

Time to spend the rest of my life in the future instead of in the past.

I jumped out of bed and punched my fists through the sleeves of the silk robe Ivy had given me. Unaware of what tomorrow held, I exchanged my fear for a fresh sense of direction, suddenly changing all my silly daydreams into a goal—a desire—to belong to Matthew.

Attempting to remove the tired look from my face, I added a little blusher and combed my hair down until it licked my shoulders. Dabbing perfume behind my ears and knees, I needed all the help I could get.

Never having been to Matthew's room, I recalled standing in the backyard and pointing to a balcony and the French doors leading out. He told me it was his bedroom, and the balcony gave him a full view of his property, adding only the cleaning ladies and Ivy had ever been inside. At the time, I wondered if his last comment was for my benefit.

After opening my bedroom door, I peered down the long, dimly lit corridor connected to another short hallway ending at Matthew's bedroom door. The next few hours would determine the direction of my life. My house shoes slapped the bottoms of my feet, and my robe flew out behind me. I arrived at his door, stood momentarily, breathing deeply, and knocked.

No answer.

I knocked again. A little harder.

When the door creaked open, his groggy face appeared. The thick hair on his bare chest was salt-and-pepper, like his beard. He must've thrown on the denim shorts because I couldn't imagine him sleeping in them.

Matthew

I thought I was dreaming until the knocking woke me. Falling out of bed, I nearly tripped, pulling on my shorts. My heart beat as though I'd run a marathon. When I cracked open the door, I couldn't believe she was standing there, smiling.

"Andie? Is everything okay?"

"Yes. I'm sorry to wake you. I couldn't sleep."

"What time is it?"

"Two in the morning. I'm sorry, I'll let you go back to sleep."

She turned to leave.

It was one of those moments when I knew there was a God. A God who gently reminded me that life goes on. It'd been a long time. *Could this old peacock still spread his feathers?* She smelled of jasmine, and suddenly, I felt wide awake.

"Don't you dare leave. Come in. You want to talk?"

"Yes, I do."

Andie

I stepped into a room resembling an exotic place and time. He had centered his carved mahogany bed in the middle of the floor. Its four posts supported a grand canopy. Dwarfed by the enormous room itself, the bed's splendor caused my breath to catch in my throat.

Matthew lit a fire, then walked over and switched on a lamp. Hanging next to massive bookcases that brushed the ceiling, a Civil War musket glowed in the firelight as if burning to tell its story. Either Matthew or his decorator had tossed animal print pillows and chenille throws over an overstuffed loveseat in front of the fire. *Architecture Digest, Field and Stream*, and his Bible lay on another old trunk used as a coffee table. A man's room. Pictures of his family in brass frames lined the mantle under a twelve-point whitetail buck's head mounted on the stone.

Matthew excused himself and walked to his ensuite bathroom. I sat on a wingback chair to wait. When he returned, he had pulled on a fresh T-shirt, and I smelled the minty fresh scent of Scope. Definitely a gentleman.

He approached me and held out his hand. "Please, Andie, come sit by me."

My eyes swept over him as I moved to the loveseat with him. He was shiver handsome, and I ached to feel the brush of his soft beard against my skin.

Matthew reached out and ran his fingers through my hair. Silently, he leaned forward, and I drank in the sweetness of his kiss, a slow, drugging kiss that sang through my veins. And then I pulled back. "I need to talk," I said, my cheeks hot as he explored my face with his lips.

"You bring a list?"

The world shrank to the room about us. My emotions whirled and skidded, and I lightly pushed him away. "Please, Matthew. I'm self-conscious—about my body. I've had three babies. I'm not nineteen anymore."

"Neither am I. And your body is fine," he said with an edge, which meant I was annoying when I talked that way.

He cradled my face in his hands. "Your cheeks are soft as a baby's," he said. And then he loosened his embrace and smiled. I think he realized I really needed to talk.

MATTHEW

Her eyes were as blue as the tiny slippers on her feet. My heart beat faster, needing her, wanting her.

"I had no right to move so fast."

Opening my mouth to apologize again, she surprised me by laying one finger gently against my lips. "Yes, you did." Her sincerity moved me to tears. "You had every right. You saved me from prison, from insanity—and from Hell."

It was hard to breathe, and I shook my head slowly. "How can this be happening?"

"I don't know," she said. Confusion clouded her countenance briefly, then cleared. "But long ago, I learned some things you can't explain. They're simply true."

I couldn't stop myself. I kissed her again, a succession of slow kisses that forced me to come up for air. When I moved to sweep her back into another kiss, she pulled away again, gasping to catch her breath. "I—I can't. What time is it?" She sat up, dazed. "What am I doing?"

"Kissing me," I said. Whatever else she had put on her list needed to wait. I reached for her again, but she held me off.

Her face flushed, and she pressed her hands to my chest, this time pushing firmly and then to her cheeks as if trying to cool them. "Godamighty—I mean—I hardly know you—"

"—I believe you know me." On that point, I was sure. I smiled and tucked a strand of her hair behind her ear. "I feel we've known each other a long time."

At that, she gave me a shaky laugh. "You're right. I knew your hands a long time ago," she whispered, as if speaking to herself.

With an inward start, I recalled she had mentioned my hands before. I knew there were things she had not yet revealed about herself. But then, there were a few things I'd not told her either.

"Although," she continued, "I *want* to know *more* about you."

My thoughts jumbled, and I took a deep breath. "Of course you would. What an idiot I am." I raked my defective hand through my hair. "My name is Callahan," I said. Matthew Wayne Callahan. At your service, I need hardly add. Oh, yeah. I think I said that already."

Laughing, Andie pulled herself up and leaned against the arm of the loveseat, resting her head in her hand. "Tell me more about Matthew Callahan," she said.

"Well." I cleared my throat twice and tried to calm my neglected libido. You know about my mother. I've three brothers: Mark, Luke, and John. And a sister-in-law: Mark's wife, Patsy."

"You're kidding, right? Mathew, Mark, Luke, and John?"

"I never kid about my brothers. Remember, my mother is a pastor. My father, Court Callahan, died when I was very young. Actually, he was murdered. I grew up fast." It was a punch to my gut to tell her. To say it out loud. I didn't think of my father often.

"Murdered? How horrible for you! You didn't stay a child long."

"I haven't been a child since I turned six, and a liquored-up swamp-dweller in Morehead City blew him away over a land deal. Dad owned property in several Southern states. Mother refused to sell his holdings after his death. Her second husband, Jack, was one of the first men in North Carolina to sign a prenup. My mother is a smart gal. I think I told you that. But Jack didn't care what Mother owned. He was a chef, catering meals for the racetracks from New York to Florida, including the Kentucky Derby. A happy, handsome Italian man, a veteran like Dad, and a Catholic who converted to Pentecostal Holiness. Can you imagine? A preacher married to someone who spent his life at the tracks. But," and I laughed, "it worked. He was a good guy, good to Mother and me."

I sat and allowed some of what I said to sink in. Andie didn't seem phased by any of it. "I was an only child until Jack and Mother had the rest of the rascally bunch of males I call brothers. John loved him the most—followed him everywhere. My stepdad died in 1986, a year before my daughter passed away. Their deaths were hard on Mother. But she had her four sons and a small congregation who have loyally sat their butts in her pews for years. I want to take you there soon. Would that be okay?"

"Maybe. I'm not a church-goer these days," Andie said. "But your family sounds like wonderful people."

"They are." I looked into the fire, feeling the pain of loss. "Hey, now. Tell me about why my hands looked so familiar to you."

Andie spoke slowly, as though brushing away the cobwebs from her memories, relaying in detail the story of my hands, fighting for her life and the life of her unborn child.

"That's why you let me into the apartment."

She took my defective hand and pressed a kiss into my palm. "The *only* reason."

I caressed her face, then stood and stoked a gentle fire. "Now, I've got something to tell you. You asked me how I lost this finger." Sitting beside her again, my heart swelled with affection as she leaned against my chest, waiting intently for more.

"I lost my finger field dressing that deer." I pointed to the buck hanging over the fireplace. "I had been hunting all morning and got careless with my bowie knife. They make those knives to cut through bone. Unfortunately, it sliced right through mine. The top of my finger dangled by a flap of skin, and I nearly passed out. Thank God that Tobias was with me. He administered first aid, wrapped it, and then flew back to the house five miles away. You should've seen that man run. He looked like Jesse Owens reincarnated. Ivy called the paramedics, but I'd lost pints of blood by the time they got to me. You ready for this?"

She nodded, and I continued. "This may sound familiar to you, and even as I tell it, it sounds ridiculously similar to your experience. In the hospital, after my surgery, I had a dream, vision, or whatever you want to call it. I saw a gold ring sparkling in the shallow part of our pond, down by the edge of the meadow near Ivy's house. The next day, I telephoned my daughter; she was only eight. I told her to go to the pond, to the rock where she fished with her brother. To look near the edge for a gold ring. Of course, she found it. She meant to keep it. But when Jessie heard about an auction at Baptist Hospital, she donated the ring. She had spent many weeks at Baptist. It surprised me my eight-year-old daughter would donate that ring, but—she did." My voice trailed off. "Anyway, that was the last we saw of the ring. The strange thing about that gold ring—it looked very much like the one you're wearing."

Andie sat in sheer astonishment. "I have to tell you. Daddy worked for R. J. Reynolds. He supervised a committee to raise money for the hospital's building fund. They put together several auctions, and at one of them, he bid on this ring as a gift for Dixie. But my fussy mother didn't like the plainness of it, so she gave it to me. I never wore it much until I realized Joe was stealing my jewelry. Then I put it on my right hand and never took it off. I know it's stamped; I thought it had something to do with the gold content or the maker."

"Let's check inside," I said. "There may be initials. C.S.K."

Andie pulled the ring off her finger. "You look. I think I need glasses."

I held it up to the firelight. "You need glasses?" We both chuckled as I reached for my readers on the table. Holding the ring toward the light, I smiled. "C.S.K. This is the ring. I'll be damned."

Her lips parted in surprise. "This is all too much. Day after day, the fate of our meeting becomes more and more obvious. Now I *know* I'm in *The Twilight Zone*."

"Andie. C.S.K. isn't the maker. It's the initials of the original owner."

"You know who owned it?"

"I do. Ivy told me. Coretta Scott King."

"THE Coretta Scott King, wife of Martin Luther?"

"That's the one. The Kings and their entourage traveled through North Carolina in 1967 and stopped for about an hour to visit Ivy and Tobias. Of course, Ivy and Tobias didn't live here in '67;

they lived on a small farm near Mother. Ivy told you how closely they worked with the Civil Rights Movement. Anyway, Doctor King wished to thank them personally and give them a token of appreciation. A letter signed by him. Tobias framed it. It hangs on the wall in his den. Ask to see it whenever you get up to the house. But Coretta had used Ivy's bathroom to wash up and left her ring on the sink. When Ivy contacted her, Coretta told Ivy to keep it. Years later, Ivy thought she had lost it and worried herself into a tizzy."

Andie slid the ring back on her finger. "Oh, poor Ivy. How devastating for her to lose a ring like this."

"Years later, Ivy told me the story, but it was too late. I would've returned the ring to her, but Jessie and I had already donated it and other items to the hospital auction. But Ivy felt better, knowing we found it and donated it to a good cause. She accepted its loss. Now, here it is, on your hand." I kissed the ring on her finger. "On Andie Oliver's right hand."

Andie stared at the ring. "Ivy never mentioned it. Do you think she noticed?"

"She saw it the moment she met you. That's how she knew you were supposed to be here. She said she'd let me tell the ring story."

The clock read four a.m. "We've been talking a long time. Do you think you've heard enough about me for one night?" I asked.

"Yes," Andie said.

I certainly hadn't imagined the quickening of my heart as I looked into her eyes again. Or the unusual quiver low in my belly, a sensation that made me shudder repeatedly. That night, there were no shadows across my heart as Andie stood and untied her robe, letting it fall to the floor, revealing perfumed and powdered naked flesh.

Chapter 18

The Joining of Souls

June 1993

Matthew

I stood and pulled off my shirt, letting it fall on the loveseat behind me. My eyes roamed her body; she wasn't skinny, but she certainly wasn't overweight. I took in the soft roundness of her hips and her small waist. Pulling her into a warm embrace, I felt her bare breasts against my chest, making my heart thump erratically. For a second, I toyed with a blond wisp of her hair trailing down to her shoulder, my mouth grazing her earlobe. I skimmed my palm down her back, and she arched against my caress like a sleek cat.

Looking into her expressive face, I smiled as she blushed. "I can't believe I'm saying this," she said. "I'm in love with you, Matthew. Every day, I list reasons I shouldn't be, but this feeling deepens and intensifies." She trailed her fingernail down my bare chest.

I retook both of her hands and held them, prayer-like, in mine. "I want you to know I'm not only committed to your cause, Andie, but to you. I not only love you, but I'm also giving you my heart and my life. I want you with me." Holding her close, I nuzzled her ear again. "I want you in my bed."

"Just for tonight?"

"Tonight and always."

Covered in gooseflesh, she slipped under my blankets. I smiled, pulled off my shorts, and climbed into bed beside her. Slowly, my hand moved downward, skimming either side of her body to her thighs. I was too emotion-filled to speak. The blood pounded through my chest as I kissed her soft lips, neck, and ample breasts, then ran my tongue over her round belly and down to the velvet parts of her, caressing her with my mouth, adoring her with my tongue.

Andie's breasts rose sharply as she drew in a breath. I moved back up her body, and she shivered. Taking her hand, I laid it on me, wanting her to feel me. "This is what you do to me," I said.

"Then love me," she said. "Discover every inch."

I smiled, watching the faint outline of her as she spoke.

"Nothing would please me more." We lay in my heavily quilted bed, kissing here and there, wherever our eyes lingered in the dim, wavy light of the fire-lit room. Finally, I moved on top of her, and she wrapped her legs around mine. I felt the tips of her breast crush into my skin, hardening.

Her arms closed gently about my neck. She whispered, "Matthew—I need all of you."

I shuddered. "You have me, Andie."

We moved slowly, unhurriedly, like two people whose pent-up passions now begged to be released, shattering the remains of every wall and any fortress built.

Andie's hands ran smoothly and slowly along my neck and shoulders, down to the small of my back, then up my spine. I cupped my hands under her buttocks and brought her up as I forced myself deeper into her, bringing me to the pinnacle of orgasm with her.

We lay still in the absolute quiet of the room, our breathing and hearts beating as one. "The first of many," I said, nuzzling her.

"Can I believe you?" Her breaths were short and fast.

"Yes. Always."

We dozed lightly until Andie had to get up to find the bathroom. The fire had gone out; darkness filled the room. Lying in my warm bed with her scent on my skin, I couldn't wait until she returned. Even the thought of her grew pungent. The morning sun was minutes from dawning, but my bed felt empty, and I prayed it wasn't a dream.

Finally, I felt her again. I snuggled her into my arms. Her small breath warmed my shoulder, and her hand pressed against my chest. Within minutes, she had fallen asleep, catching each loving, fragile beat of my heart in her hand, receiving my spirit with absolute sleeping innocence.

And just like that, I was a giant again.

Aside from the lucky sheet twisted around her thigh, she was naked and uncovered. The sun rose, pouring in through the shutter's slats, bathing her in a subtle ray and tracing the silhouette of her legs, back, shoulders, and neck. A silver key on a chain snaked between her breasts. A key to her lockbox she'd told me about, or perhaps a key to her heart. I propped myself up, studying every inch of her fair and delicate skin, my fingers fluttering over the swell of her hip. A sliver of grace, a love song, a statuette carved by unseen hands. Andie was, undoubtedly, the centerpiece jewel in God's crown.

She stirred and rolled over in the warm sheets, and my hand found the smooth curve of her shoulder. I pressed my lips to her neck and my groin to her naked buttocks. Everything fell into place. We lay there like two exquisite pieces of porcelain, broken and glued back together.

At that moment, we only needed one heart. I whispered in her ear, but up came her hand, a bouquet of fingers, and touched my lips in the muted morning sun. "Quiet," she said. "If I'm dreaming, I never want to wake up."

Lying amid sex-tangled sheets, I stroked her silky skin and pulled her closer. She smiled. "Maybe we *should* get up; what time is it?" Her clever fingers slipped down between us, encircling me. "Won't Ivy miss us at breakfast?"

I yawned. "Does it matter?" I was finally ready to sleep.

"I think you should bring breakfast back to bed," she said.

"Sounds great, and I'd be happy to, but let's rest first."

She snuggled back into my chest and then copied my yawn. "Good idea." I watched her fade. Within minutes, she had fallen back to sleep yet again. Her spirit had finally calmed itself, and I followed close behind.

♥

At nine in the morning, I slipped out of bed, showered, and took off for the kitchen. I intended to surprise her. Our first morning of breakfast in bed, as she requested. I would spoil her for the rest of our days. She had lived a horrible existence with a man who did not love or appreciate her, and for the life of me, I could not imagine such a monster. The epitome of everything I longed for and never believed existed. Andie proved a woman could love me for all the right reasons, despite my shattered dreams. Rushing down the staircase, I caught myself whistling. I hadn't whistled in years.

Introduced to hundreds of beautiful girls worldwide, I had my pick of eligible, single ladies. But that little woman lying in my bed had no clue as to the extent of my wealth other than what she saw around her. And she didn't care. All she ever wanted was for someone to love her, to love her children, and to work together to provide a comfortable life.

Somehow, I knew Andie's ability to love me back towered higher than the mountain I lived on. My mother never hid her prayers about her boys. For me, she prayed for God to show me the path to the right woman's door. He had done that and more.

"Snoring away?" Ivy asked.

Amused, I kissed her cheek. "A regular buzz saw in a barnyard."

Ivy knew. Of course, she knew. I never slept late. When neither Andie nor I showed up for breakfast, she had peeked in Andie's bedroom and found it empty.

"Did you tell her?" Ivy's inquisitive eyes burrowed into mine.

"No. I will. Today." I sighed. "I promise, Ivy. Okay?"

Tobias sat at the breakfast bar, drinking Ivy's buzz-worthy coffee. He winked at me as if I were still the twelve-year-old boy who followed him everywhere.

Ivy made a face at her husband. "What you looking at, Toby? You not think a man Mattie's age can love again?"

"Ha, woman. The older the bull, the stiffer the horn. Every man knows that."

"You wish," said Ivy.

Chapter 19

Handwriting On the Wall
June 1993

Andie

I opened one eye when I heard Matthew close the door behind him. Laying on the bed, I stretched, then searched for the remote on the nightstand. Half-hidden in an armoire that matched his bed, the TV offered no diversion from his magnificent bedroom. In daylight, the room seemed less mysterious. I loved the deep reds, soft ivory, and russet-brown accents and how the colors reflected Matthew's masculinity and style. I wanted to know everything about him.

My heart was light. I had found him. A love like none other. The name *Matthew Callahan* filled me, and I rolled over to bury my face in his pillow. *Intoxicating.* I savored the satisfaction he left in me. He had freed me in a burst of sensation, hurtling me past the point of no return. I never dreamed his hands could feel so gentle. Or that his words could hang in the air between us like vows.

I switched off the television. The thought grew like a seed, planted only hours before, exploding in the room's silence. The great love of my life wasn't Joe, after all. It never was.

I lay there, wishing Matthew would forget breakfast and return to bed so I could cradle in his arms. For him to move inside me again. I had never known lovemaking to be so incredible. The desires and urges I thought I'd lost had pumped into overdrive. It was exhilarating to be held so closely, loved so deeply, and then discover I wanted more. Delicious thoughts of him ran thick inside my head, pulsing through my squirming body.

I looked around the room again, noticing every little thing that was him. In an instant, my love for Matthew became boundless. I crawled out of bed, slid my arms through my robe, and strolled to the fireplace, wanting to look at every photograph on the mantle, hoping there was one of his mother. I smiled, going from picture to picture. A family who clearly cared for one another.

Then my eyes widened. *Oh God. It can't be. It can't possibly be him.* I tore open the frame, pulled it from behind the glass, and turned it over. *Little brother, John Rossi, 1987. It's him!* Quickly, I surveyed the rest of the mantel. Pictures of Matthew's brothers lined up one after the other, including three of John. The finger of God had reached down and carved it on the wall of my heart. It was time to tell Matthew what I knew.

But why didn't Matthew tell me about his brother? What does he really want from me?

The best night of my life suddenly grew twisted and full of frightening questions. Something Matthew said on the mountain struck me like a fist. I hadn't put it together or even considered it until that moment. '*We both know the pain—of losing someone we love to a monster.*' He was talking about John!

I sat on the loveseat, digging into my memory, desperate to recall my conversation with Johnny Rebel so many years before. John had mentioned his family, '. . . *my mama—salt of the earth.*' That's where I first heard that phrase—from John! And that his brothers did not accept his homosexuality, but his oldest brother supported him. The words played like a tape recorder. I gripped the picture for all it was worth. It was him. *John!* I snatched the remaining photos off the mantel, including a picture of Matthew and John standing in front of a Christmas tree. Someone indeed led me to Shiloh. Meeting Matthew was no coincidence, but was it divine or a set-up?

Andie. I heard my name called from outside. Loud and clear through the French doors. I didn't stop to think. Anger propelled me forward quickly, fearlessly, and I flung the doors wide open. Thunder rolled in the distance, and the wind whipped the trees back and forth as if all of nature had suddenly become frantic. My feet froze on the edge of the bedroom carpet, refusing to move out to the balcony. The hair on the back of my neck rose. I yelled into a churning sky. "Who is it!? What do you want? What? What!"

Static filled the air as a deep, solemn weeping rolled down the mountain. *"Avenge—us—all,"* the wind cried. In a blustery gust, the doors slammed in my face.

Terrified, my heart rattled inside my chest as I screamed and bolted out of the bedroom and down the hallway, *"Matthew!"*

Seconds later, he caught me as I collapsed in his arms.

Roused by Tobias's voice, I felt as if my bones had turned to rubber. "Get her to your bed," he said.

Matthew lifted me, whisking me down the hall and into his room, laying me on the sheets. I shook my head and sobbed as if waking from a nightmare. Sitting on the bed beside me, he waited and watched my every move. Pulling myself to a sitting position, I yanked the quilt over my legs and stared at the mantle, wiping my tears on my sleeves. Ivy handed me a Kleenex from the nightstand. She had walked around the room, finding the photos scattered on the floor where I had dropped them. She held one up to Matthew. "I told you, Mattie, you should have told her. She knew him."

Matthew took the photo from Ivy's hands. "You're right, Ivy, as always. I'm not sure why I kept it from her. Talk to me, Andie, honey. What frightened you?"

Ivy and Tobias positioned themselves on the bed. I blushed. Matthew smiled and smoothed the hair out of my eyes. No one but my mother had ever done that for me. "It's okay," he said. "They know you stayed with me last night."

Ivy handed me another tissue. "Nothing to fret about, Andie. God brought you here. He only used Matthew to drive the car." I appreciated her trying to lighten the mood. "It is the natural order of things, loving Matthew," she said. "Tell us what happened. You have a bad dream?"

I reached for a pillow and hugged it to my chest. "No." My voice cracked when I pointed to the pictures of John that Ivy had placed in Matthew's lap. "It's those."

"What about these, Andie? My brother John?"

"Yes. Why didn't you tell me? You never bothered to mention his last name. It's Rossi, isn't it? Your mother's last name is Rossi."

"It is, but everyone calls her Pastor Bobbie. People seldom use her last name because some old-timers at church still think she's a Callahan. I don't know why I didn't talk to you about John. I hoped you knew him, and yet—I hoped you didn't. I think I was afraid to ask. John's murder—it's still painful for me. Even more painful than Jessie's death because of the cruelty of it. Then I tried to tell myself it didn't matter if you knew him. Did you know John?"

I stared straight ahead.

Matthew sighed, exasperated. "Andie?"

"What!?"

"Did you know my brother?"

"You could say that. Yes, I knew him. He was the Assistant Chef at the Praise Buffet. They didn't allow him to attend services. It was cruel, you're right. Cruel and inhuman, what they did to him."

"Then you knew he was—"

"—Gay? Yes. And he was warm and wonderful. Funny and full of life and hope. He was desperate to get the man he loved out of there. Peter, the head chef." Glaring at Matthew, I tried to stop the tears from flowing down my cheeks like a steady stream of anguish, but I couldn't. The memory of John refreshed in my brain; it felt like his murder happened yesterday. "He loved you all. I had no proof of Calvin's utter debauchery until I met John. Until then, until John told me his story, I only suspected the evil in him. I—I talked to John for a long time that night. The night he died."

The color drained from Matthew's face. "What else, Andie? What else do you know?"

"I didn't know he was your brother. I didn't. I never wanted to talk about what I saw to you or anyone. I was afraid because if they knew—I had to protect my children. Do you understand that? I had to keep Dillion and Gracie safe."

"What, Andie? What did you see?" Matthew asked.

Hesitating, I clutched my pillow. "I saw him shot by Evan Preston and Silas Turlo. *I* am the eyewitness. *I* called the police to report his murder. *I'm* the one they were looking for to come forward. The one you were *all* looking for." The tears lodged in my throat, and I coughed to speak clearly. "Oh, Matthew. I'm sorry. I'm sorry you lost him. But you should've told me! Damn it, why didn't you tell me?" I bawled into the pillow like a frightened child.

Matthew rolled his head between his legs. "I think I'm going to be sick."

"Sweet Jesus!" Ivy's hands shot over her head, her chin quivering as I watched her stagger. Her entire body convulsed in a full-blown Pentecostal moment. "Yes, Lord! It was God and Johnny who guided you to her, Matthew! She's here to help you bring those wicked men to justice!"

Tobias rushed to the bathroom for a glass of water to give to Matthew while he reeled from my revelation of his brother's killer. Finally, Tobias put it all into perspective. Wrapping his arms around his wife, his eyes filled with tears. "After all this time, all our prayers, God has delivered the only witness into your hands, Matthew."

Matthew sat close, his liberation palpable. "It's been years of torture—to not know the truth." Holding me like a father comforts his child after a nightmare, he kissed my forehead. "Tell me everything, Andie. Start at the beginning. Don't be afraid."

As the storm outside grew in intensity, we all moved to the sitting area near the fire in Matthew's bedroom. I settled into the loveseat beside Matthew and scooted to the edge, gripping the cushions so tightly I thought my bones might snap. I told them about the few hours I spent with John. Looking back on that night, I felt like I was trekking alone across a vast desert. Sand and dirt whirling up behind me. Afterward, my heart pounded with pity for Matthew's look of desolation. If his eyes had looked tired before, they suddenly appeared haunted.

I watched him attempting to gather his thoughts and turn them into words. "I'm sorry." His voice sounded scratchy and filled with agony. "I should've asked you if you knew him. You had no idea John was my brother. The few pictures I own of him I displayed in my room, and until last night, you had never been in here. Please understand, Andie. I was desperate for a long time to find my brother's killer and almost gave up. I never knew for sure, but I always suspected that church had something to do with it."

"Now you know," I said.

He sighed. "Yes, now I know."

The room grew quiet except for the popping embers in the fire. We each sat there for a while, locked in our remembrance of John. Purely spectators at that point, Ivy and Tobias only nodded occasionally and raised a hand as if to testify.

"Why didn't you help him, Matt? Like you're helping me."

"John was a private man, as you can imagine. He had to be. My brother never let on how bad things were for him there. I guessed he wasn't happy and asked him more than once. But he hid his misery from me. I had no clue of the real danger he was in. Or his pain. If I had, I would've swooped down there and carted him back to Shiloh, but I think he knew that and wanted to stay near Pete. I should've listened to my gut. I have a sixth sense about death; I should've listened." He looked at me. "Where is Peter now?" he asked.

"On the night he left town to live with his mother in Florida, Peter stopped at my house. He had seen me talking to John that night. Peter figured I knew who did it. Peter Collins bought his way out with AIDS. Once they knew he was dying from AIDS, they didn't want him there. They allowed him to leave. A year ago, Peter told me he had six months to live. He gave me a videotape Calvin didn't know about. And some cash. I think it was his attempt to make some sort of restitution for how he treated John. I don't know what's on the tape; I never watched it. But it's in my lockbox at the bank. Joe knows I have it, and—they also know I saw Evan kill John. I told Joe I saw Evan murder him."

Tobias wiped his eyes with his hankie and finally spoke. "You're a strong woman, Andie. Your path to our door—it's a miracle you survived. And I'm sure we don't know all of it."

"No, you don't," I said.

Matthew gripped my hand. "You only need to tell what you want to, Andie. I want peace for you now."

We watched the fire again and listened to the rain pelt the roof and windows. Tobias looked at Ivy. "You remember Pete? They often visited when he and John worked in Charlotte before joining that church. Stayed with us while Mattie traveled. Bobbie always came to our house to see them. You remember that Ivy?"

"Sure do. But Mark and Luke did Johnny wrong. They—"

"—I know, Ivy. Believe me, they know, too." Matthew sat forward and leaned on his knees. "Mark and Luke feel they are as much to blame for his death as the man who shot him." Making a fist and holding it to his heart, he turned to face me head-on. "Artury will never, ever touch you, Andie! I will follow him to Hell before he or any of his assassins lay a finger on you. Ivy is right. Destiny, fate, call it what you want; we came together for a purpose. I love you, Andie. Harm will never darken your door again. I can promise you that."

I watched, stunned, as Matthew wept great masculine tears that fell and caught in his beard stubble. He sobbed as few men know how to do. Tobias reached over and rested his hand on Matthew's knee to comfort him until he could speak again.

Matthew's voice choked. "I want to thank you for being John's only friend and for loving him in his last hours. That's why, I am sure, God led me to you—and you to us. This *was* a divine meeting. Your Mavis, our John, seems like they worked a deal with the Almighty." Finally, Matthew smiled.

I pulled in a cleansing breath, moved by his raw emotion. "I believe you're right. They did. I stood in your room with John's pictures in my hands and heard my name called through those doors." I pointed to the balcony.

"Outside?" he asked.

I nodded. "John's senseless murder filled me with rage so hot I ran to the doors and flung them open to confront whomever it was calling out my name. I didn't think fast enough to be afraid until I heard the voice cry out, *'Avenge us all.'*"

Matthew looked at Ivy, who nodded, obviously indicating I had told the truth. He pulled me to him. "What do you think, Ivy?"

"I think you best do what they've asked of you, Andie."

"We will do it together," said Matthew.

Ivy brought a tray of bagels and coffee into Matthew's bedroom. I had curled up against Matthew by the fire again. "Tell me about John," I said. "I only knew him a few hours, but I felt like I knew him all my life. He was—regal, I guess." I took my coffee mug from Ivy and smiled at her wink.

Matthew's features became animated. "Skinny as a piece of celery when he was a kid. Remember, Ivy?"

"Oh, do. Pants all the time fell off his tiny behind. The boy had no butt."

Matthew laughed, then sighed. "He was handsome, with hair like he'd stepped out of a shower. Not an ounce of fat on him, even as an adult. Six feet of pure muscle. Strong. Well-defined arms and legs. Women chased him for years. He didn't have an eye for any of them, and that's when I knew. John was a star. Until he and Peter went to work for that church restaurant."

I grinned at Ivy. "Did he learn to cook from you?"

"No," she said. "Jack, his father, was a chef. When Jack came home from a trip, he and John always cooked for the family. We thought it was only a hobby for John," Ivy said.

"I remember now. He said he gave up Harvard for culinary school."

Matthew finished his bagel and smiled affectionately. "We all thought he would follow in Jack's footsteps. Until his homosexuality split the family. For years, he was afraid to tell Mark and Luke; all hell broke loose when he did. It's been difficult for me to forgive the way they treated him. I'm still not sure Ivy has."

Matthew stared at Ivy, who said nothing, and I realized every family had their crosses to bear. "Like I said, John could've come here but he never wanted to cause trouble. He wanted none of us to suffer a moment's pain for the life he led. My brothers have to live with their regrets. But it's over. We laid John to rest beside his father. Jack loved him the most. Andie, it'll truly be over with your testimony. I vow to you we will get your children back. Bring them here to heal. I will put this madman behind bars."

Tobias perked up. "Can't work outside today with this weather. Let's celebrate."

"Good idea," said Ivy. "I'll make a grand supper to celebrate Andie and Matthew. Good love, yes?"

I blushed as Matthew kissed me. "Yes, the best," he said.

MATTHEW

At noon, Andie returned to her room to shower.

"Ivy, please move Andie's things in here with me." I pulled my old Villanova sweatshirt over my head while she placed John's pictures back on the mantle.

"Do you think she'll approve?" Ivy asked.

"I approve!"

Andie had heard the question halfway down the hall and answered it. Ivy smiled. "Good plan."

When Ivy left my room, I pulled my old friend aside. "Tobias, I need you to make calls today. Get in touch with Royster Bently at the FBI. If you recall, he and his wife had supper with Mother and Jack every month for years."

Tobias nodded and stroked his chin, mentally listing my instructions.

"Set up a private meeting with Royster in town. Call your connections at the IRS. I want another investigation started on the Praise Buffet, Peyton Broadcasting, and any other entity of Artury's not labeled as a church, including the private accounts of Artury, Preston, Turlo—and whoever that Assistant Pastor is. Let's include Joe Oliver on that list. I also want a meeting with the detectives who investigated John's murder and the murder of Mavis Dumass in New York. In the meantime, I'll schedule another appointment with the Attorney General."

"This will take some time, Matthew. We worked hard to find John's killer before."

"Right, but this time, I have an eyewitness. And we will have our ducks in a row."

"When it's over, you will marry Andie?"

"If she'll have me. When it's truly over."

Chapter 20

AN INVITATION
July 1993

MATTHEW

Ivy sat with the remote on her lap, staring into Calvin Artury's face on the small kitchen TV. Andie developed a migraine after breakfast, and Ivy had sent her back to bed. Ivy shook her head so hard her earrings swung against her neck. "It's staggering," she said. "By changing the TV channel, televangelism has touched everyone in America. Poor Andie. She struggled so to get out of Artury's pit. All her young life, wallowing in it, and it kept sucking her back in."

"I'm sure not all televangelism is corrupt, Ivy, but you can turn that bastard off," I said. "If I have to listen to him much longer, I'll be tempted to do some evil deed myself."

"Your mama is coming to supper tomorrow night, remember?"

"Make it simple. Don't fuss." I stood at the window with my coffee, soaking up the first rays of sun breaking through the clouds. The previous night's dream had upset me, perhaps more than I realized. I couldn't get back to sleep, so in the early morning, I crept downstairs to pour a glass of milk and catch up on my reading. But I couldn't concentrate. The events of the past few days were bittersweet. I'd made love to Andie and found the one witness to my brother's murder. *How do I introduce her to my family and tell my mother who she really is?* At three a.m., I crawled back into bed only to lie awake, think, and watch Andie toss and turn in her sleep.

I finished my coffee and rinsed out my cup. I wanted to talk to Andie again and discuss everything. But first, I needed to meet with Royster Bently. There was no point in discussing it further with Ivy. She would only engage in unlikely speculation and wander off into long stories about John as a boy.

Fetching my jacket, I called out that I was leaving and wouldn't be home for lunch. A vacuum cleaner whined from somewhere in the house. Not sure Ivy heard me, I called out again.

"You call me Mattie?"

"Don't make lunch for me, Ivy. I'm not hungry."

"You coming home for supper?"

"No, probably not. Tell Andie I'll see her this evening. I've got work in town; keep her busy. We had a restless night. And it's not what you think."

"Uh-huh."

"It's not." I couldn't stop my grin.

"She be fine. I keep her busy. Go on now. Be safe and get home soon."

∾

Tobias had set up the meeting with Royster, and afterward, I hoped he would start the investigation purely on my word, as I had yet to recover the evidence in Andie's lockbox.

But I needed to prepare my mother before she came for supper on Saturday. And I wanted to do something special for Andie, cementing our relationship, mission, and lives together.

I shifted my car into low as I drove into the parking lot at Valle Crucis Holiness Church. Stepping inside her tiny office at the back

152

of the church, which doubled as a Sunday school room, I recalled having to bring in more chairs every Easter and Christmas. We had wedged her desk under the window overlooking the valley and a small thicket of rhododendron and dogwood trees, each jostling for position in a patch of earth.

Mother's office had once been a storeroom. Lurking beneath the odor of newly restored floors and freshly painted walls, the storeroom's disinfectant smell seeped in from the cartons of cleaning supplies kept there for decades. I ran my hand across her old wooden desk, the color of thick honey. She had used her desk hard, with hundreds of scratches as ample evidence. I'd seen her practice sermons at that desk and change a few diapers on it, too. She was a mother and grandmother first and a pastor second. I loved that about her.

The members had recently purchased a new office chair for her. A fancy model that adjusted in more ways than Pastor Bobbie knew how to sit, her feet never touching the floor. I had paid a local carpenter to refinish the hardwood floors throughout. Indeed, the tiny church and parsonage in Valle Crucis existed because of Callahan money. I was good with that.

My mother had given her boys their inheritance early, and in return, we kept the church alive for her, even when its members dwindled. The church didn't advertise other than the sign in the front yard. Over the years, the small congregation had seen moderate growth due to a recently built fellowship hall and the addition of a youth group led by Mark and Patsy. I worried my mother couldn't handle it if it got much bigger.

There were no computers. She wouldn't know how to use one. An old rotary phone sat on her desk. Two six-foot shelves packed with books and Sunday school papers leaned against the wall. Except for a picture of Jesus preaching His Sermon on the Mount, the walls were clear of all ornamentation. Any displayed family pictures sat in the parsonage next door. Nowhere close to retirement, mother had been a country preacher from the time her first husband, my father, brought her to the area in 1952. I couldn't imagine the church or my life without her.

I followed the smell of furniture polish and found her dusting pews and hymnals in the sanctuary. "Pastor, why don't you hire some cleaning help?"

She ignored me. She'd cleaned her church for forty years and wouldn't stop anytime soon. "Who do I owe for the pleasure of your company in the middle of the day?"

I grabbed her, locked her in a bear hug, and planted a kiss on her forehead. A blush of tiny blood vessels spread across her pudgy cheeks. She was a short, blocky woman of Irish descent. At sixty-five, her broad, impassive face wore a permanent smile, and I always found her wearing a pressed housedress with matching earrings. Her white hair resembled sifted powdered sugar styled in something she called a French twist. My mother's voice was too loud, her heart was too soft, and she loved Jesus more than life. Her childlike faith pulled her through many trials and tribulations over the years. Everyone who knew her—loved her.

"I want to make sure you're not backing out on supper tomorrow night."

"Not on your life. Ivy cooking? I hear Andie is quite the cook."

"Ivy's making your favorite. Fried chicken and cornbread dressing. Andie volunteered, but I wanted her free to spend time with you."

"So, why are you here?"

"I need to talk to you about Andie."

She motioned for me to join her on the front pew.

I sat, crossed my legs, and turned toward her. "Really, Mother, this is about John." I saw her stiffen, her eyes teary. I took my time and told her about the night Andie had seen John's picture in my bedroom. Half an hour later, she remained quiet, always holding her emotions in check.

I took her by the hand and held it on my knee. "Mom, I know it was hard on you to go to the House of Praise to find out what they were saying about Andie. You've been a blessing to us both. There's no need to return."

She breathed in shallow, quick gasps. "Good. After what you just told me, I can't go back. And I think it's best we keep this from your brothers for now."

"Agreed."

She looked into my eyes. "You're in love, aren't you, son?"

I sighed. "Yes. I am."

"You're certainly old enough to know what you want. I'm eager to meet her. Give her time, Mattie. From everything I've seen and heard, she's had a rough go of it. I trust your decision. But you must remember, she has children. They seem fine, even after what they've been through. Nevertheless, you may have many challenges over the next few months. I will pray God gives you strength to bring John's murderers to justice. But please, be careful. If God brought her here, as you believe, the truth will out."

"Your optimism is what I need. And your prayers. Thanks, Mom. See you tomorrow night around six?" I stood and kissed her cheek.

"I'll be there." It hurt me to see my mother's tears fall, despite how hard she tried to hold them inside. She took my hands and clasped them in her own. "Remember this: *Many are the afflictions of the righteous: but the Lord delivereth him out of them all.*"

ANDIE

Saturday morning brought renewed anticipation. My belief that I would soon see my twins again grew daily. Walking Matthew to the door, I caught him grinning from ear to ear. "You're all smiles today," I said.

"Am I?" he asked, pulling me into his arms. "It's difficult saying goodbye to you every day."

"Then don't go. Stay with me today. I hate when you leave." I gave him my best pout.

"If there wasn't so much to do to expose Artury, I'd keep you in bed all day. I hear we're to have a taste of summer this afternoon. Enjoy it. Ivy's got everything under control for tonight."

I lowered my eyes. "I'm afraid I'll never have many guests here. Everyone I know and love is dead—or gone."

"Don't worry. I've got a plague of relatives to make up for it," he said.

"What time should I be ready for supper?"

"Five. And wear something sexy."

"Not to meet your mother! She's Pentecostal Holiness."

"Yeah," he winked. "But she's a Methodist during the week."

I mussed his hair, kissed him a final time, and shoved him out the door.

❧

Matthew and Tobias arrived home early but refused to divulge any information to Ivy or me until they *had their ducks in a row.*

I had to admit; I wanted it over with. All of it. And I didn't look forward to meeting the famous lady pastor, another mother-in-law candidate. I kept busy setting the dining room table until I felt Matthew's gaze. It traveled upwards from my black heels to my black skirt, which I tugged downward, then finally to my pink blouse. I turned in time to watch him smile.

His inspection lasted only seconds, but felt like a lifetime. Walking up close, he stood behind me, looping his arms around my waist.

"You look like the main course."

"Leave me be. I'm helping Ivy." I said, dropping a fork on the floor. He always made me as nervous as a teenager on a first date.

Matthew hitched his pants at his thighs and squatted beside me, picking up the fork. I couldn't help but notice he winced at the noise his knees made.

"Your knees sound like walnuts cracking."

"I've been younger, I admit," he said.

I touched his face. "I wish we had met years before now."

"We met when God wanted us to." After a gentle hug, we walked into the kitchen, where Ivy sprinkled paprika on deviled eggs. The front door opened before he reached the stove to taste-test the soup.

I placed my hand on his arm. "Matthew."

"Are you nervous?"

I shrugged one shoulder. *Why couldn't she be anything other than a pastor?* "My entertaining skills have atrophied," I said to give him some kind of reply.

"She'll love you. Almost as much as I do."

A voice I didn't recognize boomed from the entryway. "Where is she?"

A stout little woman turned the corner and reached up to pat her snowy-white hairdo, which probably added a couple inches to her height. "There she is! You must be Andie. You were right, Tobias. She doesn't look a day over twenty-five!" Tobias had ushered the pastor into the house on his arm.

"Thank you." I blushed.

Matthew stepped in to offer a proper introduction. "Obviously, this is my mother, Pastor Roberta Rossi."

"Oh, call me Bobbie. Everybody does. Andie, thank you for giving Matthew here a new lease on life."

"It's my pleasure to meet you, ma'am. Matthew saved my life, though. And I thank you for all you've done for my children and me."

"No need! I am proud to have been of service, especially now that I've seen you."

We walked to the living room, and Matthew served wine. It thoroughly stunned me that a holiness preacher drank real wine. Tobias joined us with a pilsner glass of beer while Ivy busied herself in the kitchen, putting the final touches on supper.

I grew quiet as the room hummed with happy chatter. Light conversation that flew right over my head while I looked back on the past few months in awe. I'd met the dearest people in the world. Matthew's mother had put me at ease for the moment. She reminded me a little of Maudy. Sweet and religious, the pastor had a continual apple-blossom smile and bluish-gray eyes that sparkled when she talked, and I wondered if all women her age liked to wear earrings that matched their dresses.

I grabbed my third glass of wine from the bar as Ivy's voice erupted through the doorway. "Supper's ready!"

Matthew offered his arm to his mother. I took hold of Tobias's arm as he held it out.

"Does the church keep you busy, Pastor?" I asked.

"I should say so. Since Jack died, I have had more than my share of work. It's hard to find reliable help." She winked at me, then turned toward the table.

I didn't ask who the church slackers might be and didn't much care. Maybe I'd visit her church, but I wasn't joining it. Or any church. Not for a long time. If ever.

"Will you come to service tomorrow morning with Matthew? I'd love to show you off."

I swallowed my thoughts. "If Matthew goes, I'll be with him. Thank you, that'd be nice." *Damn my good manners.*

Matthew held the chair out for his mother, then pushed her up to a table set with fine linens, crystal, silver, delicate chinaware, and fresh flowers. He then sat me while Tobias pulled out a chair at his regular spot, and Ivy served.

I had never been around formality to that degree. I almost forgot—they were people of a different class. *I* should've been serving the food, not Ivy. My parents seldom ate at their dining room table, preferring their breakfast bar or TV trays. And until that evening, meals with Ivy and Tobias had been relaxed and casual.

Suddenly, I felt out of place and unclear how to act or which fork to use, like the silk purse made from the sow's ear. My hesitation showed.

Matthew's mother whispered to me as she sipped her wine. "It's all for show, darlin'. We're all just country folk. Like everybody else, we put our pants on one leg at a time." She smiled and placed her napkin on her lap. "I must say, after four visits to the House of Praise and their Hollywood production they call a church service, I was sure glad to get back to my little old-time house of worship."

Lifting my chin and squaring my shoulders, I returned her smile, adjusted the napkin on my lap, and drained my glass of wine.

"Your children are beautiful reproductions of yourself. So well-behaved. Just lovely young people."

That did it. I teared up. But Pastor Bobbie reached out and squeezed my hand. "Trust the Lord with all your heart, darlin'. Don't try to figure it all out. God will work His wonders. I know the man upstairs personally. He loves to show off. Let's say the blessing, shall we?"

We bowed our heads while the pastor prayed. "Lord, please bless this food and the hands that prepared it, and forgive me, please, for any embarrassing words that shoot out of my mouth. Especially anything stupid I say to Andie—and thank you for bestowing Ivy with her exquisite culinary talent. Amen."

Everyone replied with a hearty, "Amen."

But Matthew's mother raised her hand and shouted, "Oh, shoot! I forgot! She looked at Ivy and smiled. I heard Matthew sigh and put down his fork. She waited until we all bowed our heads again. "Lord, You still on the clock? Today is a rather special day because we are darn happy Andie is here with us. Safe. Keep her in

Your loving arms. We pray a hedge of protection around her and her children. I do hope that when I pass through those heavenly gates, you got me a welcome home party waiting with folks at least half as excited as we are today. In your precious and Holy Name, we do pray. And amen again."

I nearly laughed out loud. I nodded and whispered a *thank you* as she patted my hand. I suddenly forgot my uneasiness. Hearing a prayer like I'd never heard, it was as if these people truly knew God better than anybody.

Ivy ladled tomato bisque soup into small bowls, then passed cornbread dressing, wild rice, and sweet potatoes on antique platters. Fried chicken, green beans, a plate of deviled eggs, and a basket of steaming biscuits rounded out the meal. I suspected it was a special occasion.

"Ivy! I thought I told you not to fuss. This is the best meal ever! Tobias, did you make the chicken?" Matthew teased.

Tobias chuckled, and Ivy poked him. "Mattie, you know Toby only knows how to eat chicken, not fix it." Poised gingerly on her chair, Ivy sat ready to rise whenever someone needed a fresh glass of ice water or more of anything. I missed Lula and silently vowed to find her once my quest ended. But I was more than touched by Ivy's servant's heart. A woman who was no more a servant than anyone at the table. A woman whose education rose far above us all. A woman whose choice it was to serve those she loved, no matter what color she was, or we were. In return, Matthew had given her and her husband part of his farm, more money than they could ever spend, and had made them his family.

❦

We ate our meal and exchanged the usual polite remarks. I felt relieved I hadn't said anything inappropriate during the conversation. As I spooned another serving of rice onto my plate,

I tried to keep my emotions in check, not wanting to break down in tears. Apart from the gentle scraping of silverware on plates and the soft background music, a sense of quiet prevailed over the table.

Matthew, his spoon clinking against his wineglass, broke the silence. Clearing his voice, he leaned back in his chair as a flush of color spread across his cheeks. His eyes sparkled with a feverish intensity that moved me. His words, however unbelievable, were perfectly clear.

Turning to me, he gently placed his hand on mine. "Andie, I'm acutely aware of the brevity of our relationship. We've discussed this, and the fact we've both reached a point in our lives where we know what we want. But I know, without a doubt, that I want you. Yes, this may seem sudden, and I had intended to wait, but I find myself unable to resist the pull of my heart. My otherwise cautionary approach has eluded me. You have breathed life back into me. And love. Love I so desperately yearned for. What I'm trying to say is that I want to share the rest of my life with you." With that, he reached into his pocket and produced a square red velvet box.

"I discovered this in one of my favorite stores today. It's ancient. I know you love antiques and anything vintage." He stood and stepped toward me, got down on one creaky knee between his mother's chair and mine, and opened the box. He spoke with his eyes first, then held up a ring. A large diamond surrounded by platinum scrollwork. I couldn't help but gasp, my breath catching in my throat at my first glimpse of it as he moved in closer.

"Made at the turn of the century, one of the Vanderbilts wore it. A jeweler friend in Ashville kept it in his safe for decades," he said as he held it between his fingers. "Now, I realize Dillon and Gracie must live here before we proceed, but when they are finally at Shiloh, and we have accomplished all we have set out to do—please, will you marry me? Be my wife." This was not just a proposal, but a culmination of our shared determination to face the trials we knew were yet to come. The ring was a testament to our unwavering commitment to each other and our mission.

I gently lifted it from his fingers, feeling its weight and history in my palm. A slow smile spread across my face, erasing any trace of distress. I managed a nod, my heart pounding in my chest. Matthew, his eyes filled with love and anticipation, took the ring from me and slipped it onto my finger. I stared at this thing that had taken over my hand. "Okay," I whispered, my voice trembling, tears welling up in my eyes, and a rush of heat flooding my cheeks.

"*Okay?*" everyone said in unison. Giggles rippled around the table.

Overcome with a swirl of emotions, I felt my head was about to spin off my shoulders. "I—I love you, too, Matthew. You know that because I've been open with you since we met. And I would love to marry you. Someday. After the children are here. And when Reverend Artury and his accomplices are behind bars." I stated the stipulation of my engagement. Everyone knew it. *My* prenup. Even though he had already said it, I enforced it. I would become Mrs. Matthew Callahan only after we had accomplished our goals.

The table of on-lookers broke out in applause. He stayed on his knee and reached for my face, trailing his fingers lightly down the sides of my cheeks, whispering into my ear while the others chattered on. "I wanted the people I love most to witness this. I hope you're okay with that."

My face continued to burn in a hot blush. "I'm fine with it. I only wish those I love could be here as well."

"They will. I promise you."

"Please don't make promises you cannot keep," I whispered back.

"I never have. I never will."

"How can I thank you for all you've done for me, for the twins—"

"—Your love is more than enough. We still have a job ahead of us, but tonight felt like the right time to do this."

As Matthew embraced me in front of his family, I recalled over twenty years before when I had promised God I'd never love another. I sat there, realizing God knows our promises aren't worth a lick. I only hoped Matthew's promises were better than mine.

A round of congratulations filled the room, but pure pleasure registered on Ivy's face. "I will serve dessert in the living room," she said. I asked for another glass of wine as the talk remained light for the next hour. I appreciated that. My life, being what it was, there wasn't much to say that didn't include sorrow, death, or pain. When the evening wound down, Matthew asked his mother the question I had also been thinking.

"Is it safe to bring Andie to church, Mom? I mean, I'd love for her to meet Mark and Patsy. And Luke, but—"

"—There isn't a soul in my congregation who knows anyone related to that damnable House of Praise. She's as safe at Valle Crucis Holiness as here in this house." On that point, Pastor Bobbie was clear. "We'd love to see you tomorrow, Andie, darlin'. And welcome to the family."

"Thank you. I'm eager for you to know my children."

"So am I. They'll love it here. A new start for them." Bobbie turned to Ivy. "Thank you, Ivy, for a lovely supper, as always. Can I help you clean up?"

"No, go home and get your sermon ready for tomorrow."

"Andie, before I leave, I want to say something. We have not mentioned John tonight, but Matthew told me about your unfortunate experience. That you witnessed the murder of my youngest son. Thank you for coming into both of my sons' lives when they needed you. God has brought you here to us. For that, I am grateful."

"Pastor, once again, it's me who's grateful. Truthfully, I'm not sure I'm ready to return to any church. I think I've been hiding from God for a long time."

Her smile turned into a quiet chuckle. "You can't hide from God, darlin'. He'll hunt you down, grab you by the seat of your pants, and nail your backside to the church wall. I've seen Him do it. I'll see you in the morning."

"Yes, ma'am."

Chapter 21

VALLE CRUCIS HOLINESS CHURCH
July 1993

ANDIE

I paused, staring at Matthew's mother's church with grief on one side of my battered soul and guilt on the other. The sting of laughter and pre-recorded music drifted through the stained glass windows and bounced off the bright blue sky, and I fought the impulse to turn and run from the white steeple pointing to Heaven, reminding me of my past.

Imagining the cool darkness of the sanctuary, I felt a wave of nausea. *Sanctuary, a place of safety and refuge.* The church was supposed to shelter those who pursued its protection inside its sacred and secluded walls. *Was that even possible for me?*

Walking through the front doors, I gazed at the engraved words above the altar. They registered a measure of comfort: *Come to me all ye who labor and are heavy-laden, and I will give you rest.* I identified with the heavy-laden outcasts Jesus sought, although resting inside a church was not something I had experienced.

Pastor Bobbie waddled into the lobby and smiled. "We're serving donuts and coffee," she said and pointed. I couldn't believe my eyes. Several boxes of assorted donuts and paper cups for coffee covered the table in the corner. "Enjoy, but watch for sticky little hands that may have touched your pew before you sit."

Did I hear her correctly? Donuts and coffee served in the church?

I smiled as Matthew stepped up to shake his mother's hand. In a flowing royal blue satin robe, the pastor threw her arms around my neck. "Andie! I saved a front pew for you both."

"Mom, I want Andie to meet the family. Do you know where they're hiding?"

"Getting ready for Sunday school, I presume. Don't be late for my sermon."

Matthew grinned. "She can make me feel twelve sometimes, I swear."

I laughed my first genuine laugh of the day, which eased the gnawing in my gut. Excusing ourselves as Pastor Bobbie greeted other members, I felt a strange comfort, as no one seemed to look twice at me. It was refreshing, to say the least. Walking toward a tall man in mirrored shades, a black cowboy hat over a self-inflected haircut, and sitting on the hood of his car, I saw hints and flashes of John in the way he moved.

"Luke. I want you to meet Andie."

He tossed his cigarette into the gravel, slid off his souped-up '59 Thunderbird, and hoofed it to me with extended arms. "I heard! Congratulations! She's a purty thing, Matt."

I smiled at the brother called Luke, who obviously had seen one too many Johnny Cash concerts. His black shirt, black jeans, and matching black jacket appeared slept in. He was not as classy and composed as Matthew, but I immediately felt his warmth and liked him, and especially his curly-blonde hair, which also reminded me of John.

It took little to realize he didn't give a flip what anyone thought of him and his country boy persona. Matthew had called him a man with plenty and no responsibility who lived in a constant laid-back state of mind and loved fast cars, fast women, and his family. And definitely in that order. A heathen who followed NASCAR and Jesus but couldn't commit to either of them.

"Nice to meet you," I said.

And then there was Mark, whose classic allure also reminded me of John. But he was no hick. All the brothers had the same washboard build with a different presentation. Mark's dark complexion made Luke's appear pale and sallow. His ebony hair, cut short and gelled, glistened in the sun. Mark spun his sunglasses in his right hand, and I suspected his put-together look reflected his personality. Straightforward and no-nonsense.

His wife, Patsy, smiled with riveting dark eyes. She had styled her jet-black hair almost like her husband's. They were the new youth pastors. A swarm of teenagers gathered around us, and I longed for Gracie and Dillon to be there—join in. I was so close to a normal life, and yet the reality of one still evaded me. But Mark proved as kind as the rest of his band of brothers, offering me a hug and excusing himself and his wife. "See you after church, Andie?"

"Yes, stay for lunch!" Patsy shouted, herding her group inside for Sunday school. "We're having a potluck in the fellowship hall." The rowdy teens quickly harnessed her attention. "Hush, now," I heard her say.

"You have a great family, Matthew. I miss mine."

"I know you do. Someday, we'll gather both families here. On the day you marry me?"

"Okay," I said. But as I stepped into the church, haunting memories hit me in the face like a heat blast from a casting oven. Fire-breathing sermons at the House of Praise, years of torturous sorrow, and the insanity it created. I stopped in my tracks, couldn't speak, and my vision blurred. My legs gave out from under me. "I can't do this," I said.

Matthew assisted me to a folding chair in the lobby.

"I'll get her some water," said an older woman who stood at the back handing out church bulletins. By the time she returned, the color had returned to my face.

"I'm sorry," Matthew said. Clearly upset, he squatted in front of me and wiped my forehead with his handkerchief. "I should've thought more about this. I was so overcome with you, wanting you to meet my family and my church family, that I didn't think of the effect a church, any church, would have on you. Do you want to go home? Let's go home."

"No, give me a minute. Let me sit here. Just let me breathe. Can we sit in the back? I can't walk down to that front pew."

"Yes, of course. Mother will understand."

Scooting into a back pew, a children's choir lined up on the altar, ready to sing. *A children's choir. How beautiful, how simple, how Christ-like.* To calm my beating heart, I closed my eyes a moment and imagined my twins sitting next to me.

MATTHEW

I asked God to give Andie strength, to direct my path, and to guide my steps in the days ahead. *A righteous man's steps are ordered by the Lord.* I'd read it and heard my mother quote the scripture many times. Andie didn't see how similar our lives were—both of us were raised in church. Just two entirely different churches.

I had carefully selected my suit and tie that morning, my first occasion in years to stand before the congregation with a woman on my arm. Andie looked beautiful in the pale pink suit Ivy had purchased for her. Her pearl bracelet hugged her wrist, and her diamond, round to match the shape of her face, flashed as it caught the light. Wrapped around her finger, the lucky ring was where I wanted to be.

I planned to call Conner, to come to Shiloh and meet Andie. I suppose if anyone had asked me at that moment if I were happy, I would have had to say I was genuinely happy for the first time in over a decade.

But I had to remember Andie's pain had been far greater than mine, and I felt a fool for pushing her back into a situation possibly too familiar than the one she nearly died trying to get out of. I would never do that again. What I *would* do is love her and her children back to wholeness—give Andie and myself a family again as soon as we put Calvin Artury and his cohorts in prison where they belonged.

Special Agent Royster Bently had started his investigation, considering the evidence I assured him we had. Several other officials also promised to turn up the heat on the House of Praise. Cases reopened or began anew. Having friends in high places was about to pay off.

ANDIE

"Thy word is a lamp unto my feet and a light unto my path." The children's cherub faces quoted the scripture before singing it with every ounce of elation they could muster. As the song ended, their Sunday school teacher herded the first and second graders off the platform, and the next ensemble, a handful of teenagers, took center stage. Mark and Patsy's youth group belted out their well-practiced Amy Grant number, *El Shaddai.*

I wept bitter tears. Those young people, who reminded me of my two, sang their hearts out, over and over, echoing the love of their Creator. Ten or so throaty bells tuned each to the other, a few raised hands, and some faces lifted to the ceiling. They sang to God, not to each other or the congregation. As Patsy played the piano, Mark accompanied on the guitar and semi-conducted.

The congregation cheered and applauded, but I sat, stunned, unable to move. I'd been robbed of more than I knew. It was worship in its purest form. I'd felt it once before, the day Mavis sang at the Baptist church in Winston-Salem, but I was too young and stupid to recognize it. The battle to eliminate my anger over wasted years had begun.

MATTHEW

My mother preached for forty-five minutes. I checked my watch and whispered to Andie. "It's almost over."

"How can you tell?"

"At precisely twelve-twenty, our organist will walk to the Hammond. Bernice fixes roast chicken for her family every Sunday. It's been her sacred duty for thirty years to end the service. *What a Friend We Have in Jesus* is her signal to Mother to quit talking so she can get home before her chicken burns."

I watched Andie's eyes widen as she put her hand over her mouth. She nearly laughed out loud. I thought we might get *the look* from Mother if she saw us giggling on that back pew, which only made me laugh longer.

When the organ echoed to silence, a sawing of coughs, the rustling of bulletin paper, and folks zipping up their Bible covers filled the gap. Pastor Bobbie raised her hands in front of her tiny pulpit one last time to end the service. "Go with God this morning."

The standard reply I'd heard for decades warbled back from the congregation.

But Mom had to squeeze in a few last-minute comments. "We hope you enjoyed our youth choirs earlier. The adults will be back next week. One last item. My entire family is here with me this morning. I want you all to meet Andie, Matthew's fiancée. Welcome, Andie."

Andie didn't stand, and I certainly didn't force her. She only nodded and blushed the color of her suit.

"I feel like I've never been to church before," she whispered. "And it's been a long time since I've been anybody's fiancée." She smiled benevolently while Mother swept her arm in a circle, indicating the congregation should stand.

"Let's all sing my favorite hymn this morning, *Blessed Assurance*. Because folks, when you have Jesus, you have assurance. He will turn your adversities into advantages and your darkest hours into glorious sunshine. I thank Him this morning; I praise Him because God returned seven times over what the Devil tried to take from me! Hallelujah!"

I decided someday, Mother would have to tell her story to Andie. A past that possibly rivaled Andie's.

ANDIE

I shot to my feet, and my heart leaped within my chest. This was what God was trying to teach me all along. If I learned to trust Him again, I would find more than just my faith. I would discover my way out of my darkest hours and an end to a lifetime of unhappiness.

As Tobias had said, God had found me. I was starting over because, for me, returning to church was nothing short of a miracle. A perfect beginning.

As the congregation sang, the third vision of my life caught me by surprise. I saw Mavis, standing in a white robe, alone in the choir loft, watching me. And smiling.

Chapter 22

THE STINK OF THE FISH
July 1993

REVEREND CALVIN ARTURY

In my dimly lit office, bent over my desk, sluggish, stodgy, and mottled with new liver spots, I nursed a headache, speculating whether I'd go bankrupt first or to prison.

All over the world, brokers, traders, and bankers watched my holdings and investments plummet as I struggled to put the finishing touches on the new House of Praise. A magnificent cathedral—three times as big and three times as plush. But construction and interior design had slid to a screeching halt. And that was the least of my problems. Television equipment changed and fluxed constantly. Cutting-edge video and audio purchases broke the budget every six months. Airtime remained at a premium, and we had purchased another satellite. The payments were astronomical.

Of course, a new team of high-priced pilots waited in the wings to fly the jet while several mechanics demanded top wages to maintain it. The cost of doing business had skyrocketed, not to mention the deals, coverups, and payoffs had gotten way out of hand! It wasn't my job to watch it all! How could I possibly? Lord knows, my body had yet to be glorified!

Even so, the worst wasn't over. I had maxed out my personal credit to make the last few payrolls. Over 500 staff depended on me for their livelihoods, and as of the past week, the banks had called in my loans. Loans I recently learned were in default. My billion-dollar ministry had dropped into the toilet overnight!

Where's Silas?

I had worked my whole life to protect my ministry, but suddenly, words like corruption, bribery, and fraud infiltrated private meetings with top staff members, infuriating me. I had senselessly trusted my Chief Financial Officer and his team of crack accountants to handle the finances of the church, the restaurant, the television studio, and Peyton Broadcasting! Evan suggested I put legs to my prayers, and he was right. I sent for the bank president, who handled our significant deposits, only to be told the man had disappeared. I glared at Evan, turning stiffly, almost stumbling, and seething in mindless rage. "Do something about this!"

Evan, cool as always, raised his brows to cover his smirk. "What do you want me to do? Take time from everything else to find a man probably on the other side of the world by now?"

∽

Weeks later, I spent nights combing through my files. The North Carolina Attorney General ordered me to preserve and submit all files regarding the television studios. Evan said it probably wouldn't come to a head until after the August Nigeria Crusades. But I wasn't chancing it. I'd heard about those FBI raids Jim Bakker and a few others had suffered through. They'd never televise *me* in handcuffs!

The only bright spot was that my congregation had yet to get wind of the total upheaval. Evan assured me specific allegations wouldn't leak to the press until I was safely in Africa. God only knew what I would come back to. *Come back? No.*

The bank had foreclosed on my house. Not the tiny, modest three-bedroom ranch down the street where I had lived with Vivi. It was the only place my congregation knew about and believed to be my current residence. Oh, no. I'd paid that old house off decades ago. It sat empty most of the time. The bank sent notices on the other place—my 12-bedroom monstrosity in Atlanta with acres of lavish gardens and golf course lawns. They also wanted my New York City apartment, the country place near Gatlinburg, and my two chalets in Jackson Hole that I kept for dignitaries, particular donors, and occasionally for my ministry team's use.

But that wasn't the worst of the most recent accusations. A new Forsyth County prosecutor and the IRS had begun breathing down our necks. Evan and Silas had kept it from me as long as they could. *Who was fueling this persecuting fire!?*

Mavis was dead—that much we knew. God had destroyed all enemies who threatened to defame me. Peter—dead, long gone to AIDS. No danger of lawsuits from any of the young men and women I'd taken to my bed had ever surfaced. I'd seen to that. The few staff who knew my secrets possessed plenty of their own that I would not hesitate to expose!

There was only one person this harassment stemmed from! Only Andie had evidence to force an investigation. But one of this magnitude? How could she without help? We'd not heard a peep from her in months. All reports came back the same— WHEREABOUTS UNKNOWN.

"Fannie, get me Joe Oliver on the phone."

Suddenly, it made more and more sense. She was the only demon we had never fully dealt with. She didn't show up on the tennis court that day. Andie didn't show up anywhere. My bringing her evil before the congregation led to nothing. Not one church member had seen her, or they weren't talking. It was as if she had disappeared into thin air. I'd been foolish to stop the relentless search, believing she was bluffing. *How utterly stupid on my part! How ridiculous we all had been. Someone is helping that harlot!*

"Joe Oliver on the phone, Reverend."

I picked up the receiver. "Have you found Andie? Do you know where she is!?"

"Um—no, Reverend. She's not been a priority lately. Should she be?"

"She has always been your priority, Oliver! Where are your children?"

"They're still in a foster home. I get them on Sunday mornings for service when I'm in town. I haven't seen them this week, but their mother hasn't seen them since the court took them months ago. As far as I know, she's dead. At least, I hope she is. She may have killed herself, or we would've heard from her by now. No one has even seen a glimpse of her in months. As you know, she sold her car and all her stuff. Since then, I've checked everywhere, but she was nowhere to be found, Reverend."

"You sure she's not in Charleston with her mother?"

"I'm positive. We've followed Andie's entire family everywhere, even bugging her mother's house and tapping her phone. Pastor DeSanto posted a man at every place she could turn up. She's not been near any of them."

"If you hear from her, call me. Immediately! In the meantime, tell Selma you must prepare for the Nigeria Crusade. Then *you* go look for Andie yourself! Don't stop until you find her; don't you dare return until you can prove she's rotting in her grave!"

"Is there a problem?"

"Problem? The problem is your head's going to roll unless you find her! Andie is behind *all* our problems!"

"What if I can't locate her? We're leaving for Nigeria in a week."

"I know when we're leaving! This is your fault, Oliver! You never could control her! Listen to me carefully. You will not board the plane for Africa until you find your ex-wife. I have replaced you until you can tell me, without a doubt, that she's dead. Now, do as you're told!" I slammed down the phone.

Days before my departure to Africa, I searched my hard files and computer floppies again for incriminating evidence. I still didn't know if the prosecutor was only fishing. But the blame game was about to begin.

Everyone left standing in the inner circle would profess their innocence and trade evidence for leniency the second the prosecution offered it. The irony was that Joe, my Chief Engineer, who was supposed to know everything going down inside the church and had made a name for himself within its walls and in the world of audio engineering, couldn't afford a lawyer. Not the kind he was going to need. My top brass faced prison time, regardless. I didn't care.

For me, either way—a prolonged investigation or a swift and merciless trial—as the church's sole head, I would take the most heat. *'The stink of the fish starts in the head'* rang in my ears. *Where did I hear that?* My mother, probably. Complaining about my father.

Take the cash, disappear, and don't look back.

But I *did* look back. As I reached under my desk for my briefcase, I felt something. When I discovered what it was, I clutched it so hard it bit into my palm. Vivi's cross necklace. It must have dropped off her picture on my desk.

My beloved Vivi. My angel of light. Her skeletal hands struggled to pull off her wedding set. The disease had ravaged her, turning her inside out. Only bits of hair covered her head, and her eyes stared at me, black and hollow in bile-green sockets. I was sorry she had to die for God's work to continue. I had warned her not to open my Pandora's box. But she did, and she had threatened me. She would not keep my secrets, she had said. Not a moment longer.

Vivi threw her wedding rings at me. "No—more—lies."

Her action stopped my next breath in mid-exhale. I stroked her ringless hand and cried. "You don't mean that, Vivi."

She rolled her head back and forth on the pillow. "I—I want the world to know," she said and coughed, "what you are." Unable to speak another word, she gasped her final breaths.

I turned and nodded to my private physician. To watch my beloved suffer in death, it tore my heart out of my chest. "I can't stand to see you in pain."

Within minutes, the doctor injected a glue-colored liquid into her arm. The room's light faded into the hue of death. "She's gone," the doctor said, glancing at his watch. "Time of death, nine-twenty."

"Angel of Death, take my Vivi to the mansion our Lord has prepared for her. No more pain, Vivi. No more pain." I collapsed at her bedside and stroked her body. Grieving, I cried aloud into the shroud of sheets.

The doctor stood to leave. "The coroner will rule it as a natural death due to the progression of her disease. There will be no autopsy. I will send for an ambulance."

"I loved her," I said.

He ignored me, collected his bag, and left the room.

Her wedding band sparkled on the floor. I picked it up and placed it on my pinky finger. But my tears came to an abrupt halt as grief turned to anger. "If only you had believed in me, Vivian. If only you could've seen the plan of God for my life, you would not have had to die. We could've ruled the Christian world together."

I hung Vivi's necklace back on her picture. Walking swiftly down the carpeted hall wrapped behind the substantial baptistery, I arrived at a private office few knew about. I disengaged the alarm and retired to my closet sanctuary to sulk and covertly nurse my self-pity, one shot of bourbon after another. Tapping the shot glass against my teeth, I breathed in the smell. *"Have Thine own way, Lord! Have Thine own way! Thou art the Potter; I am the clay. Mold me and make me after Thy will, while I am waiting, yielded and still."* I sang the beloved song loud and long, and then the voice of God revealed my escape route. I emptied the bottle as a plan formed in the recesses of my mind.

In that inner sanctum, a wall safe hid behind an oil painting of the Jerusalem skyline given to me by Prime Minister Yitzhak Rabin on my third trip to Israel. Crisp, green large bills, folded into wads, lay in that vault behind ledgers and more computer floppies. I gathered all of it. Piles of cash. A slush fund created to tip waiters, limo drivers, and escorts. Money used to entertain donating religious celebrities or political figures who dropped a bundle into my offering bags when in town. Cash for excursions to Paris, Rome, Morocco, and five-star hotels on the return from any Crusade. Money for the unexpected.

I needed to disappear, like Andie Oliver, and not leave a paper trail.

Flipping open my briefcase, I dumped files, come-to-Jesus tracts, and department reports onto the floor. Filling it with cash, I jammed several stacks into my pockets and the rest into a paper bag. I would also take the money from the Nigerian Crusade as soon as we converted it into dollars. If anyone believed they could send me away to rot in some hellhole prison, they had a surprise coming.

A smile tugged at the corners of my mouth. *I'll take Silas up on his offer. When the Crusade ends, send the staff home and head for an island.*

Chapter 23

TESTIMONY

July 1993

MATTHEW

Andie and I hiked the narrow footpath that wound up the mountain around rocks and underbrush. The temperature dropped the higher we climbed. July seemed easier to tolerate in cooler elevations. Gazing over the landscape at the pinnacle, I held her in my arms, watching the sun cut itself on a sharp hill and bleed into the valley. Its blistering heat was merciless on the farm and livestock below that day.

I felt an urgent need to explain precisely what lay ahead of us. Moving to a nearby rock, I sat and observed her as she crept to the edge of the overlook and peered out over the deep green waves of the foothills in front of her. "I think this must be what it's like on the open sea. I think I can see all the way to Virginia." She had fallen in love with Shiloh and the mountains surrounding it. Then she turned to me with a funny grin on her face. "I have to pee."

"There's a nice tree right over there," I said and laughed, watching her walk to a clump of bushes. "By the way, last week, the neighbor at the next farm told me he saw a black bear and her cubs roaming these parts. And watch out for copperheads."

"Oh, great. That's just great, Jungle Jim."

I simply loved her.

Later, we collapsed near the trail on a grassy knoll where we surveyed yet another panorama of the Blue Ridge. The afternoon sun dipped low. The rock under my back felt smooth, and the sun warmed my face. Andie fell asleep in my arms. I savored my time with her. She snored as she slept, relaxed from toes to fingertips. I delighted in her body's heat and the strength she gained daily. I had called her *chiseled* the previous night, exploring her with love but also with care, wanting to make sure she wasn't too thin. She was a belle. She was supposed to be round and soft. But the constant hiking and farm work had made her body hard, including her heartache. It was proving more and more challenging to conquer.

"Andie?" She lay unmoving in the space we shared, her face warm when I laid my finger on it. I moved a strand of hair from her forehead. At her temple, her pulse beat steady and strong. I wanted to touch it, to assure myself of her strength and endurance. She shifted in her sleep, and I felt her despair that, God help us, Artury find her before she could testify. I had given her the first bit of hope she'd ever had to shut him down, but from when she was a girl, grief and misfortune trailed her like a scent, always with a hungry wolf not far behind. Andie was not a natural optimist.

She slowly opened her eyes. The surrounding lines were new. They were inevitable, weren't they? I was forty-two; she'd turn thirty-nine soon. She had earned those lines.

Andie arched her back as she stretched, her small hands fisted white. She turned her face upward to mine, her eyes wide, and then she put one hand on the back of my neck and brought my mouth down to hers, kissing me until my entire body responded, and I groaned.

"Goodness," she said, checking her watch. "It's almost five. We need to go."

"Not yet," I said, pulling her to me.

A glint sparked in her eyes. "You realize the entire world can see us up here?"

"What world? Only miles of sky and trees up here—"

"—And bears and copperheads."

"Let them look. Let them all look." I kissed her again. My lungs gasped for air. I was sure she loved me despite how I found her—broken, despised, and rejected. Not because I had rescued her, but because it was the only way she knew how to love—with all her heart.

Suddenly, it took great effort to stop kissing her before it went further. I leaned against the boulder again, pulling her back against my chest. "Andie, we have to talk. There are things we must do. Now. Before Artury takes his team to Africa."

She pulled away. "Like starting down this mountain before the sun sets and the night wind turns us into giant Popsicles for those bears."

Taking her hands in mine, I pressed them to my chest and warmed them between my hands and the flannel of my shirt. "Every day we delay, we're another day behind in getting that bastard. A day further away from bringing Dillon and Gracie to Shiloh."

"I know."

I released her left hand, sliding mine inside her shirt and up her back. "We must get the evidence out of your safe deposit box."

"It's not that simple. They probably assume my evidence hides in one since they can't find me. I'm sure they're watching the banks."

"Ah, but so are the Feds. Artury would be pretty stupid to do anything in a Winston-Salem bank at this point in time. And he's not stupid. Besides, the banks are on notice. They're tightening security as we speak. If having money gets you one thing, it gets you in the back door. I know old Hootie Snitch, the president of Wachovia. We worked a deal on a tract of land near Pilot Mountain some time back. He's taking us inside your bank branch tonight at midnight. After that, we'll get your testimony recorded and log the evidence. You'll have to testify about what you saw and why you waited so long to tell it. Our attorneys will help you."

"And then?"

"The prosecution won't need you again until Artury and the rest go to trial."

"Oh." She nodded, watching a turkey vulture glide on a breeze.

It was easier for me; I knew that. I made life work my way. She never could have done it by herself. The beginning of our investigation to uncover the House of Praise and its leadership was a tremendous success. I only wished Andie knew how important she was to the effort. "Won't you at least try to call Peter again?" I asked.

"I will. After supper. I can't think about this right now." She shouldered her pack and lowered her cap on her forehead.

I pulled her into me again. "Hey, it's okay," I whispered. "We'll talk later. But we have to deal with it soon."

"I'm sure Peter is dead," she said. "If he's not, he'll be too sick to travel."

"Then we'll go to him."

ANDIE

I headed for the trail. I wanted the long nightmare over with. It had taken all my courage to survive the deaths of my loved ones and lose custody of my children. I had no clue what would happen next. *Will God turn a deaf ear again?*

But I was right about Peter Collins. He had told his mother, and it seems an aunt, too, that I might call someday. When I finally reached the aunt with the phone number he had given me, she said Peter, as well as his mother, had passed away, strangely, on the same day. But Peter's aunt also informed me someone had knocked on her door recently, asking if she knew me or had heard from me. Quickly, I thanked her for her kindness and asked her not to tell anyone I had called. I got off the phone. We didn't have a moment to lose.

At midnight, our quest kicked into high gear. The bank president unlocked the back door of my Wachovia Bank branch. It was as quiet as a tomb. Escorted inside by two police officers, Hootie Snitch turned off the alarm and kept the lights off. Matthew and I followed him to the lockbox area and stood near the security door. I recognized Jenny's cubicle, the sweet pregnant girl I met when I opened my safe deposit account the year before. A picture of her walking baby girl sat on her desk.

Mr. Snitch retrieved the master key from Jenny's desk. He spoke quietly, "Follow me."

Matthew carried an empty canvas bag and glanced around. My nerves got the best of me as it bit at my nails. "I've guarded this key a long time," I whispered, pulling it from around my neck and handing it to Matthew. His eyes sparkled in the dead silence of the room.

Mr. Snitch gave us our privacy inside the vault. Within seconds, we opened the box. The treasure chest. My written testimony of the night John died, the pictures and letter from Mavis, and Peter's videotape. The roll of film I had snapped of everything in my shed, which included pictures of Joe's briefcase filled with money— Matthew slipped every piece into the bag. I hoped all of it and my testimony were enough to put Calvin Artury away. Enough to put him in an electric chair. Enough to send him to Hell.

Royster Bently reported to Matthew and me the following day the pressure was getting to Calvin. According to Royster's sources, Calvin announced he would not preach at the House of Praise until he returned from Africa. I leaped and twirled around the room. My confidence spiraled upward as my contagious laughter lasted throughout the day. With my spirit encouraged, I was ready to nail his coffin shut.

Matthew told me of the immense manpower that had come together to force Calvin into the open, bring the evidence to light, and wallop him in his pocketbook. The tide of public opinion was slowly changing. Word of IRS audits and FBI agents seen around the church leaked to the newspapers, which flooded the massive complex with reporters from major media outlets.

I arrived at the police station with Matthew and his legal team the following afternoon. They drilled and questioned me and took my sworn statement. My rehearsed testimony was flawless. Matthew, the FBI, and the Winston-Salem detectives assigned to the case reviewed the evidence and watched the videotape, then presented it to an unbiased judge who accepted it and issued arrest warrants for Calvin Artury, Evan Preston, Joe Oliver, Tony DeSanto, and Silas Turlo. In addition, every official suspected of taking bribes from the ministry was under investigation.

Matthew would not divulge what he had witnessed on Peter's videotape. "Let's just say Peter Collins has a new star in his crown. He recorded the sins of the century. Enough to lock Artury up for an eternity."

But officials had issued the arrest warrants two days too late. Under the cloak of night, the ministry team and its executive staff had left the country earlier than expected. The authorities kept the warrants quiet, deciding to wait until Artury and his team arrived back in the States the middle of August.

Chapter 24

NO WAY BACK
August 1993

REVEREND CALVIN ARTURY

Suspecting the worst and keeping all suspicions to myself, I insisted my entourage secretly depart two days early for Africa. The non-stop flight had been fraught with terrible turbulence. Everyone on the plane had thrown up at least once, including me. I had spent millions of dollars and years in the planning the Nigeria faith-healing Crusade. God would not forsake the faithful.

But in closing my eyes, a dread born from the certainty of my mission rose like bile into my throat. Like Moses, I had failed to take God's people into a land flowing with milk and honey. And now, I would pay the ultimate price.

Plagued with problems, the massive Crusade drew record crowds. But the heat created the most havoc for staff, equipment, and me, since I refused to wear anything but my three-piece suit. And oh, the smells! Open-air toilets, overripe fruit, unburied corpses, parched meat hanging in markets, and hundreds of whores in the streets. The putrid odor of unwashed bodies saturating the sweltering air nearly buckled my knees into the Nigerian dust. The stench of sin and wickedness and a glimpse into the bowels of Hell—I wasn't sure how much more I could take.

After the first night, I returned to my hotel room in Port Harcourt and found a phone call waiting for me. The caller had refused to speak to anyone but me. A caller with the authority to push the correct buttons—my inside man in the Winston-Salem Police Department, Tyrone Neben.

"Reverend Artury, this is Tyrone. Bad news. They issued warrants for your arrest and got warrants for Evan and Mr. Turlo, too. They say they got all the evidence and testimony from an eyewitness. Don't know who. They didn't invite me to that party. It's all hush-hush. The FBI is involved. You need a top security clearance to find out anything in here. Man, I was lucky to get the information I did. You want me to call Evan? See what he wants me to do?"

A guttural hiss escaped my throat. "No. Don't call anyone. Talk to no one. Only me."

"What do you want me to do about this?" The phone connection cracked and gurgled. It became difficult to hear him.

"Nothing. I repeat. Do nothing."

"You're the boss—" Tyrone's voice trailed, and the line disconnected.

I dropped to my knees like Lot in Sodom, praying for one drop of mercy. But within seconds, I shot to my feet. That's right. I was the boss and wasn't about to let anyone forget it. I would tell no one about the warrants, not even Evan. Evan hated me. *Let him fry. Let them all fry.*

The morning of the last day of the Crusade dawned like a fire in a hearth, so gold everything seemed cast of metal. The air proved unfit for human consumption. I rolled over on a wet sheet and spat a swig of piss-warm water onto the floor. The skin on my face had turned a fiery red from the scalding sun. Preaching, prophesying, and praying for the sick in the enormous all-day events had pushed my staff and me to exhaustion.

Long-legged and nearly naked, the young Nigerian man at the foot of my bed stared at me with murky and inexpressive eyes, his shirt barely covering his voluptuous chest. His pants, unzipped, had slid down to his slim hips. I reached out, stroked his cheek, and thanked him.

The knock at the door startled me.

"One minute." I slipped into my pants and buttoned my shirt. I knew Silas stood on the other side as I opened it. "You alone?"

Silas nodded and rolled his toothpick from one side of his mouth to the other. He stepped into the room, glared at the young man spread across my sheets, and then turned his attention to me. "Are you ready, Reverend?"

"Better question. Are you?"

"We're ready. Percy knows what to do. We're moving forward."

"God will be with us. This is His plan of protection, Silas. Don't be afraid. I am here to bring you a great deliverance, a wonderful, blood-working anointing."

Silas looked back only once, then closed the door behind him on his way out.

A storm missed the hotel that morning, but with it came unbearable humidity. In the sticky hour after Silas left, I heard the vast throng of people pounding the ground only 500 yards from my room. Nigeria's heavy air reeked of human waste, and I hated the thought of fighting the dust and mud around the stage. The reclining young man in my bed smiled seductively. The beautiful creature had heard everything and nothing.

"Time for you to go." I handed him a hundred-dollar bill and watched him slip out the hotel window and climb down the trellis the same way he got in, disappearing into the sea of faces already jamming the sidewalks.

I picked up the phone and dialed the car waiting below.

"Yeah?" The static-distorted voice was almost a bark.

"It's me," I said.

"About time."

"Sorry. You know how it is."

"Who was with you?"

"Some comfort in my time of need."

"Are you ready?"

"Give me ten minutes."

Evan appeared agitated as I stumbled into the backseat beside him. He knew. Of course, he knew. Evan had his own eyes and ears within the system back home.

Whisked away in the dust and heat, the car moved slowly from the narrow alleyway to the street and into an endless mass of people, dividing them like plowing a soft field. Women balanced bundles on their heads and backs, with their children following close behind. Men carried the sick and afflicted, while others rode bicycles without tires.

An eerie silence settled inside the car in the humid afternoon air. The car dropped us off at a white cement block building used as a gathering place for staff to count the offerings, securing them in a large portable safe. A conspicuous group of bodyguards with guns surrounded the perimeter. Once inside the building, we wiped the sweat from our faces with wet cloths provided by local pastors from that God-forsaken country.

Evan placed his gun in his holster. "I need to check security. Do you want anything?"

A slight chuckle escaped my lips as I shook my head. His concern for my safety amused me. Our eyes met briefly. *I wonder what you're plotting for me, Evan? What form of death would you choose?*

"Everything okay?" he asked. Evan's eyes, suddenly dark as tarnish, spoke silent obscenities.

I knew my assistant had sensed trouble escalating months before. Leaving early for Africa was his idea as much as mine. In years past, Evan tried to reassure me it would come to this someday; someone would leak something to the media, and we would have to prove ourselves innocent. He believed all televangelists lived with the threat of exposure and would face it, eventually.

A smile spread across my face like a cancer. I didn't answer. I waved him out the door, placed a pill on my tongue, and washed it down with a warm Coke. It wouldn't take long. I clamped my jaw as waves of pain receded to a tolerable level.

I hid in the sparse room, asking not to be disturbed. A typical request: I often hid myself away, praying and talking with God, sometimes all night, for services like that. But I wasn't praying. Not that time. I walked to where Silas had told me he'd stashed the nine-millimeter silencer-equipped Luger. "For *mine* is the kingdom and the power and the glory." I slid it into my pocket. "Forever."

I stepped out into the heat and the droning sounds of the quartet singing their worn-out gospel songs. Songs made famous by Southern Christian artists over a decade ago. Songs that made no sense in that country, on that landscape, to those people.

I pulled my Ray-Bans from my shirt pocket and slipped them on to shield my red, swollen eyes from the blinding sun. A migraine engulfed my entire head. Evan stood several feet away, sweating like a migrant worker in his white dress shirt, discussing security measures with several men in uniform. I motioned to him. I was ready to press through the crowd and reach the platform.

The sun's intense, steady heat never let up. The old and the sick, a desperate lot, squatted like mice as close to the stage as possible, hoping I'd touch them as I walked by. I retched at the smell of their poorly washed bodies. Thankfully, a light breeze rose, saving me from falling to my knees. A few babies cried in their mother's arms. Suicidal dogs with their ribs protruding mingled among the crowd while hordes of grimy children swarmed like flies over the grounds. I wanted to be in any place but Nigeria.

Silas motioned to Percy, who took his place behind me. He had been proud to be the on-stage bodyguard since the incident in Germany.

Evan took center stage along with a Nigerian translator. "Good and kind people of Nigeria," he paused for translation. "I would like to introduce you to God's man of the hour, the last hour before Jesus Christ's return to earth." Another pause. "Your evangelist from the United States of America, the Reverend Calvin Artury!"

I gazed out over the immeasurable assembly. There were no seats. A million or more people stood like trees as far as my eyes could see and began to jump in place, raising their hands, praising and applauding as Evan announced my arrival. The music played, and the crowd's shouting escalated in sound and intensity.

In the distance, firecrackers exploded. A hopeful mob of the press, CNN cameras, and paparazzi from several American and British tabloids jockeyed for position to document my every word and movement.

A sudden string of drool dripped down my chin, and I staggered and stumbled halfway up the steps to the stage. I felt ill. Julia Preston lingered nearby. Evan's wife never hesitated to butt in where no one wanted her. She grabbed my arm. "Oh, my god. Reverend, are you sick?" I pushed her away, and she fell backward into the arms of a portly man from the House of Praise. I recognized him as one of my faithful church members who traveled to the Crusades on their own dime. A group of devoted followers, retirees, a mixture of bankers, lawyers, and influential business people coming to Africa to support me, testify to the Nigerians, and lead them to salvation.

Percy, close behind, shot Julia a stern look and then helped me the rest of the way up the steps. I rushed to the middle of the stage before anyone pulled at me again. Standing on legs that barely held my weight, I didn't speak. Anticipatory sweat rolled down my forehead into my eyes, and I wiped it away with the back of my trembling hand before I tore off my sunglasses. Looking out over the dark knot of people, I watched the multitude grow quiet but restless. A peculiar throng. Their mood was always unpredictable. A river of changing faces who waited impatiently for their miracles. I turned from the crowd to speak to my staff and crew.

Squinting in the bright sunlight, I scanned their faces. Singers, musicians, and stagehands; some with bowed heads, some with adoring expressions—they had given all, traveled with me for the past sixteen years, and sacrificed their lives for Almighty God. With their whole hearts, they believed the power of Jehovah moved through me. That my silence was the great miracle anointing. That prophecy was about to spill forth out of my mouth. It was the moment I decided Silas and Percy's plan of escape would not include me.

Instead, I shouted with the voice of an archangel and with the trump of God. "And the dead in Christ shall rise first! YOU who are alive and remain shall be caught up—to meet the Lord in the air—wherefore—comfort one another with these words! Prepare ye—the way of the Lord!"

I spun back around to face the vast congregation of Nigerians, pulled the gun from my pocket, jammed it into my temple, and fired.

Chapter 25

That Old Serpent

August 1993

Andie

I slept for thirteen hours after Matthew brought me home from the police department. A full day of questioning had totally worn me out. But my part was over for the time being. Still, the FBI advised us that until they had arrested Artury and his executive staff, we should not bring the children back into my life. It was too dangerous for all of us. They had planted agents outside the Darwoods' home for my children's protection and for the Darwoods. It relieved me slightly while worrying myself sick for all of them.

I kissed Matthew good morning, feeling his beard against my face. A feeling I had become addicted to. I pointed to the gun in his hand. "What's that for?"

"I'm not taking chances. You know the alarm system in the house; you remember the buzzer under my desk?"

"Yeah, so?"

"It goes directly to the police. They're on alert. We cannot be too cautious at this point. I'm sure there are leaks in the department. I don't know who might spill their guts; let someone know where you're hiding. This is my .38 revolver, and it's loaded. I keep it in my top drawer."

Staring out the window, I shivered at the creaking sounds the house made in the morning.

"Are you listening to me?"

I nodded.

He winked. "I know you can shoot."

"What are you thinking, Matt? Am I in more danger now since giving my statement to the police?"

"Probably. Ivy and Tobias have agreed to move in with us for a while. I don't want you here alone if I go off-property. Until Artury returns from Africa, until those guys are in jail, I don't even want you to walk outside unless someone is with you. I'm sorry, honey, but you know these people better than all of us. You know they'll stop at nothing to find you. My honest feeling? All of this will be over soon. These precautions—they're only temporary."

I sank into the chair in front of his desk and pulled my knees up to my chin. "I hope you're right," I said.

MATTHEW

Paranoia was a contagious thing. I caught myself staring out windows and checking doors several times daily. My fingers slid over the gun barrel, and my skin grew cold at the thought of using it. They would kill her if they found her. Not only to eliminate her testimony, but who knew what crazy church member searched for her because Artury had called her the *dark angel?* I turned away so she didn't see the concern in my eyes, the fear in me she had yet to find.

As quiet as a baby's sigh, she said, "My birthday is next week."

"Your twenty-ninth?"

"Try thirty-ninth."

"We'll celebrate here with Mother and the Brothers Grimm, okay?"

It was Andie's turn to look away from me. "I miss my children. So much."

I hurt for her. "I know you do. Hold on a little longer, honey." I leaned down and kissed her, tasted her breath, and inhaled her morning scent of lavender shampoo and Ivy's coffee. "Have I told you how beautiful you are?"

"Like a broken record. When will you be home?"

"As soon as possible. Although I'd prefer a morning in bed with you, I've meetings in Boone this afternoon and supper with Royster in Winston-Salem."

"Come home as soon as you can."

"Count on it. We have taken every precaution. I'll tell Tobias to let the dogs loose. They'll let you know if anyone is around. There's also two agents parked at the gate."

Driving away from Shiloh, I heard her words and the rhythm of her accent, and for an instant, I thought about turning the car around.

ANDIE

After Matthew left for Boone, I fried a bologna sandwich for lunch. My old cooking habits died hard. Ivy had gone home to gather her things. I disliked the house's quiet, especially with the thunder outside. Sadie wagged her tail and needed to go out. "Come on, girl. Let's head on over to Ivy's. We'll help her carry a few things back here."

I walked the flagstone pathway between the houses, feeling its warmth from the day's heat, and tried not to think of anything other than what to prepare for supper that evening. I found Ivy in her bedroom, folding clothes into an overnight bag.

"Lord, Andie! You startled me! What you doing here? You shouldn't be outside by yourself. You know what Mattie say."

"I thought you might need some help. Besides, I'm sick of living in fear. I've had enough of it."

Ivy clicked her tongue and raised her brow. Ignoring her stern look, I walked around Ivy's room—a room in bloom. Her patchwork quilt flowed over the end of her iron bed like a waterfall. The scent of lilacs and beeswax filled the air. Nestled among lush houseplants on a table under a bay window, family pictures filled the space, including one she had snapped of me.

"Fear—No. Common sense—Yes, by all means. Tobias will help me bring the suitcases later in the truck. How about some iced tea?"

Ivy's white and chrome kitchen was functional rather than fashionable. Stainless steel countertops, a well-used apron sink, and the most oversized refrigerator I ever saw stood in tight formation along the opposite wall of a commercial stove and a large pantry filled with Ironstone dishes, platters, pitchers, and soup tureens. I sat at her laminate table and looked through floor-to-ceiling windows at late summer iris beds. Regal and top-heavy, the bigheaded lady flowers seemingly stood posing as if for an unseen Victorian painter. Sadie stretched on the other side of the screen door. Her buttery ears unfurled across the porch floor, twitching and alert.

Ivy poured two glasses of tea and then planted herself in a chair. "You holding up under all this?"

"You know, I feel fearless for the first time. Calvin can't hurt me now. Matthew's scared they'll still try to kill me, but I'm not afraid. The police know everything. I'll do whatever it takes to put that beast away and get my babies back. I guess, though, in answer to your question, some days are better than others."

On better days, I didn't have to remind myself to breathe. On better days, I had completely dressed before I had the urge to crawl back into bed. On better days, I even clipped recipes in magazines to save for later. Yes, some days were better than others. Despite Matthew's love and constant attention, I knew until this was over, progressing in our relationship wasn't possible.

I smeared my fingerprints on the frosty glass, slumping in my chair, not trusting myself to continue. Ivy's quiet demeanor disturbed me, as if peering inside my head. I drank the rest of my tea and stood too quickly. My chair caught on the tile and crashed to the floor, and I almost peed my pants. "I'm sorry. I guess I am a little nervous. Best head back. You'll wait for Tobias, then?" I uprighted the chair, then made a beeline for the screen door, but stopped there. The sky darkened, the wind blew dust across the meadow, and lightning cracked in the distance. Sadie sniffed the air and rolled to her feet.

Ivy walked up behind me and leaned against the door jamb. "You must move on, no matter what happens. Even if your heart hasn't. You must put this behind you. Matthew deserves that, but you deserve it more. I don't mean to bury your anger. Let it go. Let it all go, Andie. I feel danger for you otherwise."

I nodded and pushed a bit too hard through the screen door. "Thanks for—" *Please, Ivy. Stop.* "—the iced tea."

Ivy followed me outside. She rested her hand on my arm. "You listen to Ivy. I feel things before they happen. Not see, just feel."

"Okay. I'll put it behind me, Ivy. Somehow. I promise. Come on, Sadie. Let's go. Looks like a nasty storm."

Ivy lifted her hanging ferns off their hooks and set them on the porch floor. "The wind is picking up. I'll be up to the house soon. Matthew due home late?"

"Yes. I'm making supper." I pulled Sadie off the porch.

A smile spread across Ivy's ruby-red lips. "That's more than fine with me. You should wait; go with me and Tobias in the truck."

"It's a short walk, Ivy. I'll be fine."

"Lock the doors behind you when you get inside," Ivy said.

Sadie suddenly sprinted across the field, and I followed without responding to Ivy. "Slow down, girl!" The dog's legs moved like she was running on hot asphalt. Hurrying back to the house, I recalled I locked the doors, but I'd forgotten to set the alarm. It was easy for me to forget about the alarm. I wasn't used to alarm systems. Daddy never had one in his house, and I *certainly* never had one. Setting the alarm had not become a habit like—well, like locking your door.

Whirling around and gazing back toward Ivy's house, now far behind me, an overwhelming presence swept over me. The courage that surrounded me minutes before had evaporated, leaving me feeling vulnerable and exposed. Lightning flashed again, splitting a gray southern sky. Terror prickled my skin, each hair on my body standing on end. But continuing forward, I found my backbone as the roof of Matthew's house rose above the tree-lined yard. I picked up my pace, jogged to the back door, unlocked it, and stepped inside. Everything seemed fine. The house was quiet. I opened the door again, stuck my head outside, and yelled for Sadie.

A voice crept up behind me. "She's off after a groundhog or a squirrel."

"Tobias! You scared me to death." I had nearly jumped out of my flip-flops.

"So sorry," he said. "I saw you as I came up from the barn. I let the dogs loose. Where's Ivy?"

"At your house, waiting for you."

"I'll fetch Ivy and then look for Sadie. Stay inside and set the alarm. Weather looks bad. I expect a downpour soon. Ol' Sadie runs off sometimes, but she'll be back."

∞

I kept myself busy, putting supper on the table. But I breathed easier when Ivy and Tobias walked in. Watching for the dog, I peeked out the windows occasionally while we ate. "I wish you had found Sadie, Tobias. Where could she have gone? I hope she doesn't come back muddy and think she's coming inside."

Ivy cleared the table. "Huh. Who knows? That dog! She worry Mattie to death, I swan. She thinks she's the queen around here."

Tobias leaned back in his chair. "I've got to get the horses in, close up the barn. Looks like it might rain all night. I'll whistle for Sadie again." He wiped his mouth with his napkin. "After I feed the dogs, I'll leave them loose, like Mattie said. Excellent supper, Andie."

"I'll say," said Ivy. "We must share recipes, maybe write a cookbook together."

I laughed at my new friend until I held up my hand, shushing her, my ear cocked to the doorway. "Did you hear that?"

"No. Probably the wind and this house. Mattie's old house creaks in the wind. Besides, I thought you were fearless," Ivy said with a chuckle.

"I'm a little jumpy, that's all. Matthew left his gun in the bedroom. I'll go get it."

"Uh-huh, well, don't shoot yourself in the foot. Mine's in the kitchen drawer here. We'll have a shoot 'em up time anybody messes with us."

I smiled at Ivy. Both of us, truth be told, were edgy. I took the stairs two at a time and hurried to the bedroom.

Rummaging through every drawer, I thought Matthew said he hid the gun in his top drawer. But I couldn't find it. *Maybe he meant his desk drawer.* I figured I only half-heard him, with all his security precautions and the long list of instructions running through my head.

Rushing down the staircase, I opened Matthew's office door and stopped with my hand on the knob. Someone had turned off the desk lamp and closed the shutters, which was strange. Ambling into the coldness of the study, a sudden, inexplicable chill shot down my spine as I breathed in a familiar scent, and a hand came from behind the door and across my face, clamping my mouth shut. He yanked me hard into him. "Looking for this?"

JOE!

He shoved Matthew's gun into my temple. His eyes moved slowly over me, his smile broadening with every jerk my body made to free myself from him. I tried to scream, but his grip was suffocating.

"If you so much as crack a smile, I'll strangle you," he whispered. My head against his shoulder, I smelled all of him. His foul breath, stale sweat, and hair—the odor of rancid vinegar.

I nodded, and his hand moved from my face to my shoulder. His sneer made my blood run cold. Wishing I had something to lean against, I thought I might be sick as my legs wobbled like rubber posts. "Please, Joe. You don't have to do this."

The house felt cool, but he was sweating like a prizefighter. He had lost his good looks. Middle age, years of secret-keeping, and long Bible fasts had done a number on his skin. The stress on his now gnomish face and receding hairline made him appear a decade older than he was. He wasn't the man I once knew.

Joe stared at me with a *found-you-bitch* grin. "Nice place you're living in. It wasn't easy tracking you down until I thought about your daddy's backwoods cousins in Boone. Figured you might've headed this way. When I showed your picture around town, it didn't take long for somebody to recognize you as the new girlfriend of the richest man in the state. Give me the tape and the pictures, Andie. All of it. Now. Now, damn it! Give me everything!"

Joe unloaded Matthew's gun, allowing the bullets to fall to the floor. "I prefer a good knife," he said, throwing the gun into the corner. "It's nice and quiet."

When I heard a muffled noise coming from the hallway, Joe cast a quick look toward the door, his eyes showing the slightest glimpse of fear. He obviously didn't go to Africa with the rest of the team, and he sure didn't know I'd been to the prosecutor's office the day before and handed in every piece of evidence he was looking for.

He pulled a long, serrated knife from inside his raincoat and swayed where he stood, blinking his eyes, the sweat beading like tiny pearls on his forehead. The afternoon light cast his already narrow face into hard, angular lines, emphasizing his frown. I told myself to breathe in and out as I listened to his sudden low and harsh laughter, followed by words I will never forget. Not for as long as I live. "Give me what I want, Andie," he said, "or I swear I'll cut you up more than I did Mavis."

Joe's words hit me with the force of his fist. I drew in a sharp and painful breath, doubled over, and placed both hands on my knees to keep myself erect. I broke out in a viscous sweat, and my legs finally gave out as he ambled closer. My vision blurred. But I knew if I passed out, I might as well be dead.

"Joe," I said, my voice small and shaky. "*You* murdered Mavis?"

"Don't act so surprised. I hated that bitch. She almost cost me my entire career." Another sneer stretched across his face, and he laughed. "God, you should've seen her. She looked like she'd been through a meat tenderizer by the time I got through with her. I fucked her, then I about cut her head clean off."

The vile words out of his mouth knocked the wind out of me and stabbed me in the heart. Cold, merciless fury sliced through the middle of me, and I fell completely to the floor, clenching my hands into numbness, my face contorting into twenty years of agony. "You filthy son of a bitch. You revolting, demonic creature! You killed my Mavis!"

He mocked me. "You killed my Mavis! You killed my Mavis! You bet I did, baby. And I'd do it again for a lot less money!"

"You animal! You *knew* Calvin molested children! My baby died because of what you put me through, and I lost my children because of your vicious lies! And now—now you tell me you—raped and murdered Mavis. You *lived* with me, *lying* to me all those years! *You're* the monster! Do you really think I'll hand over evidence that'll nail Calvin's ass to the wall, along with your own!?" I laughed. "And I thought I'd lost *MY* mind!"

Joe coiled back like a snake, the knife clenched in his fist. "Living with you was my sacrifice to God." He moved toward me, grabbed hold of my hair and held it tight while pointing the knife tip within an eyelash of my neck. Yanking my head backward, he pressed the cold blade against my throat, allowing trickles of warm blood to drip down my skin and soak into my shirt. "Get—the damn tape. Or I will be more than happy to slice your throat, too." He released his grip on me.

There was no time to think. I bit the inside of my mouth to appear unruffled at the mental pictures he was so quick to relay. As precisely as a debutante, I stood and felt the pressure of his hand at the small of my back, pushing me to Matthew's desk. I had to stall him. Searching for the alarm button, I felt dizzy, my stomach rolling. "I have the tape, I said. It's in Matt's office safe," I lied. "But I don't know the combination. None of you are getting away with this. The police already know."

"God will protect us," he snarled as he stumbled back to the door, slamming and locking it behind him. "How 'bout we get down to business?"

That was when I saw the blood. Bright drops of blood. On the floor and on top of his boots. I got a better look at his grimy, full-length oversized raincoat. Underneath, he wore a black suit with a charcoal shirt and tie, like a minister turned evil—crumpled, malicious, and red-eyed. A flask stuck out of his coat pocket.

I heard the noise again, like a whining pup, from outside the room.

"Now, then." He spoke calmly. "The tape and the pictures? Get them. Now, Andie."

"It's easier for you to hate than feel guilt or pain, isn't it? I told you I don't have the combination to the safe. Matthew is due back in a few minutes."

Joe shook his head furiously. The sweat rolled down his face. His eyes flickered, and he grabbed his head like he was nursing a migraine. I couldn't imagine I had once loved him so much because, at that moment, I hated him beyond belief. My adrenaline pumping, I couldn't think clearly enough to remember which side of the desk the alarm button was under. "Why?" I asked, stalling for time, feeling under the desk's ledge.

Joe stiffened. "Why what?"

"Why did Calvin want *you* to kill Mavis?" Two tears fell onto my arm.

"It was God's perfect divine will, not the permissible will, but the divine," he said, rigid and unmoving. "Reverend had a vision. We are the chosen. Jehovah-Nissi chose me. I was His hand. He used me to wipe His enemy from the face of the earth. We are special people. But I—I am God's anointed warrior."

"Please, let me understand this. God wanted *you* to beat, rape, and murder Mavis?"

"No. Just kill her. Like God killed Ananias and Sapphira in the Bible when they told their big, fat lies. Ripping her to pieces was my idea. Kind of cool, though, don't you think? That bitch deserved it. I hated her. She started all of this. Reverend only wanted her dead. But I put my own spin on it. Because of Mavis and you, though, I've lost my position, maybe my job. Everyone is in Africa but me."

I froze behind the desk. I wanted to kill Joe myself. Watch him suffer the way he made Mavis suffer. And then I looked down at the blood on his shoe and heard that curious, muffled cry again, banging against a door. *The hall closet! Shit!* He'd heard me coming down the steps and had shoved Ivy into the closet.

Staggering close to the desk, he scraped the knife's tip back and forth across his leg by his knee. It sliced through the fabric and into his skin and muscle, oozing blood into his pants and more on the floor. Suddenly, he plunged the knife into Matthew's desk. "Why are you stalling!? Get the shit, NOW!"

He would sacrifice me to his God because he was as delusional as his employer. Backing me into the corner between the wall and the bookcase, he grabbed my arm and yanked the knife out of the desk. Pulling me away from the wall toward the middle of the room, his eyes bulged. His fingers released my arm and then dug into my shoulders. Mouthing incoherent obscenities, he forced me to my knees and knelt behind me, filling me with a deep terror. Despair washed over me in waves as Joe dug his fingers into my hair again, pulling my head back. His breath came hot on my neck as he jerked me into his chest.

"I can get you everything you want when Matt comes home!" I screamed.

"This isn't *your* home," he said. "You belong in a whore house or another piece of shit apartment, covered in disease and lice. That's what you deserve, my love. Don't bother getting me what I want; I'll tear this place apart and find it myself after I kill every demon in it. First, though, I will slit your throat, then take pleasure in cutting out your tongue. It'll be my souvenir. I'll keep it in a jar of formaldehyde and display it on my audio board. Whenever I look at it, I'll smile. No more dark angel to wag her foul tongue and destroy the ministry."

His words added to the pain he inflicted as he pulled hard on my hair and forced my head back even further.

"You destroyed it, Joe. You and Calvin. It's over. Do you hear me!? The police know all of it! I was with them yesterday. They have all the evidence. All of it! Our children, Joe, think of them! Please don't do this!" I choked back a sob, but he was oblivious to my words.

"You are, by far," he screamed into my ear, "the worst fuck I ever had! And that includes a half-dead Mavis! Goodbye, Andie." He brought the knife up to my neck—

—And the door blew open!

MATTHEW

I didn't hesitate when I walked into my house and heard a man's voice in my office. I kicked open the double doors and rammed into Joe from behind. We crashed into a chair, sending it flying across the floor. Andie screamed as I smashed Joe's knife hand against the floor. But he kicked and bit into my arm as the knife spun around, landing under a table. He attempted to push me back against the couch, but I threw a shoulder into his chest, spinning him backward. That's when Andie hit him in the head with the iron cannon paperweight from my desk, causing him to turn and gaze at me for a few startled seconds, then drop entirely to the floor as if all his bones had suddenly turned liquid.

Andie ran to the desk, found the panic button, then into my arms. We both collapsed to the floor.

I had worked part-time as a social worker for thirty years. Not given to panic or violence, I recalled the last time I had to get physical on a case. It was the day I laced up my steel-toed boots and walked into a roadhouse outside of Statesville some ten years before. I'd always known my heart and fist together were powerful because there beside me was the proof. The one thing in my life worth fighting for, worth dying for. And she was alive.

Andie.

A pounding echoed from the hallway, like someone trying to open a door.

"Matt, it's Ivy!"

I sprung to my feet and bolted to the guest closet. Not knowing how badly he had hurt her, I felt panic flare in my chest.

"Ivy! Stand back!"

After one hard kick to open the door, we found Ivy with her hands bound and her mouth taped shut. I gently pulled off the duct tape. "Be careful! He's got a knife!" Ivy yelled.

Andie worked to untie Ivy's wrists. "Her hand is bleeding."

I smiled at the woman I loved as much as my mother, helped her to her feet, and quickly pulled her into the kitchen to wrap her bloody hand in a towel. "At least we will always have Ivy to watch our backs."

A swarm of police, FBI agents, and Officer Bently stormed into the house.

"I'm fine," Ivy said. "He got my hand. I would've shot him dead with Tobias's gun, but he cut me before I opened the drawer. Damn, son of a bitch! Who does he think he is, breaking into this house, all cocky, thinking he can order us around? Did he hurt you, Matthew? Andie, you're fine? Please tell me you're fine."

Andie kissed Ivy's forehead. "I'm okay. But we need to get you to a doctor. You need stitches."

Sadie appeared at the back door and barked. I let her in and threw my arms around her neck. "I came home early. Thank God. I had a feeling I should skip supper with Royster. I called him and told him to meet me here. When I arrived at the gate, Sadie was waiting for me, barking her head off. That's when I knew. She ran ahead of me all the way back to the house."

"She saved us all," Andie said, hugging her. "Good girl, Sadie."

ANDIE

The police picked Joe off the floor. Someone read him his rights while the FBI scoured the property for additional intruders. Joe was conscious when they led him out the front door. Matthew sat with Ivy in the kitchen as an EMT treated her wounded hand. Tobias had nearly run himself into a heart attack when he saw the commotion at the house from the kennel where he had been feeding the dogs. Another medical technician treated him with oxygen.

I looked at Matthew and laid my hand on his arm. "Don't worry about me. I have to do this." I walked to the front porch where the police stood, cuffing Joe's hands behind him, and I stared into the eyes of a man gone mad, his mind seemingly gone. A purple goose egg swelled on his forehead and bled. More blood dripped from his nose, mouth, and chin. His eyes fluttered, and a low animal growl emanated from his lips as he slurred his words. *"And behold, the angel of the Lord came upon him, and a light shined in the prison: and he smote Peter on the side, and raised him up…And his chains fell off from his hands!"* An officer grabbed Joe by the arm and pulled him away.

But I stepped close, inches from his face, astounded that no matter how incredibly evil Calvin had become, his sycophants believed he was right, and *they* were right to follow him to the bitter end. Joe would never admit he was wrong. He would rather die. I only thought of one thing to say: to throw scripture back at him. *"And I saw an angel come down from Heaven, having the key of the bottomless pit and a great chain in his hand. And he laid hold of the dragon, that old serpent…and bound him a thousand years. And cast him into the bottomless pit, and SHUT—HIM—UP, and set a seal upon him, that he should deceive the nations no more."*

The policeman laughed. "She got ya on that one, fella. Let's throw your nasty ass into the cruiser, get you out of these nice people's hair."

Joe stumbled down the porch steps, and then, wrenching himself free from the policeman's grasp, he bounded back up the steps, tripping and coming with a hair of me before another officer grabbed him by the back of his neck. Once again, Joe glared at me and snarled like a wounded beast. "When Reverend Artury returns from Africa, he'll deal with you."

I stared him down as I stood my ground.

"Then you haven't heard," the policeman said matter-of-factly.

Agent Bently stepped to my side. "Please, let me inform our prisoner." He grabbed Joe by the coat and pulled him back down the steps. "Your leader is dead. Shot himself. Right in the head. Over there in Africa. In front of all those poor people. Crazy son of a bitch."

Agent Bently barely got the last word out when Joe spit in his face. *Let God be true and every man a liar!*

The kind agent wiped his face on his sleeve and threw Joe into the arms of several policemen surrounding them. "You don't believe me? Look for yourself!" He pulled the newspaper from his inside coat pocket and shoved the front page of the *Winston-Salem Journal* in Joe's face. The headlines didn't lie. EVANGELIST CALVIN ARTURY DEAD IN NIGERIA. "Get this slimy bastard out of here. And this time, don't let go of him! If he tries anything, shoot him!"

Joe turned ashen white, and his body wilted as he fell into the cruiser's backseat.

The police finished their search of the house and grounds while the car holding the man who murdered Mavis Dumass drove away.

Matthew admitted the videotape Peter Collins gave me was, indeed—horrendous. He said it was difficult for even him to watch. But he also said I had to know what was on it in case they showed it during Joe's trial. Peter had secretly recorded both video and audio at several staff meetings. In one particular meeting, Calvin laughed, reminiscing with Evan about Mavis. How he gave permission for whoever Evan chose to kill Mavis to have *fun* with her first. Evan had made a wisecrack about it being an employee benefit, a *bonus*.

In another meeting, Calvin gave clear and concise instructions to Evan to do whatever was necessary to eliminate the John Rossi problem. Peter had been a brave soul to slip in and push *play*. He'd been a *very* brave soul, and no one knew it.

All of it sickened me. I couldn't turn off the light at night. I simply lay, watching the hours tick by slowly. Eventually, my body demanded its due, and I closed my eyes. But I tossed and turned with no real meaningful sleep. Matthew protested I needed rest, but my answer was always the same. "It means nothing to me that Joe will spend the rest of his life in a federal prison. Locking him up does nothing to get the pictures out of my head of what he did to Mavis. That will haunt me for the rest of my days."

We had dodged reporters for weeks. Ever since the news hit about Calvin's suicide and Joe's attack. The press had camped outside the gates of Callahan property, clamoring for comments. Although Matthew and I had steered clear of the media, soon they broadcast our names on every news program, channel, and in newspapers around the globe.

The media was clear in their view of me. *Andie Oliver, scorned former member of the House of Praise, a tireless champion of good Christians everywhere, out to destroy scumbag televangelists worldwide.*

At least we hoped the worst was over. Matthew insisted I still had to be cautious. House of Praise crazies had been spotted in Boone and some surrounding villages. Matthew hired additional private security to roam the property, but at least I didn't have to hide anymore. Finally, I talked to my sister, Lula, and Aunt Wylene. But it seemed Dixie was always out of the house whenever I called. I dismissed the excuses Aunt Wy made on her behalf. I had other things to consider as I anxiously awaited news about my children. Matthew convinced me to wait patiently. He and his lawyers needed a little more time to work their magic with the court.

The days passed slowly after Joe's arrest and waiting for word on my twins. At September's end, Royster Bently surprised us with a visit. Ivy, Tobias, and Matthew walked outside to talk to Royster and relax in the late summer evening air. A warm breeze blew softly on my face as I stepped out to the porch with a tray of iced coffee and shortbread cookies.

"I thought you all deserved a report," Royster said. His silver-white hair stood on end like he had repeatedly run his hands through it. He had shed his suit jacket and tie, but the warm expression in his eyes was comforting.

Matthew moved to the swing, motioning me to join him. "What do you have for us?"

I relaxed beside Matthew and took little sips of coffee, listening to the chains creak. It was a soothing sound compared to whatever Royster had to say.

"Thanks to Andie and Matthew, there were twenty-seven arrests."

Tobias nodded. "Thank you, Lord," he said.

Royster continued. "Since Reverend Artury's death, the remaining stressed-out church members have scrambled to take up the slack. They have no leader now. A few more innocent men on his staff attempted to rally those who showed up for service, singing songs and praying for their imprisoned leaders, hoping the truth would come out. And the truth is getting louder every week. Besides all the murder and mayhem, you wouldn't believe the rest."

Matthew sighed. "I think we would believe anything at this point. What happened to Artury's body?"

"They flew it back to the States. All those named in his last will and testament are now in jail, facing prison time. The court has contacted a distant cousin to collect his remains."

"What else can you tell us?" asked Tobias.

"More men and women of the congregation have come forward, offering stories about Artury. Seems he told them God could heal them, but only in his private office. First, they had to remove their clothes for God to *cleanse* them. It was a mode of healing that had recently become popular within certain circles in the church, especially among the youth. Many of the men in the church confessed to the police during questioning that Artury had asked to see their privates. In particular, before marital counseling. That Artury acted like it was normal." Royster shook his head. "I won't get into the fraud and money laundering, but it's all under investigation."

"Looks like the congregation has dwindled to about two hundred. Diehards who refuse to believe their leader is dead or that he committed the crimes reported by the media. Last week, those members waited inside the church, expecting the rapture or their Reverend to rise from the ashes. A few members were relieved when the police took the initiative, forced everyone out, and padlocked the doors. Justice had come, but not in the way the House of Praise folk had hoped. They're definitely a sad lot. Church construction has stopped, and they have canceled all TV programming. Sponsors and donors all jumped ship. There's a world full of hurt evangelicals out there."

Royster bit into a cookie and drank his coffee. "I thought you'd also like to know about Joe."

I looked at Matthew, not sure what to say.

"Might as well tell us," Matthew said, then turned to me. "This is all part of putting it behind us."

I nodded. "Okay."

Royster smiled again in an apparent effort to calm my nerves. "When we interrogated Joe, he said, 'You think I've committed a crime, but I haven't.' He insists he is innocent but does not deny he killed Mavis. I asked him to explain how these contradictory statements were true, and he said, 'I am God's warrior. I only do His bidding. It was the divine will of God. What I did wasn't a crime.'"

I stood, walked to the porch edge, and stared down the path to the old cemetery. "You should let them know, Royster, that in dealing with Joe, there's no argument. You cannot argue logically with him because he uses the illogical to support his beliefs." I crossed my arms in front of me. "How could a sane man, or so he seemed—" I hesitated, feeling the revulsion of him in the pit of my stomach, "—I mean, good Lord, I lived with him for years and had no indication of his crimes. Of what he did to Mavis. How could he viciously kill a blameless woman without the barest flicker of emotion? He was often cold, but I had no hint *he* was the one who raped and murdered her. I should've known; I should've felt it somehow."

Ivy fanned herself with her good hand. "But you didn't know, Andie. Until Mavis could get you all the pieces of the puzzle, which is why she and our Johnny led you here."

Royster set his glass on the table and locked his hands around his knee. "That sounds right to me, Ivy. And I believe there's a dark side to religion that's too often ignored or denied. There may be no more potent force than religious conviction, and I doubt this is the end. Faith-based violence and craziness were present long before Joe Oliver, and they'll be with us long after Calvin Artury's death. The way I see it, Artury was a zealot, a fanatic, and outwardly motivated by the anticipation of a great reward at the other end—wealth, fame, eternal salvation—but the real reward was his obsessive control and the rush he received from it. I can hardly imagine God condoning such atrocity, much less that Artury dared to seek His protection. Artury possessed a narcissistic sense of self-assurance about everything he did. I've seen this behavior before in serial killers. A delicious rage that quickens their pulse. The one thing that fueled Artury's behavior was the non-believers, their sins, and their shortcomings. People he considered lesser beings soiling the world. When he issued orders to kill in the name of God, he experienced something akin to the rapture every time he did it. Ecstasy. Killing himself was the ultimate ecstasy."

The air grew still and hot. Royster's words stirred a quiet emotion in all of us.

"Andie, they have charged Joe with the rape and murder of Mavis Dumass and the murder of Mr. Chip Atkinson." I assume you knew him.

"No, I didn't know him. He sublet Mavis's apartment when she came to visit me. He was an unfortunate bystander. In the wrong place at the wrong time."

Royster stood to leave. "That's a shame. But I should tell you, Joe is looking at a death sentence. Have you talked to your children?"

"No, I've been advised to wait. Tell them everything gradually. But we've contacted a judge. They've revoked the previous judgment, giving me back custody. Matt and I are picking them up in two days."

"Good. That's good." Royster nodded and smiled. "I don't know how much they've heard, but I am sure they're ready to come home. I assume home is here with Matthew?" He looked at the ring on my finger.

Matthew sat his drink on a table and stood. Slipping his arm around me, he smiled. "Home will always be here for Andie and her children. Andie and I have a January wedding planned."

"Yes. Royster. Will you and your wife please come?" I asked.

"We'd be honored."

"*For the Lord is good, and His love endures forever. His faithfulness continues through all generations.*" Ivy said, rocking back and forth in her chair with her bandaged hand in her lap.

Chapter 26

MAMA
October 1993

ANDIE

Matthew and I strolled past a café, its hot apple cider scent wafting out onto the sidewalk. The aroma, a perfect complement to the russet and lemon-yellow leaves on the trees, the V of geese overhead, and the Halloween candy sale signs in the drugstore window. I fondly recalled the costumes I painstakingly crafted for Gracie and Dillon when they were little. The joy of walking with my children through Salisbury's streets, collecting candy and spreading our loot on the kitchen table—it was a cherished memory.

I guided Matthew through the places I had once called home, sharing snippets of my past for therapeutic reasons. But Salisbury, it seemed, had undergone a transformation. Coot's garage was no more. Liquor stores, pizza parlors, pawn shops, and dimly lit taverns, their roofs adorned with towering dish antennas; the town had evolved with the changing times. Someone had repurposed the convenience store next to Shady Acres into a thrift shop. Beyond the city limits, the houses thinned. We passed a used car lot, a new barbeque joint, and a desolate strip mall, its concrete wasteland punctuated by scraggly trees and scattered cars. Time had left its mark on the area.

Driving past the Olivers' house with its peeling paint and missing shutters, it had been a while since I'd seen it. A *For Sale* sign sat in the yard. I tugged on Matthew's arm. "Stop. Turn around. I need to see Maudy."

He pulled the car halfway up the drive since we spotted her on the front porch. Before I opened the car door, Matthew squeezed my hand. "Be kind to her. She's the one hurting now."

I walked through unmowed, parched grass and weeds and silently climbed the steps. Unaware of her visitors, Maudy's eyes were closed behind wire-rimmed glasses pearled with fingerprints. A new metal glider had replaced her old wicker rocker. A few rusted lawn chairs sat where the dozen rocking chairs used to be. She was alone.

"Maudy?"

Leaning to the right, she opened her eyes. Maudy looked withered and thin as an eggshell. Her skin sagged in on itself, and her cloudy eyes appeared as if sleep had abandoned her long ago. A sheer scant of white, wispy hair had replaced her strawberry-blonde curls. Someone had wrapped a pale pink sweater around her now bony shoulders. She stared at me like she couldn't quite make out who I was.

I tiptoed toward her. "Maudy? It's me. It's Andie." The hum of hundreds of memories circled my head like June bugs, causing the first tear to slip down my cheek.

Her mouth twisted as she whispered. "Andie? Oh, my sweet girl. It's you. I didn't think I'd ever see you again. How are you?"

I kissed her lightly on the forehead. "I'm fine, Maudy. Are you okay?"

"Been better, sugar. Had a stroke a few months back. They tell me the cancer's back, too. You know Al passed away."

"I know. I wanted to attend the funeral, but—it wasn't possible."

"He loved you, Andie. He really did. I do, too. I always will. How are my grandchildren?"

"They're fine." That was all I could say. I hadn't seen them in a year myself.

Maudy lowered her eyes to the porch floor. "You know Joe is in prison."

"Yes, I know. Maudy, you should prepare yourself—for a life sentence."

"Prepare myself? Life is what I gave to my sons. Life *isn't* living behind bars. Some judge is going to take Joe's life from him." Her teary eyes darted around, then focused on me. "Selma is living out at Shady Acres."

"Really? Why?"

"She couldn't afford the condo payments with Joe in jail, and she lost her job when the Praise Buffet shut down. She came here for a while. Then Ray moved her skinny butt out to your old trailer. It was available for rent. Can you believe it? I think she washes dogs for a living or something strange like that."

I smiled. *What comes around goes around.*

Half of Maudy's face smiled back. "She deserves it," whispering as if the world was listening. Her hands trembled, reaching for a tissue in her pocket. "But I'm to blame."

"Oh, hush, now. It's all over."

"No, let me speak. I'm to blame. Al knew it. I think he forgave me, though, before he died. I made Joe the way he was. I pushed him to be better than his brothers. It ruined him. I'll have to live with that. But you—you, Andie, have paid the steep price to get us all out."

Maudy sighed, then took my hand and held it in her lap. Her voice shook, and I almost choked on my tears at her feebleness. She strained over every word. "I'm so glad you stopped by today, sugar. I think about you a lot, and I apologize for how my son and we all treated you. Except for Ray, God bless him. He tried to tell us, too."

"Yes," I said. "Ray and Libby have always been good to me."

Maudy turned her head as if the shame were more than she could bear. "He destroyed us, Andie. Reverend Artury destroyed my family. All but you. Please go on for us. Go on for me, Al, Ted, and Joe—God help him. Make something of your life out of this mess. You're the one who can do it. The one God has chosen to heal the wounds. I'm sorry about everything. Go on and find true love. Have a good life, sugar."

I wept cleansing tears. God had taken a scrub brush to my soul, wiping away the grime the Olivers had left behind. Maudy had put it all into perspective. Now, I could truly—go on.

"Are you moving, Maudy? I see the house is for sale."

"To Atlanta to live with my brother. You remember Dodrill? He's got plenty of room. I'll stay there until the Lord calls me home—to Heaven. At least that's where I hope I'm going."

"Of course you are, Maudy. Of course, you are."

A column of blooming chrysanthemums grew in a large terra-cotta pot near Maudy's feet. I picked an orange one. Opening my purse, I pulled a straight pin out of the tiny sewing kit I always kept handy—a carryover from my days when I mended things—and didn't throw them away to buy new. I pinned the flower to Maudy's sweater.

"Remember when you attached a flower to my high school graduation gown, Maudy? I believe you said, 'Your gown needs a little color. It's from the family because we love you.' I love you, Maudy." I kissed her one last time, turned, and walked to the car and to Matthew. I didn't look back.

"Let's go home," I said.

Almost a year had passed since the day my twins walked out of our dingy rental at the edge of Kernersville. Thinking about that day, I closed the clinic door behind me harder than necessary. Matthew and I walked through another set of glass doors into a drab reception area, where a dozen people sat on black plastic chairs lined against stark-white walls.

To keep reporters from following us, all parties agreed we meet at an undisclosed time and day. The receptionist behind the low gray counter wore a parrot green dress, bright orange lipstick, and feathered back hair. "May I help you?" she chirped.

"I'm Andie Oliver, and this is my fiancée, Mathew Callahan. I have an appointment with Dr. Fitzgibbons."

The woman peered at her computer screen through round glasses perched at the end of her pointed nose. "One moment," she said, clicking away at her keyboard. "You're not on the schedule."

"Please check again."

"Ah, someone just added your name to the computer. I see you're here to pick up your son and daughter."

I smiled at the bird-like woman. "Yes, we are. The sooner, the better."

She slid a sheet of paper toward me. "Please sign here. I'll need to see some ID."

I pulled my driver's license out of my new slim leather wallet and handed it to her.

The woman tilted her head to the left and examined it. I figured I passed because she gave it back with a smile. "It says on the screen here Dr. Fitzgibbons drove to your children's foster home this morning and should return momentarily." Handing me a clipboard, the woman's nasally voice became irritating. "In the meantime, I need you to complete this form."

Matthew found two seats between a round-shouldered, middle-aged woman and a young Hispanic mother holding a sleeping toddler. I took the form, signed my name and address, and answered other nonsensical questions. Then, I hesitated at the line marked *Father's Name*. Joe had been a father in name only, certainly not like my daddy. I wanted to write *none,* but I scribbled Joe's name and moved on.

It was easy to be angry over losing my children for almost a year, and I was. I had a right to be angry. The judge had treated me like a criminal. "Seems she punished the wrong parent," I mumbled. My case was a setup; I knew that. But it didn't make it any easier to forgive the system.

I scrawled my signature on the bottom, rose from my chair, and carried it back to the bird lady. I'd retaken my seat when a door opened, and someone said, "Andie Oliver?" A dark-haired woman in flower-patterned scrubs smiled and said, "You can come back."

I jumped to my feet and then looked apprehensively at Matthew.

"I'll be right here. You go. This is your time," he said, reaching for my hand. "I love you."

"I keep forgetting how wonderful you are," I said.

"Go get our kids."

Our kids. He said 'our kids'. It amazed me that Matthew, who had never met Dillon and Gracie, wanted them—when all their lives, their own father wanted little to do with them.

My heart pounding, I turned and followed the woman down an antiseptic-scented corridor to a small office. A plump, pleasant-faced woman in a navy blue pantsuit greeted me. "Hello, I'm Doctor Bella Fitzgibbons," she said, holding out her hand.

I shook it. "Andie Oliver."

She gestured to two black vinyl chairs in front of her large steel desk. Three diplomas on the wall testified that she'd completed college and medical school and was a board-certified pediatrician. "Please, have a seat. I have a few things to review with you, then I'll get the children."

I could only nod; my heart felt as though it were bursting.

The doctor gave me a gentle smile, then drew two forms from a brown folder and attached them to yet another clipboard. "First, I need you to sign these forms and custody papers, verifying we have returned the children to you. I'll make sure you get copies." She handed me the clipboard. I scribbled my signature across the bottom once again.

"Can I see them now?"

Dr. Fitzgibbons smiled. "Don't worry, Ms. Oliver. They're with a social worker who's wonderful with teenagers. They're as anxious as you are. But I need to ask you a few questions."

I pulled my brows together. "Like what? Is something the matter?"

"Routine questions and explanations," Dr. Fitzgibbons said soothingly.

But I refused to be soothed. Alarm bells went off. "What do you mean? What needs explaining?"

The doctor hesitated. "I need to discuss a matter with you." She tapped a stack of papers on her lap, straightening them into a neat pile. "The Guardian ad Litem reported Dillon has been, well, rather difficult."

My jaw tensed. *Screw the Guardian ad Litem. Screw her.* It was the same word Dillon's teachers used during parent-teacher conferences. I took offense to anyone sticking a negative label on my son. "Difficult, how? The Darwoods have no complaints."

"To those he doesn't know, isn't familiar with, he doesn't listen. Outright refuses to quiet down. He's been hard to handle and isn't doing well in school. Gracie also seems to have retreated inside her own little world. She won't come out of her room without being coaxed."

I'm sure Dr. Fitzgibbons saw the fury on my face because she quickly said with a smile, "However, she makes excellent grades."

"This would never have happened to them had the courts not taken them from me!"

"We agree, Ms. Oliver. Be that as it may, their resistance to human contact concerned us, so we took them to Brenner Children's Hospital for a thorough evaluation."

It sounded like everyone within the court system was trying to cover their butts in this case. The door opened abruptly, and a tall man in a white coat wearing wire-rimmed glasses walked in. Dr. Fitzgibbons stood, her face registering a grateful smile. "Dr. Vincent Starling, our staff psychiatrist, specializes in adolescent behavior. He can explain it much better. Dr. Starling, this is Ms. Oliver. I was about to review the problems we've encountered with her twins."

More problems? I shook the doctor's hand, impatient to get to the bottom of it. "What exactly are the problems? Is something physically wrong with them?" My questions demanded answering, and I began not to care about the tone of my voice.

Dr. Starling nodded a hello with a practiced smile, his gray eyes somber as he sat beside me. "We ran a complete battery of tests. Gracie's not gaining weight as she should and is developmentally behind for her age. She's sixteen but looks and acts like a child two years younger."

"And though he's thriving physically, Dillon is definitely a handful. What I would call hyperactive with an attention span problem. Stress and the situation with their father have not helped their mental state."

My anger turned to rage, running a path from my head, down my spine, and into my feet. I wasn't in the mood to play the blame game. "Again, doctor. What, precisely, is the problem?"

"Both Dillon and Gracie have developed forms of Attachment Disorder."

I took a deep breath to calm myself down before I exploded at these doctors. I decided not to give them a reason to question whether returning my kids to me was a good idea. "Okay, so what is that, exactly?"

He tapped his long fingers together. "All children need to form a strong attachment to one primary caregiver. They did that with you, but as we know, the court took them from you. Also, the events surrounding their father's imprisonment have made them both unstable. If the children don't reestablish that attachment with you soon, they may develop more severe behavioral problems."

Dr. Starling opened a file. "Both can be bright and cheerful teenagers on the outside, but they've exhibited severe lows. Of course, you know the Darwoods. They were excellent foster parents for the twins. But even though Dillon and Gracie knew the Darwoods, being removed from your custody the way they were—it's been rough on them. They do cling to each other."

I could easily solve the problems Dr. Starling described once I took them back to Matthew's farm and spent every day with them. I would call Velda and Henry. Get the actual story from them. One thing I knew for sure was that the Darwood's love for my twins had saved them.

He continued. "Dillon needs weight management and someone to work with him daily to help him concentrate on one thing before moving to the next." After flipping through his paperwork, he looked at me over his eyeglasses. "When their bond with you was broken, their progress as thriving children slowed to almost a standstill. We need to mend that bond. You must be patient. It will take time to ward off future problems. I understand you are engaged to Matthew Callahan?"

"Yes, that's correct."

"I know Matthew. He has worked with me in placing troublesome children. If it were anyone other than Matthew, this new man in your life would not be a good idea, and I would strongly suggest you take some time to live alone with your children first. However, I've been to Matthew's home. That is exactly the environment they need. Matt's a good man."

"Yes, he is." I was sure Matthew had also made considerable donations to the hospital.

"Take the rest of the school year and stay home with them. Nurture them again. Home school them. Invite other kids into the house. Then, if you choose, introduce your children to a new educational system next September."

I leaned forward. "You said something about avoiding future problems. What problems?"

"Again, mental deficiencies and challenges that need psychiatric treatment. At this stage, however, let's be thankful you got them back when you did. As I said, the twins need stability. In a year or two, they should look at colleges: they're both bright. Security, Ms. Oliver. That's the ticket. And love." The doctor pushed his glasses up and rubbed his nose.

"That's the ticket for all of us," I said.

"Yes, we understand it was a nasty divorce, filled with great anger. The twins felt all of that. I've followed the stories in the newspaper. I've also read the police reports. What they did to you was nothing short of brutality. I've counseled numerous patients who have suffered because of that cult. At least two a week since its demise. I'll be honest: I questioned whether we should return your children to you, as I needed to ensure healing had materialized in *your* life. But Matthew assured me you were the most capable of anyone he knew. You must be a strong woman, Ms. Oliver. I wish you only the best in the future. You and Mr. Callahan."

I smiled. "Thank you."

"As far as your children are concerned, be extremely patient and empathetic, and hang in there despite any fussing, fuming, and pushing away. This separation has held them back in many areas, even at their advanced age."

I wanted to ask Matthew about suing the courts, specifically Judge VanOrson, who took bribes from Artury. *But why rehash it?*

We need to go on, like Ivy said. Like Maudy said. Go on. "The twins have me now. And Matthew. And Ivy and Tobias."

Dr. Starling smiled. "They're lucky children."

"Anything else?" I asked.

The doctor lowered his glasses and issued me a final warning as if driving his point further. "The worst thing would be for the twins to be alone again."

"The system took them. I didn't abandon them."

"I understand that. Just don't get caught up in a new relationship—"

"—Stop. I know what you're saying. My children are my priority. They always have been."

"Fine. I want to see them in six months."

"Is that all?" I wanted to get my kids and go home. This guy didn't need to tell me how to care for my children.

He handed me a sheaf of papers from his folder. "That's all."

"Good." I shoved them into my purse, snapped it shut, and shot him a feeble smile.

Dr. Starling stood and circled his chair to open the door. "It was nice meeting you. Good luck." He shook my hand again and left the room.

Dr. Fitzgibbons raised her eyebrows and smiled as if the need to bring the twins back from the brink of mental destruction was a cheery thing to contemplate. "Well, now. Why don't I go get them, and you wait here. I'm sure you're anxious."

"You have no idea." I sighed. A wave of nervousness washed over me as she bustled out. I couldn't sit still, so I stepped outside the door and waited. Within minutes, I heard their Reeboks plodding down the adjacent tiled hallway. They turned the corner, and my heart swelled as if I were watching my deceased children rise from the dead. Dillon dragged his jacket behind him, and his rugby shirt hung out of his jeans. Gracie's eyes were downcast, her arms folded in front of her. Her pants were too big, and her shirt was too small. My twins were perfect.

"There's your mama," said Dr. Fitzgibbons.

I cocked my head and smiled through my tears. Reaching out to them, my hands and arms ached as I moved slowly forward, propelled by an undeniable force, a mix of excitement and apprehension. The twins ran into my aching arms, knocking me backward. For a quiet minute, the only sounds were tiny noises of affection. Sweet kisses, hugging—and sobbing.

Dillon had grown a good inch. "Mom, we missed you so much."

"Please don't let them take us away again," cried Gracie. "Please!"

"Not to worry, darlings. It's all over." Tears streamed down my cheeks. "Nobody can ever take you away from me ever again." I kissed them repeatedly and ran my hands over their faces and necks. "Look at you both; you've grown! You're sixteen! Dillon, you're taller than me! Let me look at you. You're shaving?" His smile was boyishly affectionate.

Tears glistened on Gracie's pale, heart-shaped face. Her complexion had become very sallow. "I've missed you something awful, Mom. I didn't think we'd ever see you again."

"Oh, Gracie, we'll be together, always." I wiped my daughter's tears with my hands.

Gracie had latched onto my waist and wouldn't let go. "Can we see all the Darwoods again?"

"Of course, you can see them. Anytime you want. And they can come to our place, too. They're family." It seemed strange how they thought Gracie was so distant from human contact when she clearly loved the Darwoods. But she *was* tiny and so thin! The only fat on her body huddled in her cheeks. Someone had given her a perm. It was a bit frizzy, with short hairs falling about her face— Gracie looked like a large, raggedy doll. A new retainer sat in place of her braces.

Dillon rambled on. "Mom, I got my driver's license. Velda made me eat broccoli; it's okay if you put Velveeta on it. I'm starved. Do we have a place to go?"

"We do, and it's a wonderful place. A farm in the mountains. And I've made some new friends." With uncrushable exhilaration, we cried, hugged, kissed, and jumped from one subject to the next. The great albatross of our lives had fallen from our necks, and I was suddenly delirious with relief.

Guiding my children toward the door, I nodded to a small group gathered to witness our reunion. With my arms around the twins, we walked to the lobby, where a waiting Matthew stood beside their bags.

"Best of luck to you all," I heard Dr. Fitzgibbons say as the door closed.

Chapter 27

Vows To Last A Lifetime
January 1994

Andie

Unable to fall back to sleep, I woke before daybreak. Gazing into the bathroom mirror, I found it hard to ignore the nervous blue eyes staring back at me, asking, "Are you sure?" I blinked the sleepiness away, fastened back my hair, brushed my teeth, and then rinsed my face in cool water. Like the rest of me, my face had become mature yet soft. Even the pleated corners of my eyes.

I lifted my chin after applying lip gloss and running a few determined brush strokes through my hair. "Yes. I'm sure."

Turning from my reflection, I shivered. Humming under my breath to not disturb my sleeping family, I slipped into jeans, a sweatshirt, and house shoes. I smelled coffee and headed in its direction.

A chilly day dawned. Mist rose from the forest floor, creeping up tree trunks and along bleak, leafless limbs. Like an old woman's hair, tendrils of gray fog spiraled down the back of the mountain. Later, its peaks would compete for prominence in the colorless winter sky. I had become acquainted with Shiloh and its changing expressions.

Winter in the mountains was majestic and still; its frigid night air extended into the early morning. I felt the chill in the house still hanging on with all its might. Soon, the sun shining through the windows would warm the second floor. Before long, activity on the lower level would warm the downstairs.

Ivy's two pots of coffee every morning became the norm after the kids arrived. I approached the glass French doors leading to the back porch and decks and faced my dark, shadowy reflection. Gulping down my first mugful, I felt jittery and supposed I hadn't needed the caffeine.

The good news was, most of the time, my memories were no longer haunting. I had forced the worst ones into the back of my mind and tried every day to look straight ahead. On better days now, I had to check myself to prevent a hysterical tickle from escaping my throat. If I laughed, I might never stop. But I also knew I might never be whole again despite all we had accomplished. I sensed Matthew knew it, too.

That day, though, there was no terror. No nausea. No ghosts of the past waiting to devour my children and me. No more funerals. No more thinking about death. Not that day, and certainly not on my wedding day, scheduled for the following morning. There was still lots to do. Gracie needed shoes to match her dress, and I had to tell Dillon to pick up his tux at three.

The gurgle of a fresh pot drew my attention. *Ah, another cup.* I needed more coffee, after all. Sitting in the temporary quiet of the morning, wrapping my cold fingers around the bottomless mug, I thought of the past few months since the twins had come back into my life.

Initially, it had been a little rough; they kept Matthew at arm's length while immediately warming up to Ivy and Tobias. But Shiloh was like Disney World to Dillon and Gracie. They explored the farm and the mountain, enjoyed the animals, and found something new to do every day. Living on Matthew's estate was intense therapy, waking up to their mama's voice every morning. It had taken long talks to sort everything out.

The twins called Velda and Henry regularly, and Matthew had sent a limo to bring the Darwood family to Shiloh to spend a few long weekends. But what broke through to them was the love and attention Matthew showered on me. The interaction between Matthew and me was a new experience for my children.

At Christmas, Conner came to stay for a few weeks. The glitter and magic of the season lit every room. Ivy's helpers decorated the first floor with Christmas delights, candles in every window, and wreaths on every door. Ivy's blooming Christmas cactus sat on Matthew's desk. Boughs of pine and holly and Charles Dickens figurines lined the fireplace mantles while greeting cards framed the archways in the foyer. Giant trees lit up the windows in several rooms, and Ivy's unique hand-crocheted tablecloth covered the dining room table in holiday splendor. Red and green tableware added Christmas color to every meal.

Mark and Patsy's youth group sang carols at our front door, which helped introduce the twins to many local teens. Matthew's friends and colleagues sent endless gifts, some of which included trays of candies, cookies, and lush pink and red poinsettias; it was like walking into the glossy pages of *Southern Living magazine*. It was the home of my dreams.

The boys, fortunately, hit it off. Conner and Dillon loved action movies, and Matthew bought them enough videotape and pizzas to keep them occupied and fed for a week. A house full of noisy kids and holiday hoopla simply elated Matt and me. The perfect Christmas had arrived. Even Ivy and Tobias seemed younger with the children in the house.

We slept in heavenly peace. Finally.

Gracie, thank goodness, gained a little weight. And homeschooling was definitely the right prescription. Dillon met a girl in town, Diana, and talked about her non-stop. They would all be juniors together at their new high school. Other than a few tantrum outbreaks of not wanting to step foot in a church again, I felt things had gone smoothly. We didn't push when it came to church, but after meeting Matthew's mother, the twins agreed to attend Mark and Patsy's youth group once a month. It was a start.

When I finally sat them down and told them how Matthew and I met, which included my *vision* of his hands and his dream about my ring, the twins' last resistance toward their future stepfather broke. Both shed plenty of tears, but Gracie bolted into Matthew's arms. From that moment, I had my kids back for good. The past year's events had left minimal damage on them, but I knew well that total healing for all three of us would only happen over time.

My son stumbled in for coffee, wrapped in his blanket, his sleepy eyes half open. "Geez, mom, it's cold enough to freeze a fart!"

"Dillon!" Yep. I had them back.

❧

The next day began with more frigid temperatures, but a flurry of activity warmed the house quickly. Our plan called for a big breakfast, a private and simple morning ceremony, and a light lunch after the wedding with a few immediate relatives. We had scheduled the formal reception and buffet, with a much more extensive guest list, for six in the evening at The Grove Park Inn in Asheville.

Matthew fried potatoes while Conner turned bacon in the pan and hollered at me as I walked into the kitchen. "Andie, you're not supposed to see Dad until the ceremony!"

I hugged him from behind. "That's a little old-fashioned, Conner. We'd like to have breakfast together, especially since you're cooking! But you need an apron."

"No way! Get that faggy thing away from me."

"Conner!" Matthew shook his head. "Many skilled chefs are men. And because your Uncle John was gay does not mean he was less of a man. It's not a disease. Got it?"

"Sorry, Dad. But do I have to wear Ivy's apron?"

"I'm wearing one. Put it on." Matt winked at me, and I handed Conner the apron.

The smell of coffee and bacon brought Dillon and Gracie to the table. "Mom! You shouldn't see Matthew until the wedding!" Gracie squealed.

"Geez, what a bunch of old fogies we've raised!" I said.

Tobias walked in from the outside and pulled his chair to the table. "Let's eat!"

"I love this kind of heart-stopping breakfast," said Matthew.

Everyone talked at once. Ivy laughed at Gracie's jokes; Conner and Dillon discussed their girlfriends, the Super Bowl, and NASCAR, and in that order. Matthew and Tobias debated about how much firewood to cut for the week. With great satisfaction, the loves of my life ate bacon, sausage, grits, fried potatoes, eggs scrambled in cheese, biscuits smothered in apple butter, and drank lots of rich, hot coffee. The breakfast you fix when there's a house full of children, family, and love.

I recalled what Pastor Bobbie said on the first Sunday I attended her church. *God has given back seven times over what the Devil stole from me.* I sat in stunned silence. It appeared He had done the same for me. So, I prayed silently, thanking Him as I watched my miracle at that table. *Her children rise and call her blessed; her husband also praises her.* Maybe that Proverbs woman wasn't so crazy after all.

MATTHEW

There would be no honeymoon. Andie agreed. We'd been *honeymooning* for a while, anyway. I planned to take her on a trip after the kids returned to school in September, when everyone was stable and secure at Shiloh. I'd cut back my work with Social Services. I had a family now, and they needed me at home. Admittedly, it felt good to be needed at home again. We envisioned traveling more later, but not until Andie was ready.

The truth was, I was concerned. Although she refused to admit it, she had her down days. I suggested therapy, but she resisted. Andie had significant trust issues with anyone she didn't know, her own form of Attachment Disorder. She had told me she believed in God but wasn't sure God could be everywhere all the time, if that made any sense.

It was all Andie could do to endure some days, but she hid it well. Even with her children finally back in her arms, I knew she still suffered silently. I'd seen her staring at an old picture of herself and Mavis. She had told me about Mavis, and I'd seen the scar on her palm. And her mother wasn't speaking to her. Neither of us understood why. Andie's past loomed too dark and too overwhelming. I often reminded myself that Andie's pain had been far greater than mine.

Sadly, Calvin Artury's absence did not eliminate his threats. She had locked them in the dungeon of her mind. Over the weeks, I did my best to put salve on her wounds, but all I had were Band-Aids. I needed answers, and so I started a search of my own. A search for the faintest ring of truth. Who was Calvin Artury? I had my suspicions and wondered if it were something Andie could handle. Yet I knew she needed all the facts to heal completely.

ANDIE

I sat in the room Ivy assigned to me, feeling the heat of the morning sun through the windows. A time when new life began. Life as Mrs. Matthew Callahan. I debated about changing my name, but I no longer wished to be known as an Oliver. *Andie Rose Callahan is a good, strong name.*

My suit lay on the bed, pressed and ready. Shoes, hose, jewelry, a rose; my wedding ensemble waited for me to shed my housecoat. I relaxed in the chair, dismissing the memories of my first wedding day so many years before.

Gracie pulled her long, burgundy velvet dress over her head. "Mom, did you ever think you weren't as pretty as Grandma Dixie?"

"Why do you ask me that?" I stood to zip up my daughter's dress.

"Because I've always wanted to be as pretty as you."

"Oh, Gracie Mae, you are the most beautiful girl. Not only are you far prettier than me, but you're also way smarter. You've just turned seventeen. You'll be applying to colleges soon. When I was your age, I only dreamed about marrying your daddy. I no more thought about college than I thought about the shape of Albania. Live your life for yourself, Gracie. Make your own way. Then fall in love."

"I'm happy for you, Mom. But you still haven't answered my question."

"You mean about Grandma?"

She nodded.

"It's true, your Grandma Dixie was beautiful. With my mother, I was always lacking something that would have made me nicer, prettier, thinner, and more popular by her standards. I suppose I never thought she loved me as much as I loved her."

"I know you love me, Mom."

"Well, good, because I'm late for my wedding, and I need you to tell the boys they'll have to wait a few more minutes."

"Oooh, I can hear them now. Women!"

❦

Conner and Dillon, in black tie, attempted to straighten Matthew's white one. When I walked down the staircase, Matthew's eyes glazed with tears. To the compliments of my family waiting at the bottom, I wore a white wool suit with mother-of-pearl buttons and velvet cuffs. Carrying a red rose and a picture of Daddy, I wanted him with me on my wedding day, even if I had to imagine it.

"You're beautiful." Matthew wiped at his tears as I searched for a Kleenex.

"Don't cry, you two," Gracie said. "I'll be a mess before tonight."

"Okay, Andie. How about marrying me this morning?"

All I could do was nod, wipe away tears, and hope to not smear my mascara.

Tobias drove the limousine to the church in Valle Crucis, where Pastor Bobbie stood in her white robe to perform the ceremony on that frigid January day. A small group of friends and immediate family had gathered to witness the union of two souls. The ladies in the congregation had decorated the church simply. White candles in glass sconces lined the painted ivory walls, casting a golden glow on the altar and on every face. They had trimmed the pews with springs of pine branches tied together with gauzy ribbons. There were no flowers, only the rose that I carried. Ivy placed a candle on the organ to represent the souls we missed: Matthew's daughter, Jessie. His brother, John. Both of our fathers and, of course, Mavis. No one sang; nothing was read. It didn't seem necessary.

Luke played his guitar as Matthew and I walked in together. Caroline and her new husband, Herman, and my four nieces and two little nephews huddled at the back in case they needed a quick exit. And there sat Coot and Candace; seeing them next to Lula and Clete was so wonderful. I blew Lula a kiss, which she returned with her beautiful smile.

Of course, Royster Bently and his wife attended. I felt he deserved a seat of honor because he had believed me. The Darwoods sat in the second pew behind Aunt Wylene, whose favorite color had changed to bright orange. She looked like an early Easter egg. But my mother wasn't there. Aunt Wy explained she had come down with a terrible cold. Another excuse, I knew. And once again, I put her out of my mind. Dixie still wasn't speaking to me. I refused to allow her to ruin the day.

Matthew's family and close friends sat in the adjacent section while Dillon, Gracie, and Conner stood beside us at the altar to take part in the ceremony. Our vows were short, sweet vows—vows to last a lifetime. Nothing fancy, nothing to record in a book of poetry. But they rang of truth and of a deep abiding love. There wasn't a dry eye in the sanctuary when I slipped a wedding band over the stub of Matthew's ring finger.

Soon, the steeple bell rang loud and long as Mr. and Mrs. Callahan dashed to the waiting limousine, our children following close behind in the wintery morning air. It was a grand day, despite Dixie and her continual need to get under my skin.

Chapter 28

END OF THE LINE
March 1994

MATTHEW

After the wedding, a reporter managed to snap a picture of Andie and me, together with Dillon and Gracie. An image that appeared on the front page of the Winston-Salem Journal. A newspaper that landed on the table of the Forsyth County Jail lunchroom. A table where Joe Oliver sat eating his ham sandwich. I was told the newspaper slid into his lap like a bomb, exploding his insides into soup as he stared at the picture. He spent the next three days in the infirmary with the newspaper fisted in his hands.

Andie and I agreed that her life was a fascinating study of the mysteries of God. We talked long into the night that Calvin succumbed to the same end he had plotted and planned for her. It all stood out in our minds as a miracle.

Thousands of House of Praise members who had exalted themselves were now scattered to the four winds, nursing wounds and trying to make sense of their beliefs. For Andie, a new life had begun—with me. And so, it was a shock on a particular March morning, nineteen years to the day Andie buried her baby boy, that I received a phone call from the prosecutor's office.

Besides charges of murder, the District Attorney accused Evan Preston and Tony DeSanto of drug running, organized prostitution, and pornographic film pirating with cash filtered through the church. Pastor DeSanto, they'd discovered, had worked for a New York crime family for the better part of thirty years. Joe, wanting to soak up some of the leftover money and prestige, had worked for DeSanto and Preston in a starving-man-near-a-buffet kind of way. The prosecutor needed to know what Joe knew of their operation for the upcoming trial.

Joe agreed to a plea bargain. The trial was due to start in a week, but suddenly, Joe refused to testify against DeSanto's Southern Mafia with Preston at the helm. He was no longer cooperative. Unless he could speak to Andie.

I was livid.

The prosecutor told me that Joe would trade the death sentence for life in prison and tell everything if they allowed him ten minutes with his ex-wife.

I consulted my attorneys, as well as my doctor, about the repercussions of such a meeting for Andie. I was still working on closing her wounds, and I sure as heck didn't want all we had accomplished to come crashing down because her maniac ex-husband demanded to see her.

We had become busy with daily living, running the house and farm, and handling business. Andie had absorbed a great deal of office work to lighten Ivy's load, as she and Tobias had taken on tutoring the twins. Although this unwelcome news disrupted our lives and our well-deserved peace, we all agreed to keep it from the children.

After days of discussion, Andie decided if seeing Joe would put Preston and DeSanto away forever, she would see Joe. As long as I was with her, she would hear what he had to say, put it behind us as quickly as possible, and once again, we would go on with our lives.

ANDIE

I was told Joe was in his sixth month of psychiatric evaluation and counseling. They said he had been *deprogrammed*, and that he was *remorseful*. I was about to find out.

The windowless room, painted thundercloud gray, fell quiet as a guard led Joe in like a dog on a leash and told him to sit. A chain between both ankles caused him to take small, childlike steps. I felt no fear or hate, yet neither of us knew how to start.

I tried a noncommittal nod.

Decked out in prison-issue orange, Joe simply stared at me. I folded my hands and placed them on the metal table. He might have done likewise had they not cuffed his hands to his waist.

I had no intention of ever seeing him again. But Joe, an accused murderer, had made a bargain. In exchange for information, he had demanded a private meeting with me, not Selma, his wife, but me. I had told Matthew that nobody should allow a killer to make deals or bargains.

The guard who led him in said, "You got ten minutes, Oliver."

I broke the silence. "You asked to see me?"

"Yes."

I nodded again and waited for him to say more. He didn't. "What do you want?"

Joe maintained his stare. "Do you know why I'm in here?"

"Of course, I know. You raped and killed Mavis Dumass and also murdered Chip Atkinson, and I hear they also got you for the rape of a minor."

I glanced around the room. The prosecuting attorney, seated on a nearby chair, flipped through his files; a prison guard with stovepipe arms and a chest like a gun cabinet stood behind Joe, and a ferret-looking man reeking of garlic, Joe's lawyer, sat in a corner. Matthew leaned against the wall behind me in Joe's line of sight.

But Joe only stared into my eyes. "I didn't know she was seventeen, and it was consensual sex," he whispered, as if nobody heard him except me.

"Do you realize that's your daughter's age!?" I shook my head and turned to the prosecuting attorney. "Do I honestly have to listen to this? I'm leaving—"

"—Please, Andie Rose. Stay. Please don't go—"

"—Don't you dare! Don't you dare call me that! Tell me what you need to say so I can get out of here!"

Joe babbled. "I followed him because I loved him. I loved him more than anyone in the world. I did as I was told. I believed he was who he said, a Son of God." He paused. "I gave my life to God, so it seemed to me I should be willing to *take* a life for God." His southern accent had returned.

"I know that," I said. "And you disgust me."

"I disgust myself." He sighed. "The warden here told me that out of suffering have emerged the strongest souls, and the most massive characters are seared with scars. I disagree. Reverend mentally beat us down to where there was no hope of recovery— we became as warped as him. Most of us became twisted inside, disfigured—no longer recognizable as what we once were." A faint tremor emanated from his voice, as though some emotion had touched him.

I had no sympathy. *Why am I here?* My week had started off happily working with Ivy, planning and preparing for Matthew's birthday party. But there I sat at a bolted-down table across from my ex-husband, who had raped and murdered all I held dear. I didn't care about his scars. Or his suffering. "Why did you ask for me? What do you really want?"

Joe looked like an aging, shrunken playboy with combed but unwashed gray hair. His teeth had turned cigarette-yellow, his skin leathery from years of playing by hotel swimming pools and too many long nights in windowless coliseums and dark hotel rooms.

His reward for Calvin-mandated Bible fasting was skin hanging off his body like an eighty-year-old man and internal organs that had begun to give out. Upon arriving at the jail, I'd been told the other inmates had severely beaten him. Twice. And that he'd been passing blood through his urine ever since.

"I'm going to die in here."

"I hope so," I said, then sighed. "I'm sure Selma wants to see you."

"This has nothing to do with her."

"And it does with me? She's your wife, Joe. You need to talk to *her*, not me."

Joe leaned forward. "I have to tell you something."

"Why should I care what you have to say?" I was long done with his tortuous maneuvering, his quest for an edge, his twenty-year search for a way out of marriage, and his overblown sense of importance. I had moved on.

Matthew, perhaps sensing my thoughts, had moved along the cement block where I watched him shoot Joe a warning glare.

"You think you detest me, Andie? You can't possibly hate me as much as I hate myself."

"You're damn lucky they're letting you live," I responded, giving him my best I-don't-give-a-shit stare. "Unless you refuse to cooperate."

"I know what I have to do. There's a lot to be told. But I want to see my kids. Don't I have a right to see my kids?"

At that, Matthew peeled himself off the wall. "You gave up that right years ago. You're not only a failure as a father; you're a disgrace to the cause of Christ."

Joe kept his eyes on me, not giving any sign he had heard Matthew.

Rage from the audacity of Joe's statement made me tremble to keep from laughing hysterically. He was the last person in the world I wanted around my children. To discuss visitation rights after what he had done made the bile in my stomach churn and rise into my throat, and I fought off the desire to leap across the table and scratch his eyes out.

But he kept his stare constant. I didn't like what I saw. Though his eyes were lifeless, as one would expect, I saw something else. Something beyond the vacancy. A hint of shame. A pleading. There was regret there, maybe. It surfaced quickly, which surprised me.

I looked up at Matthew and nodded. He frowned, but he knew Joe wanted to be alone with me, and I would give him that moment.

Matthew signaled to the guard and the attorneys. "I will stay here for her protection. Everyone else can wait outside."

Rising from his seat, Joe's lawyer spoke for the first time. "Anything my client says is off the record."

The lawyers picked up their briefcases and files and followed the guard out the door. Mathew sat in the corner, graciously allowing Joe to finish what he wanted to say.

I knew the guard and attorneys were behind the one-way glass. They'd all be watching.

I shrugged. "Well?"

"Mavis told me something before she died."

I put my hands up to my mouth and blinked hard. Tears formed as I held my breath.

"She barely spoke. 'Tell Andie,' she said, 'take care of my little girl.' It's been a lot of years. I'm sure she's no child now, but Mavis said her name. I never forgot it. Believe me, I tried to forget it. At first, I didn't believe her, but I've been told folks don't lie on their deathbed. Mavis said, 'Her name is Suri. Fourteenth Street, Greenwich Village.' Mavis—" Joe hesitated and took a deep breath. "—She said, 'It's Artury's child.'"

The scattered debris of Mavis's past reached across time to that moment, piercing my heart. "Why did she tell *you*, the monster about to take her life?"

"I don't know. I suppose it was her last chance to tell anybody. I kept it a secret, even from Reverend. I didn't want him to know he had a bastard child. A nigra child. It would have ruined him. I had to protect him."

Joe brought his handcuffed hands up to his down-turned face. The chains rattled as he wiped a tear from his eye. "It didn't matter in the end."

Joe was not lying. I was as sure of it as I knew my name. He had gripped my heart with his icy hand, but he was telling the truth. I shriveled in my chair, unable to absorb further shock. Matthew stood and walked up behind me, resting his hands on my shoulders for support.

I pulled a Kleenex out of my pocket. "Is that it? Is there more?"

Joe shook his head.

I remembered the first two years after marrying Joe, Mavis never left New York, not even when her mother passed; she never left that city. Everyone thought Mavis was busy working on her career. But she'd also had a baby. Her one time with Calvin as a seventeen-year-old girl landed her pregnant and in the middle of New York City.

"Why?" I held more tears in check, not wanting him to see me cry.

"I told you, I did what I was told. I was just a hitman."

"I know that." I looked up. "Why are you telling me this now?"

Joe turned his head and studied his reflection in the mirror. Looking into my eyes again, his voice grew quiet and desperate. "Hopefully, you'll help me see Dillon and Gracie. They're my only hope for sanity in here. I've no right, none, to say I'm sorry. I've said it countless times and never meant it. These months in here have cleared my head. I threw my life away to chase after a man I thought could give me a life better than the one I had with you. The best I can hope for is some kind of relationship with my kids."

Joe pleaded. "Andie, please, help me. Please. I want to see them. I need them," he said.

"Wow," I shook my head. "You *need* them. Through the years, did you ever stop to think they needed *you?* That they needed, oh, I don't know, something like love, affection, attention, a kind word? Now, you want *me* to help you have a relationship with our children? After you never wanted them in the first place, ignored them their entire lives, and then ripped them away from the only parent who truly loved them!? Sure, Joe, and we'll be one big, happy family at last." I glared at him. "I wouldn't help you dig your way out of Hell."

"Please." The anguish etched across his face changed to a guise of self-repulsion. He began to slam his forehead repeatedly on the metal table in front of him. In a flash, Matthew yanked Joe's chair away from the table while the guard flew into the room, grabbing Joe's greasy hair and holding his head at attention.

I remained seated, undaunted by his sideshow. I looked at the guard. "I'm fine. Please, let him go." The guard backed away, and Joe's chin fell to his chest.

The prosecuting attorney gave Joe a two-minute warning. "Wrap this up, Oliver."

I rubbed the scar on my palm. How do I forgive him for what he did to Mavis? Joe's head bled from his table tantrum, dripping over his eye and down his cheek. Other than anger, I didn't have a spark of feeling for him. And yet, I knew I had to forgive him to move on and have the life I wanted. I had to let the anger go.

"Joe," I said softly.

He lifted his head and stared at me again.

"Dillon and Gracie have grown up. When they were babies, they cried for you as you walked out the door every Friday. Asked me all the time where you were. They know what you've done, why you're in here. But what you've done to their mother has hurt them the most. You'll be damn lucky if you *ever* see them again. Still, they know where they can find you. I promise I won't stop them if they want to see you. As for me, take a real long look; it's the last time you'll ever see my face." I stood to leave.

"But thanks for telling me about Mavis. You've redeemed a tiny piece of yourself in some small remote corner of the universe. Maybe after twenty years of rotting in some hellhole prison, you'll have made a bit of progress toward redemption. It's up to God in the end. Will I forgive you? I suppose I'll find that out then."

Matthew put his arm around me, and we headed for the door.

"Andie!" Joe called out, panting, his voice a mixture of torment and tears. "I—I did love you once."

It galled me he still wanted the last word.

My back to him, I forced myself to laugh and walked out of the room. But after crossing the threshold, I stopped and turned to look into his eyes one last time. Holding the door open, I spoke each parting word slowly and for all to hear. "Frankly, my dear Joseph, I don't give a damn."

Joe shot up from his seat. His ankles and hands shackled, he fell to his knees, and that's when the last door finally slammed shut between us.

Chapter 29

Farther Along

April 1994

Andie

Spring had come to the mountains. Ivy's jonquils popped out of the ground along with hyacinths and tulips. The trees leaned to the east, their leaves and branches spread out in supplication toward the morning sun. Tobias set the sprinklers to pirouetting on the lawn. The soothing landscape of Shiloh had become home.

Ivy fried chicken for an after-church picnic on the grounds. Matthew had booked Luke's new gospel bluegrass band as lunchtime entertainment. It was time for church.

When Matthew and I walked into the back of the sanctuary, greeters shook our hands, spoke pleasantries, and chatted about the fine weather. Ivy and Tobias strolled the middle aisle and laughed with the members. A few deacons and elders sat like proud peacocks with their flock of grandchildren in the pews behind them.

Here, there were no rigid rules, no flashy church decorations, no ushers keeping a watchful eye for misbehaving teenagers. People came as they were, sliding across the pews to make room for friends and family. The sound of babies' cries mingled with the chatter of expectant mothers, who occasionally popped up from their seats to tend to their children's needs. In this place, nobody looked twice. It had become a safe haven of comfort and familiarity.

I sat in my family's favorite pew and smiled through my mother-in-law's sermon, which lasted only forty-five minutes. Gracie, Dillon, and Conner huddled with friends in the corners of the sanctuary. A giggle escaped my lips periodically throughout the service.

I'm happy. Really, really happy.

We sang a song that brought Dixie to mind. *Farther along, we'll know all about it; farther along, we'll understand why; cheer up my brother, live in the sunshine, we'll understand it, all by and by.* I sang it to Rupert in his tobacco field the day I told him his daughter had died. Dixie sang it to me when I was a bitty girl. I thought of my mother a lot. And wondered.

"Don't forget about water baptism next Sunday," said Pastor Bobbie. "Pray the river is a little warmer this year. In the meantime, let's all head outside. The ladies have prepared a delicious lunch, and we got ourselves a band on the lawn."

I had made it through. Just.

◦◦

"It's a church picnic, not a hanging." Matthew made me laugh, and I waited while he tugged his yellow tie loose before shaking a deacon's hand. The large double doors at the back stood open. God had turned on the sun to preheat the mountain. Steam rose from cars in the parking lot, and freshly mowed fields next to the church smelled sweet and rich. A nearby thicket of dogwoods swung gently in the last puffs of wind from an early morning storm. Everyone appeared happy and content as they rounded the corner and walked toward the fellowship hall.

I busied myself, helping Ivy place chicken platters on two rows of picnic tables covered in long white tablecloths. At least until

Matthew walked up and slipped his arms around me. "Anybody tell you how beautiful you are?"

"Matthew! People are staring!"

"Let them," he said as he nibbled my earlobe. "I love you and plan to tell you every day for the rest of our lives." His words deserved a kiss, and he got one.

"Now leave me be; I'm helping out this morning." I smiled at my husband as he walked away, allowing me to get on with the business of serving chicken and upright vases of wildflowers blown over by the wind.

A blanket of quiet fell as Pastor Bobbie requested the families gather around the Lord's table. Pleased with the day and their place in the world, my new family joined hands and looked up toward the mountains. Their benediction was a simple one. That Sunday, it was Matthew's to say. *"I will lift up mine eyes unto the hills, from whence cometh my help."*

The congregation responded together. *"My help cometh from the Lord, which made Heaven and earth."*

Matthew concluded the prayer. *"He will not suffer thy foot to be moved; He that keepeth thee will not slumber."*

Everyone replied. *"Amen."*

"Amen," I responded alone.

Later that afternoon, as I poured tea at the table, I glimpsed Dillon and Diana holding hands, sharing a plate of food on a blanket under a tree. Gracie flirted with a group of young men competing for her attention.

"Just like her mama: a beauty queen," Matthew said.

"That was Dixie, not me."

"She's you, Andie. She's you," he said as he walked off to join a group of men discussing the crop season and basketball scores.

I wandered among the tables; the air filled with the laughter of children. They swarmed around me, playing a lively game of tag. The boys' white shirttails hung out, already grass-stained, their jackets stashed somewhere. The girls' bows had come utterly undone, their hair falling out of a once tidy braid or ponytail. A three-year-old boy tugged on my skirt, his eyes sparkling with mischief. I hugged him close, remembering the sweet innocence of my children at that age, and then released him to play with his siblings.

As I meandered past the ladies, a blanket on the ground caught my eye. I couldn't resist its invitation. Lounging and lifting my face to the warm sun, I felt a warm softness hanging in the air. It was a magical spring afternoon meant for unwinding. My eyes closed, and I tried to soak in the moment, to find contentment and peace. But a dark presentiment had crept into my daily thoughts, waking me even at night. Restlessness clung to me, questions about Mavis's daughter, about Calvin's life and death. I opened my eyes, forcing a smile. It was over; I had to believe it.

❧

The late-day air grew cool. I folded the blanket, threw jackets to my kids, and helped my husband load the car.

"I've got a surprise for you," Matthew said as we drove home.

I yawned. "What is it?"

"I can't give it to you until Saturday. I just want you to know it's coming."

"Oh, that's nice. I'm ready for a surprise, but now I must wait a week?"

"The kids are off to the Darwoods' house on Saturday. Ivy and Tobias are taking Mother shopping and to supper in Asheville. We'll be home alone."

"You're not getting kinky on me, are you?"

Matthew laughed. "Not unless you want me to, sweetheart. It's a pleasant surprise. I'm having it delivered on Saturday."

"And what do I do until then?"

"You wait. You wait and see."

Chapter 30

THE KNOWLEDGE OF GOOD AND EVIL
May 1994

ANDIE

The first Saturday in May, settled across a sunlit countryside. I stood at Matthew's office window, watching yellow finches at the feeder. Against a brilliant orange sky stretching across the pasture from the west, a car barreled up the gravel road past Ivy's house and the meadow. Dust kicked up behind the tires, making it difficult to see through the sun's rays.

Matthew walked behind me, slipped his arms around my waist, and whispered, "She wants to see you. Go out and talk to her."

My knees grew weak. I gave Matthew a quick glance. He winked, picked up his newspaper, tucked it under his arm, and headed to the front door with his mug of fresh decaf.

My surprise.

Wiping sweaty hands on my jeans, I slid into my flip-flops and walked out on the porch. The sun's glare blinded me until I descended the steps and walked past the fountain to the end of the brick path, where the driveway stopped and trees filtered the evening sun. The car parked, and a familiar bubble blonde hairdo peeked above the steering wheel. "As I live and breathe." My heart leaped in my chest. "Dixie."

My mother stepped out of her car and sauntered toward me, holding something in her hands.

"Andie Rose." She nodded. "I brought you a present."

Daddy's banjo. As she handed it to me, I absorbed her immediately. She was a little older; a few more lines showed around her mouth and forehead, but she was as pretty as ever. Slim for her age, my mother had held together well. "Thank you. I haven't seen this in a long time."

"It's yours, now. He'd want you to have it," she said, laying it in my hands. Peering down at Daddy's banjo, I knew he had loved it with his whole heart. It was an immortal piece of him.

When I looked up, Dixie had already walked ahead, making a beeline toward the house. "This is quite the place. I almost got lost trying to find it." Her eyes widened as she stepped through the front door. I suspected Dixie was still as pickled in pride as she ever was. Expecting a comment from the green-eyed monster within her, I waited. But she smiled and said, "What a magnificent home, Andie. I'm happy for you. Maybe you can take me on a tour later?"

"Sure."

"I met Matthew last week."

"So I gather." I carefully laid the banjo on a side table, caressing the warmth of it before ushering Dixie into the study.

Matthew gave my mother a quick hug. "How are you, Dixie? Want a cup of coffee, a cold cola? Or a glass of wine—"

"—A glass of wine sounds great. Whatever you have. That'd be nice. Thanks."

Dixie seemed nervous, rubbing her arms, stepping to a window that overlooked Callahan farmland, and then eyeing every nook, corner, and wall filled with Matthew's things and a few new things I had purchased. "I think about the twins every day," she said. "I want you to know I couldn't find them, and I hadn't a clue where *you* had gone. Nobody told us Dillon and Gracie were with the Darwoods. Even Wy, with all her connections, couldn't get a thing out of anybody. How are they?" she asked, both of us wanting to embrace, neither knowing what kept us from it.

"They're fine. You remember the court took them from me. The twins are with me now, all grown up, nearly. They'll be excited to see you."

Dixie sat at the table as Matthew served us a glass of Cabernet. I spent the next few minutes giving my mother a quick report of the past year of my life. She grabbed my hand, and her eyes watered. Her first tear fell on her hand. Another dropped to her dress. The others left wet splotches the size of nickels on her cotton sweater. I handed her a tissue and laid my hand on her trembling knee to comfort her.

"I'm sorry," she said, wiping her eyes, "so terribly sorry." Dixie's face appeared pale and pinched. "Matthew came to Charleston to talk to me."

I looked at Matthew, who only raised his eyebrows. My voice cracked. "Are you mad at me, Dixie?"

"Of course not. I've missed you, Andie." My mother sobbed.

I rushed to her side, pulling her into my arms.

"I've been avoiding you," she said. "Avoiding the truth about my life and things you need to know. Things your daddy never wanted you to know. But we can't hold back the truth any more than we can hold back God's love. Matthew, he wanted me to tell you."

"Tell me what, Dixie?"

"It's a long story. Do you remember how I refused to talk about my past? My life as a young girl."

I nodded.

Matthew motioned for us to follow him. "Let's get comfortable. Bring your wine."

"Oh, Matthew," Dixie said as he assisted her to the sofa, "you tell her. You go first."

"What are you two talking about?" I asked.

Matthew sat next to Dixie, and I soon understood my husband possessed the resources to discover anything he needed to know. "Sweetheart," he said, looking at me. "I had to discover more about Calvin Artury than what we saw. Unbeknownst to you, I laid awake many nights, my mind racing. During the day, those thoughts weighed me down with questions about him. Who was he? Where did he come from? We knew very little about his past. After the murder of my brother and what happened to you as a result, I became obsessed to know what made him tick."

"Why didn't you tell me? Maybe I could've helped you."

"You were dealing with enough. I think it was the psychological part of me demanding answers. Not a soul has successfully investigated him. He hid his secrets well. When I told you I was in South Carolina on business a couple of weeks ago, I had driven to Charleston and then to the Goose Creek area where Artury is actually from to discover the truth about his childhood."

"Do I have to hear this?"

"I think you do."

I sighed, then looked at my mother. The pain of this truth was somehow connected to her and showed clearly on her face. "Okay, let's have it. He always said he had loving parents. I never understood how he developed into the monster he became."

Matthew's voice, low and smooth, made it clear he had prepared for this revelation. "He had loving parents, but they passed away when he was nine, not nineteen, like he told everyone. His parents died in a house fire. Suddenly, everything that was right in little Calvin's world turned wrong."

My eyes opened wide, and I stared at him inquisitively.

"It's true," said Dixie.

I sat there wondering how my mother knew that as Matthew continued. "Back then, technology didn't exist to determine how that fire started. Some old folks in town, I found out, knew the story. In particular, Artury's second cousin. I tracked him down, and we met where the house once stood. Young Calvin, an only child, was at school. A fight broke out between Calvin's grandfather, who was running moonshine, and Calvin's holy-roller mama, who wanted it to stop. Andie, are you okay?" Matthew's eyes, brimmed in tenderness, moved me to tears. His concern for me was apparent.

"Yes, please go on."

"Anyway, Calvin's grandfather threw a mason jar full of his special brew at his daughter-in-law, Calvin's mother, as she stood beside a wood-burning cook stove. It caught both the stove and her on fire. Calvin's daddy tried to save her but caught fire himself. The clapboard house went up in no time flat. Strange enough, the grandfather escaped and lived a while to become the town drunk, shooting off his mouth, telling folks how he'd killed his son and daughter-in-law. And, according to legend, the old man bragged he'd also shot his wife, Calvin's grandmother, evidently years before in front of his children. Sometime later, they found him with a bullet in his head laid out by his smokehouse. And it gets worse from here."

"Worse?" I rubbed my temples.

Matthew stood and retrieved a file from his desk. "Calvin went from being raised by loving parents to living with his father's sisters. Two spinster aunts. In my quest for the truth, I learned a lot from a little widow, a Mrs. Brenner, who lived across the street from the old aunts. I believe her story. She had no reason to fabricate it. She told me she had turned ninety the past week, and no one had ever bothered to ask her what she knew until I arrived at her door on a hunch. I was the first."

"My God, Matthew. What happened?"

"This dear lady remembered Calvin as a little boy. She was his teacher in elementary school. His life became threadbare and cramped overnight when dispensed into his aunts' care. He learned to survive by pretending, making things up, and lying constantly to anyone about everything. In school, they caught him in one lie after another. He once told her he believed having children was a great waste of time."

"Well. It's no wonder," Dixie said.

Matthew looked at my mother. "I think you know, Dixie, that both aunts sexually abused him. Repeatedly."

I gave my husband a strange look. "How would my mother know that?"

Dixie took over the conversation, her voice cracking and strained. "I'll tell you how I know in a minute. But Matthew is right. They molested him until he was fifteen years old. Then Calvin got deathly sick. He almost died. But he told me he watched Oral Roberts on TV and got healed."

"He told you? Dixie, I repeat, how do you know this? When did he tell you—why—"

"—Let her finish, Andie." Matthew put his finger up to his lips and smiled.

My mother's shaky voice further surprised me. "A year later, when young Calvin turned sixteen and was well physically, but certainly not mentally, he ran away from his aunts' home. He worked in honky-tonks, tended bar, and got blitzed about every night. Women loved him. He was truly a blonde bombshell and every bit as good-looking as Troy Donahue or Tab Hunter. He loved dancing and drank most customers under the table." Dixie coughed as if her words had choked her. As if hearing them out loud made her ill.

Matthew interjected. "He had an IQ of 180. I discovered Calvin graduated with perfect grades. You know, it takes a genius to pull off what he did. He fooled the world."

"Either that or a psychopathic madman," I added.

"True." My mother swallowed hard, then sipped more wine. "But after a year or two of sinful living, he headed for college. He hated women, mostly because of what his aunts had done to him. And then, remembering his mother's love of evangelism, he used his brain and some smooth talking to wheedle his way into Lee University, making new friends. He became charismatic and twisted."

"Dixie, how do you know all of this?"

"If you'll let me tell this story and stop asking questions, I'll tell you."

I shook my head. "Okay. Go on, then."

"I need to step in here. This part is important," Matthew said. "I sent an investigator to Cleveland, Tennessee. He found Calvin's old schoolmate, who told him Calvin believed kids were a necessary evil. That the state should raise them on farms like animals, and only after they're disciplined and educated should the government send them out into society to be productive and God-fearing. It makes me shudder to think what would've happened if Calvin had continued unchecked. He had a disturbed view of Christianity. His plan to rule a gullible Christian world may have worked had we not stopped him, Andie. The man honestly believed he picked up where *he thought* Jesus left off."

I blinked, stunned at my husband's words.

Matthew poured more Cabernet into my mother's wineglass. "Here's another shocker," he said. "There was a scandal at Lee University."

Dixie snickered. "Can you believe it? A scandal about Calvin Artury?"

Matthew smiled at my mother's sarcasm. "My investigator discovered the now sanctified young Calvin interpreted the Bible to suit himself, getting caught with his pants down around his knees. A freshman at Lee professed his homosexuality to the wrong person. Namely, Calvin."

Matthew grew quiet momentarily; I think to let it all sink into my head.

"In any case, after the administration caught them, Cal talked his way out of it. He said he experimented with homosexuality so he could preach against it someday. That, really, what they did wasn't sin. They only *rubbed against each other's nakedness*. That it was an *indiscretion* on his part. Can you imagine the bull he laid on the administration at Lee? You know me, Andie, I don't care which side of the bed a man sleeps on, just be honest about it. But it was the '50s, and the student body ridiculed him and nearly drove him insane before he graduated, which only added to his madness. So now, Dixie. Why don't you tell her the rest?"

A tinge of dread rippled down my spine, watching my mother set her wineglass on the table and scoot to the sofa's edge.

"By now, Calvin is in his mid-twenties and goes to Parkers Ferry, which isn't far from Charleston. He's preaching in this tiny church to about fifty members who know nothing about his past *indiscretions*. One day, he eats at the local diner, and a teenage girl comes in, begging for food. Looked like a runaway. Calvin sets out to save her soul. Before it was all said and done, he'd not only saved her soul, but he'd also bought her supper. The girl followed him around for weeks like a poor lost puppy. Initially kind to the girl, he soon became irritated with her. She was a kid and got on his nerves. He tried getting rid of her, but failed. She wouldn't leave him alone because—she's pregnant with his child. The girl finally figures out he isn't about to fall in love with her because he held a knife to her throat and threatened to kill her like he did his aunts if she told anyone who the father was. Frightened for her life, she runs away again. This time, from Calvin. She hits the streets, but by now, she's eight months along. With you, Andie."

I stood and dropped my wine on the hardwood floor. Shattered glass and red Cabernet flew everywhere. I bolted to the mirror on the wall. That's when I saw him in my eyes. The same brilliant blue eyes. "Oh, my God!"

I'd been blind to the resemblance. The thought of him linked to me in any way—I wasn't sure I could live with it. I reached up to tuck a piece of my hair behind my ear, and my hands shook.

It started to make sense why it was always so easy for me to get an appointment with him, why he kept trying to pull me back into the church instead of allowing Joe or his goons to murder me like they did Mavis. He had no knowledge of the child he impregnated Mavis with, but he definitely knew about me. I twirled around to glare at my mother, but only saw the torture she had endured in not wanting me to discover my lineage.

Dixie rose from the sofa, her words like a gusher—"Yes, Andie, you have his turquoise eyes. But that's all you got from him! At least you inherited my spirit and sense of goodness, a gene left out of Calvin's DNA!"

"My God in Heaven, Dixie! His blood runs through my veins! My children! It's like a terminal disease I can do nothing about! How could you? How could you keep this from me!?"

Matthew quickly pulled me into his arms as I thrashed about the room. I buried my face in his chest and bawled softly as he spoke to my mother. "She's known for some time, Dixie, that Bud wasn't her father. Aunt Wy told her years ago."

I pulled away. "I never cared to even question who my father was. It didn't matter to me. So why!? Why are you telling me now? Why are you trying to ruin my life?"

Matthew fought to keep me still. "Listen to me, Andie! Look at me! Your mother's not ruining your life. She *saved* your life. Calvin wanted her to abort you, but she refused. Bud found her roaming the streets, digging for scraps. He took her home and married her, even though she was eight months pregnant! God blessed you with a real father whose heart was big enough to cover it all. He loved you like his own. God saved your life to stop Calvin, don't you see that?"

Matthew's expression told me there was more. I fell back on the sofa with my husband still holding me close. "You need to know the rest," he said.

I nodded, fighting off waves of hiccups that shook my shoulders. Dixie sat with her hands around a wad of tissues and dabbed at her tears, feet crossed at her ankles as always. I suddenly realized this was as hard on her as it was on me. "Okay. Tell me the rest," I said.

Matthew let go of my arms and turned to face me. "Calvin was a killer, a murderer, long before he built the House of Praise. No one knew it. You were all fooled. Let me tell you more about those two elderly aunts who raised him. The neighbor lady I spoke to, Mrs. Brenner—said she went to check on the two old women like she usually did. Taking over something she baked that morning, she knocked on the door."

"After two days of nobody answering, she broke in. On one of the hottest summer days in fifty years, she found those old women hanging side by side from the upstairs banister like two sides of beef, swaying back and forth in the heat, covered with flies. He had shaved their heads, beat them, and then sliced them open like slaughtered hogs. Disemboweled right over their entryway. She said it smelled so bad she about swallowed her tongue and that she could still smell it occasionally."

Matthew paused while I leaned back and sighed heavily.

"Mrs. Brenner said she'd seen Calvin over there a week before she discovered their bodies, but never told the police because before they arrived, she did some quick snooping and found Polaroid snapshots in a kitchen drawer. Pictures they'd taken of Calvin as a little boy. Doing grotesque and horrible things to him. Mrs. Brenner said she hid the pictures from the police, took them home, and kept them. She kept the pictures because she didn't want the police to suspect Calvin; he might have returned and done the same to her—the one person who had seen him over there. In the end, the coroner ruled it a double homicide, but the police never caught the killer."

I wasn't sure I could stand anymore.

After a deep breath, Matthew continued. "She gave those pictures to me, relieved to be rid of them. They tortured him, Andie, in unbelievable ways. He killed his two crazy aunts. Not that they didn't deserve it. I believe those two old biddies transformed him into the devil he was. That's why you had to know everything. We want you to understand that not only were his problems self-inflicted, but his mental illness stemmed from what happened to him as a child. You have nothing to be concerned about in your genetics. We are all products of our environment. Calvin certainly was."

Dixie wiped at her eyes. "Matthew gave the pictures to me. I burned them."

My thoughts racing, I spit one of them out. The fierceness of my stare made my mother cry again. "Why, Dixie, did you go to his church in the first place? Why take me there when you knew he was my father!?"

My mother had trouble gathering her words, sipping her third glass of wine. "Your daddy didn't know. Not at first. He had received an invitation when the church was new. An invitation he kept in his Bible. When he insisted we go to a service, I couldn't bring myself to tell him the pastor at that church was your father."

"I remember the invitation," I said. "Mavis and I saw it when we were little. I still have it. It's still in his Bible in my bedroom."

"You kept your daddy's Bible?"

"Yes."

Dixie looked at me, perplexed. "Nevertheless, after Bud and I attended the House of Praise for a while, Calvin realized who I was, who *you* were. He approached me. Bud wanted to leave the church, leave town, in fact. But Calvin wasn't about to let you go.

Not after he saw you. Bud and Calvin went head-to-head in the church office one night after a service. The preacher had the upper hand. There was nothing Bud could do. Calvin threatened to destroy our home, our marriage, and Bud's position at work to hold you hostage and keep his secret. As it turned out, he permitted us to accompany you to church, knowing we would keep our mouths shut, and we did. But you know how your daddy was; he only attended a few services a year—hated the place. Eventually, he quit going. I went for you, Andie, and never missed a service at that damnable church until you were grown. I attended to keep Calvin from harming my family, only guessing what he was capable of, but I guessed right."

I suddenly realized countless others had sacrificed their lives to survive Calvin Artury's horrific manipulations. But the tremendous sacrifice my parents made to save me was a priceless gift. Suddenly, it explained my mother entirely.

"What Calvin never expected, though," said Dixie, "was your independent spirit. Your attitude toward him. Your determination to pull Joe out of his grasp. And now I hear Mavis had a little girl by him. That connects you to Mavis forever, Andie. Don't you see?"

My glare softened. In stunned silence, I didn't know how to respond. Would I answer her with love and forgiveness, or would I allow the anger and bitterness to continue, eventually destroying me in the end? I responded with the one thing I had never truly lost sight of. Hope.

"I've always been bound to Mavis. But I guess I have another sister now, don't I?"

Dixie nodded. "Yes, Andie. You do. Calvin's blood runs through more than your veins and your children's. There's another girl out there somewhere."

The thought of Mavis's daughter thrilled and saddened me. "We need to find her."

Matthew smiled. "We do. And we will."

"I feel a bit wobbly," Dixie said. "I should've stopped with two glasses of wine, Matthew." She stood and walked to the window again. "Do your children see Joe in prison?"

"No. Ray visits him. And, of course, Selma. It's best that way. Dillon and Gracie aren't ready to see him. Maybe not for a long time. Maybe never. They've lived through it with me. Ray and Libby see the twins during the holidays. That's about it. It's a whole new family for me, for us. Matthew and his son, Conner. Ivy and Tobias. I don't know how I made it without them. Well. I wouldn't have."

Matthew took my hands in his. "Now you know everything there is to know about Calvin Artury."

I watched as my mother stared out the window, quiet for a minute, dabbing at more tears. "It takes more than DNA to be a father," she said.

"I know that, Dixie. This is all a bit of a shock. It wasn't the pleasant surprise I was expecting." I raised my eyebrows at Matthew. But the note of determination in my following words was unmistakable. "This stays between the three of us. At least for now."

He nodded. "It's remained a secret for decades. I think Dixie would agree; this is your story to tell. No one else's."

My mother faced me. "Matthew is right. I never breathed a word of it. It's yours, Andie. To do with what you will."

"Thank you, Dixie."

"Andie. Don't you think it's time you call me Mama?"

I walked to the window, to my mother, my gaze drawn toward the old cemetery. "I'll call you Mama if you can somehow put it out of your head who my father was."

More tears filled her red-rimmed eyes. "I did that for years, darlin'. Your father was Bud. He always will be." She peered into the distance with me. "What a beautiful cemetery with its simple white crosses and stones. I can hear Maybelle Carter singing one of your daddy's favorite songs. He played it on that old banjo. Remember, Andie?"

Mama began to sing, and the accompanying emotion between us melted the crusted and hardened anger that had stuck to my heart like burnt pork roast on a stainless steel pot. *"Will the circle be unbroken, by and by, Lord, by and by? In a better home awaiting, in the sky, Lord, in the sky?"* She sang softly and then stopped. "What do you think, Andie Rose? Will that circle break?"

I opened my arms wide, and my mother walked into them. We clung to each other, woman-to-woman, bosom-to-bosom, and I smiled through tears. "No broken circles, Mama. Not if we can help it. Not if we can help it."

Chapter 31

Into the Future
October 2003

ANDIE

Matthew stopped at Starbucks. I loved Starbucks. The drive to Fripp Island was long but enjoyable, stopping our Range Rover at every antique store and winery from home to Beaufort, South Carolina.

"I told her we're on our way. Mama's turning seventy next year," I said as I switched off my cell phone.

Matthew smiled sweetly. "Yes, and you are turning—"

"—Don't say another word!"

Matthew's wrinkles had grown deeper. His hair, more salt than pepper, had receded from his forehead the past few years. He was heading toward the other side of fifty-five, but I shared his contentment. The best years are still to come, he told me. And that God keeps his promises.

I flipped the visor down to check my face in the mirror. "Do you think we can get her to come to the anniversary party?"

"If I have to fly down and get her myself, she and Wy will come."

In January, we would celebrate ten years of marriage. Our children had planned an intimate party with family and close friends. I told Gracie that Matthew and I would take an invitation to Dixie and Wylene instead of sending it in the mail. Mama and I had only seen each other for an occasional holiday throughout the years since the day she and Matthew filled me in on who I really was.

Matt and I had traveled extensively. I finally got to stick my feet in a few oceans around the world. Wylene and Mama had grown too tired to care for their large house in Charleston. They put the place up for sale and retired to a smaller home on the ocean. Fripp Island. A barrier island off the coast of South Carolina.

Paved in crushed pink granite that crunched pleasantly under the tires, their driveway wound narrowly up a slight hill to the house. I spied Mama, standing on the front stoop, waiting. Only God knew how long she'd been standing there. She waddled to the car, her frame a little shorter and wider. After years of living with Wylene, Mama had put pounds on her hips, arms, and behind. I thought I might say something to her about it, but then I decided if she was happy, the woman should eat what she wanted.

Mama didn't say *hello* or *glad you're here*. She said, "Wy's gone to the store. I told her to go yesterday, but no, she had to clean the damn house yesterday, the old bat. So today, she's got to *buy* a pie because y'all are coming to visit. My pies aren't good enough for her; she's got to *buy* a pie! Hey, Matthew, how are you, honey? You look a little tired. Why don't you come on in? I got a bed waiting for you both. How about a little nap before Wy gets back? She'll be there all day. Course, she didn't drive, you know. Can't see a thing, the old bat. Our neighbor man takes her to town, the store, and the hospital to visit friends. How's y'all's kids? Andie, you look too thin. Lord, girl, what'd you do to your hair?"

Matthew turned to me and mouthed, *Can we leave now?*

I broke into an open smile and took it all in stride. After all, I wasn't about to change her. I went about settling us into our room. Later, I found Mama mixing up pie dough in the kitchen. "Matthew's taking you up on your suggestion. He's taking a nap. Mama, how about you and me go for a walk on the beach?"

The Atlantic Ocean was as majestic to me as the mountains at Shiloh. Standing at the ocean's edge or on a mountain's summit always reminded me of God's faithfulness.

"When did Matthew sell his property on Fripp?" Mama asked.

"Oh, you remember me telling you about that, huh?"

She snorted. "I remember more than y'all think."

Mama's dementia had started the year before. It was disheartening to think of her forgetting so much. At least one more time, I would bring her to the mountains, back to Shiloh for the anniversary party, and to see her grandchildren before she forgot them.

Mama's clothes were Fripp Island casual—a sea-foam green, loose-fitting dress, and low-heeled sandals she had pulled off to carry across the sand. Her hair, a 1972 blonde bubble, curled in the front as always.

"I'm old, Andie," she said. She stopped and stood motionless in the sand. And then, for the first time, she reached for *me* and hugged *me* first. I let my mama's arms entirely envelop me. The closeness left me sad and perhaps even a little frightened.

"You're not old."

"I feel old. Wy retired, you know. Can't see anymore. The old bat is as blind as one. Oh, I think I told you that, didn't I?" She shrugged one shoulder. "Oh, well."

Mama took my arm, and we silently walked on, listening to the ocean's roar. Seagulls glided on the wind like tiny white kites while the salty smell of fish washed up with the waves. The sand felt like wet cement between my toes, and as I stepped over a starfish caught in seaweed tangled at the water's edge, I heard my mother giggle like a schoolgirl. I loved her laugh.

"Oh, my," she said. "Isn't this fun?"

Suddenly, her expression changed, and her eyes went blank, like an erased page in a notebook. We kept strolling, kicking up wet sand. "I can't drive anymore," she said, "so we don't get away much. They deliver our groceries. Unless Wy can sweet talk the neighbor into taking her to Beaufort to buy a pie. We watch the ocean a lot."

Surprised when she reached for my hand, I remained quiet, knowing she wanted to talk. "Did you hear Caroline moved again? She lives in Idaho, of all places. Herman is her third—no—fourth husband. But this one's a keeper, even if he *did* move her to Idaho. Who would live in Idaho?" Mama giggled again. "She's got six kids. They're good at giving her fits. Four girls, two boys, can you imagine? Comes around, goes around, eh Andie?"

"You gotta choose your battles, Daddy always said."

"He did?"

Dixie's life was what she had made it. Quiet. Living with her sister, walking the beach, hoping for visits from friends and children.

"What happened to you, Andie? Where did you go for the year after we left North Carolina? We couldn't find you. We were worried."

I had explained it to her years before. It had been disturbing enough to her then. After she told me Calvin was my biological father, I think she purposely put everything out of her mind. We never talked about any of it again.

"It's a long story, Mama. It's over and not worth telling now." Not to my mama, anyway. It was time for peace in our lives.

"How are the Olivers? Have you heard from any of them?"

"Maudy died a few years back, remember? I told you. They buried her next to Al in Lexington. Ray and Libby have a son, Micah, and they adopted a little girl and called her Mavis. She looks like a little Mavis. They're coming to the anniversary party. You'll get to see them."

"Where's Joe? Did he ever remarry?"

My mother had deteriorated a little more since I last saw her. "Yes, Mama. He's still married to Selma. She lives somewhere in Salisbury." That was all I cared to say about that.

I smiled at my aging mother, turning her around like a child to walk back to the house. And then, like footprints in the sand, Mama's love washed over me and filled in the gaps, taking the painful parts of my life out to sea.

With no possibility of parole, Joe languished in prison. We were told his mental and physical body had declined over the years. Ray kept us informed and stayed in touch with Dillon and Gracie, even though neither twin expressed a desire to see their father. When it all boiled down, a jury convicted Joe of the murder and rape of Mavis Dumass and the murder of Chip Atkinson, but Joe had turned state evidence to avoid the death penalty.

A jury convicted Pastor Tony DeSanto to a life sentence for conspiracy in the murder of Mavis Dumass and Chip Atkinson, transporting drugs, running illegal prostitution rings and gambling casinos.

Because of my testimony and the evidence gathered, Evan Preston sat on death row, nearing the end of his appeal process. They convicted him of the murder of John Rossi and conspiracy in the murder of Mavis Dumass and Chip Atkinson. Further indictments included money laundering, extortion, bribing political figures, pirating videos, and the making and selling of illegal pornography.

Had Reverend Calvin Artury not put a gun to his head, he would have faced charges of tax evasion and the rape and extortion of over twenty-two men and women who came forward after his death. And, of course, the list would've included conspiracy in several murders.

Silas and Percy Turlo were still at large, believed to be living out of the country with twenty million dollars of the church's money.

We were told after Calvin shot himself, they carried his body to a nearby building that, within moments, caught fire and burned to the ground. The Nigerian government shipped his cremated remains, what little they found, back to the States and to his closest relative, his second cousin in Goose Creek.

The rumors traveled around town and eventually to Matthew. The old drunkard walked to the town dump with a bottle of Johnnie Walker in one hand and the urn in the other. After emptying his whiskey bottle, he dumped Calvin Artury's ashes over the garbage dump.

In my mind, it was a fitting end.

☙

"Ten years," I said as I kissed my husband.

"How about growing old with me?" he asked.

"Think we can make it that far?"

"Sure, why not?"

Our family and friends had gathered at The Grove Park Inn to celebrate with us as we cut our heart-shaped cake. I counted the number of hearts in the room that day. Sixty-three, sixty-four, including my own contented heart. Plenty of hearts to love and finish the journey together.

Epilogue – Twenty Years Later
September 2023

Andie

There was nothing left to say.

After hearing her Grandpa Joe had passed away in prison, Glenna appeared at my door with a notebook full of questions. At my granddaughter's insistence, I began to recount the turbulent years of my life, filled with both triumphs and tragedies. The past three days have become a blur of crying jags, pots of coffee, and continuous questions she has pieced together on her laptop like one of those video games her generation can't seem to get enough of.

It's strange, though, that Dillion and Gracie only know what they witnessed, neither one wanting the full version of their mother's story. But Glenna, Dillon's daughter, an English major at Appalachian State and budding novelist, brings a unique lens to my narrative. She says she needs to hear it, all of it, from the beginning *before I am no longer here to tell it.*

And so, the time has come to put my past to rest.

⤬

Across the room, Glenna sits attentively, dressed in vintage blue jeans from the '70s and her father's faded Marine Corps sweatshirt. She is pounding away at her laptop while listening intently to my every word, probing into the deepest recesses of my memories.

Now, watching her, I realize I might have worn her to a frazzle. She stirs uneasily in her chair, and I am worried if I was wise to share these painful and unexpected revelations. Glenna seems drained and restless, having filled a wastebasket with wadded Kleenex. Maybe even a bit tormented as she tells me for the past two nights, dreams from her biological great-grandfather and Mavis have filled in the gaps. I wonder about that. But who am I to question the plan of God? Yet I'm concerned. Is she strong enough, and can she understand it in a way that makes sense?

Glenna glances my way, fighting to keep her voice steady. "What did they gain, Grandma? Money, fame, and to sit at the right hand of God? Look where it got them. Prison or death by their own hand. It's a despicable waste of human life." Rising, she stretches her long legs, knuckles her eyes, and walks to the table where she slams her notebook down, obviously annoyed.

"I'm sorry. The whole thing is infuriating. He set out to punish you in front of his church congregation and a TV audience of millions to show the world what happens to a poor soul who disobeys the voice of God—or rather, *his* voice—his prophetic ramblings. He labeled you and any woman who opposed him a Jezebel, demonizing you so that no one in his congregation would help you. He was determined for you to beg and plead for your marriage and then for your eternal salvation. But forgiveness for you, Grandma, was unattainable because you had to become someone else to achieve that forgiveness. He wanted you with him—as a trophy."

I'm impressed by her insight but remain silent, allowing her to continue.

"In the end, you followed Jesus out the church door. *You* escaped Artury's control, became his adversary, and lived to tell the tale. *You* believed in the mercies of God and circumvented His wrath to find His love was far more powerful than the thousands of fire and brimstone sermons you endured. Your strength and resilience are undeniable. *YOU* were the thorn in Artury's side. The nemesis he had not expected. The final nail in his coffin. That's how I see it, Grandma."

Ah, she may be exhausted, but now there is a newfound understanding in her eyes, a depth of comprehension that comes with acceptance. It's as if a veil has been lifted, revealing the truth she was in search of. This understanding, though heavy, brings a sense of peace to me.

The aroma of coffee warms me as I move next to Matthew at the kitchen table. The cooler air from an open window hints at a change of season. But with the changing seasons come life changes. Some of our older members have passed on, with new babies born to replace them. Even so, my family is secure in ways I never thought possible. God has kept his promise, giving me beauty for ashes, transforming the remnants of my past into something astoundingly unique, like a phoenix rising from those ashes.

Glenna pulls back her buttery blonde hair into my signature ponytail, a mirror of my own—once upon a time. Her eyes catch the light as she refills our mugs with decaf. "Do you think I could chat with Mavis's daughter soon?" Glenna's eyes, the color of the Caribbean sea, hold a hint of enchantment, and in that moment, I realize everyone descended from the blue-eyed monster shares his eyes. Even Mavis's daughter.

"Of course," I say. "Suri and her husband will be here for Thanksgiving."

Matthew reaches for his phone to snap Glenna's picture, and she protests. "Grandpa, I've not had a shower."

"But you look like your grandmother did at your age," he smiles and says. His fingers close over mine, a warm, powerful circle, and once again, I am comforted by his caring touch and protective nature.

Glenna positions herself behind Matthew, wrapping her arms around his still-broad shoulders. "I can't thank you enough. Saving her means everything to me," she says. Her voice resonates with a profound sense of gratitude and relief and echoes in the air.

I find her words curious and endearing, but I am out of words. My emotions and memories are tapped out. The three of us move slowly to the veranda to watch the sunrise. God's grace is indeed sufficient.

I am still here in the quietness of Shiloh mountain and wrapped in the love of a man who helped me rescue myself. I am still here. Serving a God greater than any enemy I faced. The road behind me is much longer than the one in front of me, but I am content. I not only survived—I thrived in the bounty of His blessings.

Now, I can rest. My story is in good hands, and I am at peace.

THE END

Author's Note – *Televenge Trilogy*

Although there are many similarities, this book is not about me. All the characters are fictional. They are not based on any person dead or alive. While many scenes were inspired in part by real life, all events and dialogue are entirely imaginary and/or wishful thinking. Any resemblance to real people or events is entirely coincidental. Although it was difficult to revisit many dark places in writing this story, it does not change the purely fictitious nature of the work.

Sorry We're Open Diner does not exist, but there is a town in North Carolina called Welcome, and Mount Zion Baptist Church in Winston-Salem is not the same church as described in this trilogy.

Southern Fried Women, a book of short stories, contains spin-offs of scenes in this trilogy, or minor characters who tell their own story: *Pigment of My Imagination*, *Beach Babies*, and *Punkin Head*.

Though it is true this book is about the dark side of televangelism, it is also about the true light of unconditional love. Writers write about their passions, what moves them, what they know. My key inspirational force is my spirituality. I wrote the **Televenge Trilogy** to reflect the realities, the long-lasting devastation, and the horrific effects of legalism.

For those who have left a manipulative situation or are thinking about it, you should know the great plan of redemption belongs to us all. No matter how desperate your circumstances, you can come out of a dark place, and into a life that is calling your name. God's mercies are truly renewed every morning, and He never, ever turns His back on us. No matter what anyone preaches from their pretentious pulpit. And that is why I wrote this trilogy.

—Pamela King Cable

For more information or to purchase go to **GracelynRose.com**

Books by this author:

Televenge
Book One of the *Televenge* trilogy

Avenge Us All
Book Two of the *Televenge* trilogy

Vengeance Is Mine
Book Three of the *Televenge* trilogy

Southern Fried Women
a collection of short stories

The Sanctum
On her fifth birthday, Neeley McPherson accidentally killed her parents. Thrown into the care of her scheming and alcoholic grandfather, she survives by her quick wit and the watchful eye of an elderly black man, Gideon. In 1959, as equal rights heats up in the South, authorities accuse Gideon of stealing a watch and using a Whites Only restroom. Neeley, now thirteen, determines to break him out of jail.

When the infamous Catfish Cole, Ku Klux Klan Grand Dragon of the Carolinas, discovers their courageous escape, he pursues Neeley and Gideon into the frozen Blue Ridge Mountains to a wolf sanctuary. There, Neeley crosses the bridge between the real and the supernatural. Giving sanctuary, the healing power of second chances, and overcoming prejudice entwines, leading Neeley to tragedy once again but also the desire of her heart.

The Sanctum is a coming-of-age Southern tale dusted with magic and set in a volatile time in America when the winds of change begin to blow.

For my parents.
Thank you for taking me on new adventures, and always leading the way with your love and dedication for me. I love you.

Chapter One

Tapping away at the keys on my laptop, I almost don't hear Mom call out for me.

"Laelia, will you please grab us our food?" Mom asks from the passenger seat, looking up from her laptop when she speaks.

I set my own laptop down next to me on the couch, and stand in search of their food. I gather a few snacks for myself, and hand my parents their food.

Dad munches on his breakfast as he cruises our motorhome down the highway, while Mom types away at her computer. The strange melody of the clacking of keys, quiet country music, and the rumbling of the road is almost relaxing.

It sounds like summer.

I spend the better part of the morning working on my writing, and I'm finished with my ten-thousand word draft by the time my name is being called again.

"Laelia, Laelia, Laelia."

I look up from my phone, and see the twins—Archer and Arden—both sitting on the floor in front of me.

"What's wrong? And why are you two up and walking around? You know that you're supposed to be sitting down while we drive." They both blink their adorable, dark brown eyes at me, and I choose to ignore the fact that they were both disobeying a house—well, motorhome—rule.

"We want you to make us food, please. Mommy said that you could make us peanut butter and jelly sandwiches." Arden says, pointing towards the fridge.

"Okay, but please go sit in your seats, boys. I don't want you falling and getting hurt."

They both immediately walk to their seats across from me, and after making sure they buckle their seat belts, I set my phone down to go make their food.

As I'm spreading the peanut butter, I can feel Dad exit off of the highway. The motion makes my slippered feet slide a few inches across the floor, causing me to hold on to the counter for balance.

Turning my wrist to view my watch, I realize that it's already two in the afternoon.

I know that we left sometime around six this morning, so it's not unreasonable that we'd be close to our campsite.

Well, if you would call it one. Yes, we're the people who spend their summers in their motorhome, and 'camp' in different campgrounds throughout the summer.

I don't really see it as camping—more like 'glamping'—but that's what most people call it.

I pass the boys their lunches, and listen as Dad talks through the window to a man on a golf cart as we arrive at the campground.

Dad pays the admission fees, and the man waves us through, calling out to Dad as he presses the gas.

"Yes, sir. Your spot is number sixteen. Enjoy your stay." Dad calls out his thanks, and slowly adds more pressure to the gas as we pull forward.

Dad parks us in our site before calling out to me.

"Okay, Laelia, you can get out now."

I step out the door, the steps opening as I walk down.

"Hey, Mom, I'm going to walk around and check this place out." I call inside the door, listening for her reply.

"Um, okay. I guess the boys will stay here with us while you look around. We're going to open slides in a minute." Shutting the door and walking away, I breathe a sigh of relief that we made it in one piece.

I notice that the people next to us have a camper that is pulled behind their truck, and not a motorhome. Which I find odd, but I'm not really sure why.

The row that we're on is the closest to the trails leading into the woods, and I scout out all of the trail heads, making note of the lengths that are displayed on the signs at each entrance.

My phone buzzes in the back pocket of my shorts, and I pull it out to read the new message from Mom. She wants me to stop by the front office and see if there are any maps of the campground. A second message appears, letting me know that the boys will want to go on a walk later.

I slide my phone back into my pocket, changing the direction of my walk and starting in the direction of the front office.

I rub my exposed arms as goosebumps flood them, the warm sun sending tingles down my spine. My purple tank top covering zero percent of my exposed arms.

"Afternoon." A woman sitting outside of her trailer calls out, lifting her arm in a small wave. I gently wave back, smiling. I remember it being like this last year. Everyone calling out greetings as you walk by. Even people you've never met before.

My light brown hair runs in a thick braid down my back, and it gently swings back and forth as I walk.

After thirty minutes of walking, I've reached the front office. The bell chimes as I walk in, alerting the man behind the counter to my arrival.

"Hello, ma'am, what can I do for you today?" He calls out as I approach.

"Oh, I'm just looking at the maps y'all have." I reply, nodding at the display near me.

"No problem. Let me know if you need help finding anything." He says, returning his attention back to the computer in front of him. I nod and turn, looking through their small store.

After grabbing some maps, and saying "Thank you" to the man, I walk out the door and start the walk towards our motorhome.

"Hey, Laelia, I put Colin and Jasper in their playpen for you." Archer says, grabbing my hand as I walk in the door.

"Thank you. Were they misbehaving?" He holds on to my hand as I walk to their playpen, and doesn't answer my question.

I peer into their space, and my two Chihuahuas rush towards me, wagging their tiny tails in the process.

"Hello, darlings." I say, sitting on the floor and allowing them to crawl into my lap.

"Here, let me hold one." Arden says, walking up behind us and reaching his hands out.

"Go sit on the couch and I'll bring them over." I tell him as I stand up.

They both rush to the couch and plop down, rocking the house ever so slightly.

I'm not really sure why I'm making them sit when Archer was obviously just carrying them, but then again, I'd rather be safe than sorry.

I set Jasper and Colin on the couch, knowing that they won't jump off by themselves.

"I need to go talk to Mom. Stay here for a few minutes." I direct, looking them both in the eye. The twins nod, but I know that they're not going to stay.

"Here are your maps." I say while I walk into my parents' room.

"Oh, thank you. You'll probably want to keep them with you, though. They're for your walk." Mom says from her bed.

I nod, losing focus of the conversation as I look outside. The window behind their bed is open, allowing me to watch the chaos unfold.

A small child—probably only three or four—is walking right behind a moving RV, and by the way it's continuing to reverse, I'm sure that the driver has no idea that he's there.

I stuff the maps into my back pocket, and sprint outside. Scrambling out of the door, I trip, trying to reach the child that's about to be run over.

Just before I reach him, a boy my age grabs the child and rips him away from the back of the RV.

He quickly moves away from the now stopped vehicle, and the driver jumps out, leaving his door open in his rush to reach us, obviously realizing what almost happened.

"Oh my gosh! I'm so sorry! I almost just ran over you guys' child!" The man exclaims.

He looks to be around thirty-five, and he's clearly in a panic. He runs his hand through his nonexistent hair, and if this wasn't a serious situation, I would definitely find it amusing.

The boy who grabbed the child walks towards us with the kid clinging to him.

"Um, he's not our child. At least, he's not mine. I think he belongs to someone a few sites down." The boy—well, almost man—says, as the child buries his head into his shoulder.

"Thank you so much for getting him out of the way. Really, thank you." He turns to the boy who picked up the child and shakes his hand, and waves at me, before he gets back in his truck and drives away.

I'm a little surprised that he's already leaving, but technically nothing happened, so there is no reason for him to stay.

"So, do you know who this little guy belongs to? I asked him, but I don't think he hears very well. He obviously didn't hear the trailer heading towards him, and was completely surprised when I picked him up." The boy tells me, his voice extremely calming even though this situation is more than a little bit nerve wracking.

"I, uh, no. I just got here. Like, maybe forty-five minutes ago. I can help you find his parents, though." I reply, glancing at the poor child's face. All I can picture is seeing him innocently playing and almost being run over.

I gulp. The boy—who looks more of a man than boy—nods, patting the child's head.

"We can walk this way. I think I've seen him over here, before. I'm not one-hundred percent, though. I've only been here for a few days." I nod, and we start walking in the direction he pointed at.

"I'm Johnny, by the way." The boy—Johnny—says, extending his large hand between us.

His slender fingers grip mine in a handshake.

"I'm Laelia. Nice to meet you." I say, as his hand envelopes mine. The touch feels electric, but I'm sure that's the adrenaline pumping through me, racing like needles through my veins.

"I like your name. It's really pretty." Johnny says, looking down at me.

It's one of the first times I've received a compliment on my name rather than someone asking why my parents didn't choose something easier to pronounce like Layla or Lyla.

"Thank you. Your name is also pretty. It really suits you."

He chuckles lightly. "Thanks. I hope that it suits me in a good way."

I nod vigorously. "Definitely in a good way. I-"

"There he is! Oh my gosh! Where did you find him?" A woman screams, running towards us. She gently takes the child out of Johnny's arms, and cradles him in her own.

She hugs the child—presumably her son—tightly before looking up.

"He was a few spots down, and was in harm's way. I grabbed him before he was injured, though." Johnny answers, making the whole ordeal way less dramatic than it had been. Sure, nothing did happen, but still.

"Thank you, thank you, thank you. I was outside with him and got called away. What almost happened to him? You probably noticed, but Noah is deaf, so he doesn't notice when he could be injured. Thank you for saving my baby. My name is Angie, by the way." She's obviously more than a little frantic, her sentences coming out in a strange order.

Johnny looks to me, as though I should answer, and I take a gulp of air, not wanting to dredge back up the horrible memory.

"He was behind a moving vehicle, and the driver didn't see him. Johnny—thankfully—pulled him out of the way in time." I finish and look towards Johnny, silently asking if he wants to add anything to the story.

"I can't thank you both enough. Is the driver still here? Is there anything I can do to repay you for saving my baby?" Angie asks, peering past us. Presumably to see if the vehicle is still here.

"No. And really, Johnny did it all. I just saw it happen, and I tried to prevent it. He's the one who actually saved him." I say, ensuring she knows that I really shouldn't be getting the credit here.

"We're about to leave, but I want you to know how thankful I am. Really, thank you so much. I don't know what we would've done if you hadn't saved our baby." Angie says, tears filling her eyes as she walks away.

"Well, that was a strange way to meet." Johnny says, a small chuckle leaving his lips. I turn and look up at him, noting the way his milk chocolate hair fluffs a little in the soft breeze.

For a moment I think he's talking about Angie and Noah, and immediately feel dumb when I realize he's talking about us.

"Definitely. Are you staying at this park, too?" I ask, looking up to study his facial features.

"Yep. We're staying for two more days. How about you? You said you got here about an hour ago, right?" He replies.

"Yeah, I did say that. I'm not sure how long we're staying for, though. I don't remember dates all that much." I reply with a sheepish laugh. He nods, silent for a minute before speaking again.

"So was that motorhome you came out of yours? Our spot is the one on your left." He asks, obviously unsure what else to say now that we've delivered Noah to his mom.

"Yeah, that's my family's. I think I remember seeing your home next to ours when I started my walk. Maybe I'm wrong, though." I say.

"Yeah, that's ours. I, uh, I have to get back, but maybe I'll see you around." Johnny says, ducking his head and waving as he turns away. "Okay. I'll see you around." I respond, feeling awkward because I have to walk to essentially the same place as him, meaning I either have to walk next to him, or a few feet behind him.

Deciding against feeling awkward, I walk in the opposite direction for a minute, and turn back when I'm sure he's reached his house, allowing me to walk back to mine.

Walking into my house, I spot the boys asleep on the couch, and shake my head at the sight. They napped all morning, but they're already asleep?

I slide one of the couch blankets over them, noticing that Colin and Jasper are asleep in the passenger seat, snuggled into their bed.

"Laelia, is that you?" Dad calls from his room.

I enter their bedroom, and notice that Mom is asleep next to him on their bed.

"Why did you leave so quickly earlier?" He asks, curiosity in his voice.

I assume Mom asked him to find out, since she was the one I was talking to before. I speak quietly, knowing that the boys and Mom are asleep.

Early rising is not something we enjoy, or do often.

"There was a kid behind a moving trailer. I was making sure he didn't get run over." He nods.

"Wow, I'm glad you were able to help. Where were his parents?" I explain Angie's explanation, and he nods after I'm finished.

I leave their room, passing the boys' unmade bunk beds on my way out.

Arden and Archer are still passed out on the couch, so I walk outside again.

I note that Dad pulled the grill out of the motorhome basement storage, making my job later easier.

He placed it on our folding table, leaving me the picnic table that our site came with available for prepping food.

I plop into an outdoor chair, and set an alarm for an hour to remind myself to start baked potatoes.

I contemplate going back inside for my laptop, but decide against it. I did a ton of writing this morning, and I'm caught up on everything. The plus side to my job is that I technically can be done a few weeks in advance.

Opening an app on my phone, I start reading the mystery novel that I've been making my way through.

Soon enough, my alarm goes off, signaling that I need to start dinner, and I quickly start the electric grill. After wrapping potatoes with salt, pepper, and foil, I lay them on the grill and unlock my phone, noting that it's four-fifteen.

I decide to start the steaks at five-fifteen, and then make the salad as they cook.

Before I know it, it's time to start steaks. I grab the food from inside, and after making a few trips in and out, I manage to get the lettuce, tomatoes, carrots, dressing, croutons, bacon, and the steaks.

Laying the meats on the grill, I get to work slicing the lettuce.

I check the time, surprised that everyone else is still sleeping. I guess the boys didn't sleep last night due to excitement, and that's why they're still out.

Pulling the steaks off of the grill and slicing the boys', I plate everything, and walk inside to wake everyone up.

"Archer, Arden, it's time to get up and eat dinner." I say, gently shaking their shoulders.

"Huh? What?" Arden says groggily. His words slurring as he sits up, drool sliding down his cheek.

I stifle a giggle, knowing he'll throw a fit if he thinks I'm making fun of him.

Archer stirs a minute later, his short brown hair tousled.

"Come outside to eat dinner, boys. I need to wake Mom and Dad up, and then we'll all eat together." I tell them, giving each of their cheeks a poke as they stand.

I grin at their cute expressions as they fully wake up.

"Mom, Dad." I call as I walk in, tapping their doorframe as I do so.

"Dinner is done. I have the boys outside, already." I say, already halfway out of their room.

"Thank you, Laelia." The boys say as I place their plates in front of them. After watching their first few bites of steak, I sigh in relief knowing that I sliced it small enough.

Mom and Dad come out within a few minutes, and pretty soon we're all eating.

I feel a strange sense of being watched, and when I look up, I lock eyes with Johnny.

I smile at him, and he does the same.

His full smile is dazzling.

He's near the front of his RV, a black lab leashed next to him. His dog wags its tail as Jasper playfully barks at it.

He starts walking away, and from behind him, his parents appear. They're both brown haired, and both considerably shorter than Johnny. I find it strange, but I rein my attention back to dinner as Archer starts talking.

"This chicken is so good." He says, pointing at the steak. I purse my lips to avoid smiling, not wanting to hurt his feelings or start a meltdown.

"That's really good. Do you want to know the proper name for this meat?" I ask, Mom flicking her eyebrows as I respond.

"Um, maybe." Arden answers for Archer.

"This meat right here is 'steak.'" I say, emphasizing the word. He nods, going back to his food.

Ten minutes pass as we eat, silence stretching between us.

"Excuse me, would you mind if I were to pet your dogs?" I look up to see Johnny's mom gesturing towards Colin and Jasper, Johnny and his dad behind her.

"Oh, of course not. Here, let me pull them out." I pull Colin and Jasper out of their stroller, and sit down in one of the outdoor chairs, allowing her to do the same. She reaches out and pets them, smiling as she does so.

"Would you like to hold one of them?" I ask, offering her Colin.

"Oh my goodness, you're just so cute." She says as Colin licks her chin. "Oh, I'm Katherine, by the way." She says, extending her hand in a greeting.

"I'm Laelia. Nice to meet you, Katherine." I say, a smile forming on my lips.

"Boys, you can go inside and either read your books or watch television." I hear Dad say behind me, as he and Mom come sit down with Katherine and I.

"I'm Lucia, and this is Chris." Mom says, reaching across the empty fire pit and shaking Katherine's hand.

"Lovely to meet you both. James, Johnny, come over and say hi." Katherine says, turning her head and nodding toward us.

As they walk over, I notice that Johnny has put his dog in their house.

"Hi, I'm Johnny. Nice to meet you." He says, shaking my parents' hands before turning to me.

"Hi, Laelia." He says, grinning at me as he sits next to me.

"You two know each other?" Mom asks looking between the two of us.

"Yeah, we uh, met earlier today." I respond.

"That's so nice. Here, I think he wants you back. He's so wiggly." Katherine says, passing Colin back to me.

"This is James." Katherine says, motioning at her husband who sat down next to her.

"So that's your place?" Dad asks, pointing at their truck and RV.

"Yes, sir." James answers, pride in his voice.

"It looks nice. We thought about something like that, but we decided to go with a motorhome." Dad responds. James nods, swiping his eyes over our house.

"A motorhome is probably better for a bigger family. More space while driving, you know. My sister has one, too. It works well for them. She has three kids, too." He says. Mom nods, agreeing.

"Definitely. We needed something… other than a car or truck to travel in. This definitely works amazing for us. Did you have to remodel anything in yours?" Mom asks.

"Oh, definitely. We live in ours full-time, so there were definitely some things that we had to fix. It took us six months to get it mostly livable for us. We bought it knowing we would have to adjust, so it wasn't horrible." Katherine responds, gesturing towards James and Johnny.

"Tell them what we had to change, Johnny." Katherine says, leaning forward to see across from me. I shrink back, feeling in the way, even though I'm just sitting normally.

"We replaced pretty much everything, and added and adjusted everything else. Beds, everything in the kitchen, the seating. Dad and I spent a ton of time fixing it all." Johnny says, grinning at the end of his sentence.

I sit in silence as the conversation flows around me, and while I'm glad that we're "meeting" again, I feel mildly awkward not knowing just about anything on our house, and that's the only topic of this conversation. I prefer to stay out of the whole vehicle thing. My attention wanders for a second, and I'm snapped back when my name is mentioned.

"-Laelia is sixteen, so there's a ten year age gap between her and her brothers. What about you, Johnny? How old did you say you are?" Mom asks him, staring intently.

"I'm seventeen. I'll be eighteen in a few weeks." He responds with a smile, and I admire his easygoing nature and calm manner of speaking.

"That's lovely. I'm sure your parents are ready for you to be out of the weird in-between stage where you're not quite an adult, and not quite a kid. I know we are with Laelia." Mom says with a chuckle.

"So, Laelia, are you homeschooled, or do you attend in-person school?" Katherine asks me, curiosity in her tone.

"I actually go to a private school. What about you, Johnny?" I ask, turning to him.

"That sounds cool. I'm homeschooled."

"Really? That's neat. How does it work? I know some people do textbooks, and some do it online." I ask, vaguely hearing our parents having a conversation in the background.

"Mine is online. I'm enrolled in a completely online academy, where I pick and choose my classes, grade level, and so on. Well, my parents technically choose my classes, but I can add a few that interest me. Like, there's specific courses on engineering things that I really like. It's obviously not like being in-person, but it's still super nice."

I nod, the animation in his voice making it all ten times more interesting. "That sounds so cool. Do you think you'd like being in an in-person school more, or do you think this suits you better?" I inquire, genuinely curious.

"Um, I've never been in public school, but I definitely think that I like this better. My attention span isn't… great, and I take breaks in between classes, so I probably wouldn't 'fit in' with public school schedules." He says, chuckling nervously.

"I definitely get that. Will you graduate this year? I know you said you're almost eighteen."

He sucks in a breath before answering. "Short answer, yes. It kind of depends on if I decide to take a few more classes before I officially graduate. There's a few extra curricular classes that I'm thinking about taking. What about you? Are you close to graduating?"

I shake my head. "No. I'll turn seventeen in August, so I'm kind of far from graduating. I mean, I could add more to my work load and try to graduate early, but it's not really worth it right now. Who knows, maybe I'll pick up summer school and try to get ahead." I say, giggling a little.

"Ah, that would definitely be something. I'm sure you'd go back to school a grade ahead."

"A whole grade, you think? Wouldn't it take me a few more months to do that?" I tease.

He grins at that, and I'm definitely not expecting his response.

"No, not really. You don't need eight hours a day to complete a lot of school, to be honest. Completing grades quickly is actually pretty easy. I mean, you really could finish a whole grade in three-ish months if you were consistent." He responds, sincerity in his face.

"Really? That's wild to think about. What's the shortest amount of time it's taken you to complete a grade?"

"I'm not sure. I know I've done a few of them quickly. Maybe my mom would know." He replies.

"Oh, okay. Hey, do you want to hold him?" I ask, motioning to Jasper, as he tries—again—to jump into Johnny's lap.

"Sure. What's his name?" He asks, Jasper looking even tinier than normal in Johnny's large hands. He licks Johnny's hand like a rabid animal, and I duck my head in embarrassment at my dog's horrible manners.

"That's Jasper, and this is Colin. They're Chihuahuas."

He nods, amusement in his smile as Jasper continues licking and wagging his tail.

"He's pretty… energetic. He's cute, though. How old are they?"

I smile at his compliment. "They're around ten or eleven months old, so basically full grown. They're pretty small, though. I saw you with a dog, earlier. Is it yours?" I ask.

Johnny smiles in typical dog-parent fashion before speaking. "Yeah, she's mine. She's a Labrador. Her name is Berry. When my parents got her for me, I wanted to name her 'Bear' but my mom persuaded me to make it Berry, so it would be 'more feminine.'" He says, laughing at the end of his sentence.

"That's so cute. How old were you when you got her? I'm guessing you were a little bit younger?" I ask, noticing how he smiles when I say this.

"I got her for my twelfth birthday, so yeah. A little bit younger. I occasionally call her 'Bear,' but Berry seems to suit her pretty well." He says with a shrug.

"She looked pretty adorable when I saw her. From what I saw, Berry fits her."

"Pretty destructive, you mean. As a puppy she destroyed everything. My parents probably had gray hairs after we got her." He laughs.

"Are you sure she was the only destructive one?" I tease, knowing how my brothers are right now.

"Probably not. I wasn't a super 'easy' kid to raise. I really had my fair share of destructiveness. We were probably a terror together." He says with a chuckle.

I laugh at his honesty, his complete realness refreshing.

"Laelia, please go check on the boys and make sure they're changed into their pajamas." Dad calls to me, jolting me back to reality.

I nod and stand, deciding to just take Colin with me.

"Oh, I'll hold him for you." Johnny says, reaching out with his left hand, Jasper asleep in his right.

"Thanks. He's a little bit more feisty than Jasper, good luck."

Walking inside, I see the boys sitting on the couch sharing a bag of mini popcorn, and watching their favorite train show.

"Okay, let's take a pause and put on pajamas. Afterwards you can go back to your show."

They both huff and fold their arms. Even though they just turned six, I'm still surprised when they're so in sync with each other.

It *still* catches me off-guard when their synchronization is so on point.

"No. I'm not going to put on pajamas. Neither is Arden." Archer says defiantly.

I roll my eyes before walking to their drawers and pulling out two sets of pajamas.

"Come here, please. If you don't come in here and get changed you're not going to be watching television when you're done."

Usually I have a little bit more patience when it comes to their antics, but I want to get back to my conversation, and I feel slightly bad for being short with them.

They both reluctantly change, but immediately after, they go back to watching their show.

Walking back outside, I gather the plates and silverware, even though I desperately want to go back to my conversation with Johnny. Hurrying through after-dinner chores, it only takes me about fifteen minutes to finish up.

Sitting next to Johnny again, I smile, seeing both Colin and Jasper asleep in his hands. The veins on the back of his hands and wrists are pronounced with the way he holds both of my dogs, and with the position they're in, I can only imagine that it's not all-that comfortable.

"I think they both like me." Johnny says, motioning with his head to Colin and Jasper.

"I think so, too. They're pretty standoff-ish most of the time, so I'm surprised that they let your mom hold them, and fall asleep in your hands."

"Wow. Should I feel special, then?" He says with a chuckle, his thumb brushing lightly on Jasper's back.

"Something like that." I reply with a chuckle.

"Johnny, I think it's time for us to go back, we don't need to intrude on their night, anymore." Katherine says while standing.

"Oh, you're welcome to stay longer, if you'd like." Mom says, waving her hand in the air in "a don't be silly" gesture.

"No, really, we should go and do our evening things, and let you do yours." She says.

"Oh, isn't that precious. Look at Johnny and Laelia's dogs. So cute!" Mom exclaims.

"You must have some special touch with them." Katherine says, patting Johnny's shoulder.

"Here you go. They're super sweet." Johnny says, handing me back my dogs, care in his motions to keep them asleep.

His hands brush mine as he passes them back, and it must be the warm air, because my whole arm immediately feels warm.

Chapter Two

Rolling over, I check the time on my phone, and the illuminated numbers scream six-fifteen.

Pulling the blanket over my head, I snuggle Jasper and Colin closer to my stomach, wanting to sleep longer.

Sleep doesn't come easy, neither did it last night as I had laid down. I was plagued with thoughts of the little boy, Johnny rescuing him, Noah's near-hysterical mother, Johnny talking about his school, it becoming a jumbled mess in my tired mind.

I curl up, hearing Mom tell the boys to lay on their made beds for five minutes, knowing that they'll fall asleep as soon as they've been laying down.

I guess they're what woke me up.

Apparently, Mom, too.

I lay awake until about seven-fifteen, when Colin and Jasper wake up, and they alert me to the fact that they want to eat and drink, by attacking my face with kisses.

Swinging my legs over my bed and walking into my bathroom, I get dressed, and put my hair in double braids, my thick hair falling down my back. I let the dogs run freely in the house while I start breakfast tacos, the smell filling the house with the warm scent of tortillas.

Wrapping everyone else's in foil and placing them on the table,

I walk outside with mine, with the intention of sitting in the rising sunshine and reading a book.

I've barely shut the door when I see Johnny walking out of his house with his dog, Berry.

"Hey, Laelia." Johnny says with a smile and a wave, continuing the direction of his walk.

"Hi, Johnny. Do you mind if I come pet Berry?" I ask, taking a few steps towards him.

"Sure. Be warned, though. She's super friendly, and also super wild." He says with a chuckle.

"That's perfectly fine. She's so cute, oh my gosh." I say, crouching down next to Berry as he holds her leash. While I rub her extra soft fur, she wastes no time wagging her tail and licking every inch of my face.

"You're just precious. Yes, yes you are."

Johnny laughs and restrains her from slobbering me up anymore, and I have to imagine that it takes more than a little bit of strength to do, with a wild Labrador like her.

"Sorry, she gets more than a little excited when she meets new people." Johnny apologizes.

"It's totally fine. She's so sweet. Are you taking her on a walk?"

He nods. "Yeah. That's the only way to keep her energy down a little bit. You're, uh, welcome to come along with us. It probably won't be a super long walk because she's getting older, but you're still welcome." Johnny says.

The offer is extremely nice, but for the briefest of seconds, I remember that I've barely known him for a day. I push the worry away, deciding to be bold and take the offer.

"Sure, that sounds fun."

Johnny nods, and ducks his head seeming both happy and embarrassed.

"So, do you like this campsite? I think it's nice, but I'm excited for the place we're going to tomorrow." Johnny says as we walk, obviously trying to find something to talk about so we don't walk in an awkward silence.

"Yeah, it's cool here. I think I'm going to take a walk with Archer and Arden through one of the footpaths later. They love going on 'nature paths' as they call them." I say with a small laugh.

"That's kind of cute. I bet they like going on walks with you. How old are they again?" He asks.

"They turned six in April. So, they're a little bit less than eleven years younger than me."

Johnny nods, his hair flapping a little bit as he does so.

"That's so cool. I've always wondered what it would be like to have little brothers. I feel like it would be especially cool if they were quite a bit younger than me, like yours." Johnny replies, a wistful tone in his voice.

"I guess it's pretty fun. I mean, they're rotten, and don't listen ninety percent of the time, but I still love them. There's definitely a big difference in our dynamic, seeing as they're twins, but I feel like we get along pretty well."

Johnny bends his head sightly to listen, and for some reason, I blush.

"Oh, I'm sure. Is it true that twins have 'telepathy' or a different connection? I've always heard that." He says with a laugh.

"Definitely. It's so crazy. I'll have to show you, later. They're *so* connected. Sometimes, it's a little bit scary. Like, last night, I told them that it was time to put on their pajamas, and they both folded their arms and huffed at the *exact* same time. They're like mirror images when they do things."

"No way. Do they finish each other's sentences or something?" Johnny asks.

"Yes! That's something, too. It's always weird when they do that."

We walk for a moment in silence before Johnny speaks again.

"So, what's that you're carrying?" Johnny asks, motioning to the wrapped tacos in my hand.

"Oh, I made breakfast, and was going to eat it outside." I answer.

"Oh, sorry for taking you away from your breakfast, then. What'd you make?" Johnny apologizes, running his hand through his hair.

"I made breakfast tacos. There's eggs, sausage, beans, onion, avocado, and bacon in them. Here," I unwrap one and lift it in his direction, "try it. They're pretty good, I think."

"Are you sure? I don't want to take your breakfast." Johnny says.

"No, no, I probably wouldn't have finished it. Really, try it." I say, genuinely meaning it, seeing he's about to decline.

"If you're sure." He answers, and I'm pretty sure he's only saying this because I've offered more than a few times.

His large hand brushes against mine as he takes the taco.

I look up as he takes a bite, and I'm worried when he completely stops and stares at me. He swallows quickly, looking intently at me.

"What did you say is in here?"

He doesn't like it. I'm sure. I cringe, feeling mortified.

"Egg, sausage, onion, bacon, beans, avocado. I'm guessing you don't like it, sorry." I say, feeling so awkward.

His face quickly turns in confusion. "What? No! This is the best taco I've ever had!"

My eyebrow raises in skepticism. "Really? You're just saying that. There's no way you actually think that, right?"

He raises the half-wrapped taco and points at it. "This is amazing. Seriously, this is so good."

His compliments raise a hot, red flush in my cheeks, and I'm sure he can see it.

"You really think so? No one has ever said that."

His jaw drops and his eyebrows shoot up. "No way. This is really, really, good."

A smile grows on my face, and I try to not look as stupid and giddy as I'm sure I feel.

"What makes this so good?" Johnny asks, and I fight the urge to laugh at his energy.

"I'm not sure. I just started mixing foods I like. I really love avocado, onion, and beans especially, so I try to put them in as many foods as possible."

Johnny smiles as I talk, nodding the whole time.

"Well, apparently, your taste-buds can really pick out which foods go well together, because this is wonderful. Life-changing, actually."

I'm sure I look like an idiot with my smile, but for some reason, I don't care. Usually I care when I look dumb and giddy. Yet, right now, I can't find it within me to care.

"I'm really glad you like it. No one's ever had that reaction when they've eaten my food. Thank you."

"No. Thank *you*. I feel like I need to find some award to give to you. This is a more Latino food? I've had these foods separately, but never together."

I nod, pretty excited that he asked. "Yeah! It's more Mexican than anything else, but I'm sure other countries have something similar. My mom is Mexican, and her parents immigrated from Mexico to Texas before she was born. She doesn't really do any cooking, but before my grandparents died, they taught me cooking tips and tricks. If you're not leaving today, I could make some sort of lunch." I offer, looking up at him expectantly.

He smiles throughout my rambling, finishing the rest of the taco in one bite.

"Yeah, we're not leaving today, but I wouldn't want you to feel forced to cook. Also, it's super cool that your grandparents are from Mexico. My dad's mom is Japanese, and my mom's dad is Korean. I really like that we have that in common. Not a lot of kids I know have that in common with me."

"Oh, that's really cool! I figured you had some sort of Asian descent, but I wasn't sure. I'm sure you could tell I have Latino genetics, though." I say with a small laugh.

"Yeah, my family always jokes that both of my parents are adopted, because most of their features don't represent any of the Asian in them. My grandparents only claim relation to us, because we're a good mix of my parents *and* grandparents." Johnny says with a chuckle.

"Well, you're the only one who got doubled up on the genes, though." I laugh.

"My sister, too." He adds.

My jaw drops.

"Your sister? What? I haven't seen her, yet."

He lets out a small laugh. "Yeah, I have an older sister. I sometimes forget to mention that when I meet people. I feel like they just *know* that I have a sister. She's in college right now." Johnny says, ducking his head and chuckling.

"Wow. Is she close to graduating?"

He shakes his head, his hair doing a little flip again. "She's a sophomore, so she has another two-ish years left. Her name is Julianna, by the way."

"Oh my gosh. That's such a pretty name. Do you talk to her often?"

Johnny nods, pulling his phone out of his pocket. "Yeah, I think so. We usually text once or twice a day, and we video chat pretty often. Here's a picture of her."

He turns his phone to me, and my jaw drops.

The photo is one of Johnny and Julianna standing together at what looks to be a wedding. She has her long, brown hair in an up-do, and is wearing a knee length blue dress.

Johnny is standing next to her in a dark suit, equally as beautiful, probably more.

His hair neatly combed, and his stunning smile on display.

"Wow, you're both so pretty. I definitely see the family resemblance. Like, I can definitely tell you're siblings, but have some obvious differences, too." I say as he slides his phone back in his pocket.

"Hey, uh, I kind of need to be getting back. I promised my mom I'd run by the grocery store and grab some things for dinner. Sorry." Johnny says after a few more minutes of walking.

I check my phone, and notice that we've been walking for more than thirty minutes.

"Oh, no problem. I should probably be getting back, too."

Turning around, I feel a sense of longing. Longing for a longer walk with Johnny. Longing for more time to talk and more time to get to know him.

I push those thoughts away, and try to focus on thoughts of *my* dinner.

What did I have planned for tonight?

Casserole. That's it.

"So, what are you making for dinner?" I ask Johnny.

"Oh, I'm not making dinner. My mom is making soup for dinner. I-" He ducks his head in a slightly embarrassed gesture and gives a nervous laugh. "-don't really cook. I mean, I *can* cook. I do cook sometimes, but not really. It's just not my thing, you know?"

I nod.

"Yeah, I totally get it. I really meant it when I said that I can make some foods for you to try. It would be cool to show some of my recipes to someone else." I say, looking up to watch his reaction.

I *want* to show him my recipes.

I *want* him to try some of the foods I love.

Why?

"I mean, I wouldn't be opposed to trying your food. At all. But, I'm not sure when I'll have time. We *do* leave tomorrow. Hey, why don't I let you know if I have time later today."

Chapter Three

With my eyes and nose red as tomatoes, thanks to the onion I'm cutting, I swipe the onion into the hot pot of jalapeños, salt, and pepper. After stirring them until they're browned, I add the refried beans with the onion and jalapeños, sending the aroma of it all into the kitchen.

Finishing the rest of the quesadillas, I make myself a plate and walk outside.

I text Mom and Dad, letting them know that their food is done, not wanting to awaken the boys until they decide to wake them up. Mom texts me back, letting me know that she's going to let the boys nap for a bit longer before awakening them.

After contemplating it, I choose to eat at the picnic tables shaded by the trees fifteen or twenty sites down.

I go back inside for Jasper and Colin, putting them into their stroller and walking down to the empty tables.

Sliding my cheese, beans, and chicken, quesadillas onto the table and pulling my lemonade bottle from the stroller cup holder, I close my eyes, taking in the fresh air.

Opening them, I notice Johnny walking in our direction on the sidewalk.

I'm deciding on if I'm brave enough to wave, but he saves me from my shyness by waving as he nears.

"Hey, Johnny." I say, motioning for him to join me at the picnic table.

He obliges and sits down across from me, Berry at his heels. Her tail wagging, and her tongue flopping out the side of her mouth.

"She's *so* cute. I love her tail, and the way it looks like an otter tail." I say, motioning as she wags her tail even harder.

"I love it, too. She's pretty amazing. So are your little guys." He says, motioning at Colin and Jasper, who are sleeping peacefully in their stroller.

"Ah, they're pretty good, too. I really love them."

"So, are you eating lunch?" Johnny asks, motioning towards my plate on the table.

"Yeah. I made quesadillas. Do you… want to try them?" I ask, looking hopefully at him.

I pull another lemonade out of the stroller—I never go without one or two extra drinks—and set it in front of him.

"Are you sure? I mean, this would be the *second* time I'm stealing your food." He says questioningly, about to decline my offer.

"I don't mind at all. Really." And it's true. I don't mind sharing it, especially since he really liked it this morning.

"I mean, my mom would tell you I've never turned down food in my life before, so… yeah. I'd actually really like to try it."

I can tell I'm smiling excitedly, but I don't care all that much.

"Okay, so, these have beans with onion and jalapeño, Oaxacan cheese, and chicken. It might be spicy to you, but I'm not sure. That lemonade is for you, by the way." I say, pulling out a napkin—I keep an abundance of things in the bottom of the stroller—and accidentally knocking a deck of playing cards out in the process.

"Oops."

I set it on the table as I put one of the quesadillas on the napkins, and hand it to Johnny.

"You have to let me know what you think. Totally okay if you hate it."

He laughs, shaking his head.

"Why are you so sure I'm going to hate it? I loved your taco this morning. Also, I'm pretty sure I've only hated one food before, so chances are I won't dislike this." Johnny says, taking a bite of it.

His face immediately changes, and It's all I can do to not jump around in happiness as his expression obviously says he likes it.

"Oh my gosh. What are you doing to me? This is so amazing."

I smile, feeling pride rush through me because of his words.

"I think I need to get your recipe book and pick up cooking." He says, with a laugh.

"I'd have to make one, but I wouldn't mind sharing it as long as you swear to never share it." I tease, reaching across and patting his hand in a teasing gesture.

His hand tenses under mine, and I rip mine back, realizing what I just did.

I try to play it off by swiping a stray hair away from my face, but my hand is still tingling from embarrassment.

After finishing our quesadillas, I reach to put the cards away, Johnny surprises me by reaching for them, too.

"What card games can you play?" He asks, opening the deck and shuffling it.

"Um, quite a few. Which ones do you know how to play?" I ask, turning the question back to him.

"Hoola and Mighty are some that I play, but those aren't too popular. Do you… do you know how to play go-fish?" He asks ducking his head and chuckling. I purse my lips, tying to suppress a laugh, too.

"Of course. Who doesn't?" I tease.

"So, do you want to play it? Or we can figure out a different game that we both know." Johnny says, all the while continuing to shuffle the deck.

"No, we can play go-fish. I actually play it pretty often with my brothers. I hope you're not rusty, because I'm a pretty good player." I say, wiggling my eyebrows, and feeling instantly stupid afterwards.

You can't actually be a 'good' player in a non-strategic game.

"I like to think I'm pretty good, myself." He jokes back, wiggling his eyebrows, too.

I grin and duck my head, moving my emptied plate aside.

He deals the cards, and soon enough, there's more bantering between us than there is playing.

"Do you have a seven of diamonds?" I ask, knowing full well he does, because he asked me that two questions ago before I picked up this one.

"Yes." He says in a pretend sour voice, passing it to me.

Once the round is finished and we count up our books, we end up with an even amount of points.

"No way!" Johnny laughs, being over-dramatic and pretending that I wounded him.

I laugh at his antics while he pulls all of the cards back to his hands and shuffles them again.

"Hey, you're pretty good at that." I comment, noticing the way his hands expertly shuffle the cards in some non-traditional way.

"Yeah, my grandfather is a card master. He knows about a billion card tricks, and never stops creating new ones." Johnny responds, pride and love mixed in his voice.

"That's so cool. My grandfather definitely played, but he wasn't a card fanatic or anything. He was really in to reading, more than anything. That's probably where I got it from, to be honest." I say with a small chuckle.

"You like reading? What are some of your favorite books?" Johnny asks, looking up from the shuffling cards and raising an eyebrow.

I stare into his dark, chocolate eyes for a few seconds longer than normal before answering.

"Um, I really like reading cozy mysteries. I love them even more if there's a romantic subplot, too. What about you? What kinds of books do you read?"

Johnny purses his lips for a second before responding.

"I, uh, don't really like reading, to be honest. I don't hate reading, or anything, but I don't really see pictures or whatever when I read, so I don't find it really enjoyable. Does that make sense? My parents both used to wish that I would read more, but we've kind of all accepted that I'm not quite that person." He finishes.

I nod.

"Yeah, I can get that. Everyone is different, and some things just aren't for some people. I mean, I suck at all types of math, but I'm really good at reading and writing."

"Really? I'm so good at all of the math stuff, and while I do a decent job at my English lessons, I still don't enjoy it all that much.

It's nice that we're opposites in that aspect, you know?" Johnny replies.

"Yes, totally. It's good when people are different, I think." I say, reaching over and stroking Jasper's nose.

My phone dings on the table, disturbing our semi-silence. Picking it up, I see that it's from Dad. He's asking if I can take the twins to the playground.

"Hey, I need to go back and take my brothers to the playground." I say, looking up apologetically.

"That's not a problem. I probably need to be getting back, anyway." Johnny says, thankfully seeming not offended by my abrupt end to our picnic-of-sorts.

"I'll still see you before you leave tomorrow, right?" I ask.

In some ways, it feels like I've known Johnny for forever, but in some ways, it feels like I've only just scratched the surface of him.

"I'm sure. We should be leaving at about seven-thirty, tomorrow, so you might not be up then, but we're still here all of today." He says with a grin.

"Okay, thanks."

Johnny picks up our trash and disposes of it at a nearby trash can before we leave.

Walking side by side, Berry walking ahead on her leash, and Colin and Jasper in the stroller, I suck in a deep breath, and commit the moment to my memory.

Chapter Four

"Okay, boys, it's time to head back. I need to start dinner." I call out to the boys after a few hours of play time on the playground.

I hope they're worn out enough to not cause trouble for the rest of the day. I'm sure once they shower, they'll watch television or something.

"Are you sure? Do we actually need to go back now?" Arden asks, obviously wanting more play time.

"I'm sure. Archer, please come over here so we can leave." I say, standing from the bench.

"Hey, excuse me, miss, I would just like to say that I love that your kids are bilingual." The woman seated farther down the bench says, smiling as she says so.

I briefly realize that our short conversation had been in Spanish, but I'm quick to respond.

"Oh, thank you. They're not my sons, but thank you." She nods, turning her attention back to the magazine she's reading.

As we walk I ponder the woman's words. I realize that ninety percent of the time that I talk to the boys, I speak to them in Spanish. I guess I've never realized that before.

After sending the boys to Mom and Dad's room, I start dinner. Since it's a relatively short process, I have dinner in the oven within twenty minutes, and I'm outside with my laptop.

I've been working on a new document for a little bit of time, when I hear Johnny's voice.

"Okay, Mom. I'll be sure to check."

I try to listen without being obvious, but all I hear is Johnny—or, who I assume is Johnny—walking around their home.

I look up from my writing when my alarm notifies me to check the food, and I set my laptop on the table in front of me.

Deciding that the casserole needs a few more minutes, I pull bowls, forks, and napkins out the the table, and bring the food out shortly afterwards.

"Dinner is ready!" I call into the open screen door, turning back around to see Johnny and his parents coming outside to eat their dinner, too.

Johnny is setting the table, and when he looks up, he locks eyes with me and smiles.

His full smile is so dazzling to look at.

I smile back, and walk the few steps to their table.

"Hi." I say, noticing how lame that sounds as it rolls off of my lips.

"Hey." Johnny replies, taking a step closer to me.

"Oh, Laelia, hi." His mom says, coming a little bit closer to us.

"Hi, Katherine." I say, turning to give her a warm smile.

"Are you about to eat dinner, too?" She asks, motioning to our table behind us.

"Yes, my family is just about to come out, too." I say, turning slightly to see if they're out the door.

"If it wouldn't be a bother to you, we would love it if you joined us for dinner. I know I made some extra soup, but I see you have food out. You could just bring it over if you'd like." She says, looking excited by the idea.

"I'd love to. Let me go ask my parents if they'd like to, as well." I say, turning and speed-walking back into our home.

"Hey, Mom, Katherine would like us to join them for dinner. They're eating outside, too." I say, barely making it a few steps in before almost crashing into her, Dad, and the boys.

"That sounds fun. Sure." She says, walking past me and out the door.

I'm plating our food at our table, everyone else already sitting out Johnny's table, when I hear footsteps.

I look up to see Johnny walking over, his hands in his front pockets.

"I figured I'd see if you need any help carrying over your dishes." He says, tilting his head as he talks, making the sentence even sweeter.

"I'd love that. Thank you." I say, scooping the food into the last few bowls and setting forks into each one. "If you would carry these two over there, I can carry these three." I say.

But, before I can pick any up, he picks up three of them and winks.

I press my lips into a half grin and grab the other two.

Setting each bowl in front of Mom, Dad, Archer, and Arden, I pick up mine, but I notice the only open place is next to Johnny.

After a minute of our parents talking, I turn to talk to Johnny.

"So, are you excited to leave tomorrow?" I ask, trying to make conversation.

"A little. We go to that particular place every year for a summer thing. That's why I enjoy it so much. I like this place, though, so I'll be a little bit sad to leave. What about you? Are you leaving here anytime soon?" He replies.

"Yeah, I get that about tradition. I don't know, though. I'm kind of along for the ride. I enjoy traveling, but it's not about the destination for me. It's about the journey. I mean, I'm happy wherever we stay as long as I can cook, read, and write. I'm pretty simple." I say, forcing a small laugh at the end of my sentence as I realize how lame I sound.

"No, that's cool. Not simple. Well, maybe simple like the actual term, but not in a bad way at all. Being content is something not a lot of people can attain. It's admirable, really. You'd be surprised at how many people want to be just 'along for the ride' and content." Johnny says, tilting his head to look me in the eyes as he says this, his hair flopping ever so slightly as he talks.

His gaze is intense, almost like he's urging me to really absorb his words and realize that I'm not 'simple.'

"I, uh, I guess you could be right. People have always told me how 'simple' and 'easygoing' I am, so I've tried to be as flexible and easy as possible." I say, ducking my head in slight regret after admitting that.

I take a bite of food, giving me an excuse to remove my eyes from Johnny's intense gaze.

Johnny's head is still tilted, and his eyes look curious.

At least we've been talking in barely more than a whisper, and no one's heard me spilling my guts to Johnny.

Why am I allowing myself to be so open with him?

I hardly know Johnny.

He's essentially a stranger, and yet he already knows way too much about me.

"I don't think you were looking for this type of response, but if you're not naturally as 'easygoing' as you, I guess, are… you shouldn't shove down the part that's less… desirable? Not that I, or anyone, should find it less desirable, but I don't know a better word to use."

I nod, taking a bite of my food, not knowing how to answer his bold statement.

"Laelia! Did you hear that? You're going to take Arden and I on a walk! Right now!" Archer calls from between Arden and Mom.

I look up questioningly to Mom, and she nods.

I quickly eat the last few bites of food before standing and taking my empty bowl back to our table.

"Okay, come on, boys. Let's go get Colin and Jasper, and then we'll walk."

I jog inside and grab my dogs, their small barks comforting as I put them in their stroller.

"Johnny, go ahead and grab Berry, it would be good for her to get her evening walk in."

I hear Katherine say, her voice drifting through the screen door as she gives Johnny the instruction.

Katherine asks me if it's okay for Johnny to tag along as I walk outside, and I assure her that the more the merrier. Once I've said this, Johnny nods, turning and jogging back towards his house.

It's not long before we're joined by Johnny and Berry, their identical looks of eagerness almost making me laugh.

"Let's go!" Arden calls out from the sidewalk.

"We're coming, buddy." I say, walking up behind them, Johnny next to me.

"You'd think that after all of that time at the playground, they'd be worn out and wanting to go to sleep." I comment to Johnny, smiling as a look up at him.

He laughs before responding.

"If you think this is wild, you should have seen me as a six year old. Looking back, I don't think I have any memories of ever wanting to take a nap. Even now, I don't think I've lost my energy level."

I nod, understanding what he's trying to say.

"Yeah, I get that. I'm not sure I was ever bursting with energy, but I'm sure I wasn't the calmest child, either. I'm sure I've mellowed out a little bit, though. Having two younger brothers will definitely do that to you." I joke, fully meaning it.

"I wouldn't doubt it. I'm sure that's what Julianna would say about me. She claims I've shaved half of her life off after all of the crazy things she's witnessed me do." Johnny says with a chuckle.

"Is it bad that I want to hear a few stories?" I ask with a laugh, genuinely interested.

He couldn't have been *that* much trouble, right?

"Ah, now that's a question. I don't think I ever did anything *outrageous*, but she would say that the time I decided to cliff dive into a lake when it was the two of us was dangerous. I was fifteen, then. She would also say that the time I impulsively spooked a moose that had no clue we were there, is another time she definitely wanted to kill me. Then again, I was thirteen, and completely did the opposite of whatever she wanted me to do. I'll admit that. I'm sure she could tell you a billion stories like that, but most of them didn't stick with me because I didn't find them dangerous or something."

He looks over to me as he ends, surely noticing my mouth

hanging agape.

"You… what? Oh my gosh, you weren't kidding. Wow." I say, his laughter almost drowning out my words.

Archer and Arden look back from in front of us, curiosity displayed across their faces. I make a gesture for them to keep walking.

"Yeah, I guess some of my ideas back then weren't the… brightest. I'll admit that much." Johnny admits with a laugh.

"I have no doubt Julianna has some years shaved off after that." I joke.

"I'm sure she wanted to shave some off of mine, too." He laughs.

The sound is just so contagious that I can't reply, only laughter escaping me.

"Hey! Jamie! We want to show you this bug!" Archer calls out, waving his hands wildly.

Johnny purses his lips in a suppressed laugh as he walks ahead of me and squats down to look at the bug or whatever. I stop a few feet behind them, not wanting to take part in their insect things.

"I'm Johnny. What's your name?" I hear Johnny say, still crouched to their levels.

He sticks his hand out for them to shake, and it's the sweetest thing ever.

They tell them their names and put their small hands in his large one. I can't hear the rest of their conversation, but Arden and Archer start walking again, and I catch up to Johnny.

"They seemed to like you. Maybe they'll remember your name, now." I comment, looking up at Johnny's face as I talk.

"I think so, too. They were so excited to show me their bug—it was a harmless beetle by the way—that they were almost stepping on it in excitement. I think my name is a little bit outdated." He replies, his chuckle at the end sounding like music.

"Outdated or not, it's still really nice. And, yeah, they're obsessed with bugs and gross things like that. Actually obsessed."

Johnny nods his head.

"I'm sure. I think every little boy is obsessed with them. Bugs, snakes, frogs… I actually remember bringing a frog to Julianna's bed one night as she was going to sleep. I'm pretty sure the entire national park heard her screams of horror." He says with a laugh.

"No! You didn't do that!" I gasp, my mind unable to conjure the image of Johnny doing something so horrible. Disbelief flowing through my sentence.

"Oh, I did. Ask Julianna about it, and she can give you every detail. From the date and time, to the pajamas she was wearing. Looking back, it maybe wasn't the best idea." He says with a smirk.

"I… can believe that. Us girls have impeccable memories when it comes to things like that, you know." I say with a laugh.

"Trust me, I know. Growing up with an older sister definitely taught me that lesson." Johnny says.

"Hey, at least you know it." I joke.

"True, true." He replies, his voice drifting as he watches the boys ahead of us.

"Do you like outdoor activities? Like, hiking, scavenger hunts, and stuff?" Johnny abruptly asks, curiosity brimming in his voice.

"Um, yes? I think so. Why? What do you mean?" I ask.

"I was just curious. There wasn't really a reason." He replies, although I'm pretty sure he's trying to fill the silence with conversation.

"What are some of your favorite outdoor things like that?" I ask.

"I really like pretty much everything. I like hiking and swimming a lot, too. What about you? What do you enjoy?" He replies.

"I really like swimming. Hiking is pretty cool, too. I'm not sure if it really counts, but I also really like sitting around a bonfire or something." I reply.

"Nice. Sitting around a campfire or bonfire is relaxing, too. My parents have always laughed at the fact that as soon as I'm sitting by a fire, it's like a switch has been flipped, because I'm so calm." Johnny says, chuckling.

"Really? I mean, it is pretty relaxing to sit and hear it crackling, but what about you?"

"For me, the mix of crackling and the way the flames look, that really… captures my attention? I'm not really sure, honestly. I just sit and think or something." He says.

"That makes sense." I reply, not really sure what else to say.

Johnny nods, pursing his lips and then biting his bottom lip.

As the sky grows darker, I have more trouble seeing the boys ahead of us. It's that weird, in-between stage, when you can see, but you also can't see.

"Hey, boys, let's turn back. It's getting close to bedtime." I call out, waiting for them to turn around and get ahead of us on the way back.

"What time do they go to sleep?" Johnny asks, checking his watch.

I notice from the glow that it's seven-thirty.

"They're supposed to go to sleep at about eight-fifteen. Any later they're a nightmare in the morning." I reply.

"Oh, okay. Gotcha." He says, nodding his head.

We don't talk much on our way back, but I find myself wishing there's conversation filling the silence.

"Ah, you're back." Mom calls out, her cheery voice carrying over to us as we walk towards the cluster of their chairs.

"Archer, Arden, please go inside and get ready for bed." Dad says to the boys as they come and sit on his lap.

"Are you sure it's bedtime? Like, *really* sure?" Arden asks, looking up at Dad, and giggling as he speaks.

"I'm pretty sure. Why don't you go put on your pajamas and come out and we'll check the time together. How does that sound?" Dad says, patting their heads and nodding towards the door.

Once they're inside, I sit down next to Dad, and across from Johnny. The cold fire pit in between us.

I catch his eyes across the low light that's highlighting and shadowing parts of his face, making his ultra dark eyes stand out.

He grins and lowers his eyes, reaching down to pet Berry.

"Did you two have a nice walk with the boys?" Mom asks, glancing between Johnny and I, sending a wave of butterflies through my body.

I'm not sure why, but I can only surmise that it's because of the suggestive look she's giving us.

"Yes, we did. I think we all had a nice time." Johnny replies, raising his head to look her in the eyes as he speaks.

As the adults talk, their conversation drifting from topic to topic, my attention wanders, leaving me to watch Johnny.

His eyes follow their voices, but his brow is furrowed in deep concentration that can't have anything to do with their conversation.

I only realize that I've been staring at him like a stalker, when his head suddenly turns to mine.

He smiles, and I wonder how long he's known that I've been staring at him.

Blushing furiously, I smile back, turning my head, trying to chill the flames of my cheeks.

Out of the corner of my eyes I see Johnny chuckle, his hands clasped in front of him, his elbows on his knees.

Why must I be so weird?

"Johnny, do you mind going inside and finishing up the last few things that need to be done before we leave, tomorrow? There's not much else, but I want us to be gone bright and early." James asks, looking over at Johnny as he speaks.

"Sure, Dad." He responds, standing and nodding his head towards my parents.

"Bye, Johnny. Nice meeting you." Mom says, signaling that she won't see him again.

"Nice meeting you, too." He says with a smile.

Dad reaches out to shake his hand, and Johnny leans down to shake it.

As he walks away, I want to ask him to stay, ask him for a few more minutes of time.

He's definitely the only real friend I've ever had, but what's even crazier is that I hardly know him.

He walks Berry around the side of their home, and I drop all of my embarrassment and do something I'll probably regret later.

Chapter Five

I jump up from my chair, and half jog, half speed-walk around to the other side of their home, hoping to catch Johnny before he walks inside.

"Hey! Uh, wait!" I say, rounding the side.

Johnny looks up surprised, an easy smile appearing at the sight of me.

I stand in front of him for a second or two before I realize that I need to say something to avoid looking even more dumb than I already do.

"I, uh, wanted to say 'bye' before you left." I finally say, looking up into his eyes.

Before Johnny says anything, I impulsively—what is with me being so impulsive lately?—reach out and wrap my hands around his ribs, hugging him.

Johnny stiffens for a second, but gently wraps his arms around my shoulders, his long arms encircling me.

I feel immediate warmth and comfort, and for some reason, that surprises me.

He lets out a long breath, warming my shoulder, sending chills down my back. We hug for an all-too-short amount of time, before I pull away.

"Um, bye. Thanks for spending time with me these last two days." I say.

"No, you don't need to thank me. I enjoyed it. Bye, Laelia."

I look up at Johnny's face, his beautiful eyes, and commit it to memory. There's a large chance I won't see him again.

I turn and leave, feeling exceptionally stupid as our parents give me questioning looks.

I scoop up my dogs who've been patiently waiting in my chair, and make a beeline for the door.

As I shut the door, I notice Katherine looking directly at me, and she gives me the smallest of nods before turning back to her conversation with Dad.

I put my dogs away and grab my clothes to take a shower. I need to wash the fuzziness away from my brain.

I need to remove any thought of not seeing Johnny again.

After washing myself clean of any thoughts, and standing in the fire-hot water for way too long, I lay down in my bed, in hopes of sleep taking me under.

It doesn't.

I shouldn't be this attached to someone so new to my life.

Maybe it's because he's so different from everyone I've ever met? I've never had a friend like Johnny.

I've never had anyone so… genuine in my life.

How is it that I barely know this boy, and I'm acting like this?

I can't be like this.

I flop over, facing the wall, and slam a pillow over my head, committing to going to sleep.

It's not much longer until I hear Mom and Dad walk inside, their half-whispers tempting me to roll over and eavesdrop on them. I only catch a few words, but the ones I hear make my stomach roll.

"-Laelia and Johnny-" And that's all I hear before their voices carry into their room.

———————————

Sitting under a grove of trees underneath the warm, early summer sun is really the best thing ever.

I'm a few feet away from the table that Johnny and I sat together at yesterday, but today, I'm on a blanket reading a book.

Archer and Arden are a few feet away from me on their shared blanket, peacefully asleep.

Mom and Dad needed to go grocery shopping, visit a nearby bank, and run a few other errands before we leave and head to a more permanent place to stay for a few weeks.

So, the boys and I are spending the afternoon together.

Trying to decide on what to spend the rest of the day doing, my mind drifts to Johnny and I playing cards, and laughing at our silly banter.

I'm not a total loser that knows one person, I do have a small group of people I know back at school, and around town, but no one super close.

A sigh escapes me, filling the quiet atmosphere with the heaviness in it.

"Hey, boys, it's time to go back and spend some time at the house." I say, gently shaking their shoulders and waking them.

The rest of the afternoon is spent with movies and popcorn, and I try to commit it to memory.

The twins are only this young once.

And something about Johnny speaking so fondly of Julianna, makes me want to have more impact in the twin's lives.

Chapter Six

"Lae, would you please come in here?" Mom calls from her room.

I raise my eyebrows in curiosity as I set down my phone.

"So, we're considering leaving this place already, and finding somewhere else to spend time at for the next few weeks. What do you think?" Mom asks as I lean my shoulder against the door frame.

"Um, sure. Do you have any idea where it will be?" I question.

"Not really. We're just… bouncing a few ideas around right now. Just wanted to get your opinion on it." She pats my arm, signaling that our conversation is over.

"Okay."

Weird.

The place Johnny is staying at flashes through my head as a place to visit, but I quickly shove the thought out away.

Why must he be a constant thought in my head?

He's *just* a boy.

A *nice* boy.

A nice *friend*.

I haven't really ever had any guy friends before, so in a way, Johnny is… special. It's not that I'm against having male friends, I just haven't found any that I just *click* with.

And, to be honest, I don't really have any female friends, either. We may call each other friends, but in reality, we're not close.

I set my laptop up at the table and I open a new file.

I'm a nonfiction writer.

I mean, that's what makes me money. And people *like* reading it, so I can't seem to figure out why I'm staring at a blank page and feeling the urge to write something outside of what I'm familiar with.

I peck at the keys for a close to an hour, the words flowing.

It's only when I read back on the past eight hundred words do I realize that I hate it.

It's horrible.

I erase it all, feeling disgusted with it.

No one would even read this trash. Why am I writing it?

Shutting my computer with more than a little aggression in my movements, I slide it across the table.

Away from me.

I sigh in defeat and open a book to pass the time, but it doesn't keep my attention for very long.

I opt to power on the television, a romcom currently playing.

Chapter Seven

A week later, I take off on a jog, needing to clear my head, the jogging doing a good job of it until I jog directly into the path of an oncoming bicycle.

I stupidly stop almost directly in front of it.

"I'm so sorry. I-I wasn't paying attention and I should have-"

"Hey, it's okay, Laelia."

I raise my eyes from the tire of the bike, recognizing the familiar voice.

"Johnny? I- how…"

He gives me a goofy grin, and my frazzled nerves calm by a few notches.

"It really was my fault, by the way. I wasn't paying attention to my surroundings, and I should have been keeping my thoughts on my path ahead. I'm sorry."

I look at him for a few seconds, unable to grasp the fact that we're at the same place as each other. I suddenly remember the state of my face and I swipe any tears that might still be there, and brush any stray hairs.

"Are you…"

Johnny doesn't finish the sentence when he sees my face cringe at the question he's surely about to ask.

"How have you been?" I ask, not wanting the attention of our conversation to be on me.

Maybe it's selfish, but deflecting is the easiest way to avoid any awkward conversations at the moment.

"I've been… pretty good. How about you? Have you visited any new places since we last saw each other?"

I shake my head.

"No. Just that one place. How about you? Did you just come straight here?"

He smiles and nods.

"Yeah, we've been here since we left."

"What have you been up to? Is your summer thing over?" I ask, needing to find a topic of conversation.

"Not yet. It actually starts soon. You can probably still sign up, actually." He offers, and I realize I made it sound like I'm interested in it.

"Oh, well, I mean, I'd have to see more about it before I do." I say, and mentally slap my forehead as I realize I've just added more fuel to the fire by insinuating that I'm going to sign up.

Ugh.

"Nice. Well, I'll let you-"

"Actually, can you show me where I would sign up for this summer thing?" I ask, feeling impulsive.

I'm going to hate myself for this later, but oh well.

"Sure. Have you… looked into Teen Summer Fest at all?" Johnny asks, questioning me with his eyes.

"Um, not really, no. Should I?" I ask as Johnny looks at me quizzically for a moment, his eyebrows wrinkle, confusion obvious.

"I guess not. I can show you where to sign up and stuff if you have time right now."

I'm really going along with this.

"Sure. I have… time." I purse my lips remembering the reason I'm even out here.

He dismounts his bike and clips his helmet to the handlebars, walking next to me.

That was considerate.

"It's just this way. Not too far at all." Johnny says, gesturing with his free hand.

"No problem. I really do have plenty of time to spend today." I say, looking up at him and squinting my eyes from the sun as I do so.

He smiles at that, as a result, eyes crinkling shut at their corners ever so slightly.

I don't care who you are, that's cute.

"Do you know how long you'll be here?" Johnny asks, as if just coming to the realization that I might not be here for a long time.

"My dad said that we'll be here for at least a month and a half, but I don't know precise dates."

He nods, and mumbles something to himself that I don't quite catch.

We walk the rest of the way in silence, but it's not comfortable.

At least, for me that is.

Not because it's awkward, but because I *want* to talk to Johnny.

I don't even know what we would talk about, I just want to talk to him.

"Let me chain this real quick, then I can show you how to sign up for TSF." Johnny says, making quick work of chaining and locking his bike.

The front office building is nice, or from what I can see from the outside.

We walk towards the front doors, and Johnny jogs a few steps ahead to open the door, giving me a sly wink as he does so.

I feel my cheeks redden slightly, and I silently thank the manager here for having the air conditioner on, cooling the soft flames in my cheeks.

"Here's the board that has all of the information on Teen Summer Fest." Johnny says, striding across the room to a wall that has various pictures, notes, and announcements.

Teen Summer Fest.

I'm not going to lie, the name is a little bit… unoriginal. Whatever.

It's not like the name takes away from the actual event.

After reading for a few minutes, I gather that the events take place over a few weeks.

Essentially, it's a way to get teenagers into the great outdoors.

The events start tomorrow, actually.

There's a kayaking race, a scavenger hunt, a few bonfires, hikes, fishing, a paintball fight, and a few other things.

Cool.

There's a fee, but it's not that much, so I just glance over it.

"So, there's teams for some things, like the kayaking, scavenger hunt, paintball. Basically, everything. Are you interested in signing up? There's winners at the end, where you and your teammate get a sweatshirt, and a gift certificate for the park. It's not really about the prizes at the end, but I figured I'd mention it." Johnny says, breaking the silence.

"Um, yeah. This sounds pretty fun. Do I have to go over there and sign up?" I ask Johnny, gesturing towards the front desk.

"Yep. I'll help you get signed up, if you'd like."

"Sure. Let's do it now."

I'm all in now, I guess.

We approach the young man at the desk and say hello before asking about registration.

"Okay, and you'd like to sign up for our Teen Summer Fest?" He verifies as he types a few things into his computer.

"Yes."

He nods before going back to his computer.

"And what about you?" He asks looking Johnny up and down.

"I'm already registered, sir." He says politely.

"Alright, that'll be twenty-five dollars, ma'am. Would you like to add your email here? We'll be sending out emails each day with our schedule." He says, looking expectantly at me.

I nod and relay it to him, pulling my wallet out of my cross-body pouch and passing him my card.

He looks at me strangely for a moment, but he swipes it anyways.

"So, are you two going to be teammates?" He absently asks as he punches a few buttons.

"Um," I look over at Johnny hoping that he doesn't already have a teammate.

Darn.

Why didn't I consider that first?

"Yeah, we're going to be teammates." Johnny answers smoothly.

We are?

Yay, I'm glad.

"Cool." He says as he passes me my receipt and my bracelet that has the bold letters 'TSF.'

"Thank you." I say as we turn and leave.

"No problem, have a nice stay."

Once we're outside, Johnny turns to me, and with a grin, he says, "This will be a pretty awesome summer."

Chapter Eight

Johnny catches my eye as I walk past his site, his floppy hair standing out in the slight breeze.

I hadn't realized I would be passing his house when I'd started my walk, but I'd immediately recognized it as I walked closer.

Johnny must've seen me just as I saw him, because he—in the midst of putting a forkful of pasta in his mouth—raises his hand and waves.

I raise mine in a half wave, too, feeling slightly self-conscious when his mom waves me over.

She stands as I reach her, dinner seemingly forgotten.

"Hello, Laelia. How lovely to see you again. How are you doing? And your family?" She gushes as she pulls me into a gentle hug.

"Hi, Katherine. It's really nice to see you again, too. My family and I are really good. We're very excited to be here and see you." I reply, genuinely happy to see her again.

"Would you like to join us for dinner? There's plenty of food, you wouldn't be imposing at all." Katherine asks, gesturing towards the table excitedly.

How should I say that I've already eaten dinner?

Do I just sit down and take a small amount, and then look

rude?

Do I take a normal size and not finish it and look even ruder?

"Oh, I was actually going to run over to the, uh, restrooms, but I'll come back over here and sit with you after. If that's okay?"

Katherine nods. "Of course, I'm sure we'll still be here."

I smile as I turn to leave, my face flushing.

Of course the pipe that would allow our home to hook up the septic is broken, meaning that for the unforeseeable future—until the park can fix it—we'll be using the bathhouse for the showers and restrooms.

At least the place is clean.

I make my way back to their site, having already texted Mom that I'll be hanging out with the Sawyer's for a little bit.

Katherine smiles as I approach, motioning for me to sit next to Johnny. They're all—thankfully—mostly finished with their plates, so I don't make myself anything.

Not that the food looks bad, but I've already made and ate dinner, and wouldn't be able to eat anything more.

"Hi, Johnny. James." I say, bending my head in a little nod as I address them.

"Hello, Laelia. Nice to see you again."

"Yes, it's really nice to see you again, too." Johnny gives me a small grin before returning to the remainder of his food.

"So, do you have any plans for tonight?" Johnny asks, turning to me as he places a forkful of pasta in his mouth.

"I don't think so. I'll probably end up sitting outside reading."

His cheeks puff slightly as he hurries to swallow his food, taking a quick gulp of water after.

Katherine stands and starts clearing dinner before Johnny can respond, motioning for James to help her.

Now, this all happens within a few seconds, but she meets Johnny's eyes and they have a mini conversation with them, both of them making quick glances at me.

She turns to go inside, James behind her, all of their dinner things cleared within seconds.

"Oh, I was just wondering if you wanted to hang out or something. I mean, we'll be hanging out with each other tomorrow, so it's fine if you don't want to." Johnny says, leaning his elbow on the table, resting his head on it. His mouth forming a small smile as he waits for an answer.

I gaze into his eyes for what can only be a few seconds, and for some reason, I'm suddenly very aware of how close we are.

It feels like there's miles between us, but only inches at the same time.

Why am I suddenly aware of how his breathing has slowed slightly, and mine picked up pace?

What's happening?

His eyes are gazing into mine, and I feel everything fading around us.

As if it's only Johnny and I in the world.

A pot clattering inside snaps us out of whatever trance we're in, and I immediately search for an answer to his question.

"I, um, I'm kind of tired. Maybe we can hang out, um, tomorrow? I have a slight headache."

Why did I just say that?

What a total lie, Laelia.

His smile deflates only a little bit, making me feel insanely guilty.

"Oh, that's totally fine. I don't want you to feel pressured into doing things when you don't feel great. I'm, uh, going to go help with dishes and dinner cleanup. Have a nice evening."

Johnny says as he stands, giving me a smile. I smile back as I stand and leave, feeling so guilty for lying.

Why did I get scared?

Why didn't I just stand up to my racing breaths and pumping heartbeat?

I walk more than a little dejected back home, trying to remind myself that I'm the reason I'm walking alone.

Chapter Nine

I drag myself out of bed at six-thirty, and quickly brush and style my hair into two long braids, mentally trying to find an outfit for a scavenger hunt—whatever that entails.

The email I'd opened this morning had been more than a little cryptic regarding what type of scavenger hunt we'd be doing.

I end up deciding on shorts and a T-shirt, sliding on my sneakers and grabbing my bag with my essentials as I walk out the door.

I text Dad that I'm leaving, our agreement from last night.

Even though he's not awake and won't see it for another hour or so, he'd asked me to message him.

I haven't walked more than a few steps before I see Johnny making his way over.

I mentally cringe at how I left things last night, and I hope he isn't harboring any hard feelings.

"Hi, good morning." I say as we reach each other.

"Morning." He says with an easy smile.

"Hey, do you want to give me your phone number or something? I just realized this morning that I don't have it. I wanted to text you and ask where we should meet up." Johnny asks as we walk.

"Yeah, of course."

I pass him my phone and he enters his information as we walk towards the front office. There's already quite a few other teenagers hanging out around the building as we approach.

"Here, you can add your stuff to mine." Johnny says, passing me his phone.

I add my full name and phone number, passing it back to him. As he reads what I put in, I check what he added to his contact in my phone.

"Johnny Rain Sawyer. That's really pretty." I say, looking up at him as he grins.

"Laelia Isabelle Layne is rather pretty, too. Not as pretty as the girl who owns the name, though." Johnny says with a wink.

I instantly feel my cheeks heating in a blush, and I let a small squeak of surprise out.

I look up to find him smirking, and I quickly avert my gaze, not wanting my cheeks to flush any more than they already are.

I don't have a chance to respond to Johnny—not that I'd have a good reply anyway—but because the director of today's activities starts speaking.

"Hi, everyone. I'm Rory. I'll be the director for most of the duration of our Teen Summer Fest, and I'll have help from my assistant, Janelle."

Rory looks to be around sixty, with short, gray hair framing her face.

Janelle is probably about twenty, and has blonde, wavy hair that's a little bit longer than shoulder length.

"This morning we're doing a scavenger hunt to kick of the fun, and this will be a partner event, as will most of activities. If you don't have a partner, please make your way towards me."

There's only a few other pairs besides Johnny and I, and we end up sitting on one of the benches as Rory and Janelle sort out pairs for the other forty-ish teenagers.

"This will be pretty fun, I think. What do you think we'll be looking for on this scavenger hunt?" I ask, wanting to fill the silence with conversation.

"I'm actually not sure. I'm sure we'll be able to find all of the stuff on it, though."

"*All* of the stuff? That's a little over-confident, don't you think?" I ask with a smirk.

"I don't think so. Do you really think we won't be able to find whatever they put on the list?" Johnny replies, a twinkle in his eyes as he speaks.

I purse my lips and pretend to think about it, but I can't keep up my façade when Johnny starts laughing at my antics.

I have to join in after a few seconds, because his laugh is one of those laughs that you can't just ignore.

It's the special kind.

The kind that can make anyone laugh, and the kind that can draw onlookers from anywhere.

"Okay, people. Now that we've partnered you up, come over to Janelle and get your sheet. It has all of the items you'll need to find, and references on where you might find some of the stuff."

Johnny and I stand and get in line to get our paper, the few people ahead of us quickly grabbing theirs and immediately walking away.

"Here you go. Have fun and come back up here once you have everything, or you've decided to turn in your paper early." Janelle says, passing me the paper.

"Okay, so we have a *lot* of items to find." I say, lifting the paper so Johnny can see it, too.

"Ah, that *is* kind of a lot. It'll be fine, though. I think we'll find the woodpecker, rose, and acorn over this way, towards their forest." Johnny says, pointing towards the mountains and the forest.

"Cool, you can lead the way." I respond, glancing up and squinting at the sun at his back.

He nods and starts walking, and I follow.

"So, do you feel better today?" Johnny asks, glancing down for a brief second as he speaks.

Oh, he hasn't forgotten about that.

Perfect.

He doesn't sound like he didn't believe my story, but I'd still rather forget the whole thing. I don't lie, and it makes me so uncomfortable to do so.

"Much. I think that it was just my allergies flaring up for a little bit. I'm definitely better today. Sorry for, um, ditching you… last night. I just didn't want to be a… bummer or anything." I reply, and I have the audacity to sound guilty.

Like I *wanted* to stay.

Well, I *did* want to stay, but I wasn't brave enough to.

"Don't worry, I'm not mad or anything."

I'm eternally grateful to the woodpecker that attracts Johnny's attention, distracting him from asking about last night.

Whatever last night was.

He quickly pulls out his phone and snaps a picture, crossing it off of the list.

We find a few more of the items on the list before we talk again.

"You know you don't have to do all of the activities, right?" Johnny suddenly asks, looking down at me seriously.

"Um, yeah? Do you not want to do some of them?" I ask, worrying that he doesn't want to do the scavenger hunt.

"Oh, no, I just didn't want you to feel pressured into doing any of them that you don't want to do." Johnny quickly responds, taking a breath before he continues.

"I'll do all of the ones that you want to do, and I don't mind missing the ones you don't want to do." Johnny says sincerity in his voice.

"I don't think there are any I'll be against doing, but it means a lot that you don't mind skipping some activities for me. I don't mind skipping any that you don't want to do, either." I reply, hoping my voice conveys my sincerity.

"Thanks. I don't have plans for skipping any, but thanks. Hey, there's the sign we need to take a picture of!" Johnny says, pointing towards the "Welcome to your next vacation!" sign on the side of the path.

"Wow, did you just know that it was going to be out here?" I ask, surprise filling my voice as he takes a picture of it and crosses it off of the list.

"Maybe." Johnny says, wiggling his eyebrows jokingly.

"Did you really?" I press, genuinely wondering.

"Kind of. I had an idea that it would be down this road, seeing as it's the entrance road." I nod, only now coming to the realization that we're far from where we started.

We must be at least a mile away from our site areas.

Cool.

"So, I think we'll turn around now because there shouldn't be anything past this. The only place this leads is the highway, and I'm pretty sure they don't have flattened teenagers on the scavenger hunt." Johnny says with a chuckle, turning as he talks, staying on the side closer to the road.

We walk for a few more minutes before it dawns on me how *alone* we are.

I mean, I knew how alone we were five minutes ago, but now it's at the front of my brain.

"Do you have a drivers license?" Johnny asks a few minutes later, curiosity seeping into his voice.

Oh my gosh, I can't do this right now.

"Um, no. No, I don't. I don't really need one. You do, right?" I say, changing the question and flipping it on him as fast as possible.

"Yeah, I do. I do some of the driving when we're on road trips when my dad is tired." Johnny responds.

"Oh, nice. That's cool." I say, wanting the topic to drop.

Silence stretches between us for a few minutes, but it's broken once Johnny starts talking.

"We only have three more things to find, which, hey, isn't a lot at all." Johnny says, examining the paper, looking up with a smile and happy eyes.

"Wow, you're-"

I break my sentence when I hear a vehicle motor whizzing behind us at an extremely high speed. I turn to see a truck pulling a travel trailer racing up behind us, whipping around the bends in the road as the driver seems to accelerate even more.

"Whoa, that guy is coming up really fast." Johnny says after watching him for a few seconds and assessing what's happening.

When the driver doesn't slow as he approaches dangerously

fast, I instinctively move far away from the road, the trees scraping my arms and legs as I press into them way too fast.

My head is spinning and my hands are shaking.

"Hey, Laelia, those thorns are super sharp!" Johnny says, running the few feet towards me as the truck whizzes by, loose rocks and leaves landing near my ankles.

Johnny gently grabs my upper arm and pulls me out of the brush, concern in his eyes as he looks me up and down.

"Hey, what happened? Are you okay?"

He seems to notice my trembling hands as he says this, and he encloses both of them in his large hands.

"I was… worried the truck would hit us or something, and I accidentally tripped into the brush."

Half lie, half truth, I guess.

It's not true that we were too close to the road and in the path of danger, Johnny had put a safe distance between the road and him.

He still hasn't removed my hands from his, and he's still staring into my eyes.

The warmth and comfort from his hands are seeping into mine, and his soft, dark chocolate colored eyes are addicting.

My breaths are coming in fast, and my heartbeat is picking up pace.

I can feel Johnny's calm pulse on his wrist, and the way he's breathing is nowhere near as erratic as mine.

His breaths are calm and steady, just like his hands that are still enclosing mine.

Johnny's hair is moved by the breeze, and it's catching on his beautiful eyelashes as he blinks, his dark eyes never leaving mine.

I'm in a daze as I try to take in every detail of his face, everything about him drawing me in.

His slightly thick eyebrows and the way they perfectly complement his eyes and nose.

His eyes, and the way the pupils are dilating as he watches me intently, and his puffy lips.

His lips.

It's as if I'm shocked by electricity, and I'm ripped away from my daze.

I jerk my hands away from Johnny's, and I avert my gaze.

I don't even know how long we've been standing here for.

"Hey, I'm sorry for reacting that way towards the vehicle, we should probably be making our way back, don't you think?" I say, only looking up far enough to be looking at his nose, not wanting to make eye contact after… whatever that was.

"Um, yeah. We should probably make our way back." I take a few steps, Johnny falling into line beside me, his hand so close to mine.

We've been walking for about five minutes with no words exchanged between us, and it's painful.

Why did I pull away?

Why did I make things awkward?

My hand feels like it's been set on fire when Johnny's hand brushes against it, sending waves of warmth up my arm.

I keep my head straight, but my eyes shoot downwards.

He subtly pulls his hand closer to him, firmly planting it against the side of his leg, never changing pace.

Maybe he's just not affected by me.

Maybe when he was holding my hands, he felt nothing.

"Look." Johnny says, pointing at a small weed with yellow flowers.

"That's what we need to take a picture of. We'll only have… one more thing to get a photo of. It's a license plate, so I'm betting it's Rory or Janelle's car, which we'll probably find it in the main parking lot." Johnny says after snapping a photo of the weed.

"Wow, okay. Where would I be if I wasn't your teammate?" I ask jokingly, knowing full-well that I wouldn't have signed up for this by myself.

It's not that I did this fully for him, but I wouldn't have had anyone to pair up with.

"You'd be with another teammate that's not near as awesome as me." Johnny replies, a smirk playing across his lips as he teases back.

He's right, though.

Chapter Ten

"Hi, I'm back." I say to my family as I walk back into our site.

It's already one o-clock, and they're eating sandwiches under the shade of the large trees.

"Hi, honey. How was your first event?" Dad asks, offering me a sandwich from the platter.

I take a few bites before responding, the granola bars from this morning not enough after all of the walking I've done.

"Oh, it was so fun. We were actually the team to find all of the items on our scavenger hunt list. The lady, Rory, was surprised to see us back so early; she said that she was expecting close to another hour before seeing teams show up." I say, gushing with pride and excitement.

"Wow, isn't that nice. You're on a team with that boy, John, right?" Mom asks, looking up from the book she's reading out loud for the boys.

"Yes, I'm on a team with Johnny. He's a pretty great partner." I say, taking another few bites.

I'd emphasized Johnny's name, but not enough to make it seem as though I was being rude.

"Oh, yes, Johnny. Sorry, dear." Mom says before reading again.

"That's great. I'm glad you're having fun here. I'm really enjoying it here, too. There was a fun little trail that the boys and I walked on earlier, and we really liked it." Dad says, taking a sip of his water after he finishes.

"That sounds fun. There's supposed to be a lot of fun trails and stuff. Johnny said there's a ton of outdoor activities to do here. I think there might even be a swimming pool here." I say, whispering the last part so that Archer and Arden don't hear me.

Dad nods, taking a few more bites of his sandwich before picking up his book and reading.

I finish my food and walk inside, taking Colin and Jasper out of their playpen and placing them on the couch with me as I pull open my laptop.

They lick my fingers for a few seconds before laying down and napping while I write.

I'm conflicted on which draft to open, but after a few minutes of deliberation, I open my newer draft and let the words suck me in.

It seems like no time has passed by the time my phone alarm buzzes.

We've already eaten dinner and been on a family walk, and everybody except for me is in my parent's room, watching a movie.

"I'm leaving." I call through their bedroom door, Mom and Dad nodding as I turn to leave.

I walk outside into the cool night air, not having an idea on where the bonfire will be taking place.

The main office will probably know.

Sure, I skimmed the email with all of the details about the bonfire, but I'm sure there wasn't any information on where to find it.

I walk into the office a few minutes later, feeling slightly jumpy after walking alone in the dark.

The guy behind the desk is the same guy from a few days ago, and after asking for directions, I'm on my way across the park. He said it's near the back, so after around ten minutes of walking, I'm glad to smell smoke, and see the firelight.

"Hey, you made it." Johnny says walking towards me, the firelight at his back shadowing his face.

The shadows somehow making his face even more beautiful.

"Yeah, I did. I had no idea where I was going." I say with a laugh.

"Oh, sorry about that. I should have gone back to walk you over, sorry." Johnny says with an apologetic voice.

"No, no, it wasn't your fault or anything. I should have known where I was going *before* I left." I reply, not liking how he's blaming himself for it.

"Everyone, gather around, please." Rory calls out, interrupting our conversation.

We walk the few steps towards everyone, and are pressed close when a boy to my left knocks me into Johnny, the force making me hit him much harder than a slight jostle.

"Hey, Jayden, watch out."

Someone next to the boy that knocked into me says.

I look over, thinking someone messed up Johnny's name—or somehow confused me for Johnny—realizing that the boy who bumped into me is named Jayden, and the boy who spoke is his friend, and is lightly scolding him.

Johnny grabs my arm to steady me, but doesn't look away from

Rory.

He also doesn't release my arm, his hoodie sleeve brushing my bare arm, and his large hand wrapped around my arm, slightly below my elbow.

"I'm so glad to see so many of you attending our Teen Summer Fest. Really, it touches my heart that you're taking time out of your summer to spend time with us."

Johnny's hand slips lower down my wrist, his fingers loosening ever so slightly.

The warmth from where his hand just was leaving tingles in its wake.

"When we started this event a decade ago, we had a mission to bring more teenagers out into the world of nature and teamwork. Never did we expect so many eager faces, both new and old."

Johnny's hand slides even lower, and my breathing becomes irregular.

Is he… holding my hand?

Not really.

His hand is still near the top of my wrist, but that does nothing to calm my racing heartbeat.

"I want to take a few minutes to go over our rules and expectations for this summer. One thing that we really prioritize is safety. If any of you feel uncomfortable or you don't want to continue, please come to me and we can figure something out. If you want to speak to me about anything, come to me. We want to make this an amazing experience for everyone, so please don't hesitate if you need any type of help."

Johnny slips his hand lower, his hand wrapped entirely around mine now. I suck in a breath, and I hear Johnny let out the smallest chuckle.

I'm sure that my cheeks are red, and that he can feel my pounding pulse on my wrist.

"With all of that being said, let's kick off our Teen Summer Fest!" Rory says, excitement in her voice.

I'll be honest, I couldn't care less about what she's saying, because just then, Johnny slides his fingers through mine, and now we're holding hands.

I risk looking down at our joined hands, and look up to see Johnny looking down at me.

Neither of us say anything, the shuffling of people around us and the crackling fire all becoming background noise.

Our eye contact doesn't last for more than thirty seconds, but it seems like an eternity.

"Everyone, you can pull your chairs out and set them up while Janelle and I open the s'more stuff." Rory calls out, breaking Johnny's focus on me.

"Hey, let's pull out our chairs." Johnny says, sliding his hand up my arm and wrapping it around my shoulders.

Oh my gosh.

We walk towards the chairs that everyone had brought, and I just now come to the realization that I forgot my chair.

"Oh, shoot." I say, feeling mortified because of my carelessness.

"What's wrong?" Johnny asks, reaching down to pick up his large camp chair, his arm sliding from my shoulder.

"I forgot my chair. I'm going to walk back and grab it." I say, turning to walk away before Johnny gently grabs my wrist.

"You can share mine if you want. It's a long walk back to our campsites." Johnny says.

Share the chair?

I mean, it *is* one of those large puffy ones, but… share?

What are the chances that I could erupt into flames?

"Oh, sure."

Why did I just say that?

Am I crazy?

Yes, yes I am.

He smiles as we walk to an open spot around the fire, and he opens the chair.

Oh my gosh, there is no way we'll be able to just *share* the chair. We'll be sitting pressed against each other.

"Do you want a s'more? I can make you one, if you'd like." Johnny says, obviously coming to the same realization that I just did.

He seems to be only realizing this now, and if the moment weren't so mortifying, I might just laugh at him for only realizing now.

"Um, yeah, that sounds nice. Would you toast the marshmallow only a tiny bit, though? Like, the slightest bit golden." I ask, a hopeful tone in my voice.

"Sure. How many do you want? I can put them on a plate so they don't get messy if you want more than one." Johnny's thoughtfulness brings a smile to my face.

"Two, please. Thanks."

Johnny gives me a joking salute and he turns to make the s'mores.

My chest flutters as he walks away, but I brush the feeling away. I sit down in the soon-to-be-shared chair, and I pull my knees up to my chest.

I really like right now.

The thought swirls through my mind as I wait for Johnny.

"Here you go, ma'am." Johnny says, carrying two plates of s'mores, passing me one.

I squeeze into the back of the chair, pressing myself into the side, trying to make room for Johnny.

He delicately sits down, pressing himself to the other side of the chair.

I take a bite of the s'more, trying to dismiss the fact that Johnny's whole left side is pressed against me.

"Hey, this is *perfect*. You toasted it just how I like it." I say, turning my head and lifting my s'more some so he can see it.

"Ah, really? I always make mine almost black, so I was worried I'd make yours too toasted." Johnny says, a small laugh at the end of his sentence.

"It's perfect."

I move my legs slightly, trying to not make it seem as if they're as uncomfortable as they are.

"You can put your legs… on mine." Johnny says, not looking at me as he talks, surely feeling as uncomfortable as I do.

I suck in a breath, mustering up the courage to move them.

Do I really want them to stay crushed against the side?

No.

It's honestly *so* uncomfortable.

Do I want them to be… on Johnny's?

Not really.

But, it's the better of the two options.

I gently lay them across his, my cheeks flaming as I do so. I move my eyes enough to see Johnny's face… flushed?

No.

He's so calm and collected, there's no way this is embarrassing to him.

He takes a bit of his second s'more, avoiding eye contact with me.

He has no right to look this calm during this tense moment.

I relax as the minutes flow by, the crackling fire and peaceful night atmosphere working their charm on me.

"Did you like the scavenger hunt this morning?" Johnny asks, turning his head towards me, folding his paper plate into methodical lines, folding them over and over as he watches me.

"Yeah, I did. I really like it here. It's… different. I've never been somewhere with this vibe. I don't know how to describe it. It's just special here."

Johnny nods, silently agreeing with me.

"It is different here. I've always felt like this place had something different about it, too. I'm not sure what we'll be doing tomorrow, but I think you'll really like the trails around here. They're pretty cool."

I don't have a chance to respond, because Johnny's phone makes an alert noise like he has a message.

He pulls it out and opens it swiftly, chat messages showing up.

"Sorry, my mom wanted to check in with me, seeing as it's night and all." Johnny says, showing me the screen as if I asked for proof.

"Is this in Korean?" I ask, my eyes skimming over the message that I can't read.

"Oh, yeah. Sorry. My mom only speaks to me in Korean—messages, too—and my dad only speaks in Japanese to me. That's how they've been doing it since Julianna and I were born. Do you speak in Spanish with your mom and brothers, too?" He asks, quickly typing out a message in Korean, his fingers flying across the screen.

I purse my lips, not enjoying the direction of the conversation.

"Um, some. Not really though. My grandparents taught me. They're not around anymore." I say, not wanting the conversation to continue, because I can feel my throat tightening and my voice dropping.

Johnny nods, stuffing his phone into the chair pocket.

"I'm sorry. I didn't mean to upset you or anything." He apologizes.

I nod, the knot in my throat loosening.

We sit in a comfortable silence, both of us staring into the fire, the chatter of everyone else filling the air.

I shiver slightly in the cool evening air, my T-shirt not doing much in the warmth area.

Johnny notices and wraps his arm around shoulder, the motion allowing me to lean my head lightly on his shoulder.

He rests his head on top of mine, the weight of it feeling… right.

Everything about this feels right.

Johnny's fingers brush against my arm, sending small goosebumps over my arm, but I chalk it up to the cool air.

Johnny does it again, and the same thing happens. He sucks in a small breath, resting his hand on my arm.

"Is anyone interested in the history of this place?" Rory calls out as the talking thins, and the only amount noise is coming from the crickets and bonfire.

A few calls of "yes" come from the crowd, and Rory clears her throat before she starts speaking again.

"It's kind of a twisted story that not many are interested to hear, but it's pretty interesting. About twenty-three ago years, the owners and creators of this place were scammed, and 'double bought' this place, if that makes any sense. Maryanne and Carter, the owners, had individually bought the place, both with intentions to create some type of resort slash campground. The original owner had swindled them, and sold it to both of them individually, making double the amount of money he would have made if only one of them bought it, and tried to flee the country."

She pauses for a sip of water before continuing.

"In the process of all of this—don't worry, the seller was placed in prison soon after—out of spite for each other, they both started construction on their dream place—mind you, they pretty much hated each other—but after a while, they softened a little, realizing they could benefit from each other's ideas. That's how this place came to be. Not many places have a place to hike and a swimming pool, for one example. Soon enough, they fell in love and got married, their baby, Janelle, coming soon afterwards. If you didn't know." Rory winks, before continuing. "Janelle is my grandaughter."

Janelle gives a little wave next to Rory, and there's a faint blush playing across her cheeks. There's a chorus of "aw" and "wow" throughout the crowd, my own voice included.

There's a few moments of silence, and I realize that Johnny's breathing is now completely relaxed and normal, and while everything feels 'right,' there's still tension in my shoulders, and my heartbeat hasn't fully settled.

"The fire will probably be burned out within the next fifteen minutes, so, to any of you that are itching to get into your nice warm beds, you're completely free to depart." Rory announces, waving to the people who start to pack up their chairs.

"Do you want to head back?" Johnny whispers in my ear, making all of the hair on my neck stand up, goosebumps erupting along my neck and shoulders.

Does he want to go back?

"Sure, I'm pretty tired." I admit, internally panicking thinking about how awkward it's about to get.

How are we going to stand up without making things extremely weird?

I quickly place my hand on the side of the chair and essentially jump out of the chair, fanning my hair around my face to hide.

Thank goodness I didn't fall into the burning embers or something when I launched myself out of there.

Johnny stands, and quickly folds the chair into it's carrier.

He nods his head slightly, motioning in the direction that we need to walk.

"So, did you like the bonfire?" Johnny asks after a few minutes of silence.

Did I?

Well, now that I'm overthinking everything that just happened, maybe.

Who sits in the same chair as someone else, practically— scratch that actually—cuddling?

What was I even thinking?

"Yeah, for sure. Thanks for making me the perfect s'more." I say, looking up at him as he grins.

"What can I say, s'mores are a talent of mine." Johnny jokes.

"Obviously."

When the approaching shadow of a man walking alone appears ahead of us, I press close to Johnny, feeling slightly alarmed.

Why?

I'm not sure.

Maybe it's the lack of sleep, or the events of tonight, but I'm on edge.

Johnny wraps his free arm around my shoulder, pulling me even closer than I'd dared to be. The woodsy-sweet smell of his hoodie inches from my nose.

We don't say anything for the rest of the walk, Johnny's arm staying firmly wrapped around my shoulders.

Johnny stops us so he can drop off his chair, insisting that he walks me the rest of the way home.

Without much warning, a light sprinkle falls from the sky, dampening us within seconds.

I don't know what comes over me, but I laugh and look up at Johnny's amused smile as I gently pull away from him, and I do a twirl in the rain, my hair becoming plastered to my face.

I don't care.

We're the only people out here now, just us in the middle of the road and the rain.

"Let's get you back home before you become any more drenched." Johnny says, gently wrapping his fingers around mine, and pulling me as we run, the rain around us making it hard to see anything.

I don't care, though. I trust that Johnny's not going to trip or lead us into a dip in the road.

That he's going to get me back home safely.

Within what feels like seconds, we're back at my house, and Johnny is pulling away.

"I'll see you tomorrow. Goodnight." Johnny says, giving me one last wistful look before he turns and jogs back home.

I slowly walk inside, careful to not wake anyone. I end up pulling on fuzzy pants, too tired to change anything else.

Chapter Eleven

"Hey, honey, your alarm has been going off." Dad says, gently rubbing my shoulder, awakening me from a deep sleep.

I immediately sit up, my blanket wrapped around me like a taco.

"What? Oh, okay." I say, still in my delirious sleep-like state.

"Yeah, I just dismissed it, but you should check and see if you have anything to do if you're going go back to sleep." I nod, rubbing my eyes as I pull out my phone.

There's a cooking class at twelve, but it doesn't specify what we'll be cooking.

I flop my head back down on my pillow, and the events of last night come flooding back.

What if Johnny brings up the chair and essentially cuddling?

I hardly know him, and I'm this comfortable with him?

What is wrong with me?

I bury myself deeper into my blankets.

After a few moments of deliberation, I decide to take a shower now, and I make a quick run the to the bathhouse to take my shower.

I start breakfast after I've showered, and by the time it's finished, I've deluded myself into believing none of yesterday happened.

I take my computer outside and I pull out my new manuscript, sucking in a few deep breaths before I start writing. The few hours that I have to spare are quickly used on my writing, and it's time for me to get ready for the cooking class.

I take the few minutes to braid my hair before I leave, the two braids reaching down my back.

"Mom, Dad, I'm leaving. I'll see you later." I call through the screen-door, my tennis shoes slapping against the steps.

I walk in the direction of the outdoor event area, expecting to see Johnny any time now.

I spot him as I approach the tables that have been set up, ingredients on each table.

Johnny smiles when he sees me, and he jogs over from talking to Janelle.

"I've pried the recipe from Rory." He announces as soon as he's near.

"Oh? Were we not supposed to have a recipe?" I ask, slightly confused on if he's joking or not.

"Well, we're supposed to have it, but only when everyone else does, too."

I nod.

"Ah, got you. When will everyone else be here?" I ask, looking around for more people.

Johnny shrugs his shoulders.

"I'm not sure. The class starts in ten minutes, so hopefully soon. We're making homemade pasta, by the way." Johnny says, gesturing towards a table that has two aprons and measured out ingredients in cups and bowls.

A few minutes pass by as more and more kids show up to the

class, and soon enough, what looks to be everyone has shown up.

"Okay, please have a member of your team come get a recipe, and everyone put on your aprons." Janelle calls out.

Johnny flips the recipe up and winks before he gives me an apron, and I hate that I blush at the action.

"Hey, can you tie this?" I ask Johnny, flicking the apron strings on my back.

"Sure. Will you tie mine, after?" He asks as he pushes up his sleeves and gathers the long strings and gently pulls it tight around my waist, his fingers brushing my back as he ties it off.

He quickly turns so that I can do the same for him, and it does feel a little strange to be doing this. I pull the strings tight, and my hands shake a little as I attempt to tie off the ribbons.

Why?

I don't know.

It takes a few times before I make a decent bow, and as soon as I'm done, I rip my hands away, even though that's the last thing I want to do.

"We'll be making pasta, and I know it sounds hard, but it's really easy… after you get the hang of it." Janelle calls out cutting the tension with her voice, sounding like she regrets offering to help with this activity.

"That sounds promising." Johnny jokes as he picks up the recipe and passes it to me.

"Yeah, I know." I reply, scanning the recipe before reaching for the flour.

We work without talking for a few minutes before I realize that Johnny is completely taking the lead and mixing the ingredients with intense concentration.

"Have you made pasta before?" I ask after a few minutes of his concentration and my watching.

"Oh, yeah. I have a few times. Julianna had a 'making things homemade' phase, and somehow I was persuaded into making her homemade pastas while she did the sauces." He replies as he uses the fork expertly.

What has this boy not done?

He's actually great at everything.

"Wow. I bet you're silently thanking her for the experience now, huh?" I ask as he motions for me to give it a try.

"Do you want to do this?" He asks, moving his hands in the dough.

"What do I do?" I ask as Johnny pulls my hand into the doughy stuff, the texture extremely strange under my hands.

I tense my hands, not wanting to mess anything up.

Wordlessly, he moves his hands on mine, the gentleness in his motions making my hands tingle as he shows me how to move the dough.

After a few minutes of this, Johnny pulls our hands back.

"Okay, we need to stretch it and cut it. Then, we can cook it." Johnny says, pushing the few things on the table out of the way.

I stand back as he stretches it, the breeze making the few flyaway hairs brush my face. I brush the few pieces away with my hands, a few of them sticking to my eyelashes.

Sure, I like cooking, but this is a *little* out of my comfort zone.

"Here, this is how you stretch it. It needs to be super thin." Johnny explains, showing me what to do.

Oh, he wants me to do this, too.

I follow his motions, and after a few minutes, it becomes easy.

"Do we need to cut it? We can over stretch it, right?" I ask after it's pretty thin on my side.

"Um, yeah. I'm trying to remember how-" Johnny starts, before stopping when a girl a few tables down starts screaming at her partner.

"I told you that's *not* how we're supposed to do this! Now look at where we are!" The girl screams at the guy with her.

"I'm just trying to remember on how to tell if it's ready to cut and cook." Johnny finally finishes, a confused expression on his face.

"I can ask Janelle or Rory. They would know." I offer.

"Yeah, let's ask them and see what they say. I mean, I *think* it's done, but I don't really know for sure." Johnny says sheepishly.

I nod as I turn towards Janelle and Rory.

"Hi, do you mind looking at our pasta? We're not really sure if it's done." I ask Rory as she walks away from another table.

"Of course, dear. You're over there with Johnny, right?" Rory asks as she starts towards our table.

"Yes, we're partners." I reply, walking in step with her.

"Ah, your pasta is looking lovely. It looks about ready to cut and cook." She comments as she examines the pasta.

"Thank you, we'll cut it, now." Johnny replies.

"Okay, if that's it, I think Janelle might need help with that pair over there." She says gesturing at the pair that had been yelling at each other a few minutes ago.

"Thank you." I call out as she walks away.

I turn to Johnny, the grin on his face contagious.

"Well, it appears that our pasta is turning out pretty well." I say, surveying the stretched pasta.

"Do you want to cut it? There's a few tools to cut it with. We could also make some cool shapes, too." Johnny says, motioning at the knife, scissors, and pizza cutter.

"Sure, maybe you can cut the first few pieces?" I say, putting my hands behind my back in a clear 'you go ahead' motion.

He nods as he uses the scissors and cuts two long strips of the uncooked pasta.

"Here, you try now. It's really not hard. I'm sure it'll be easy for you." Johnny says, sliding the tool into my hand, his warm hand sending an electric current up my arm.

I cut two strips before I lay the scissors down for Johnny to cut the last few pieces. "Do I just… scrunch it up when I make a shape?" I ask Johnny, looking up questioningly.

"Yes. You can kind of make those bow pastas if you do… this." He says, moving his hands on mine and making a bow shaped pasta with one of my pieces.

His large, veiny hands completely covering mine.

"Oh okay, that kind of makes sense the way that you did it." I reply, pressing the other piece into another bow looking piece.

"That's really good. You're already an expert." Johnny says looking down with a grin.

I smile back, having to look up through my eyelashes and squint against the sun.

Johnny starts a pot of water, and within minutes it's ready for us to cook the pasta.

"Ooh, this is the exciting part." I say, peering over the edge of the pot as Johnny drops a few of his pieces in the boiling water.

"Yeah. I have a feeling these will be pretty good." Johnny says after a few minutes as he removes the cooked pieces, laying them out on a plate.

"We should ask Janelle or Rory to come judge them before they're sticky." Johnny mentions as he removes the last few pieces from the water.

"Oh, yeah, we should. I was about to offer my services as a taste tester." I reply with a laugh, embarrassed that I almost offered to eat it before it had been judged.

"Oh, your pasta looks amazing." Rory says from behind me as she comes by.

"Thank you. Do we need to do anything else to have it judged?" Johnny asks, folding his hands behind his back.

I walk around the table to do the same beside him, giving Rory a full view of our pasta.

She looks down at the pasta and back up at us a few times before using one of the forks on the plate to take a piece of pasta and dip it in the tomato sauce before popping it in her mouth.

"Wow, absolutely delicious. You two definitely passed this cooking class. Good job." Rory says before turning to go to the next table down.

Johnny turns and looks down at me, his wide smile excited.

I smile back up at him, excitement surely in my gaze.

"Oh, you have a little bit of the pasta dough on your eyelash." Johnny says, gesturing towards my face.

That must've happened when my hair got stuck.

I rub at it for a second, surely getting it off.

"It's still there... it's probably dried." Johnny says.

Oh my gosh, this is so embarrassing.

"Do you mind getting it off?" I ask, feeling somewhat shy.

Johnny nods, and I feel the gentle brush of his finger on my eyelid as Johnny tries to remove the dough, the touch sending little bolts of electricity through my face.

It only takes a few seconds for him to remove it, but it feels like an eternity.

Johnny gently slides a few hairs behind my ear as he pulls away, the motion setting my cheeks on fire.

"There, it's all gone."

I look up at Johnny's soft smile, mirroring it with my own.

"Thank you, my knight in shining armor." I say as I turn towards the table, and fork a piece of pasta into the sauce before dropping it in my mouth.

"Hey this is pretty good. I think we're a good team." I say, turning to find Johnny stepping forward, his hands still behind his back, curiosity and something else playing across his face.

He takes a piece for himself and nods while eating it.

"I agree. None of my pastas have tasted this good." Johnny says after swallowing his piece.

"Do you have anything planned after this? We could go on a walk or something. I mean, if you have something else, that's totally fine." Johnny asks as he absentmindedly swipes excess flour from the table into a trash bag, quickly stringing on the last part of his sentence.

Do I?

"I can go on a walk. That sounds… nice. Maybe we can have a picnic or something?" I ask.

"Yeah, that sounds great. There's a nice area—kind of by where the bonfire was—that has picnic tables and an open area where people play frisbee and stuff." Johnny adds as he finishes wiping the table.

"Cool. If we're done here—we can ask Rory if we are—then we can make our food and then walk over to the place you mentioned?" I say, reaching behind me to untie my apron, but the tie isn't some ordinary bow.

Johnny slips his off easily, leaving me fumbling with mine.

"Oh, sorry." Johnny says, noticing my fingers fumble the tie.

He reaches out and pulls the strings a few times before the tie comes undone.

"Thanks." I reply, folding the apron as Johnny walks over to Janelle and asks her if we're free to leave.

"We're good to go. Apparently we're one of the few teams to actually get past the dough phase." Johnny says with a small chuckle.

"Yikes. Then again, no one else had your pasta skills on their team." I say, a joking tone in my voice, but truthfulness behind it.

He ducks his head and smiles at my compliment, stuffing his hands into his pockets.

"Do you want to head out? I think I'll need to take out Berry before we eat." Johnny says.

"Oh, yeah, for sure. Do you want to bring her? I wouldn't mind if you brought her along. I could bring Colin and Jasper, too." I ask, a smile forming on his face as I pose the question.

"Yes, I could definitely bring her." Johnny replies, nodding as he speaks.

We walk back in a comfortable silence, Johnny stopping at his place as I walk the distance to mine.

I notice the car is gone, meaning Mom and Dad probably went into town to the grocery store or something.

I make myself some sliced fruit and vegetables, and a sandwich, before taking Colin and Jasper from their playpen and placing them in their stroller outside.

I set my lunch and water bottle in the bottom of the stroller as I walk towards Johnny's house.

I see Berry's familiar black coat as I approach Johnny.

He has a small bag slung across his shoulder, presumably carrying his lunch.

I reach down and pat Berry's head, her long tongue licking my hands as she wags her tail.

"Lead the way." I say from my lowered position as I pet Berry.

He's smiling down at us—Berry, really—and I stand so he can start walking.

"So I know that you've been coming here for a while, but what started the… tradition? Are there other places that you visit this often, too?" I ask after a few minutes of walking, just as Johnny starts speaking.

"So, why do you use a stroller for them?" As he motions towards us.

We look at each other for a second before Johnny's lips press together in a concealed laugh that he can't contain.

"Sorry, what did you ask?" He questions after a second.

I repeat it, and he nods as he listens.

"Um, really, I think it's because this time of year the weather here is super nice, there's tons of stuff to do, and… I'm not sure. There are other places that we like to visit at least once a year, like, we always try to go to Montana and California. I don't think we really meant for it to become a tradition, but here we are."

I nod, not really knowing how to respond. Nothing he said was bad or anything, just… what am I supposed to respond with?

"Cool. What did you ask me? Sorry, I don't remember."

"Oh, I asked why they have a stroller. I don't think—no offense in any way, really—I've ever seen dogs in a stroller before." Johnny says, genuinely nothing judgmental or rude in his voice.

"Well, when I got them they were so small, and I was afraid of them being… I don't know, stepped on? Knocked over? When I went on walks, so I actually have these sling things for them—kind of like something you'd use on a baby—but I also got this because sometimes it's easier to just push them around instead of carrying them. And, it's nice that it's sort of two layers, because I can put things down there like drinks, snacks, their food and water, I think I still have cards in there. Wow, I sound like a total dog mom. Don't judge me." I say, adding on the joke at the end.

"That's cool. Do you use the carrier things more? Maybe when you go on a hike or something?" He asks, not sounding judgmental or anything, simply just curious.

I nod.

"Yeah, actually that's when I most use them. I'm sure you guessed that this thing is more than a little inconvenient to use when it's an unpaved path."

Johnny agrees with a nod of his head, but his lips are pursed as he looks ahead, something else obviously the object of his attention.

"Do you go on hikes often? Is it something you enjoy?" Johnny asks as we approach the tables under the large trees, their shade making the breeze feel even cooler than before.

"Yeah, for sure. As long as it's not super rough terrain or anything, or if it is, I'm properly prepared. One time, I went on a school field trip, and for some reason, the person organizing it wasn't paying attention when the website said that it was an intense hike, and we ended up being on this rocky, side-of-a-mountain trail for five hours, and before we were even halfway in, everyone was out of water. There was also no cell service." I reply, realizing that my answer was much longer than necessary.

Johnny is laughing as I finish his hair flopping as he does so, obviously finding my story funny.

As if he's reading my thoughts, he tries to contain his laughter as he talks.

"I'm really not laughing at you, really, but I have to imagine that by the end everyone was ready to commit crimes to be off of that trail. Once you run out of water, it's not fun and games anymore." Johnny says through small spurts of laughter.

"Oh, for sure. I would have committed crimes for simply a sip of water. Let's not forget this was an end of the semester trip, meaning it was essentially summer." I say, pulling my food out and laying out across from Johnny as he does the same.

I notice that he has everything neatly placed in his food container, his sandwich, sliced fruit, peanut butter, and chips—surprisingly similar to what I packed—all in their own unique sections.

Johnny and I both say a quick prayer before eating, and he picks up a slice of his apple and dips it into his peanut butter.

I take a bite out of one of the halves of my sandwich, the other triangle still neat on my plate.

"Hey, we have almost identical lunches." Johnny comments as he takes a drink from his water bottle.

"Yeah, we do. What sandwich did you make? Mine is just an onion, lunch meat, cheese, and avocado." I ask.

"Well, some people find it weird, but mine is a grilled cheese with sliced pickles inside. I don't know, I read about it one time and had to try it. Now, it's my go-to sandwich." Johnny says, ducking his head in a laugh as he does so.

"I mean, it sounds… interesting. Maybe a *little* weird, but I haven't had one so I won't judge you until I make and try one." I say, trying to keep a neutral face, when, inside, I'm seriously questioning this boy's taste buds. Of course I'm never going to make one, but I added that part for his benefit.

"Oh, well, you can have this half if you want to try it." Johnny says, motioning down at the other half of his sandwich in the container.

"Are you sure?"

"Yeah, for sure. Really." Johnny looks hopeful that I'll try it, and I *am* slightly curious as to how it tastes.

"Sure, I'll try it, but you have to try half of mine, too." I say, motioning down at the uneaten half of my sandwich.

"Okay, cool. Deal."

We swap sandwich halves and take bites at the same time, both of us quiet.

"Review time. Do you think it's gross?" Johnny asks, curiosity in his voice.

"I mean, honestly, it was good. I don't think I'd just make it for lunch, but I did enjoy it and would eat it if it was served to me." I genuinely say.

Johnny nods, and states that he really enjoyed my sandwich, which, I don't know if it's a good or bad thing, but my stomach does a little flutter when he says that. It must be his sandwich doing that to me.

"Hey, do you want to play a card game?" Johnny asks, and I'm instantly transported back to when we first met.

"Yeah, I'd love to. What do you have in mind?" I ask as he pulls cards out of his bag.

"Well, I can teach you a game that Julianna and I made on one of our many hours-long road trips." Johnny offers, shuffling the deck.

"Okay, that sounds fun. What is it called?" Johnny bites his lip before answering.

"Ice Cream. We both wanted ice cream that day, so it fit. I think we both expected to forget it, but we ended up wanting to play it all the time afterwards."

I have to purse my lips and hope that my cheeks don't betray me and turn pink, because, oh my gosh.

How am I supposed to even respond to that?

Something *that* cute?

Johnny explains the rules and I'm not sure I fully understand it, but we begin a round.

Berry laying next to Johnny's feet in the cool shade, and Jasper and Colin fast asleep in their stroller.

We actually go back and forth a few times without me messing up, and I have to admit that fourteen-year-old Johnny, and seventeen-year-old Julianna made a pretty fun game.

We both continue eating our lunches, almost no words between us.

What must their relationship be like?

A small pang of jealousy runs through me when I remember that they're so close in age that they always had a friend.

They seem… close.

I mean, creating games together?

Johnny pops a piece of his fruit in his mouth just as I lay a card down, and without hesitation, he picks it back up and slides it back into my hands, our fingers brushing as he does so.

The tingling still hasn't stopped as he pulls a card from one of the sets laid out in front of me, and sets it in the discard.

"You want to get rid of these cards first." He says gently after swallowing his food.

"O-okay." I say, completely fumbling for words now.

I run the rules of the game over in my head again, and I come to the realization that if Johnny let me discard the one I originally had tried to, he would've benefited from it.

"What do you do in your free time?" I ask, and I'm not quite sure where the words come from.

I didn't consciously decide to ask Johnny that.

I'd just been thinking about how it would be cool to know what he does with his time.

What he enjoys, spends time on, what interests him.

He looks up from his cards, his expression going from ultra-focused on his cards, to me.

"Um, I go on walks, study, ride my bike, and fish, really. Those are the first things that come to mind. Why?" He responds.

Why?

"No reason, really. I was just curious as to how you spend your time since you probably don't stay in one place long enough to have a grounded hobby, you know?" Johnny nods.

"That's actually a question I get a lot. I guess I never really think about it like that. I kind of keep to myself most of the time—not that I don't get out into whatever community I'm in—but I have my things that I enjoy doing, and I'm pretty good with that. What do you do in your free time? Is there a difference in your hobbies compared to when you're going to school and at your house versus when you're traveling?" He asks, laying down a card as he waits on my answer.

Johnny keeps to himself most of the time?

"I usually read and write, but I also enjoy cooking. When I'm back at our house and in school, I participate in some clubs, but not much. Like I said before, I'm easygoing." I say, a little bit of a different meaning than when I'd originally stated them.

Johnny purses his lips and lays down a card before answering, a calculating look playing across his face.

He doesn't reply to what I've said, and I'm not sure why that disappoints me.

"I'm going up to the lake after this, do you… want to come? I might just walk around the water and hang out for a little bit. Tomorrow is the kayaking thing, and my dad is encouraging me to check out the lake ahead of time. He wants to know what the water is like before I kayak tomorrow. You could see the place before it's time for you to get in the kayak." Johnny asks, looking up into my eyes as he speaks.

"How far away is it? I'll need to be back by about five." I question, wanting to go.

"It's a little bit away, but only about a thirty minute hike after we get to the trail head."

That's plenty of time.

And, seeing as Mom and Dad aren't here, they won't need me to watch the boys.

"Yeah, sure. That sounds cool. Thanks for offering. Do you want to leave soon?" I ask.

"Um, yeah, we can. That way you get back with plenty of time to spare. Let's pack up and we can put the dogs away, then we can leave."

I nod, agreeing.

We pack up and go back to our homes, and I hurry to fill my water bottle and grab my bag.

When I walk inside, to my absolute horror, I see Johnny pulling up in front of my house in his truck.

What?

How did he forget to mention that the 'little bit away' meant that we had to be in a vehicle?

The front windows are rolled down, and he's put it in park as he waits for me.

I can only stomach the idea for a few seconds more, before I run back inside, the door slamming behind me.

Chapter Twelve

How am I going to do this?

I can't just skip out on Johnny, now.

Can I?

No, that's not an option.

Johnny isn't in his truck anymore, he's waiting a few feet away from it, almost as though he's trying to decide if he should come knock on my door and check on me.

"H-hi." I rasp out, ducking my head slightly.

"Are you… okay? I-" I cut him off before he can finish his sentence.

"Um, yeah. No… no problem." I start towards the passenger door, and Johnny easily passes me and opens the door for me.

No.

I can't do this.

He stands next to the open door as I have a mental battle with myself.

I reach for the handle to pull myself up, and my sweaty palms slip.

My eyes burn as small tears form in them.

Why am I doing this?

I can't do this.

I can't do this.

I can't do this.

The only thing that makes me pull myself in is Johnny's quiet breaths behind me.

Never changing pace.

Almost like a calming sound or noise you put on when you're stressed.

Once I'm inside the truck, Johnny gently closes the door behind me, and walks around the back when he comes around, giving me a few extra seconds to press the tears away.

I suck a few breaths, filling my empty lungs with the oxygen they're screaming for.

He opens the door and climbs in without looking at me, and I try to convince myself that he has no idea that I'm having problems.

"We don't have to g-"

I cut him off again, and this time I feel really bad about it.

"No, I want to go." I say, trying to force a note of calmness in my voice, when I really sound like I'm being strangled.

He nods and slides the gear shifter into drive, and my heart literally jumps into my throat.

Johnny must hear the sound of my heart.

There's no way he doesn't.

The pounding that's filling my ears must be audible to everyone here.

The pounding actually hurts my throat and chest, and for a few seconds, I wonder if my heart can explode.

What if this kills me?

What if I'm sitting here and Johnny looks over and I'm dead?

That sends my breathing that I maybe had the slightest bit of control over out of control.

"What music do you like?" Johnny suddenly asks as he pulls out of the park and onto the—gulp—freeway.

His eyes never leave the road, and the only indicator that he spoke is his hand moving towards the screen that controls the radio and bluetooth.

"What?" Is all I can choke out.

Gosh, if I wasn't about to vomit all over Johnny's truck, I might be laughing through the pain.

"What music do you listen to? What artists or songs are your favorites?" Johnny asks again, the calmness in his voice maybe rubbing off on me.

"I-I don't know?" I say, not really able to speak.

He doesn't say anything, just flips through channels until he finds one playing trending pop music.

I can recognize most of the songs—mostly from hearing them all over social media and at school—but I'm not all too familiar with the lyrics.

Does he even realize that I'm mid-panic attack?

My breathing slows slightly, and I try to focus all my attention on the world outside and forget that I'm in here.

"I kind of liked that one, what about you? The lyrics were strung together… nicely." Johnny says as the channel host starts talking.

The lyrics?

"Um, yeah. It was nice." I say, and to my shock, my words come out mostly even.

My heart is still pounding and I'm pretty sure I could pass out at any given moment, but my words are actually coming out with some sort of calmness. I don't actually remember a single lyric, but who cares.

Another ten or so minutes pass without either of us talking, but somehow, the silence is comfortable.

Well, my heart is still pounding and my stomach is still swirling, but maybe I'm not quite so close to passing out.

Johnny exits off the highway with extreme focus, and before I know it, he's pulling into a gravel parking lot.

A sign reads 'Welcome to Lark Lake trail' above the trail head, and I breathe a giant sigh of relief.

Johnny shuts the truck off, but doesn't make a move to open the door.

I hate it, but a tear slips down my cheek with relief that we've made it.

I pull my knees up to my chest and wrap my arms around them, and out of my peripheral vision, I see Johnny turn his head and watch me for a second. He then looks out the windshield and leans back in his seat.

"What's wrong?"

Are his only words. They're not angry or rude, just softer than his usual tone.

How do I even talk about this?

"I… I want to talk to you, but… can we just get to the lake first? I need time to breathe, and think, and-"

"Yes, you can do whatever you want. You don't even have to talk if you don't want to." Johnny says, opening his door and stepping out, pocketing his keys as he does so.

I quickly hop out, too. Not wanting Johnny to come around

and open the door for me.

I grab my water bottle from where I'd thrown it on the floor, and I softly close the door behind me.

Johnny opens and shuts the back door, and meets me at the front of the truck with his water bottle in hand.

"This way." Johnny says, gesturing for me to take the first steps onto the trail.

We walk in almost complete silence, and the only words that are spoken are us pointing out wildlife for the other to see.

When we reach the lake, I immediately walk towards the large, flat rocks that sit right near the water.

Johnny doesn't say anything, he just starts walking down the shoreline as I take my shoes off and pull my knees to my chest.

The warmth from the sun relaxes me way more than I would've thought possible.

Johnny walks about a thousand feet away, but turns around as the distance between us grows.

When he's close enough to hear me, I say his name softly, not really expecting him to stop.

I'm not sure why.

Maybe it's the face he's making.

It's the face he makes when he's concentrating.

He doesn't say anything, just comes and sits next to me, only a few feet away from me.

"Are you okay?" Johnny asks, turning to me as he talks.

I see this out of the corner of my eye, but I don't have the courage to turn my head.

"Truthfully, kind of. I... I don't struggle with a lot of things, but being in a car... I do." I take a deep breath before talking again, and while I'm still looking across the water, Johnny is still watching me.

He brings his knees up to his chest and rests his cheek on them, his full focus on me.

"The week after I turned sixteen, my parents encouraged me to get my drivers license—and I'm not blaming them at all—but I was… nervous. More nervous than I should have been, I'm sure. But, things were actually going well. We were on our way back, me in the driver's seat, and the instructor in the passenger." I pause again, sucking in a deep breath, my lungs gasping for air.

"There… there was a light. Like, I had a green light and was good to go, so I did. When I was almost across the intersection, a drunk driver ran his red light, crashing into our car. When we crashed, his car had been in the perfect position to crush the driver's door, and it did. I-I was hurt, but also trapped. Somehow— I'm not sure how, I've never looked at any pictures of it—with the way he had crashed into us, my whole side of the car was crushed, and the airbag went off, and with me being buckled, as well as injured, I couldn't get out. The instructor passed out after her airbag hit her, and it was agonizing hours—really, probably only minutes—before we were pulled out, but it still haunts me. This is the first time being in a vehicle that's not our motorhome or the school bus. Even then, I'm still on edge while I'm in them." I say, ending my story, turning my head and resting my cheek on my knees, mirroring Johnny.

He doesn't say anything for a few minutes, instead, he just matches my gaze.

"I'm sorry that happened. I really didn't know asking you to come would do this to you, and… I'm sorry."

I purse my lips.

"No, don't apologize, please. I-I am the one who decided to come, and before you deny it, you tried to let me stay back there. I made myself come."

I take a pause, and before Johnny can open his mouth, I speak again.

"And… maybe I should be thanking you. This is literally my first time being in a car—truck—since the accident. I'm a little bit proud of that." I say, genuinely meaning it.

"You don't need to thank me. Ever. If you're proud of yourself, then I am, too." Johnny says, the corners of his mouth pulling up slightly.

I don't know what really crosses my mind, but I stand and pull my shorts up on the leg that's scarred, almost really on my hip, but my shorts are loose enough that I manage.

That's where ninety-nine percent of the damage is.

I run my finger along the circular scar, the long streaks that seem to stream away in every direction of it.

Johnny looks up at me, and there seems to be… awe in his eyes.

"You're brave. Not many people would confess one of the darkest parts of their past, but also show their scar from it." Johnny says, true admiration and kindness in his voice.

I let my shorts slip back to their normal length, and I sit down next to Johnny, closer than we'd been before, but still in our original positions.

"It looks like the sun, you know. Your scar, I mean." Johnny says, he bites the inside of his cheek as he watches my reaction, as if only now realizing that I might feel insulted or something.

But actually, it's the opposite.

"Really?" I ask, not believing that he could picture something so beautiful like the sun on me, especially that part of me.

"Really." Johnny says, reaching over and gently moving a few stray hairs behind my ear.

Goosebumps erupt along my neck and shoulders, Johnny smiling as he pulls his hand back, turning his attention to the lake.

There's a soft breeze that's creating ripples across the lake, and the warmth from the sun is enough to balance it out, making it the perfect temperature.

I watch the lake, an overwhelming sense of contentment washing through me.

We sit in silence for an unmeasurable amount of time.

Maybe five minutes, maybe an hour.

I'm not sure at all.

"We should get back. Your parents will be wondering why you've been gone for so long. Mine, too." Johnny says softly, standing and offering a hand to me.

I take it, and after a few moments of me pulling on my shoes, we're making our way down the mountain.

It's mostly quiet as we walk, but about five minutes before we reach the truck, Johnny starts talking.

"You can put your bluetooth on my truck, that way you can play music or something. We don't have to drive off the minute we get in the truck." He says reassuringly.

The offer is so kind.

"Um, okay. I almost think that since I've gotten this off of my chest, it'll be easier. And, I trust you." I say, looking up at him as we walk, the sun highlighting his facial features, his jawline, full lips, and eyelashes that form long shadows on his cheeks.

The picture perfect face next to me is so mesmerizing and beautiful, that I trip over my own feet.

Embarrassment flows through me as I realize that I was checking Johnny out and got so flustered with his looks that I tripped.

Who does that?

Johnny opens the passenger door and I climb in, and almost all of my nerves are gone.

Am I even the same person I was two hours ago?

Johnny climbs into the driver's seat, and doesn't even reach to put the key in the engine.

"Will you be okay?" He asks.

I nod, sliding my hands under my thighs, pressing them into the seat.

Johnny starts his truck and pulls out of the gravel parking lot, everything about him calm and collected.

My heart starts pounding as soon as he pulls onto the highway, but at least I don't feel like I could faint at a moment's notice.

The drive passes much faster than I had pictured, and even though I'm desperate to remove myself from the truck, I almost rather spending time inside the truck than going back home.

I don't even know why I'm thinking like this.

Johnny pulls up in front of my place, and I have to take a few deep breaths before talking.

"Thank you. Really, thank you." I say, slipping out of his truck before he has a chance to respond.

Dad and the boys are sitting outside, all three curiously watching me.

Archer and Arden both have awe in their eyes—probably because of Johnny's truck—and while Dad looks curious, he looks more confused than anything.

I give them a quick greeting before going inside, needing a few minutes to myself after everything that's happened.

Chapter Thirteen

"Do you care to let me know what all happened this afternoon, Laelia?" Mom asks as I'm clearing the dinner dishes, Dad and the boys inside reading a book together.

I freeze for a split second, not knowing which part she's questioning.

"What would you like to know?" I reply as calmly as possible.

"Well, your father let me know that when you came back from wherever you were, you were in a truck with that boy." She says, a strange tone in her voice.

"Um, yeah, we went to visit the lake that we'll be kayaking in tomorrow." I say.

"That's interesting, how did that go?" Mom asks, trying to sound disinterested now.

"It went well. I'm sure we'll have fun tomorrow." I say, gathering the last few dishes and walking inside.

That was… random.

Mom doesn't especially take much interest in what I spend my days doing, or who I'm with.

I read the message from Johnny asking if I'm ready to leave for the lake, and I quickly message back a 'yes.'

I'm pretty excited to see him, seeing as it's already two o-clock and we haven't seen each other yet.

Ugh, that sounds so needy, but we've been spending almost all hours of the day together recently.

Can I be blamed?

I have on athletic shorts and a T-shirt over my bikini top, and my hair is braided a few different ways to give me a bun at the base of my neck.

I already know that somehow, someway, I'll be in the lake soaking wet at some point today.

Johnny is waiting at the passenger side of the truck for me, and I notice that he's wearing a plain black T-shirt and some sort of swim shorts as well. I guess we both know that we'll end up in the lake one way or the other.

I climb inside, setting my water bottle and bag down by my feet, and buckling all before Johnny has time to climb into the driver's seat.

Before bed last night, Johnny had texted and asked me if I'd rather ride with him in his truck, or ride in one of the vans that Rory and Janelle are driving for the kids that don't own cars.

After I'd said his truck, we agreed to leave earlier than necessary to give us some time to get there and hike up the trail.

As Johnny releases his foot from the brake, he looks over and gives me a quick smile before turning his attention to the road ahead.

I smile back even when he can't see me, and I try to not dwell on the fact that I'm actually in a vehicle and not having a panic attack.

My heart is still pumping a little bit harder than it should, but other than that, I feel… normal?

Did I really just need to get in a vehicle to get over my fear?

Is that really all it took?

"You can swim, right?" Johnny suddenly asks as we near our spot to exit off the highway.

"Of course. You can, right?" I reply, only slightly indignant.

"Yes, I can. I just realized that even though they'll have a lifeguard or designated person to save us, but we could potentially be far out and be in need of someone who has no chance of getting to us. I mean, I could save you if you were drowning or something, but I didn't think it would be smart to get into the lake if you couldn't swim." Johnny says, flicking on his turn signal and exiting.

I nod.

"I'm glad you asked, because I completely wouldn't have thought of asking you that." I say.

"I assumed you could swim, because, really, how many people sign themselves up to be in the middle of a lake when they can't swim, but I had to make sure." He says, pulling into the gravel parking lot.

We're the only ones here, which means we still have time to walk to the lake.

"Do you want to wait for everyone else or just start walking now?" Johnny asks, checking the time.

"Whichever you prefer. I don't mind either way." I reply.

Secretly, I want to walk now so that I can sit on the warm rocks for a few minutes.

"Let's just start walking, that way we can find a place for our stuff." Johnny says, hopping out of the truck and grabbing a backpack from the backseat.

After I'm out, he locks the truck and slides the keys into a front, zippered pocket of the bag.

I sling my crossbody bag across myself, the weight of my phone, charger, snacks, and other essentials slapping against my ribs.

Johnny motions for me to take the first steps onto the trail, and I'm not sure why I'm only now realizing it, but Johnny really is a gentleman.

I make a mental note to try and notice every time he does something like this.

Why?

Why do I want to know every time he opens a door, or walks on the side closer to the road, or allows me to walk first?

The answer prods at my mind, like a sharp blade cutting me from within.

I *do* know why, but- no, enough. I command myself to stop. I can't do this to myself right now.

"Have you ever kayaked before?" I ask Johnny, wanting to fill the silence with his voice.

"Yes, quite a few times, actually. How about you?" He replies.

"Oh, um, no, I haven't. I guess this will be my first time." I say, looking up with a somewhat sheepish smile.

Johnny chuckles before responding.

"Oh, then we'll definitely end up in the lake, then. I kind of assumed that since we've never kayaked together that we'd be in the water a few times, but I know now that we'll be in there a couple times."

My jaw drops.

"And you're just sure of that?" I ask, half teasing and half indignantly.

"One-hundred percent. If it makes you feel better, the first few times I kayaked, I probably spent more time underwater than in the actual boat." Johnny says with a laugh.

I had also assumed that we'd be in the lake at least once, but Johnny stating that he just *knows* that we'll be in the lake irks me slightly.

Not enough to be upset or angry, but I'd appreciate *some* vote of confidence.

"Our first teams that will be taking a loop around the lake are Johnny and Laelia, Jay and Kourtney, and Graham and Gracie. You'll just take a loop around the lake, get a feel for all of this, as I'm sure a few of you haven't ever done this. Our lifeguard, Silas, will be monitoring you every step—er—paddle of the way, so don't worry about that. Here are your life jackets, please be sure that you choose a size that fits you properly, not one that's comfortable." Rory says, ending her speech with a motion at the pile of jackets.

Johnny picks up one and slides it on, and I do the same.

The kayaks are all at the edge of the water, three lined up.

Can I actually do this?

This looks more intense than I imagined.

"You should sit in the front, because the more experienced person is supposed to sit in the back." Johnny explains, wading into the water and holding on to the front of the kayak.

"Okay." Is all I'm able to say, noticing how the kayak is *really* rocking in the water.

Johnny was totally right.

We're absolutely going to flip.

Johnny holds the kayak still as I climb into it, and I'm suddenly aware of how close we'll be in this death trap.

"I'm going to let go and climb in, and listen, when I do, it will rock. A lot. You're going to think that it's going to flip."

I already think that, I almost say.

"We shouldn't, but don't move your body and try to stabilize it, that will be what actually makes us flip." Johnny says in a calm, gentle tone.

"Okay, but just for the record, I completely believe you. We're going to flip." I say.

Johnny chuckles.

"One, two, three." Is all he says, and then he's in the kayak.

I gasp as we rock far enough that we should have flipped.

I don't say anything as he adjusts himself in the seat behind me, because I'm sure that the movement from even something as small as that will be enough to unbalance us.

"Hey, you can breathe now." Johnny says, picking up his paddle.

I notice that we've drifted quite a few feet away from the edge of the lake, and that's enough to make my chest seize in panic for a few seconds.

What if we can't paddle this thing back?

What if we get stranded in the middle of the lake and have to live there forever because we can't paddle back?

"Hey, I've done this so many times, we'll be fine." Johnny says, as if reading my thoughts.

As he talks, I notice the other teams immediately flipping into the knee-deep water at the edge, the second the last person tries to climb in.

"That's comforting, because it feels like talking is enough to flip us over." I say.

We drift a bit further out, and the water seems to almost be calmer the further we are away from the shore.

"Yeah, I guess it kind of does." Johnny says, and I whirl my body around to see if he genuinely means that, and that was a horrible idea.

"Whoa, that might be what actually flips us." Johnny says, laughing as I yelp.

He's right though, that *actually* felt like we almost flipped.

"In all honesty, it did feel like anything would make me flip the first few times I kayaked." Johnny says, dipping his paddle into the water and gently moving us a little bit.

I'm tempted to ask how Johnny knows so much about kayaking.

I dip my paddle in, and I'm surprised at how hard it is to draw it all the way back.

"Oh, that's a little bit difficult." I say out loud.

Johnny makes a sound of agreement, and we fall into a comfortable silence, the slapping of the water against the sides of the kayak and our paddles soothing.

"This isn't as bad as I thought it would be. It's actually kind of relaxing. Besides the fact that the sun is really really hot." I say, and I look up from my paddle to see that we're about halfway back.

"It's pretty fun once you get the hang of it, and it's a good way to kill time while still having fun."

We paddle in silence for a few more minutes before Johnny speaks up, almost like whatever he's about to say has been on his mind for a long time.

"Why do you trust me?"

My hand slips on the paddle for a second, jostling us a little.

"Like, kayaking?" I respond slightly confused.

Johnny chuckles slightly, and I can almost imagine him shaking his head as he does so.

"Um, sure. I kind of meant in general, but I guess that works, too."

Why do I trust him?

I think for a second on this, and I don't really know how to respond.

"Um, I guess when I saw you risk your life for that little kid, I don't know, I guess I just saw something good in you. Then, it seemed like we were bumping into each other left and right, and every time you were the same person. I mean, obviously you were Johnny, but you didn't change the way you acted, and you were always… genuine?"

I'm not sure why I leave my words sounding like a question, when I know that he's always been genuine.

Johnny doesn't say anything for a few minutes, and I have to restrain myself from turning around and potentially flipping us.

When he doesn't respond after a few more minutes, I don't press him for a response.

How would I respond to that?

Would I be able to respond to that?

We reach the spot that we started off from, but we're a little further away from the shore.

The water will probably be about waist deep.

At least the water is almost crystal clear.

"I'm going to try to get out without flipping us, but, fair

warning, it's really hard to get out from the back with someone in front."

I nod, not really listening.

"Wait, fair warning that I'm most likely going to flip?" I blurt out a few seconds later.

Johnny laughs before answering, my delayed response probably amusing.

"Yeah, fair warning that we're most likely going to flip. On the count of three, I'm going to hop out." He counts down, and I hold my breath and tense as the boat rocks violently.

Johnny lands in the water with a splash, water droplets spraying across my face.

He stands in the water and holds the kayak as I climb out, but as I do, my foot catches on the edge, and I completely flip into the water. The water is a cold slap, but I'm not really submerged due to the life-jacket, I'm just in a weird half-floating, half-sputtering water out of my mouth state.

Not embarrassing at all.

Johnny grabs my arm as I right myself, gently supporting me.

Ugh, why must I be worse at every challenge we have?

Life is not the slightest bit fair.

I avoid eye contact with Johnny, only to save myself embarrassment, but I don't think that's really possible at this point.

Once we're on dry land—or, wet sand—I pull off my life-jacket, and my T-shirt, leaving me in my shorts and bikini top.

Which—thankfully—is more along the lines of a sports bra than actual bikini top.

I'm slightly self-conscious of the fact that I'm not wearing a shirt, but I comfort myself by remembering that the majority of girls are wearing some type of swimsuit as well.

I turn to face Johnny as we walk towards the rocks.

"Well that was fun." I say, not really sounding it.

Which, to be fair, isn't really nice of me, since I was having a great time until I flipped.

"It was. In no time, you'll be a pro." Johnny replies easily.

I smile at his kind words, finding it hard to really listen.

"If by a pro, you mean flipping us into the water again, then yeah." I say with a slight smile.

"Hey, I mean, you did really well for your first time."

I look up, the sun shining behind him, reflecting off of the water droplets in his hair.

"I don't really think so, but thanks. I did actually have fun, though." I reply.

Johnny smiles, the dimples in his cheeks appearing.

"Then that's all that matters . If you had fun, and you did learn some, then we can call today a success."

I smile, hoping that Johnny knows his words are comforting.

As the next group of kids comes to take our kayak, Johnny and I sit down on the rocks, watching them climb inside and start paddling.

I lay my shirt out on one of the rocks to dry at least a little bit.

"Y'all did great out there!" Rory calls out from the pier.

"Thank you!" We call back.

We stay seated, though.

Not wanting to leave the rocks and sand.

My mind goes back to Johnny's question out on the water.

What made him ask me that?

I almost bring it up twice as we watch everyone on the water, but I chicken out every time.

"Do they really expect us to compete in a race when we're just learning all of this?" I ask, only half jokingly.

"I guess so. I think they're really expecting people to just have fun and not really race, you know?" Johnny replies, looking over at me, squinting his eyes against the sun.

I nod, only slightly listening, mesmerized by the look in his eyes.

The way that the sun reflects on his brown eyes turning them into hazy gold-brown is maybe the most beautiful thing I've ever seen.

We gaze into each other's eyes for a few more seconds, neither of us breaking contact.

I'm not sure what it is about the moment, but it feels different.

Johnny clears his throat and looks the other way, breaking our moment.

Time flies by quickly, kids getting out of the water, trading kayaks, and watching others paddle.

Johnny and I don't say anything else, rather we just sit and watch as the sun sinks lower and lower against the tree line.

When it's finally time for our race, Rory calls out to us, and we get into the boats again.

I'm not sure why there's silence between us, we almost never have moments where we're not talking, but I think it might be a combination of Johnny's question in the kayak, and whatever our moment was on the beach.

I try to not be hyper aware of the distance between us, but something feels different than it did the first time.

"Line up on this shoreline, please." Rory calls out from the pier.

Johnny does most of the steering towards our starting point, and I'm happy to let him do that.

I'm not sure how we're going to get through this race without any communication but, I guess we'll figure it out.

"We're good, right?" I ask, turning my head slightly to look at Johnny.

He nods.

"Yes."

The team up against us seems to be siblings, possibly twins, a boy and a girl, their features identical.

"One, two, three, go!" Janelle calls out.

Johnny and I start paddling, and we're immediately ahead of the other team, but they're not far behind.

Even though we've fallen into a rhythm with our paddling, I still feel a wall between Johnny and I.

I resist the urge to ask why he's been so quiet, the thought of flipping into the water again because I'm not paying attention flashing through my mind.

The team behind us gains momentum, so I just keep my sight on the finish line that we're rapidly approaching.

With a few final strokes through the water, we cross the line first.

"Yay!" I say, turning and reaching my hand behind me and toward Johnny to offer a high-five.

Johnny gently claps my hand back, and I turn my head to see a full smile playing across his face.

"You did really well!" Johnny says, sincerity laced through his gaze as he meets my eyes.

Me?

I wasn't even the one attacking the water with my paddle, back there.

Johnny really was the one who did all the work.

"Thank you. You did really well, too. We're a pretty good team together."

Johnny grins at this, and I hope that whatever happened between us, stays behind us.

We get out of the boat with a little bit more grace than last time, and make our way back to the pier where Rory and the rest of our group is waiting for us.

The rest of the teams shuffle and take their turns racing, all while we watch.

"What time do you need to be home by?" Johnny asks after a few more minutes of silence.

"I don't know. I told my parents that I could be out for a while, so I didn't ever actually give them a time that I would be back, though." I say, looking up at his face as he stares out towards the water.

"It's five thirty right now, so if you want to leave now while everyone finishes up, we can." Johnny says.

"Honestly, we can leave whenever you want. I don't have to be home anytime soon. As long as it's not, I don't know, midnight when I get back, we should be good."

Johnny smirks as he turns to look at me.

"I'll be sure to get us back at eleven fifty-nine, then." He says with a wink.

I purse my lips and let a small laugh escape, my cheeks heating with a blush. I know he's just joking, but I'm still entertaining the idea of spending a few more hours with him.

Wait.

I should absolutely *not* be doing that.

Why am I thinking like this?

"We can leave in a few minutes, that way I'll have time to help my mom with dinner stuff. I think she also wants to go on a walk with me later, so I don't want to keep her waiting." Johnny says after a few more minutes of silence.

"Okay, that sounds good. I'll grab my stuff and we can let Rory know that we're leaving early." I say, standing and grabbing my stuff.

I pick up my still-wet shirt, and drape it over my arm, knowing that I won't be able to wear it for a while longer.

Johnny lets Rory know that we're leaving, and we start our way down the trail.

She mentioned that the winners of the kayaking competition will be announced via email.

Once we're further down the path, and the sun isn't shining on us, I become increasingly colder. My wet hair, lack of clothing, and semi-wet skin all adding up.

Goosebumps run along my skin, and my teeth chatter a little.

I slip on a loose pebble, and Johnny reaches out and grabs my arm as I balance myself, his hand instantly warming that one small portion of skin on my arm.

"Wow, you're freezing. Is your shirt still wet?" Johnny asks, gently releasing my arm from his hand as we continue walking.

"Yeah, it's still pretty wet." I say with a small laugh, not wanting to let on how cold I'm feeling.

Johnny does some shuffling with his backpack, and pulls out a long sleeve white shirt.

"Here, you can wear this while your shirt dries." He says, passing it to me.

"Oh, um, thanks." I reply, taking it and sliding it on.

It's definitely too big, but hey, it's warm from being in his backpack, and it's super soft.

While I know the path hasn't grown since this morning, I'm tired from all of the rowing, and could definitely use a break.

Soon enough we're back at the gravel lot, and in Johnny's truck.

Most of the drive back is silent, but there's occasional conversation between us.

"What activity are you most excited for?" Johnny asks as we near the park.

"Um, I'm not sure. I think the painting thing might be fun. What about you?"

I shy away from mentioning the dance, because I'm not really sure how that will go.

Yeah, we're partners now, but does that mean we're going to be dance partners?

Will there even be dance partners?

Will it be formal? Informal?

Until I know more, I'm not going to be mentioning that as one of the activities I'm looking forward to.

"The painting one does sound cool. I think the hiking and paintball sound pretty cool. There's even supposed to be night hikes, so we might be able to find cool wildlife then, too." Johnny replies, enthusiasm in his voice.

I turn my head slightly, trying to watch the poorly concealed excitement on his face.

It's actually pretty cute to watch him become immersed in

these activities.

I guess that's not really something a lot of people—boys especially—my age do.

It's refreshing.

As if he feels me watching him with a smile, he turns to me for the briefest second and smiles, before turning his eyes back on the road.

My face heats with a blush, and I slowly—and hopefully inconspicuously—turn my head to look out my window.

Out of my peripheral vision I'm pretty sure I see Johnny look over at me a few times, and that sends little butterflies through my stomach.

Ugh, I cannot be getting butterflies from Johnny.

Not that he's in any way bad, but we don't live even remotely close to each other, I'm sure I'm definitely not his type, and I'm not even sure I'm ready to have a relationship.

Relationship?

Where did that come from?

How did I go from butterflies to relationships?

Thankfully we arrive back at my place, and I barely restrain myself from leaping out of his truck.

I can't spiral any more, especially when I'm less than a few feet away from Johnny.

Before Johnny can come around to my side and open the door, I climb out, making sure my few things are tucked under my arm.

The nearly-setting sun makes a beautiful backdrop with the trees, Johnny the centerpiece.

"Thank you for driving us, I had an amazing time." I say as I stop in front of Johnny, both of us standing at the hood of his truck.

"So did I."

Johnny clears his throat, and I look up at him, my body tensing as I realize he's looking directly down at me.

We stand there for what could be hours, or merely seconds. Neither of us break the silence, rather we stay still.

After an unknown amount of time, Johnny's face widens from a small grin and into a full smile.

"Have a great night, Laelia. I'll see you around."

And with that, he turns, smile still in place, and climbs into his truck.

I scurry inside completely in shock as to what just happened.

Mom, Dad, and the boys are all playing a board game, and under my charged emotions after what just happened between Johnny and I, I feel a pang of guilt for not being home and spending time with my family.

Yes, we have our issues sometimes, but I've been completely immersed in Teen Summer Fest, and I've hardly spent any time with Mom, Dad, and the boys.

I brush past them at the table and find clothes to change into.

I need to take a shower, because no doubt the shower I took in the lake earlier wasn't the most hygienic.

I let Mom and Dad know I'm going to shower, and I make my way towards the bathhouse. I cringe at the thought of having to walk past Johnny's place, but I much rather the idea of taking the straight path and not getting myself lost.

As I undress, I realize I'm still wearing Johnny's shirt, which, if I'm being honest, is still super warm and soft.

For a split second I imagine wearing it after I've showered, but

I shut that small part of my brain down as soon as the thought crosses my mind.

After I'm out of the shower, it's basically dark.

And, while I'm not scared *of* the dark, I am slightly scared of what's *in* the dark.

For the most part, everyone has campfires and some type of music playing.

As I start walking, the sounds of crackling logs, laughter, and music erases any worry I had earlier.

And although I have my towel around my shoulders, my previous clothes in a small bag, and my hair is in two messy and wet braids, I feel the urge to walk around and enjoy the night.

It's so peaceful and calming, that I lose track of time and only make my way inside after a half-hour of mindless strolling.

Mom and Dad have put the boys to sleep, but they're both still lounging on the couch when I enter.

"Hey," I say, walking to the bathroom and placing my clothes and towel in their respective homes, deliberately placing Johnny's shirt on a hanger aside, reminding me to wash it tomorrow.

I make my way back to the living room, sitting down across from them in one of the reclining chairs. I pull a blanket up to my chin and tuck my legs underneath me, resting my head against the arm of the chair.

"How was your kayaking thing?" Mom asks after a few minutes.

I nod my head, a wave of tiredness sweeping over me. My arms and shoulders have become increasingly sore.

"It was really fun, actually. I didn't think I would love it, but we actually had a great time."

Dad nods, beating Mom to the question I was betting they

would ask.

"You were with that boy… John, right?"

It does agitate me a teeny bit when they refer to him as "John" but I refrain from saying something. Instead of correcting him, I nod again. "Yeah, *Johnny* and I were partners, seeing as we're partners for this whole event."

I place only a slight amount of emphasis on his name, not wanting to sound sassy.

"Oh, yes, of course. How was that? You've been spending a lot of time with him recently, don't you think?" Mom says, and it's less of a question, and more of a statement.

"Yes, we've been together quite a bit, we've made pretty good teammates, which, to be honest, I didn't expect. Not that he's given me any reason to think otherwise, but I figured since we're so different, we would struggle." I say, quickly patching the last part on before they assume Johnny had made me feel like we'd be bad partners.

They both nod, seemingly satisfied with the conversation.

I almost wonder if they think there's something going on between us, and if I'm being fair, I would assume the same thing if I was a parent of a teenager spending so much time with someone of the opposite gender.

They both say a quick "Good night," before retreating to their room, and I make my way to my bed a few moments later.

Chapter Fourteen

"Laelia, do you want to come with us?" Mom calls out from the front door, snapping me from my trance.

I look up, blinded by the sunlight, and see her and Dad, each with one of the twins.

"Where are y'all going?" I reply, still in a slight daze after only staring at my computer screen for however long I've been out here.

"We're going to the pool. The boys really want to swim, and your dad and I are wanting to spend some time in the sun. It might be good for you to get your feet wet, too." She replies, stepping down the stairs, her sundress billowing around her legs.

"Sure, I'll get changed right now. Y'all can go ahead, I'll catch up." I agree, closing my open document and shutting down my computer.

"Okay, we're going to take the car. Your dad already packed plenty of towels."

I nod, standing and stretching before making my way inside. They drive off to the pool, which can't be too far away, and I change into my swimsuit, layering a sundress over it.

I braid my hair into two long braids that lay over each shoulder, and after grabbing my sandals, I'm out the door.

It's much warmer than it was this morning, and I'm grateful for the large trees everywhere, shading the paths to the pool.

I follow the few signs directing me to the pool area, and after about ten minutes, I'm at the entrance gate.

I find Mom and Dad on the lounge chairs at the far end of the pool, and I drop my stuff in the chair next to them.

I pull off my sundress in the locker rooms, and sit at the edge of the pool, dipping my toes in and deciding if I want to commit to another hair-wash shower later.

After a few minutes of splashing my feet in the water and watching Archer and Arden, I take the plunge and hop in the pool.

The pool itself is large, and there's volleyball nets in the deep water.

The twins and I are only in the three to four feet deep area, and I'm having fun splashing around with them until I see a familiar figure playing volleyball.

Johnny and a few of the boys I recognize from the Teen Summer Fest activities are playing volleyball.

I feel like a stalker for watching them play for a few minutes, but their banter and competitiveness is pretty fun to watch.

And, I'll admit, Johnny is pretty cute, too.

Ah, where did that come from?

Cute?

I turn away and focus my attention back on the twins, clapping as they show off their "gymnastics" in the water.

They're both arguing over who's handstand was better, when I hear Johnny—sounding extremely close—say my name.

I whip my head around, finding him only a few feet away.

His hair is plastered to his head, and he's wearing a wide smile.

I instinctively touch one of my braids, it being only slightly damp from the boy's splashing.

I smile back when I see him, suddenly unable to speak.

"Hi," is all I finally reply, after an embarrassingly long silence.

I'm sure it was only a few seconds, but it still felt like an eternity.

"I didn't notice you until now, I'm not sure if you saw, but I was with those guys playing volleyball." Johnny says, seeming to realize that he has nothing to say.

I nod.

"Oh, yeah, I think I saw you over there. I'm watching my brothers right now, so I haven't been over there."

Lies, but whatever.

Johnny nods, and I take this moment to look over at my parents who both seem to be dozing in the warm air, their umbrellas open.

"Hey, Johnny! Watch us do gymnastics!" Archer calls out a few feet away, waving his hands wildly before launching into a poorly constructed handstand, Arden right behind him.

Johnny chuckles and crosses his arms over his chest as he watches them.

His muscles flex as he does so, and I'm quick to change the direction of my line of sight.

There is no way I'm going to be caught staring.

When they emerge, he claps for them and reaches over to give them individual high-fives.

They convince him to watch another one of their tricks, making sure to let him know that his head has to be underwater to watch.

"Hey, he might want to go swim somewhere else." I let them know, not wanting Johnny to feel obligated to watch.

He turns to me before dunking his head underwater to watch

them, and says, "Don't worry about it. I don't have anywhere to be."

Then, he ducks his head to watch them, holding his breath as they do some sort of underwater flip.

Once they both emerge, Johnny emerges and flips his head back to remove the hair from his face, running his hand through it to get the last few tendrils away from his cheeks. Water droplets running down his face as he does so.

I feel my face heat with a blush as he notices me watching him, and I hope that the blinding sunlight is the only reason he thinks my face is red.

"Do you usually braid your hair?" He asks after a few more minutes of watching the twins perform.

What?

"Usually. It depends, but for the most part, it's the easiest way to keep all of it away from my face and in some sort of style." I reply, looking over at him and squinting at the sun.

Johnny nods, seemingly considering this reply.

I'm still wondering why he was curious as to my hair patterns, but before I can ask, Arden launches at me, and Archer at Johnny, sending me toppling into the water, and Johnny staggering backwards.

I emerge from the water only a few seconds later, Johnny grabbing onto my arm and helping me up.

I'm slightly gasping for air, since I just inhaled the whole pool into my throat.

He drops my arm a second later, the warmth from his grasp staying.

The baby hairs framing my face are now sticking to my cheeks, and my braids are now drenched.

"What was that about?" I ask the boys as they throw their little heads back in laughter.

"We just wanted to knock you guys over." Arden barely makes out through his giggles.

I smile and hold back laughter, not wanting to reward them for conspiring against us, but as soon as Johnny lets out a chuckle, I can't hold back my giggles either.

They swim a few feet away, splashing each other and ducking their heads underwater.

"I would make them apologize, but they're having too much fun." I say, turning to Johnny with a sheepish smile. "I'm sorry, though. They're rotten, sometimes." I finish, feeling slightly mortified now that I'm not choking on water.

"It's fine, really. I remember being that age, too. They're just having fun." Johnny says, moving his hand in a "don't worry about it" gesture.

"Do you know what the next event will be? I haven't checked it since this morning." I ask, knowing that there's not going to be one today, but maybe one tomorrow.

"Yeah, I think there's supposed to be a paintball war tomorrow. I'm pretty excited for that one. The guys that I was playing volleyball with were pretty excited, too."

Oh, that will be intense.

"Wow, really? That'll be fun. I wonder where it will be held." I reply.

Johnny nods, excitement in his smile.

"I think somewhere near the tree line or possibly even in the woods. Somewhere far away from their sites, I'm sure." He says easily.

"Good point." I reply, brushing a few stray hairs off my face as a breeze floats through.

"I'm pretty sure they're going to release the final events list any day now, seeing as TSF will be coming to a close soon." Johnny says a few minutes later, and my head snaps over to him in shock.

"What?" Is all I can reply.

"I'm pretty sure they're going to release the final events list. Teen Summer Fest ends soon, and each year when there's only about eight or so events left, they send out the final list." Johnny repeats, and I have a hard time keeping my jaw shut.

Of course I know that Teen Summer Fest doesn't last forever, but these last few weeks kind of made me forget that.

"Oh, they do? Cool." Is all I'm able to say for a few minutes as I regroup my thoughts.

Johnny nods, biting his lower lip.

I don't say much for the next fifteen or so minutes, I just watch Johnny and the twins play in the water.

I don't know why this is so difficult for me to wrap my head around.

I'd *known* that Teen Summer Fest only lasted for a few weeks, but I'm still reeling from the thought of not hanging out with Johnny almost every day.

And what about after we part ways?

It's already July second, and I can almost guarantee that we won't be staying at the same place again.

I'm chewing on the inside of my cheek when Johnny comes over to me.

"You look like you've sucked on a lemon." He teases, surely referencing my sour face.

"I happen to like lemons." I tease back, plastering a smile over my previously sour expression.

He laughs, and I splash water on him, diverting attention from my sourness.

"Hey, Laelia, we're going to be heading back now." Dad calls out from the edge of the pool, reminding me that he and Mom are still here.

"Okay." I agree, motioning to the boys that it's time to leave the pool.

"I think I'm going to head back, too. It was fun seeing you here." Johnny says, giving Dad a wave as he makes his way back to the stairs.

"Yeah, I'll see you tomorrow, then." I reply, and he nods while holding on to Archer's hand, helping him out of the pool. Arden grabs his other, and he pulls him out, too.

Oh my gosh, that was actually pretty cute.

I mentally slap myself for thinking that *twice* today about Johnny.

I can't be thinking these things when our time together is so limited.

I can't be developing feelings for him.

Especially not now.

It's way too late in our time together to be crushing on him.

I climb out, too, noticing that Johnny is talking to my parents, each of my brothers holding one of his hands.

All three have towels wrapped around their shoulders, and for a second I do a double take.

If I could only see their backs, I'd assume they were brothers. Their hair is pretty much the same color, and their skin tone is pretty similar.

Huh.

I grab my dress and change in the women's locker room, my bag across my chest, and sandals on my feet.

I emerge from the room to find Johnny and my Mom still in conversation.

"Hey, what do you think about walking your brothers back to the house? Johnny would surely go with you, right?" Mom asks, glancing from me to Johnny.

Johnny nods, agreeing to her words.

Okay, then.

"Yeah, sure. Are you and Dad going to drive back?" I ask.

"Oh, yeah, but we just figured the boys would have more fun with you and Johnny." She replies.

I nod in agreement, and she and Dad walk to the parking lot, leaving us four to walk.

"Okay, lead the way." I say after a few seconds, motioning for the boys and Johnny to start towards the trail.

As we walk, the boys faithfully hold onto each of Johnny's hands, and I feel like a stalker for watching them as they walk.

It's literally so adorable how small their hands are in Johnny's large ones.

They chatter in front of me as they walk, Archer and Arden competing for his attention as they try to impress him with the various topics they have interest in. Mostly meaning their favorite television shows and children's books, but Johnny still listens intently to each of them, engaging in their conversations.

My dress swishes at my knees as I walk, the greenery around us bringing out the vibrant colors.

It's not until we're on a larger path that Archer and Arden drop Johnny's hands and walk ahead of us, picking up small rocks and sticks, comparing them as they walk.

I pick up my pace and fall into step with Johnny.

"Hey, you weren't joking about liking lemons." Johnny teases, and it takes me a second to realize he's referring to my earlier remark about liking lemons, and the lemon pattern on my dress.

"You thought I was joking? I actually do love them." I reply, a small laugh escaping me.

The trees surrounding the path rustle in the breeze, almost as if they're laughing too.

Johnny laughs.

"Do you want to have breakfast with my family tomorrow? I was supposed to ask you a little bit ago. My mom insists that you have a meal with us. Your whole family is invited." Johnny asks a few minutes later, rushing the last few sentences.

"Yes, I'd love to. I'll talk to my parents about them and the boys coming, but I'll be there. What time are you thinking?" I reply, inwardly giddy with excitement.

"Does eight work for you?" He questions, rubbing the back of his neck when he asks.

I nod excitedly, agreeing with the time.

"My mom will be excited to hear you accepted. She's been wanting to spend more time with you and your family." Johnny replies, and for the briefest second, I think I see the tips of his ears turning red.

My smile comes from both his words and the thought that he might be excited by the idea, too.

Chapter Fifteen

All too soon, we're back in the main area, and we say our goodbyes to Johnny and continue the short walk to our house.

Dad takes the boys to take showers while Mom and I hang out in the living room.

Mom on her laptop, and me on mine.

I plan on taking a walk to the bathhouse to shower later, but the temptation to have clean, chlorine-free hair is too strong.

I end up passing Dad and the boys on the way to the bathhouse, me on my way there, and them on their way back.

I'm in the middle of shampooing my hair when a woman opens the curtain on me, mid-shower.

Obviously, it was an accident, but it still caused me to release a small scream. Besides that, my shower is nice, and my hair is fully rid of chemicals.

Like last night, I have the urge to walk around and explore again.

Something about the setting sun and rustling of trees while campfires crackle, calls to me.

After a few minutes of mindless wandering, I hear a few pebbles skid across the ground, and I take that as my cue to go home.

I'm not sure what's behind me, but I don't necessarily want to find out while I'm alone in the dark.

I go inside to find everyone eating pizza.

Mom and Dad are on the couch, both of them with a slice of pizza on their plates.

I serve myself and sit across from them, eating a slice of pizza before announcing our breakfast arrangements.

"We've been invited to eat breakfast with the Sawyer's, and I told Johnny we'd be there." I say, biting into another piece.

"Oh? How lovely. What time are we expected to be there?" Mom asks, looking up from her food as she speaks.

"Eight. And I'm sure you've seen, but they're not too far away." I reply.

"That sounds good, I guess we'll be getting up a little bit earlier than expected, but I'm sure it'll be worth it. Don't y'all have one of those events tomorrow?" Dad asks.

"Yes, we have some sort of paintball thing. Johnny knows more about it than I do. I still have to check my email to learn more about it." I say, taking another bite of pizza.

"That'll be fun. Are you sure you're up to that, though? That might be a little bit more intense than you think." Dad asks.

Ouch.

Of course I've already come to the conclusion that I'm going to suck, but someone else voicing their thoughts on it stings.

"It'll be fun, I'm sure." Is all I reply. And while I know the comment wasn't a dig at me, I still feel hurt.

Chapter Sixteen

My alarm buzzes, and after a few seconds, I will myself to sit up and rub my eyes, our breakfast date immediately jumping to the front of my mind.

I'm getting dressed in leggings and a slightly cropped sweater when I hear Mom and Dad's alarms waking them.

My hair is still in last night's protective braids, and I decide to undo them, allowing their natural waves roll down my back, only tying back a few pieces near the top of my head, leaving a few face-framing pieces.

I know I'll have to tie it all back later when we play paintball, but for now, it's going to have a rare moment of freedom and full-display.

I'm waiting outside in the cool air, my sandals leaving my feet chilly as Mom, Dad, and the twins emerge.

There are already plenty of people outside cooking their breakfast on their grills and griddles, children wrapped in blankets and in cushy camp chairs.

Johnny waves to us as we grow near, and he's wearing an apron, frying bacon on their grill.

The sight both adorable and attractive at the same time.

"Hi, guys. Feel free to sit down. My parents are just finishing slicing fruit inside, they'll be right out." He says, his usual, wide, smile on display.

Everyone sits down and his parents emerge, setting pancakes, fruit, orange juice, coffee, and scrambled eggs on the table.

I walk over to Johnny and stand next to him as he places the last set of bacon on the grill.

"Good morning." I say, giving him a shoulder bump, which I immediately regret.

Instead of giving me time to wallow in my embarrassment, Johnny bumps my shoulder with his as he flips a few more pieces of bacon.

"Morning."

There's silence between us for a few more minutes as Johnny pulls the last few pieces off of the grill.

He motions for me to walk ahead of him as we move to the table, and as I'm sitting down, he brushes past me.

"Your hair looks nice." He says in a low voice, his breath tickling my ear, and sending goosebumps down my neck and shoulders.

I smile and before I can respond, he's sitting across from me, setting the bacon down next to all of the other food.

As I'm serving my plate, he reaches to serve himself, too, everyone else already served.

Our parents chatter about everything under the sun, Archer and Arden contently eating their breakfast.

I take a bite into my pancakes, and if food wasn't currently residing in my mouth, my jaw would drop.

"These are so good, Johnny." I say, noticing how a shy smile plays over his face as he ducks his head to take another bite of food.

"Thank you. My mom is a pretty great chef. You'll have to tell her that you like them." He replies.

I nod, acknowledging that I will.

I pop a piece of bacon in my mouth, glancing over and finding Johnny and his mom making eye contact, their mouths moving in rapid Korean, almost no noise coming from them as they seemingly lip-read each other.

I look away just before they notice my eavesdropping, and even though I don't understand any of it, it still feels rude to have been intruding on their conversation.

It's only a few seconds later that Johnny turns to me, his lips pressed as though he's trying to contain a smile.

I catch Johnny grinning at me when my head is turned to listen to James talk about their homeschooling, and how amazing it's been for them. I'm becoming more and more fascinated with the idea of it.

The speed at which he learns, how many extra classes he's able to take, the fact that he doesn't have to sit in class for eight hours, and the freedom of traveling.

I'm tracing the table's wood and noticing the patterns when I feel Johnny's shoe knock into mine under the table, and my finger stills on the wood.

Out of the corner of my eye, I see Johnny stifle a laugh, discreetly covering his mouth with his arm.

And even though it's only our shoes touching, it's still enough to send my heart racing.

Johnny is still watching me, and the fact that he's messing with my head and has the audacity to be holding in a laugh, almost makes me demand to ask him who he thinks he is.

It's a nice thought.

Calling him out and demanding a reason for doing this.

I finally look up and meet his eyes, and I'm met with a smirk.

Gosh.

I refuse to break eye contact.

"Laelia, did you hear me?"

I snap my head towards Mom, her eyebrows poised in a questioning look.

"Sorry, can you say that again?" I say, placing a smile on my face.

"I think the boys want to take a walk, and it might be nice if you took them, that way us adults can talk, and the boys don't have to sit here bored."

I nod, standing and placing my silverware neatly on my plate before I leave.

Johnny's mom says something to Johnny is Korean, rapidly speaking and flapping her hands at him.

Johnny smirks and laughs, standing, too.

"Would you like company on your walk?" Johnny says, walking over to the the boys and I, his hands swinging freely at his sides, an easy smile on his face.

I open my mouth to say yes, but the twins both shout "yes!" and pump their fists in the air.

"After you." He says, motioning with his hands at the path ahead of us, leading us away from their site.

I will my cheeks to not betray me, but I feel warmth creeping up my cheeks.

I steal a glance at Johnny as he falls in place next to me, and I'm genuinely surprised to see his ears are tinged with pink.

"So, I'm guessing you were sent to walk with us?" I say, it coming out as more of a question, rather than a statement as I'd originally intended.

"Something like that." Is all he responds with, and I notice his ears turning a deeper crimson.

"Last night my mom said she saw you walking hurriedly around dusk and was worried about you." Is all he says after a few minutes of silence.

I rack my brain for what I did last night, remembering my shower and the woman opening the curtain.

I'm sure she hadn't realized I was in there, but still.

I laugh a little at the memory now, and I realize I just laughed after he'd mentioned his mom being worried.

I clap my hand over my mouth as I realize what I've just done.

"Oh my gosh, I was not just laughing at your mom, please don't think that." I hurriedly say, looking up to see a confused expression on his face.

"I showered last night, and a woman opened the curtain on me, and that's what came to mind when I was recalling last night. I wasn't laughing at your mom, I swear." I say, the words tumbling out of my mouth as I try to reassure him.

His eyebrows raise and his mouth drops a little, as if horrified, too.

"I know, right? Can you even imagine that?" I say, relieved that he seems to believe me.

His mouth drops a little more before it snaps shut.

"Um, are you sure you want me to imagine that?" He replies, and it's my turn for my jaw to drop.

He did not just say that.

Now, I'm the horrified one.

"Don't worry, I'm not." He says, turning to reassure me.

"I'm glad." Is all I can stutter out, realizing I've made a complete fool of myself for bringing that up.

Why can't I just keep my mouth shut?

Silence stretches between us for another few minutes, both of us embarrassed over our previous conversation.

"So, paintball is later…" I say, breaking our silence.

Johnny nods, and I give him a few seconds to find a response to my not so respond-able sentence.

"It is. It shouldn't last all that long, which is nice. I mean, I like doing these events, but I'm tired today, you know what I'm saying?" Johnny says, and I get the sense that he's rambling now.

Which, honestly, I haven't heard him do much of that.

I guess I never figured he would be someone who rambles, but over these past few weeks, I've started to come to the conclusion that he might be someone who rambles when he's comfortable.

A shadow of doubt crosses my mind, and I feel silly for a second.

I mean, who am I to be coming to these conclusions about Johnny's personality?

I shouldn't be analyzing his traits and patterns, no matter how subconsciously I may be noticing them.

"Yeah, I do know." I finally say, giving him an answer to his question.

I have to admit that I'm tired, too.

I did sleep last night, but I think the activities and added stress of my writing is catching up with me.

It's not too long before we've made a loop around the area of

Johnny's site, and we're back where we started.

"Oh, you're back already, wow." Mom says, noticing us approach.

I nod, unsure of what to say.

"I guess we'll be heading out. Thank you so much for that wonderful meal, we all appreciate it." Mom says, giving a hug to Katherine.

As Mom, Dad, and the twins walk away, I hang back for a second, wanting to thank Katherine personally, and mention my love for her pancakes.

"Thank you for breakfast, all of the food was delicious. Especially, the pancakes. I loved them." I say, looking into her eyes and seeing gratitude for the compliment.

"Oh, thank you, dear. I'm glad you enjoyed the food. We loved having you over, and would love to spend more time with you and your sweet family. Johnny, James, and I, enjoy your company, and I love seeing you and Johnny spend time together."

I allow myself a smile, but inside I'm jumping up and down with happiness.

I've never thought that Johnny's parents dislike me, but I'm not sure if they've ever said that they *do* like me.

"That means so much, I love spending time with Johnny. It's been so fun to have him as a teammate these last few weeks. He's an amazing partner. I'm really glad we're staying here at the same time. I'm even more glad Johnny wanted to be teammates."

Katherine is beaming by the time I'm finished talking, and I'm glad.

I really do care what his parents think of me, and having a good impression on them means a lot to me.

"Me too, honey. I would love to keep talking to you, but I need to finish putting away breakfast with Johnny, and then I have to run to town and pick up more groceries. I'm having James drive me."

I nod, understanding she's in a slight rush, and she gives me a quick hug before carrying dishes inside.

I leave their site and walk home, smiling the whole way.

Chapter Seventeen

"That's the end of our lesson. Let me know if you have any questions before we begin." Janelle calls out, waving her hands in a "get in your positions" gesture.

Johnny and I are paired with three other teams, our color being red.

To say I feel dumb is an understatement.

Understatement of the year, actually.

We're suited in black jumpsuit-type clothing, and helmets that remind me of what a motorcyclist would wear.

Again, I feel dumb.

I probably look even dumber, too.

We all take our positions on our side of our "battle field," which consists of equal parts woods and open field.

Johnny turns to face me, seconds before Janelle blows her whistle, and gives me a thumbs up before reaching his hand out for a fist bump.

He starts to say something, but it's lost in the noise coming from the whistle.

The paintball gun feels strange in my arms, but I do know how to handle it, thanks to Janelle's lesson earlier.

The other team scrambles into the trees, and we do the same.

We're barely into the woods before the blue team rushes at us, blue paint flying towards me.

Our team scrambles, all of us hiding behind trees, boulders, and everything else imaginable.

Shock floods throughout me as I manage to land one of my paint balls onto an opposing team's member.

The blue team retreats as our team continues to land paint on them, and within a few more minutes, we're pushing them back.

I aim my scope at the torso of someone from the blue team, and my finger is reaching for the trigger when I hear a shout behind me.

"Laelia! Duck!" I do as Johnny calls out, and I hear the rush of a ball whizzing above my head. I whirl my head to see Johnny take out the opposing team's member who tried to eliminate me, and my cheeks heat with blush as I realize that he just saved me, and took out my attacker all in the same moment.

What a gentleman.

I force myself to focus on the game again, and after another fifteen minutes, we lose only three members of our team, and we end up finding their last two players, and win the game.

I immediately pull off my helmet, running my hands over my head and pulling any sticky-from-sweat hairs off my face and behind my ears.

Johnny does the same from a few feet over, and I can't help but notice how soft his hair looks, even in its slightly disheveled state.

He shakes his head a few times, his hair basically styling itself back into its usual form, his middle-part allowing the few stray hairs to frame his forehead and upper face.

Johnny notices me watching him, and I meet his smile with

one of my own.

I tuck my helmet under my arm and use the strap on my paintball gun to allow it to hang freely from my shoulder. Johnny is doing the same, and we fall in step as we walk back to our starting point, our other teammates pairing up with their original partners and doing the same.

"You saved me." I say after a minute, my statement coming out of nowhere.

Johnny nods and smiles, mostly concealing the proud smile that plays across his face.

"I did."

I'm not sure why, but the simple confirmation of him saving me makes butterflies flutter through my stomach.

"Do you want to get ice cream together after this?" Johnny asks a few minutes later.

"Yes. Isn't there a small restaurant somewhere near the pool?" I ask, racking my brain for a memory of seeing it sometime in the last week.

"Yeah, they have all sorts of small meals and desserts. Burgers, sandwiches, things like that. Their desserts are usually cookies, ice cream, and pies. It's a good source of revenue for them this time of year." He responds, and just him mentioning food makes me hungry, since I haven't eaten lunch yet.

A foolish move, yes, but I'd been so full after breakfast that lunchtime came and went without me being hungry.

Now, I'm paying for that.

"Oh, that sounds cool. I think I've only seen the outside only once or twice. I've never been inside." I say, looking up at Johnny as I talk.

"Cool. After we get back, we can change, then go get something from there." Johnny replies, a hint of eagerness flowing in his words.

I agree with him, and after we've given our gear back and walked to our site area, we split off into our houses.

I decide to leave my braids in, considering they're still ninety-percent intact, the few stray pieces framing my face.

Changing into a skirt and loose shirt, I slide on sandals and grab my purse, walking out the door and giving Arden and Archer a kiss on their cheeks as I pass them outside. Dad reading a book to them as they lay out on blankets under the trees.

I'm walking towards Johnny's house, and find him walking towards me.

He's changed into jeans and a white T-shirt, and looks pretty cute if I have to admit it.

"Hey," he says, giving me a smile as we reach each other.

"Hey, Johnny." I reply, returning his smile, and he falls in step with me as we walk to the cafe.

The crunch of small pebbles under our feet as we walk, blends with the chirping of birds and rustling of leaves.

Johnny's hand brushes mine as his arm gently swings, and it's like I've been struck by lightning.

I barely stop myself from jerking my hand back, and I have the strongest urge to look up and study Johnny's expression.

Did that have the same effect on him as it did me?

Is this all in my head?

I lose willpower and look up, and Johnny is looking down at me.

We've both stopped now, the only sounds on the deserted path are nature, and the sounds of our breaths.

I raise my hand ever so slightly, but drop it, unsure what I was even going to do with it.

Johnny takes a deep breath, searching my eyes before speaking, his expression almost unreadable.

"I-" He sucks in another breath and closes his eyes, opening them a second later.

"May I hold your hand?" Johnny asks, reaching his opened hand towards mine.

I genuinely want to pinch myself, and ask if this is real.

Instead of doing either of those things, I place my hand in his, nodding.

I don't comment on the fact that we've essentially held hands before, knowing that this is somehow different.

Instead, I reply with the most honest answer.

"Yes."

He smiles, and turns, and now instead of walking with our arms hanging freely, they're connected.

The tingling in my hand hasn't stopped, in fact, it's doing the opposite. It's spreading from the tips of my fingers across my whole body. The feeling is that of an electric current.

Humming and buzzing, constantly in motion, leaving me feeling charged.

Neither of us have said anything, and I can't tell if Johnny is nervous or not.

If he feels the electric current that's pulsating from our joined hands, he's concealing it well.

Time flies, and it feels like only mere seconds have passed by the time we reach the entrance to the cafe.

"Snack Shed" reads across the chalkboard next to the door, the vibrant colors and mini illustrations on it bright in the shade of the umbrellas they have placed on the outdoor tables and chairs.

Johnny reaches for the door, opening it for me and walking in himself.

The small bell above the door jingles as we walk in.

Our hands are still connected as we walk towards the counter, and I can't help but feel that everyone is watching us.

I mean, I'm sure they're not.

But it still feels that way.

"Hello!" the girl behind the glass counter says to us as we approach, her bright blonde hair shining under the hanging lights they have installed throughout the cafe.

"What can I get for you today?" She asks, cheeriness in her voice.

She places her hands on the glass counter, and leans forward towards us, an expectant smile playing across her face.

I do a quick search of the menu, and decide on fries and ice cream.

Johnny speaks first, ordering fries and a milkshake, and looks at me, letting me know he's done.

I tell the girl, Aubrey, my order, and she asks us to give her a few minutes as she makes it.

We oblige and walk over to the other end where there's the cash register and other condiments.

"This place is so cute." I say swinging my hands a little, momentarily forgetting that one is still connected with Johnny's.

He drops my hand as soon as I swing it, and I can't help but feel a tinge of sadness at the realization that I'm the reason our hands have been disconnected.

I open my mouth to say something like "I didn't mean to do that," but the words don't make their way out.

Aubrey rings a bell and calls our number, giving us our order.

Johnny reaches for his wallet, and I reach for my purse, fully expecting to pay for my own food. But Johnny tells Aubrey that it's all on him, and I feel slightly surprised at his actions.

"Are you sure?" I question, looking up at him.

I search his eyes and he gives a fully-sure nod, not taking my question into consideration.

He just swipes his card, and grabs both of our food before asking if we want to eat inside or out.

"Outside. It's pretty nice out, and there's still a breeze. Unless you want to eat inside, I vote for outside." I say.

"No, I'm happy to eat outside."

I smile, excited to eat my food, but also spend more time with Johnny.

My recent realization that we won't have forever together this summer has been hitting me.

I'm determined to make every moment last with Johnny.

I take a few extra steps to get ahead of Johnny and open the door, the bell ringing again.

We pick a table that's a little bit further away from the entry, and he sets down our food on the table.

We sit down on the ice cream chairs across from each other, the umbrella flapping a little in the breeze.

"Thank you, Johnny. You really didn't have to pay for my lunch, though." I say.

His ears turn pink around the edges, and I almost want to press my cold ice cream against my cheeks in hopes that the rising blush cools.

Even though my cheeks are slightly pink, I'm seriously loving every moment of today.

Today almost feels like a dream.

Johnny picks up his milkshake and I pick up my ice cream cone and we tap them against each other in a "cheers" motion.

I lick the top of my ice cream cone, the huckleberry fudge flavor flooding into my mouth.

I've never had huckleberry ice cream, much less huckleberry fudge, but oh my gosh, this is amazing!

I look up with a smile, to see Johnny looking at me at the smile of his own. His full smile on me, his milkshake almost disregarded in his eyes.

I smile back at him, both of us watching each other for longer than necessary.

"How's your ice cream?"

I can't remember what flavor he got, but judging by the big sip he took a second ago, it must be good.

"Super good. I got strawberry-chocolate." He says, considering something before speaking again.

"You can try it." He says, reaching his hand with the shake across the table.

Is this really happening?

Sure, the sound of it sounds good.

But sipping after him?

Isn't that something couples do?

I decide to not hurt his feelings, and pop the lid off, using a spoon to take a small amount out, placing my mouth.

The flavor, oh my gosh.

"Wow! This one is really good too. What are they putting in their ice cream?" I say with a laugh, passing him his milkshake back.

This is seriously the best ice cream ever.

Johnny takes another sip of his milkshake, and then pops a french fry in his mouth after. The purple brown color melting of my ice cream reminds me to offer some to Johnny.

"Do you wanna try some of my ice cream?" I ask, a small amount of shyness seeping in my voice.

I can tell he's about to say no, so I rush to add,

"Really, you should try it! It's so good!"

Johnny smiles as he gives in, resulting in a smile of my own.

"Sure. You got huckleberry fudge, right?"

I nod.

"Yeah, I did. It's so good. I've never had huckleberry ice cream before, but this is seriously amazing."

He picks up a spoon, and scoops a small amount of ice cream out, sliding it in his mouth.

Johnny swallows, nodding his head approvingly.

"Wow, this is really good." He says.

"I know, right? I guess since it's summer there's a lot of berry ice creams?"

I'm not sure if he knows the answer to this, but I still bring it up because I'm curious.

After dipping another one of his fries in ketchup and placing it in his mouth, he nods his head, yes.

"Yes. There's actually a few farms around here that have giant gardens specifically for growing fruits that local restaurants will buy for their desserts. I bet that this is really fresh. Like, probably made within the last few days."

I nod, taking another bite out of my ice cream before responding.

"Wow, that's so cool. I wish there was a lot more of that where I live." I comment.

Johnny nods before responding.

"That's what I love about traveling everywhere, I've seen so many things like this, and it never fails to amaze me. How long have you and your family been traveling, again?" Johnny asks.

"Oh, we only travel during this summer, remember? The rest of the year we live in our house, and since I'm in school, we occasionally go on small weekend trips."

The more I think about going back to our boring, everyday life, with me being in school almost twenty-four seven, and never experiencing new things, the more I'm starting to wish that we live more like Johnny's family.

Always traveling and finding new adventures.

More involved in events like these, where we do things outside and inside equally.

"Oh yeah, sorry, I forgot. Do you enjoy being in school and living in one place most of the time?" He asks after a small moment of silence.

Ah, the question I've been dreading.

A month or so ago, I would have said yes, but now, I'm not really sure. It feels like this time with Johnny has been my whole lifetime, but also, no time at all.

Now, I can't imagine a day without spending time with Johnny.

I feel as though I'd give anything to keep this summer going on forever.

"I'm not sure, honestly. I probably would have said 'yes' a while back, but now, this life is kind of growing on me. Old Laelia probably would have laughed at hearing me now, but something about these past few weeks has really shifted something in me." I answer as truthfully as possible, watching his expressions rapidly change as he processes my answer.

"I can understand that. You haven't ever done any type of event like this while you've traveled, right?" He asks curiously.

"Yeah, this is my first time doing some sort of event like this. I'm really enjoying it."

Johnny smiles before placing a few more fries in his mouth.

I look down and realize that my ice cream is rapidly melting, and it's already dripped a few small drops from the bottom of the cone onto the table. I spoon quite a bit of the top into my mouth, and I feel myself getting a brain freeze as it touches the roof of my mouth.

"Ah!" I say, the brain freeze really hitting me now.

Johnny looks up from his food surprised.

"Brain freeze." Is all I say, and Johnny nods his head a small laugh escaping his mouth.

"Hey, not funny!" I say jokingly.

I hurry to finish my ice cream, all that's left now is my fries.

I dip the salty fries in the ketchup before placing them in my mouth, their flavor pretty good for being just french fries.

"I'm definitely coming back here before this is all over." I say, one hundred percent meaning it.

Johnny smiles, a small laugh escaping him.

"We should definitely come back. I haven't been here since last year."

Wait, did he just say "we"?

I only said that I would be back.

Not that I would object to him coming, but I'm intrigued by the idea of him assuming we'll be back together.

I try not to let any thoughts of us doing more things like this together flow through my mind, but it's almost impossible.

We literally held hands.

We shared ice cream.

What does all of this mean?

"Yeah, we should." I respond, and I try to watch his face for emotions, but his face stays pretty much blank.

Ugh.

Johnny, why must you do this to me?

We finish up the last few fries we have, and stand to throw them away in the outdoor trash can.

"We should probably be heading back. I spent almost no time today with my parents, and I'm sure my mom would like to go on a walk with Berry and I." Johnny says after we leave the enclosed area of the outdoor cafe.

"Yeah, we probably should. I had a lot of fun with you today." I say, a smile filling my voice.

Johnny smiles at this, his eyes crinkling at the corner when he does so. It's seriously the cutest thing ever.

I know it happens to me when I smile, but it's one-hundred times cuter when it's on him.

"I've had a lot of fun with you today, too." Johnny says, sincerity in his voice.

And even though I'm unsure of my feelings with Johnny right

now, it makes me happy to hear that he's enjoying his time with me.

The walk back feels like no time at all, and Johnny insists on walking me the rest of the way to my place after we reach his, but I assure him I'll be fine, and I walk the rest of the way back home, alone.

The car is gone when I get back, meaning at least Mom or Dad is gone, probably both of them, and the boys, too.

After walking inside, I'm sure that everyone left, so I end up hanging out on the couch with the dogs until they get back.

Mostly reading, and occasionally watching the television that Mom or Dad left on.

It's dinner time when they get back, and I prepare tacos, setting up the dinner arrangement on the outside table.

I made homemade guacamole, sliced limes, onion, and cilantro for toppings.

Mom explains during dinner that they left to buy the boys new shoes, since they've already outgrown their old ones. And, with the Fourth of July coming up, the boys will be spending all day on their feet.

They must be going through a growth spurt.

I know there's a decent sized city about forty miles away, and I wonder if that's where they went.

I don't ask, I'm not all that interested as to where exactly they went, but I am interested as to what the cities around here look like.

It feels so isolated from the outside world here, that I almost have a hard time believing that there's any type of cities around here.

Which, of course, is crazy.

But that doesn't stop my mind from thinking like that.

After dinner and dishes, I read to the boys before bed, both of them falling asleep easily.

It's only a few minutes before ten-thirty, but I'm still feeling a little restless.

I decide on putting the dogs into the stroller and taking them on a small walk.

The windows are open in here, and I can hear the chirping of crickets, and the whistling of a small breeze.

It's calling to me.

It's completely dark outside, and I'm only in a T-shirt and shorts, but I'm still determined to go on a walk.

I take off in a direction I haven't really explored yet, and of course the paths around here are all interconnected, so in one way or another, I'll be back home.

Mom told me to be careful on my way out, but I'm not sure she really knew where I was going.

I mean, heck, I don't even really know where I'm going.

I've only been walking for a few minutes when I see someone up ahead, the dark silhouette of a woman and a dog.

Of course there's no reason for me to be nervous, but I am alone in the dark, so I'm slightly on edge when the person ahead and I cross paths.

As the woman grows closer, I notice that it's Johnny's mom, Katherine.

I consider talking to her, but decide to leave her in peace on her walk.

She calls out my name from the other side of the road as she passes. Our closeness must have allowed her to see that it was me, and I give her a small wave.

"Hi, Katherine." I say, stopping, seeing as she did, too.

She walks over to me, deciding that she wants to talk further.

"Hello, dear, how was your afternoon?" She asks, Berry on the end of her leash. "Pretty good. Johnny and I had a good time at the paintball event, and I was just feeling a little restless, so I decided to go on a short walk. How about you?" I ask, reaching down to give Berry a pat.

"I'm just out for a little bit of air, and decided to bring Berry along."

I nod understandingly.

"I understand. Are you out here alone?" I ask looking around to see if Johnny or James is out here with her.

"Yes, it's just me and Berry. I'm glad you and Johnny had fun today. He really does enjoy your company."

Her mentioning this again sends a thrill throughout me, and I smile, glad for the darkness that is surely hiding my blush.

"Oh, thank you. I'm glad to hear that."

She smiles, and the small amount of light there is peeking through the trees, reflecting off of the moon, allows me to see it.

"I hear there is a painting class or something the day after tomorrow." Katherine says.

"Yeah, there is. I'm pretty excited for that one. I wouldn't really call myself an artist, but I do enjoy painting or drawing a little bit here and there. You know?"

She nods.

"Yes, dear, I do understand. I'm glad Johnny will be trying this out too. His sister, Julianna, is a little bit more artistic, and he always felt like he was never as talented as her in the drawing and painting area. Although, in my eyes he's still amazing. But, that discouraged him from doing a lot of artistic activities. I've noticed he's been more open to things like this since being around you." She says.

My eyes widen a little at this, completely taken aback by her comment.

Really?

"Oh, really?"

She nods intently.

"Oh, yes. Very much so."

I'm surprised by this, but I'm not sure why I am.

I mean, Johnny has pushed me out of my comfort zone, without even realizing it.

I've heard the saying "iron sharpens iron" but I hadn't really thought about it with Johnny and I until now.

"Is there anything else he's tried that he wouldn't normally try by himself?" I ask, unable to restrain my curiosity.

"Yes, I know for sure cooking the pasta was hard for him. See, he used to make it sometimes, and he was pretty good, but after a few failed batches he kind of gave up on it. I was surprised to hear he made it with you."

Wow.

He made it sound like he had made it before and it had been nothing.

"It's nice to hear that we've been a good influence on each other." I say, truly meaning it.

Katherine nods her head, approvingly.

"Yes, I agree. It's rare for him to open up this much with a stranger."

My eyebrows raise in surprise, I'd been expecting Johnny to be a bit more social than he'd been with I.

"I mean, you're not a stranger to him anymore." Katherine says, realizing how her words might have sounded to someone else, moving her hands in an apologetic motion.

"I knew what you meant, don't worry. I guess I expected he was a bit more social."

Katherine moves her hand in a "more or less" motion, and I have to wonder what that means. I'm about to open my mouth to speak again, when Katherine receives a notification on her phone, and she realizes the time.

"Oh dear. I'm so sorry for keeping you this long, your parents must be wondering where you are. I must be getting back now. It was nice talking to you." Katherine says before continuing her walk back.

I give her a quick good night, and I take a slightly different path back, allowing Katherine to have silence on her walk back.

After I'm back inside, I prepare for bed, and I'm laying down within a few minutes.

Thoughts are swirling wildly in my head, and while I usually have some level of control on my thoughts before bed, tonight, I don't.

My thoughts are a stream of Johnny and I during breakfast, Katherine and I talking after breakfast, Johnny and I taking the boys on a walk, and our conversation from then, the paintball event, our walk when we held hands, and our lunch—which was a lot like a date—where we had a somewhat deep conversation, and everything else since then.

Chapter Eighteen

Pulling my hair into a long ponytail, I slide on my baseball cap, looping my hair through the ponytail hole.

I smile at my reflection in the mirror, the glitter I placed lightly under my eyes, shines in the bathroom light.

"Mom, are you ready?" I call out, sliding on my shoes, then helping the twins tie their laces.

"Almost. I just need to send this email, then I'll be out." She calls from her room.

From the open screen door, I can hear the happy cheers of children, and the sound of music playing over speakers.

To be honest, the Fourth of July completely slipped my mind.

Of course the park hadn't forgotten, and instead, they're throwing a mini festival.

Archer grabs a fistful of my red tank top for balance as I set his foot on my bare knee, tying his laces.

Standing, I brush my hands off and lead them both outside, sitting them down on the bench as we wait for Mom.

Dad is making a quick trip to the front office for ice, and then we'll all make our way over to the event area. Since he has the car, he'll be taking our cooler and anything else we'll need over there for us.

"Hey, sorry I took so long." Mom apologizes as she breezes out the door, taking the hands of both Archer and Arden and setting off in the direction of the festival.

"No problem." I say, falling in step with her and the boys.

We're passing the Sawyer's house as they're leaving for the festival, too.

"Oh, hello, Katherine!" Mom calls out, stopping to allow the three of them to catch up to us.

"Lucia! How lovely to catch you. We were just leaving." Johnny's mom says, falling in step with Mom, allowing Johnny and James to walk a few steps behind them.

I slow my pace, walking next to Johnny, now.

"Hey." I say, looking up at him with a smile.

He smiles back at me, excitement in his eyes.

"Hey." He replies, glancing over at his dad who seems to be in a whole world of his own.

"So, what can I expect from this event?" I ask, wanting to fill the silence between us with conversation, my curiosity brimming within me.

Mom and Katherine are ahead of us, chattering away as they walk.

"There's music—obviously—and a lot of carnival type booths." He replies, referring to the music that only grows louder and louder as we near our destination.

"Cool. Do you want to explore the booths together?" I ask, a hint of shyness seeping into my voice.

"Sure. I don't know exactly what there will be, but I'm sure we'll have fun." He says as we reach the open field.

This seems to be the place that houses all of the park's events and parties. It is the best place to host them, I just find it funny that all of these events get held at the same place.

After leaving our parents behind—Dad was arriving just as we did—Johnny and I are off to explore.

Music blares over the sound system, and the sound of children screaming playfully fill our ears as we enter the maze of booths that are set up.

"I think the first thing we need to do is find snow cones and popcorn." Johnny says, grabbing my arm just below my elbow and sliding his hand down, leaving our hands intertwined.

I smile up at him and nod, and Johnny immediately finds a vendor selling snow cones.

He buys two large cups, and we move to the flavor stand.

"Okay, what flavors are you going to get?" I ask Johnny, doing a quick survey of all of the options.

"I'm going to go with blue raspberry. How about you?" He asks, drizzling the flavoring over his ice.

"I'm going to have… cherry and lemon." I decide, adding the flavors to my ice.

We find a popcorn stand a few booths down, the buttery smell wafting through the air.

Johnny buys a bag, and we munch on it as we walk.

A few minutes later, we're walking through the booths when I spot the "knock the bottle over" booth.

"Oh, look at those stuffed animals!" I say, using our linked hands to point in the direction of the booth.

Johnny smiles and leads us to the small line.

I take another bite of my snow cone, the sugary-sweet syrup and the crunch of the ice sending a chill through my body, even though the day is fairly warm.

"Come on, man." The boy that just lost says to the attendant.

"Son, it's just the rules." The elderly man says apologetically, gesturing for the boy to leave and make space for the next person.

"Come on, Quinn." The boy who lost says, stalking off, his friend—or brother—following him.

The girl in front of us makes an impressive throw, and wins one of the stuffed kittens.

She leaves with a satisfied smile, and then it's Johnny's turn.

"Do you mind holding this?" He asks, motioning to the cup and bag of popcorn that he's carrying.

"Yeah, of course." I say, taking it from his hand as he steps up.

After paying the small fee, he picks up one of the balls, and throws it directly into one of the bottles.

Since I'm unable to clap with both of our cups in my hands, I just wait until he's done.

He smiles, picking up his next ball.

Again, his throw knocks down one of the bottles.

A few cheers and claps come from behind him.

He picks up his last ball, and before he throws it, he turns to me for the briefest second, and gives me a wink before turning and throwing it, knocking down the last bottle.

"Good job, son. Now, which prize would your lady over there like?" He asks, gesturing over at me.

My cheeks heat with a blush, and I step forward as Johnny gestures for me to pick a prize.

"Which one do you want?" Johnny asks me, gazing into my eyes as he speaks.

"Um, how about one of the bears? You pick." I say, gesturing at the assortment of teddy bears that line one of the shelves.

"How about the one with the heart eyes?" Johnny says, pointing at the last one of its kind on the shelf. I nod, and the man picks it up and passes it to Johnny, who in turn gifts it to me.

"Oh my gosh, thank you." I say, tucking the bear under my arm after squeezing it against my chest.

Johnny just smiles, taking the last bite from his snow cone.

I smile back, taking the last bite of mine, Johnny chucking the cups in the trash can a few feet away.

He picks up my hand, and we wander throughout the booths, no real direction in mind.

"We should get fries." I say, leading Johnny to a vendor that's selling snacks.

I pull out my wallet, reaching to pull out money, but Johnny beats me to it, sliding his money to the cashier first.

"Hey, I was going to pay for that. You already bought the snow cones and the popcorn." I say, looking up at him.

"So? Those things weren't detrimental to my wallet. Seriously, just let me pay." He says, nodding at the cashier to use his money.

I huff, giving him a side eye.

In return, he just smiles his award winning smile, ignoring my objections.

Chapter Nineteen

I swing my legs off of my bed, and they hit the cold floor, sending a slight shock through my body.

I guess today is a little cooler than it has been, and I'm somewhat surprised when there's a chill in the air as I change.

I braid my hair into two long braids that will stay firmly behind my shoulders, keeping them safe from the paint.

As for my clothes, I wear an older set of loose jeans, and a gray T-shirt.

Dad is up by the time I'm finished changing, and he's working on making breakfast.

Within fifteen minutes, he's made egg muffins and placed them on the table.

I'm kind of surprised that the twins aren't up yet, but hey, I'll take it. They're usually jumping off the walls by this time.

We eat in silence, Dad reading on his e-reader, and me with my paperback book in my hands. He's probably reading one of his sports papers that he has a subscription for on his e-reader.

Since he can't be home and cheering on his teams from the local television station, he does the next best thing by reading up on their wins and upcoming games, all from his e-reader.

His dedication to it is admirable, but I can't say I really

understand it.

Sports are nice and all, but they're just sports.

I've ruffled a few feathers saying that back home at school, since we have a football, baseball, and soccer team that our school basically worships.

I finish eating, and I pull my laptop out to write for a few minutes, only having about fifteen minutes to spare before heading out.

"Bye, Dad." I say as I slide on my tennis shoes and walk out the door. He calls out a goodbye, and I'm on my way.

The e-mail had stated that the art class was at the picnic tables over where Johnny and I had eaten lunch the other day, before we went and visited the lake, and where the mini festival took place.

It's as though the festivities from yesterday never happened, the only traces of the events are the occasional candy wrapper, and popcorn kernels.

When I arrive, Rory, Janelle, and a few other kids are already there, setting up the tables by covering them with plastic tablecloths, and setting out paints, pencils, canvases, and other various items.

I offer to help, and I'm on my first tablecloth when I see Johnny approaching.

He's probably here to set up too, and I notice that it's something he's done multiple times now.

Sure, it's not asked—or even expected—that you help set up the events, but Johnny's helped with a few of them already, and I find it admirable.

"Hey, Johnny!" I say, raising my hand and a wave, happy to see him.

His full smile comes out, and that causes me to smile too.

"Hey, Laelia, how are you doing?" He grabs the other end of my tablecloth as he talks, tucking it under the table and using the clips to secure it.

I didn't even have to ask him to—not that I would have—but he just instinctively did it.

"I'm good, how about you? I loved seeing your Mom, yesterday. She's so sweet." I reply, fully meaning it. Johnny grins and nods.

I find it so cute.

Probably because most kids would disagree and complain about their parents, but not Johnny.

All of the small moments and interactions I've seen between them shows their deep affection for each other.

"I'm glad you like her. She's pretty cool. I know she really likes you, and I'm pretty sure she's ecstatic that you enjoy talking to her." Johnny reveals, a smile playing on his face as he talks.

"That makes me happy to hear. I really like her. I can see where you got your sweet personality from." I say, looking up through my lashes as I speak.

Johnny grins, and his ears turn a pink.

It's true.

I can completely see why he's so kind.

I don't know much about James, but from what I've seen, he's nice.

You know when you can tell when someone was raised in a loving home? That's completely what I see in Johnny.

I can tell it that shaped him to be more confident, happy, and kind towards others.

"Thank you. It's an honor to have my personality compared to hers. My mom really is extremely kind, I'm glad others see that in her, too."

I smile, agreeing with him.

Johnny opens his mouth to say something, but it's interrupted when Rory calls out, asking everyone to come gather around her table for further instructions.

Johnny and I stand next to each other as Rory discusses what we'll be doing, and, like I expected, it's more just painting what you feel like, and less of a lesson.

She says to come to her if we want any instructions, advice, or anything like that, but I'm sure many of us will just paint what we feel like doing.

Johnny and I sit down at the table we placed the cloth on, and it's the furthest away from all of the others.

We each have a canvas, but we share brushes, paints, pencils, and erasers.

I'm not sure what I'm gonna paint, but I want it to be special. I stare into space for a few minutes, all thoughts leaving my brain as I try to find something to paint.

I look over to see Johnny, scratching away with a pencil on his canvas, giving himself an outline.

I watch him for a few more minutes, not realizing the time is passing rapidly.

Johnny suddenly looks up, a smile on his face as he realizes I'm watching him.

I blush, not sure what to do.

"What are you working on?" Johnny asks, nodding over at my empty canvas.

"Oh, I don't really know yet. What about you? What are you

working on?" I ask, redirecting the attention from myself.

"If I told you, it wouldn't be a surprise." Johnny says, looking up with a smile.

Surprise?

What does he mean?

"Okay, then. I'll figure out eventually." I reply, giving him my best nonchalant face.

Johnny laughs, my face probably amusing.

I mean, I'm not all that nonchalant.

Even when I try to be.

He turns on his side of the bench, facing his canvas away from me.

Darn.

I really do want to know what he's painting now that he's made it a secret.

I decide to try and recreate the picture from when we were at the lake, both of us on the boulders, the sunlight glistening off of the lake, and the soft waves lapping against the sand.

Although I'm not that talented when it comes to painting, I do have to admit that it is coming along. We've been here for close to an hour already, and there's been almost no talking, just the sound of pencils and paint brushes against canvases.

It's interesting how such a small activity can really entertain everyone. After two-and-a-half hours, Rory calls out for everybody to place their canvases down, and come meet over at her table.

I'm surprised to see her painting a scene, but even more surprised to see what the scene is.

Since her table is at the front, and ours are all placed in front of her, she has a good view of all of us.

On her canvas, there's a skillfully painted picture of all of us painting, all of our heads dipped, bent over our own work.

"How is everyone's work coming along?" Rory asks, meeting each of our eyes as she talks.

There's a chorus of "great" from most of us. Rory smiles at this, and seems to note that none of us have said we're done yet.

"If you're done, or want to be done, let me know and you're free to go. If not, feel free to stay as long as you'd like and finish your paintings."

We all disperse back to our tables, and as I sit down, I quickly pick up my painting, not wanting Johnny to see it yet.

Not that I've said mine is a surprise, but if I can't see his, he can't see mine.

After a few minutes of concentration, I notice that Johnny is quietly singing and humming under his breath.

I can't understand the lyrics, they're either in Korean or Japanese, but through his quiet voice, the melody is pretty.

I only realize after a few more minutes, that I'm moving my brush strokes to the rhythm of his voice.

He seems to be singing the same song over and over, or maybe it's some type of nursery rhyme that basically never ends.

I wouldn't know, seeing as I can't understand it, although I do understand the melody and tone.

I can tell that it's meant to be sung quietly and gently, and that makes it all the more special that Johnny is singing it now.

Of course he's not singing it for me, but the fact that he's singing it around me, where he doesn't know if I can or can't hear it, that's what makes it special.

He moves on to another song, and it has the same tone, sound, and simple melody.

I'm convinced this one is maybe not so much a nursery rhyme, but maybe some sort of ballad, or something that might be a little bit older.

I realize that I've almost completely stopped painting, all of my attention on Johnny as he sings and hums, his brush strokes gently floating over his canvas.

After a few more minutes, my painting is almost done.

It's more rough strokes, rather than precise alignments, but I still find it beautiful.

I decided to only do what my view was, excluding me, and having Johnny, the small beach, lake, trees, mountain, and all of the other nature included instead.

I face it away from Johnny, allowing the sun to dry it.

I want it to be mostly dry by the time he's done with his, since I'm kind of worried of dropping it and ruining it.

Since I wouldn't dream of leaving Johnny while he's finishing his, I watch him paint, the way that his mouth moves in the gentle lyrics of his song, and the way his long fingers hold the paint brush, allowing it to stroke freely across his canvas.

After a few more minutes, the curiosity behind what he's painting starts nagging at me.

It's only a few more minutes before he places his down, intentionally facing it away from me.

Okay then, fair enough.

Mine is facing away from him, too.

He brushes off his hands, then places his elbows on the table, resting his head in the palms of his hands.

"Are you done?" Johnny asks, nodding over to my painting.

"Yes. Are you? You seemed to be in the zone while you were painting it." I reply, teasing him just a little bit.

He chuckles, looking down the table before looking up again at me. "Yeah, I was. I just wanted it to be perfect." He says, giving me a smile.

"Okay, I'll let you see my painting, as long as you let me see yours. In fact, actually, we should show each other ours at the same time." I say, offering a deal.

I reach my hand over the table, offering it in a handshake. Johnny chuckles before reaching out and firmly shaking my hand, the tingling from where his hand grasped mine lasting even after our hands separate.

"You have yourself a deal, ma'am." Johnny says, reaching for his painting.

Ma'am?

Oh my gosh, why was that so cute?

I reach for my painting, and we flip them over at the same time.

I'm surprised to see Johnny's painting, and I can tell he's surprised when he sees mine.

Where mine is more rough strokes, generalizing the scene, Johnny's is precise. Almost as though he'd drawn his lines with a ruler.

Where my painting is all as it was, nothing sharper or clearer than something else, Johnny's is almost blurred in the background, giving the illusion that the only real beauty is the un-blurred part.

Which is… me.

In the painting, it's me sitting on one of the ice cream chairs, smiling and looking up at Johnny, my ice cream cone in my hand, only inches away from my face as though I just taken a bite.

I tear my eyes away from his painting, and see that Johnny is still staring intently at my painting, and I wonder if he's surprised by the scene I chose.

I'm surprised that he painted me, but I guess he probably feels the same way.

All of the angles and proportions are perfect in his painting, and I wonder if that has something to do with the fact that he's skilled in more math-type academics and exact measurements.

Whereas mine gives off the impression that it was done by someone who sees the full picture, and wants everything to be shown.

The stark contrast between ours is beautiful.

Seeing how our painting style is so different because of how different we are, but how beautiful they each are in their own way makes me emotional.

"Yours is so beautiful!" I finally say, truly meaning it.

Johnny's ears burn red, and he ducks his head.

"If there was a competition, yours would definitely be the winner. The way you painted it all is so unique."

I quickly shake my head back and forth, letting him know I disagree.

"No, I think yours is a thousand times better."

Johnny opens his mouth to reply, surely to disagree, but he never gets the chance to speak, because Rory calls out for us to join her again.

"Is everyone just about finished up? We're running a bit over than what I would normally allow a class overrun to be."

Almost everyone says yes, and she tells everyone who's done to bring their paintings up to her, and everyone who's not, to go finish theirs.

Johnny and I both grab ours, and return to her.

"Oh, wow, These are beautiful!" Rory exclaims, when she lays eyes on them.

She looks between the paintings, then looks up at us, as if realizing we've painted each other. She smiles, and we do the same.

"Do you mind if I take a picture of these? I'd love to have you both in them, and have them for later when I'm judging the paintings."

I look up at Johnny, silently asking him if he's okay with it, and he nods.

"Okay, step back a little bit, please. I'd like to get a full picture." Rory says, pulling out her phone and opening her camera.

We stand next to each other, and just before she snaps the photo, Johnny wraps his hand around my waist, pulling me closer to him. I'm only shocked for a moment, but when I look up and smile at him, my eyes sparkling, and he looks back at me, a full smile and shining eyes looking down on my face, I forget that Rory is taking a picture of us.

We snap back to reality when she calls out to let us know the picture is fabulous, and thanks us for allowing her to take a picture.

"These are some of the best paintings I've had here. You two did a marvelous job, and you've been an excellent team so far. You're one of the few teams I haven't seen constantly fighting, and arguing over minuscule things. In fact, I don't think I've seen you two fight at all. Good job." Rory says, giving us both an admiring smile.

"Thank you." Johnny says, smiling back at her.

I too, say thank you, and she lets us know we're good to go, and we're entered to be judged at the end.

Johnny and I both pick up our pieces, and start the walk back to our homes.

"I really like your painting." Johnny says, looking over at me as we walk.

I feel my face heat a little bit, a blush creeping in.

"Thank you, I really like yours, too. I think Rory is right, we're a really good team together." I reply.

Johnny smiles, and I have to wonder where he got the idea to pull me closer as Rory took the photo.

"I agree, I think we've done really well together." Johnny replies, a smile playing across his face.

"So…" I say, and Johnny looks over and smiles.

"So…" He says, mimicking me.

I don't know where I'm getting the confidence, but I look up at him before I speak.

"So, when Rory took the picture…" I say, not really wanting to finish my sentence, the small amount of shyness I have in me coming out.

Johnny smirks, looking down at me, before looking straight ahead again.

I'm questioning whether or not he's going to make me finish my sentence, but just as I'm about to speak again, he starts talking.

"I hope you're okay with that. It was a… spur of the moment idea. I am glad I did it, though."

My head snaps up to face him.

What was that supposed to mean?

Yes, I'm okay with it, but the end of his sentence?

Sir, where is the shyness you were just displaying?

"Yes, I'm fine with it, I was just… surprised I guess."

Johnny smiles, and I almost swear I hear him mumble under his breath the words, "Yeah, me too."

One minute, he's bold and doing things like that, the next, he's acting all shy.

Since we're already having this conversation, I almost demand to know what all these small moments between us have been for him.

Does he think this is just friendly behavior?

Does he like me?

What is the effect of these small interactions between us for him?

Because the longer and harder I try to convince myself that these are just small coincidences, the more I realize they're a lot more than that for me.

I look up at his beautiful face, and it finally dawns on me that I like him.

Like, really like him.

I'm not sure why I'm only realizing this now, but I really like him.

And that scares me.

It shouldn't, but thoughts of the summer ending, life back home, and everything else that could be a problem, make me nervous about my feelings.

I refrain from asking him these questions right now, but the longer and longer we're together, the more these questions burn at me to ask.

I look over at Johnny, and notice that he's taking his eyes back to the path ahead of us, as though he'd been watching me as I'd been lost in thought.

Everything is beginning to seem monumental, even the smallest things.

Whereas, before, I wouldn't have noticed all that much when Johnny watched me, but now, I'm hyper aware of everything he does.

I'm watching him as we walk now, and the small expressions he makes as we walk, the way his eyelashes flutter as a small breeze kicks up a little bit of dust, everything, everything he does important to me now.

If he wasn't walking right next to me, I would probably be smacking my forehead with my hand telling myself to stop these thoughts.

But, here I am, walking next to the boy of my dreams, and forbidding myself to ever tell him I have feelings.

Chapter Twenty

I can't let Johnny know that I like him.

The summer is almost over, and we live in two different worlds. We'll never work.

There's no way our differences and opposite lifestyles will allow us a chance.

I look up at him one last time, committing his face to memory, allowing myself to admire his features one more time before telling myself that our relationship is strictly a friendship.

Nothing more.

Once we're back near our houses and we've told each other bye, I give Johnny a hug, allowing myself this small moment before walking back to my house.

I don't know why I only realized how strong my feelings are today, but the time between me realizing how much I like him, and me deciding that we can be nothing more than friends was too short.

As I change into lounge clothes, I lay down in bed, feeling… grief? At the idea of only now realizing my feelings.

Yes, I'd had an idea that I maybe liked him, but now that I've come to my senses and realized just how much I like him, I'm upset that I didn't realize it sooner.

I want to go back to earlier, when I was giddy and happy at the idea of Johnny possibly liking me.

I want to go back and realize how amazing Johnny is sooner.

I want to have the opportunity to swoon and smile because of Johnny.

I can't allow myself that now, but I want to go back in time to a moment when I would've allowed myself to.

I'd always expected there to be some grand moment when I realized I liked someone. But, today, it felt as though I'd already known.

Almost like there'd been somewhere deep within me that had known I really like Johnny.

But, it had only been subconscious knowledge.

It's always been Johnny, and I'm not sure why I didn't realize it sooner.

Why didn't my feelings make themselves known all of this time before?

I could have fixed all of this if I'd only known sooner.

We're so close to never seeing each other again.

Our time here is almost up.

This bubble that being here has created around me has popped, and it's like I've awakened from a deep sleep.

I eventually fall asleep, my thoughts swirling and circling like a hurricane, only, the eye is Johnny.

Johnny and his smile, his sweet personality, his gentlemanly ways. Everything swirling around Johnny.

Chapter Twenty-One

I wake up at around seven o'clock, the smell of dinner being cooked outside floats through the open windows.

I get up, and after fixing my hair and sliding on sandals, I walk outside. I'm horrified to see James, Johnny's dad, talking to Dad by the grill.

Mom and the boys are sitting at the table, and they seem to be playing a card game.

"Oh, good, Laelia, you're here. Katherine and Johnny will be over in a few minutes, we invited them to dinner." Mom calls out when she sees me. I look down at my sweatpants and T-shirt, looking up at her horrified.

I go back inside, needing to change as soon as possible.

Why must the one day that I decide I need to distance myself from Johnny, did they invite his family over for dinner?

I put on one of my sundresses, taking out the braids in my hair, and letting it fall in loose waves over my shoulders and down my back.

I put on mascara to hopefully disguise the puffiness under my eyes from sleep, and smooth out the few wrinkles in my dress.

I walk back outside, feeling more confident about dinner, now that I've changed and done something with my hair.

I sit down next to Mom, smoothing down my dress and taking a sip of the lemonade that's placed in front of me.

Mom has already set the table with lemonade and cutlery, and it's not long before Katherine and Johnny arrive.

I find myself immediately sucking a breath, regretting my decision to keep Johnny in the friend zone.

I'm not going to change my mind, but it still hurts.

He smiles at me, and the knife in my heart twists more.

He sits down across from me, of course, and gives me a smile. I give him a friendly smile back, and remind myself that I'm still allowed to be friends with him.

Nothing more.

The twins both welcome Johnny eagerly, and I have to smile at their excitement.

At least some of us can be excited he's here.

Mom and Dad plate the food, steak, baked potatoes, and salad for dinner.

After everyone is seated and eating, I finally look up at Johnny after ignoring all of the small glances he's been giving me.

Johnny looks up just as I'm finally looking at him, and it takes all of my willpower to look away.

I can tell he's confused by my lack of eye contact, and the all-out avoidance of him tonight.

He hasn't really tried to talk to me yet, but in any normal circumstance, we would be talking or doing something together.

Something.

Instead, here we are.

Me, essentially ignoring him, and Johnny seeming confused by my behavior.

Dinner passes and what seems to be no time at all, but also an eternity.

After I've washed the dinner dishes, and I've done a quick clean on the house, I lay down in bed, pulling out my phone and with the intention of opening my reading app.

Instead, I see the e-mail from Rory, and it's her alerting Johnny and I that we won the painting competition.

I click out of the app and shut my phone off all together.

I'm finally starting to doze off when Mom walks by and tells me good night. I wish her the same, and roll over, facing the wall.

My last thoughts before I succumb to sleep is of Johnny's confused face after dinner when I'd just said a quick "bye" and walked inside.

Chapter Twenty-Two

As I pull on my tennis shoes and grab my bag, I prepare myself to see Johnny.

I'm going to be meeting Johnny at his truck, and I take a deep breath before walking out the door.

It's been two days since I've realized that I like Johnny.

It's also been two days since I told myself I can't like Johnny.

To say it's been a rough two days is an understatement.

And, here I am, getting ready to be in the same vehicle as him, giving us less than a few feet of distance.

Being alone with him as we drive to the lake for the fishing competition is going to be difficult.

If it wouldn't hurt Johnny, I would completely drop this whole Teen Summer Fest.

We haven't done another activity since the painting, and frankly, I'm struggling with the idea of continuing them.

Now, I have to spend this time with Johnny.

And, if fighting with my feelings while being around him won't be hard enough, I have to also try to focus on being a good teammate.

And, while it's not Johnny's fault, I have a small amount of resentment towards the idea of spending time with him.

Not the actual spending of time with him, just the idea of trying to fight my feelings right in front of him.

He's still the same Johnny.

I'm the one who changed when I realized my feelings.

At least, that's what I tell myself.

That I'm the different one.

The last time we talked was last night, when he texted me asking if we were going to drive to the lake.

Besides that, I've done a pretty good job of avoiding him.

Take yesterday for example: as I was walking back from the main office—I'd needed to do a check in and ask when our site would be fixed—I'd seen Johnny. And, of course he waved at me, but I'd pretended to not see him, and hightailed it back home.

Yes, I'd felt extremely guilty after, but I'd been freaked out and not ready for any interaction with him yet.

After dinner the other night, when I'd been completely blindsided by him being there, I've made a point to make sure that if we're going to interact, it needs to be planned out. Giving me enough time to prepare myself.

But, alas, hiding only works for so long.

So, here I am, walking out the door to meet Johnny.

The minute I see him my heart skips a beat, and my stomach swirls.

This is already so much harder than I'd expected. I want to turn around and go back inside, leaving him out here.

It's so strange that the last time I'd felt so much aversion to going to the lake, it had been over a fear, this time, because of feelings.

I almost wish he's easier to dislike.

Not that I could ever dislike Johnny, but the idea of being able to dislike him is easier than confronting the fact that I like him.

And that's a hard pill to swallow.

"Hey." Johnny says, and the the sound of it makes the knife in my heart twist a little more, and I almost rub my chest, hoping the feeling will go away.

"Hi, Johnny." I reply, giving him a small wave as I reach him.

I continue walking around to the other side of the truck, and Johnny follows, doing a few, extra-long steps to get ahead of me and open the door.

I give him a smile as I climb up, and he smiles in return.

He makes sure that I'm fully inside the truck before he shuts the door, and he rushes around to the other side, climbing in, himself.

I remind myself that I'm still allowed to talk to him and be friendly.

Our friendship isn't changing.

Or, at least I hope it's not.

We drive in silence for a few minutes, and by the time Johnny pulls on the highway, it feels like my insides are going to implode if I don't talk.

"So, what have you been up to?" I ask, looking over at Johnny, yet again amazed by his beauty.

Oh my gosh, why is he so cute?

He's making this way harder than it has to be, and the worst part is, he's not even trying.

How fair is that?

"Not too much. How about you? I haven't seen you around these past few days." He replies, looking over at me.

Thankfully, I'm looking straight ahead out the windshield, and I only see him out of my peripheral vision.

Yikes.

I guess I haven't been as subtle as I've been trying to be. My complete avoidance, obvious.

"I've been busy with work things, and I've been looking into my classes for the upcoming semester." Which isn't a complete lie, but also not the complete truth, either.

I have been doing more writing, although I'm not satisfied with it.

On the classes part, I've only checked them once, and that was when I received the e-mail with my teachers and class list.

So, maybe I'm making this up a little bit, but can you blame me?

"Cool. I've been doing some school, and figuring out the next few things I'm going to be doing." Johnny says, and I almost swear that I can hear a hidden meaning in his words.

Maybe not relevant to me, but relevant to why every time he speaks about being busy, he seems to have some aversion to it.

And, I'll give him credit, he's good at concealing when he's upset, but after hearing him talk normally about his school, and just regular life things, I can tell that this isn't how he normally is.

He's usually way more upbeat and excited when talking about school, and just everyday life. It's almost like when he asked about my school the other day, he just seemed to know that there was an underlying, inward battle involving the issue.

"That's exciting." I reply, completely wanting to ask him more about it.

My questions are on the tip of my tongue, but I remind myself that I can't become closer with Johnny.

We're just friends.

Nothing more.

If we become any closer, my resolve might crumble.

I resort to looking over at him, wanting to let words tumble out of my mouth and tell him everything.

As if feeling the tension in the air, Johnny reaches for the radio, and flips to a pop station.

It feels like our first drive together all over again.

Except, then, I wasn't having a war within me.

Well, I was. But for different reasons.

Reasons that I would gladly take over these.

I'd rather go through that fear one hundred times over again than keep denying my feelings.

I nod my head to the melodies, not really paying all that much attention to them.

Multiple times, I open my mouth, wanting to talk to Johnny, wanting to feel the comfort that I feel when I'm talking to him, but I stop myself every time.

I can see the tension in Johnny.

His jaw is clenched, and his hands are tight on the steering wheel, causing the veins in his hands and arms to pop out more than they already do.

I watch as he takes caution when passing people on the highway, and I almost laugh at the thought of being scared to be in a vehicle with him.

Besides the tension that could be cut with a knife, I'm relaxed. I'm not worried about crashing anymore.

If someone told me that a month ago, I would've laughed in their face.

Chapter Twenty-Three

"Have you ever been fishing?" Johnny asks, breaking the silence.

I'm surprised by his sudden question, seeing as there's been no conversation between us for the last ten minutes.

"Um, when I was like five, or something. Not anytime recently. My grandfather loved fishing, but we quickly learned it wasn't really something I enjoyed. You fish sometimes, right?" I say, ending with a question.

To be honest, I haven't really thought about fishing with Abuelo for a while.

It's kind of something I've... forgotten about.

While I don't usually feel pain when I think about Abuelo and Abuela, since I usually only think of happy memories, it's only at times like this when I remember small things that I've near forgotten about. Memories like those bring a wave of sadness as I recall them.

"Yeah, I do try to fish often. I don't get around to it as much as I'd like, but I still love it. I brought two of my poles, so you're welcome to use one if you'd like. I figured they might be easier to use than the older poles that have been used a thousand times, and have old line and hooks that Rory and Janelle will be bringing."

I smile at Johnny's explanation of why he brought his poles.

It's cute to see his knowledge and thoughtfulness.

Cute on a friendship level way, of course.

I repeat this in my head to remind myself of my vow to not develop any deeper feelings.

"Wow, you've thought of everything. Thanks. I'm sure the other teams will be jealous of your expertise and fishing." I say, giving him a smile as I talk.

Johnny smiles, and the tips of his ears turn red, my over-the-top compliment going to his head.

For a second, it's like the days before everything had come crashing down on me.

Before I realized my feelings.

I snap back into reality when a small part of my brain reminds myself that we're only friends, and it's not good for either of us for me to be complimenting him like that.

While I'm unsure of his feelings, I have an idea that he might like me, and it's not fair to lead him on.

I could be completely off, but some—most—of his actions point otherwise.

It's not fair to unknowingly lead him on, just because I'm being careless.

Especially since I know I have feelings.

"Thank you. Hopefully, we'll do well. And, maybe, you'll like fishing and want to go again. It's pretty fun. Even if you don't catch anything, it's still fun to be by the water and just relax." Johnny says, chuckling as he finishes speaking.

I let out a small laugh, unsure of what else to say. It's highly unlikely that I'll enjoy it. I might enjoy sitting out there on the dock, but the actual fishing?

The worms are gross, and the fish are slimy, slippery, and floppy.

And, on top of that, your bait always gets stolen by fish that don't even stay on the hook.

It's cheating.

A memory pops up, and it's of me and Abuelo.

In it, I'm in my small princess chair, my child-size princess fishing pole in the shallow water.

Abuelo was sitting in his normal camp chair, his normal size pole also in the water.

I remember the tugging on the pole as a fish was hooked, and me jumping up and down in excitement, not even reeling it in. Abuelo had helped me reel in, the patience of a saint with my excitement.

When we had finally reeled in, it was a small fish, but I had been so excited.

I remember Abuelo picking up and handing it to me, and the second it touched my hand, I screamed and dropped it.

Of course I dropped it close enough to water that one small flop and it was back in the water, swimming away, and forever scarring my fishing experiences.

We'd gone a few more times after that, but I'd been quite stubborn and determined to catch a fish.

And when I didn't catch one the next few times we went, I swore to never fish again.

And I haven't.

I feel a small amount of anger at kid Laelia for not going fishing with Abuelo even after that, but I try to remind myself that I was a kid.

I didn't know better.

I wish that I can go back and offer to go every time he went, just like I wish I can go back and say "yes" every time Aubela asked if I wanted to help her with her quilting and crocheting.

I'm lost in memories, and only yanked out when Johnny's voice breaks through my barrier.

"-don't you think?"

Is all I catch, and I feel slightly embarrassed when I ask him to repeat what he said.

"Oh, I asked if you have been thinking about any of the upcoming events, and if you've taken any special interest to any of them." Johnny says, giving me an easy smile.

I rack my brain for the list of upcoming events, and the only ones I can remember are the dance, cleaning up around the park, another bonfire, and a few night hikes.

I think the hikes have something to do with the constellations, and that's why we're doing a few of them.

"Oh, I've been excited for the night hikes, and another bonfire. The last one was pretty fun. How about you?" I ask.

I specifically leave out the dance, not knowing how to approach that topic.

"I think the night hikes and bonfires will be pretty fun. Last year we did a bonfire before the two night hikes, so there might be multiple. There's also a dance—that's mostly a party—thing, too, but..." Johnny trails off as he realizes he's bringing up a dance, and I almost giggle when I see his pink ears and shy smile.

"So there's multiple bonfires? That's pretty cool. I really did like the last one. There's something calming about being around a bunch of other people when you're all pretty quiet, just enjoying the outdoors and dessert, you know?" I ask, looking over at Johnny.

"Yes, I really do know."

After another few minutes, we're pulling into the gravel parking lot again, and I'm yet again reminded of our first drive here.

We both hop out, and I grab my water bottle, hat, and bag. Johnny grabs his backpack, and goes to the bed of his truck, pulling out two fishing poles and two camp chairs that I hadn't noticed earlier.

He slings both chairs over his shoulder and holds both poles in the other hand.

"Are you ready?" Johnny asks, gesturing in the direction of the trail.

"Yep."

I start walking at the trail, and I'm reminded of the last few times we did this.

I offer to carry one of the poles and chairs, and Johnny laughs.

Yes, *laughs* at the idea of that.

"No, they're light. It's no trouble to carry both sets." He replies after another small laugh.

"What's so funny about me wanting to carry a pole and chair?" I ask, fully wanting to know why he finds it funny that I want to carry my weight. We *are* a team after all.

"It's literally no trouble for me to carry both of them. Besides, you have your water bottle and bag, you don't need something else to carry, too. I have these." Johnny says, and I can tell he doesn't mean his words as an insult, more of just a statement of facts.

I can tell he doesn't think my water bottle and bag are any weight at all, and the only conclusion I can come to is that he's just being a gentleman.

If anyone is overloaded, it's him.

Johnny has a relaxed expression on his face as we walk, and I can feel my face doing the same.

I look over at him a few times to make sure he's not struggling under the weight of anything extra, but I immediately feel silly, remembering how muscled Johnny is. While he does have a slightly more narrow frame then most boys his age he's still pretty muscled and strong.

It's a little bit warmer than it was the other day, so I am a little warm by the time we get to the top, and for the second time I turn to check on Johnny.

There's one other team here, but we saw their car in the parking lot earlier so it's not much of a surprise. It's a team of brothers, and they already have their poles in the water, fishing for the fun of it before it becomes a competition.

I pull out my phone and check the time, noting that we're fifteen minutes early.

Johnny gives them a quick greeting before quickly unfolding the chairs and making sure the line on the poles is correct.

One of the brothers—I believe his name is William—notices Johnny unpacking everything and elbows his brother.

"Hey, Ben, why can't you be like Johnny and treat me like your girl, and carry all of my stuff, too."

They both chuckle, and I can tell it wasn't meant as an insult at us, but Johnny freezes when he mentions the 'your girl' part.

Obviously, William thinks that Johnny and I are a couple.

Johnny smiles and continues working, and I just turn to face the water and suck in a few deep breaths, feeling both embarrassed and slightly interested on why he assumed I'm 'Johnny's girl.'

I turn to see Johnny sitting down in one of the chairs, and I do the same.

It's not long before Rory, and the rest of the teens arrive.

Pretty soon the pier is filled with kids and their chairs, and the poles Rory brought along for them. Quite a few people are talking, and I can bet that this event will be mildly noisy.

I mean, we're just going to be sitting until someone catches a fish.

She gives out instructions, also the rules.

Basically, there's no rules except don't sabotage anyone.

I don't think any of us would sabotage each other—much less know *how* to sabotage each other—but, I haven't spent almost any time with the rest of these kids. So, I don't really know them well enough to say for sure.

Rory gives the go-ahead, and a few people start casting, some are struggling with the bait, and selfishly enough, I kind of want Johnny to just handle most of this.

I can already tell that my hopes won't be fulfilled when Johnny extends a pole in my direction.

It doesn't have bait on the hook, and it's definitely not in the water.

Johnny chuckles as his gaze lowers, surely noticing my confused look.

"Don't worry. I'm going to do mine, and I'll teach you all of the steps, then I'll help you with yours." Johnny says, seemingly noticing that I'm more than a little bit lost.

"Okay, first thing, there's already a hook and the reel is fine, so all we need to do is bait and cast."

I nod, and he reaches for the can of worms.

I cringe both inwardly and outwardly, the sliminess and

wiggling is making my skin crawl.

"So, this is probably gross, but you need to break it in half."

My jaw drops and I clamp my hand over my mouth.

"Johnny, you're joking, right? You don't expect me to break one in… half, do you?" I ask, completely horrified.

Johnny releases one of his beautiful laughs, and while he might find it funny, I definitely don't.

"I mean…" Is all Johnny replies with.

I look away as he snaps it in half, but I can still picture it.

"Okay, the hard part for you is over now. Now you need to hook it, then cast." Johnny demonstrates how to hook a worm—which isn't much better than the previous step—then picks up his pole.

"This is the hardest part for people when they're learning how to fish, but it's easy to pick up on. You want to always check your surrounding areas, because this small hook can cause a lot of damage to someone's face. Then, you hold it like this kind of behind you, your finger holding the line in place, since you've opened the reel, and, when you cast, you let go when it's a little bit past the side of your face." Johnny demonstrates, his line flying far into the lake, his hook landing out with a satisfying plop.

"Now you'll close you reel, and wait until you feel a bite. Then, of course, you'll start reeling in."

Johnny turns to me, hands on his hips, as though proud of his demonstration.

I have to admit, he's extremely cute.

Everything was so precise, and his knowledge and instructions were kind of attractive.

No.

Stop yourself right now, Laelia.

Right now.

"Are you ready to do yours?" Johnny asks, motioning at the pole that's still in my hands.

I blush and nod.

Why must Johnny be this attractive?

Not even just his looks.

His whole personality is attractive.

Everything about him is attractive.

It's not fair.

"So, first thing is your worm." Johnny says, motioning at the remains of his worm.

My eyes widen.

"I hate to break it to you, but I don't think I can do that part. I've never been… good with worms." I say, giving Johnny a hopeful look.

I'm not sure what I mean by "good with worms" but Johnny just purses his lips and nods.

"Okay, I'll do this part. It's really not that bad, but you don't have to do it."

I sigh in relief as he quickly hooks it, taking way less time than when he hooked his.

He stands, brushing his hands against his pants.

"Do you think you can cast it, or do you want help?" I look around at everyone on the pier, and all I can imagine is sending my sharp hook through someone's face or limb.

"Maybe you can help? I'm more or less freaked out by the idea of hooking a person, and not a fish." I say, sheepishly looking up at Johnny.

"Sure, I can help, but just for the record, I don't think you'll hook someone—you're too careful for that—but I did have to tell you that because it is a possibility. And, side note, you'll want to keep your eyes peeled for anyone else's misguided hooks. Anyways, here, place your hands here and… here." Johnny says, looking at my hand placement for a second.

"Sorry, I'm used to doing it myself. It's one of those things that you can do, but teaching someone how to do it is hard."

Johnny stands behind me now, the softness of his breath on the back of my head and on my neck.

He moves one of my hands and covers it with his as he places it on the pole. The warmth from his hand is burning mine, but saying something isn't even an option.

Besides the fact that I'm maybe just a little bit enjoying this, there's no air in my lungs for me to speak.

"And the other goes here." Johnny says softly, his long fingers wrapping around mine, and placing it lower than our other hands.

"We'll pull this behind our shoulder, and then cast."

Johnny guides our bodies, sliding his finger under mine to release the line, allowing it to successfully land in the water, only a few feet away from Johnny's line.

"Hey, we did pretty good." I say, turning, slightly surprised by how close our faces are now.

Close enough to… stop!

I pull away from Johnny, and while it pains me to do so, I remind myself that I never should have let him get this close. I'm supposed to be distancing myself, not doing things like this that bring us way too close.

Johnny pulls back, and steps the few steps to his chair, sitting down and facing the lake. I sit in the chair next to him, and every few seconds I look over at him, expecting... *something* from him.

Again, I want to ask him what our small moments—like the one that just happened—mean to him.

Maybe I'm just looking too deeply into this, but friends don't usually do things like that... right?

Then again, while I don't see him as anything more than a friend right now, I would be one hundred percent lying if I said that I don't want to see him as more.

Is this how it's really going to be from now on?

Me, longing and stealing glances at Johnny, and him unaware?

Am I giving him too little credit?

Does he know that I like him?

"I'm pretty sure you have something on your line." Johnny says, tapping my rod with his finger, pulling me from my thoughts a few minutes later.

My rod is bobbing against the wooden railing, and I instinctively grab it.

"I just reel it in, right?" I ask, feeling the fish pulling against the line.

"Yes, you'll want to reel pretty fast right now. When you see it flipping over the top of the water, you'll need to be careful you don't accidentally let it free. Um, you might want to start reeling it in now." Johnny says, motioning at the still bobbing pole in my hand.

"Oh, yeah, on it." I say, reeling as fast as my hand allows.

Within a few seconds, my fish is flopping in midair, and I don't make a move to pull the remaining line towards myself and unhook the fish.

I move my gaze from my still-in-mid-air fish to Johnny, silently asking what to do.

Why didn't we go over this part already?

A few people are starting to watch, and it almost feels like a scene from a teen movie where the main lead does something embarrassing, and then she looks around to find everyone watching her.

This makes me freeze even more, knowing that any small mistake I make, other people will be watching.

Johnny seems to realize my hesitation, and immediately reaches out to grab the poor fish.

I feel bad now that it's in Johnny's hand. I've been unintentionally shortening it's life.

"Here, you just gently remove the hook, and hold it like this. Super easy."

Johnny gently explains, swiftly moving his hands as he speaks, and when he lifts his head, an easy smile is on his face.

I melt a little.

"Well, Johnny, you're the first to catch a fish today. Can we do a quick measure on it before you release it?" Rory says from behind me, startling me slightly.

I'm willing to let her give the credit to Johnny, but he quickly corrects her.

"Oh, Laelia caught this one, I'm just helping unhook it. Sure, let's measure it, then Laelia can release it." As he's finishing his sentence, someone behind us shouts that he's caught a fish.

"Wow, good catch! Fourteen inches! I need to go measure this next one, but don't worry, I'm keeping the books and will get this down for you." Rory says before rushing to the other end of the pier.

"Here's your big moment. You can just hold it around like this, I don't think you want to hold it the normal fisherman's way." Johnny says, transferring the fish into my hands, wrapping my hand around the slippery body.

I immediately almost drop it, but after a second, I'm giving Johnny a small smile. I surely look freaked out, but Johnny gives me a full smile.

"I'll take a picture of you. You're going to want it later on." Johnny says, quickly pulling out his phone and snapping a picture before I can protest.

"I- um- can we put this one back in the water?" I ask, feeling it struggling against my hands.

"Yeah, you don't want to just drop it in the water, because that will shock it. Just gently put it in. You're going to want to get on your knees or something so you can reach through this bottom rail and be as close as possible to the water."

I do as he says, and I breathe a sigh of relief when I see it swim away.

I stand, brushing my hands on my shorts, feeling the slime from the fish now. I must be making a face, because Johnny reaches into his backpack and hands me a hand wipe.

"Oh my gosh, thank you. For this," I motion towards the wipe, "and for helping me unhook it and stuff." I say, fully meaning my thanks.

Johnny nods, and I can almost swear that I see his ears turning a deep crimson color. The sun reflecting off of the lake behind him makes it hard to be sure, but I'm almost positive.

"It's no big deal. You did most of the work yourself. And, by the way, for that certain fish, fourteen inches is pretty long. I doubt there will be many fish caught that match yours."

I want to protest that he did most of the work, and all I did was reel it in, but I know he'll gently argue back, saying he only did a small part.

Instead, I look down at my now-empty hook.

"Now we just wait for you to catch one, right?" I ask, glancing out to see his line peacefully still in the lake.

"No. Well, yes, but don't you want to cast again? Who knows, you might be lucky and catch another one. The competition has a few different categories. There's a winner for the first fish—which is you—the largest fish, and the most. These are of course team wins, but most people count them as personal wins, too."

I nod.

"Oh, yeah, we can cast it again. Maybe we'll get another one." I say, hoping that from now on Johnny is the only one that catches anything.

Yes, it was fun, but I don't think I can hold another one for at least a little while.

That last one was *so* slimy and floppy.

"Can you… maybe bait mine again? I don't think I have it in me to hold a worm." I ask sheepishly.

Johnny nods, and within seconds, he's baited my hook again.

"There you go. And when you cast, just remember when to let go." Johnny says, stepping back and giving me a 'go ahead' gesture.

I give him a thumbs up, feeling his gaze on me as I prepare to cast.

I do my best, and although it doesn't go as far as Johnny's, it comes close.

Yay, I don't look like a complete fool.

"Perfect. Now, we're good to wait." Johnny says, seating himself back into his chair. I do the same, leaning back into the chair.

A breeze rustles in the trees all around us, and our lines move a little bit in the small ripples of the lake.

Johnny and I are in complete silence, and while I'd tried to prepare myself for hours of awkward moments, I'm completely at-ease now. The way I always am with Johnny.

It's like he has an aura of peace and calmness around him. And while I know he has energy and excitement, that's not what I mean.

I mean the way he seems so in control and in sync with his emotions.

I can feel myself slipping back and not reining in my emotions.

I can feel every bit of resolve and self-control leaving, and I force myself to look anywhere but Johnny.

Think about anything other than Johnny.

Essentially, convince myself Johnny doesn't exist.

And, while I'm failing miserably, I'm not confessing anything to Johnny. I'm not giving him any signals that I like him.

Well, at least I hope I'm not.

I've never really liked a boy, and even if I'd had a silly crush or something on someone, I've definitely never felt this way about any boy.

Ever.

I can only hope that I can continue my little charade for as long as we're together.

That I can keep my emotions and feelings at bay.

At least, when I'm around Johnny.

Then, I can just forget about him after we part ways.

A scoff escapes me, and I don't dare to look over and check to see if Johnny heard me.

Let's be real, he did.

And while I'm staring out into the open lake, out of my peripheral vision I can see Johnny checking me out.

Checking me out?

Where did that come from?

Not checking me out, probably just wondering why it looks like I'm having a conversation with myself.

Seriously, though, I'm not going to ever forget Johnny.

I'm not going to forget a single thing he's said or done.

I've been telling myself that I'll be able to forget him, this summer, everything, but I already know I never will.

There's only silence between us, and the few sounds coming from the chattering of other people, the babbling of the birds, and the wind rustling the branches and rippling the water.

I guess that's why we don't realize Johnny's pole has caught something.

Because, within a few seconds, Johnny's pole is yanked almost completely over the edge of the pier.

He launches and grabs it, and pulls back.

He starts to set it back down, but then realizes there's something on the line.

I stand, feeling excited that he's finally caught a fish, too.

I mean, wouldn't it be ironic that the fisherman doesn't catch any fish, and the person who hasn't been in over a decade catches one?

He reels it in, and within a few minutes, there's a fish flipping and flopping on the line that's still hanging over the water.

I risk a look over at Johnny as he unhooks his fish, holding it and looking up at me with shining eyes and a full smile.

"Wow, yours is so large!" I say, noting that it's much larger than mine probably was, and I don't have to continue guessing, because Rory measures it, and it's not so surprisingly larger than mine.

Not by much, just a mere inch.

"I'm going to go write this down. You two have caught some pretty large fish, already. Good job." Rory says, smiling before walking away.

"Wow! Good job." I say, giving Johnny a smile.

"Thank you. I for sure thought that you would be the winner of the largest fish."

I duck my head, slightly embarrassed for no reason.

"Do you want a picture with your fish? Maybe someone like your mom would like it?" I ask, reaching for my phone.

"Bold of you to assume I don't want one for myself." Johnny says with a smirk.

My jaw drops, and I feel heat rushing to my face.

He seems to notice my face, and quickly rushes to add on to his previous statement.

"I'm joking. My mom would love it." He says, and I feel relief flood through me, washing away my worry.

I snap a photo of Johnny holding his fish and smiling, and I can feel a smile rising on my face, too.

Chapter Twenty-Four

"Perfect. I have the photo." I say, sliding my phone back into my bag and zipping it.

"Thank you." Johnny says over his shoulder as he drops his fish back into the water.

He stands and brushes his hands against his jeans, and I don't make a face, but the idea of not thoroughly wiping my hands off after holding a fish, completely grosses me out.

Thankfully, I'm not him.

I try to remind myself to not be so cynical of others, and maybe that will relate to me being so much less cynical of myself.

Hey, it's worth a shot.

I mean, even if it doesn't work on me, at least I'm being a little bit nicer to other people.

Johnny re-baits his hook, and casts again.

He does this all within a few seconds, and I'm amazed at his expertise and speed.

Then again, he is an expert, and I haven't done something like this in years.

I think back on my past few summers, and all of our small expeditions in our motorhome, and realize how I haven't done anything.

All of this time we've been 'soaking up the great outdoors,' but really, we haven't done anything.

It's almost like we've been living in this sheltered version of camping and spending our summers outdoors.

Yes, I admit being in a motorhome isn't exactly camping, but we're still so close to nature, yet so far away.

Which surprises me.

We've been on hikes, and visited lakes, but we've never been this immersed in the world around us.

It's all because of Johnny that I'm doing this.

I feel completely different than I did when we started this trip.

I wouldn't ever call myself outdoorsy, but I'm definitely enjoying our small escapes into the peace and wonder of nature.

"Don't you think it's crazy that both of us have caught fish?" Johnny asks, looking over with curiosity in his eyes. "I mean, statistically speaking, a few more people should have caught fish before both of us on the same team caught fish, right?" Johnny adds, his eyes flashing as he seemingly runs numbers in his head.

I fight the urge to giggle, his complete immersion in the statistics both fascinating and cute.

Cute?

I need to stop this.

Every five seconds I seem to forget that I'm supposed to be pushing all thoughts that could qualify as 'more than friends' as far away as possible.

Even though I'm failing miserably, failing isn't an option.

Not when it's something as serious as this.

The day drags on with Johnny and I both catching a few more fish, nothing as large as our first ones, but still decent.

"Okay, everyone, it's time to start wrapping things up. The competition is officially over, and I'll be going through scores on our way back. If you'd like to know your score immediately, feel free to wait in the parking lot back over at the park, where I'll be announcing them personally. Otherwise, feel free to go straight back to your homes, and wait for an email." Rory calls out, clapping her hand against her clipboard to draw everyone's attention.

Johnny and I both reel in our lines, and after he secures his hook on the pole, he reaches for mine and does the same.

"Thanks." I say, reaching down to fold up my camp chair.

Within a few minutes, we're ready to leave, and we thank Rory before starting the walk back down.

There's a few other kids that are walking a little ways in front of us, and behind us.

Since not everyone took the bus, a few pairs of people are able to start the walk back early.

Johnny is carrying both camp chairs, and his pole, and I insisted that I carried mine. I had tried for the chair, but Johnny wouldn't hear of it.

I look over at him as we walk, and I can't help but blush as I take in his expression, and the way his hair flops over his ears and forehead. Why does he have to be so adorable and attractive at the same time?

It's not fair.

At all.

"Hey, Laelia, good job on your fish." A boy says as he passes us.

I look over, surprised and unsure of who the boy next to me is.

"Thanks." I reply, looking over his face again, desperately trying to remember his name.

"It's Jayden. I've been doing this Teen Summer Fest thing, too." He says, his blond undercut peeking out from under his hat.

"Cool. Yeah, sorry I didn't recognize you. I haven't been hanging out with many people recently." I say with a shrug and an apologetic smile.

I glance over at Johnny, noticing he's been silent since Jayden arrived.

"Hey, if you need someone new to hang out with, let me know." Jayden says with a wink as he jogs to catch up with his teammate. My jaw drops, but I clamp it shut as Johnny snaps his head up.

He whips his head towards me, but only focusing on me for a split second before staring daggers into Jayden's back.

I'm horrified at what Jayden just said, and what he was implying, but I'm even more horrified by the fact that Johnny just witnessed that interaction.

Being alone with Jayden and him saying that would've been mortifying enough, but with Johnny here?

I'm pretty sure whoever said you can't die from embarrassment was lying, because I feel close to dying.

Jayden and his teammate's pace is faster than ours—rather mine, seeing as Johnny is walking at my pace—and within another few minutes they're out of sight.

"We won't be taking this trail for our night hike tomorrow, right?" I ask, trying to bring some life back to the rest of our walk.

Johnny's head lifts when I start speaking, listening until I finish.

"No, it'll be over on one of the trails that are connected to the park. I think the last night will be on this one, and we'll go past the lake." Johnny replies.

"Oh, cool. I haven't really been on the trails by the park. Have you?"

I mentally smack my forehead, realizing how dumb I must sound.

Of course he has.

Johnny smiles and nods.

"Yes, a few times. It's been a while, but I did bike on one of them a few weeks ago. Actually, that was the day that you got here." Johnny says, as if he's recalling a large detail.

I vaguely remember that day, and it feels like years have passed, since.

"Really? It must be pretty fun to bike these trails." I comment, truly meaning it.

I rarely bike, although I do have one back home.

It might be a good way for me to get out of the house, and I have a feeling that when I go back home, I'll be longing for the freedom of being outside of my home.

Honestly, I'll be longing for the freedom and feeling of this summer.

We reach Johnny's truck, and Johnny loads the few things into the bed before climbing into the driver side, and me and the passenger.

I tuck my legs underneath me, resting against the door, my head propped on the window.

A wave of drowsiness washes over me, the warm air and eventful past few days catching up with me.

I tell myself I won't fall asleep before we get back, because that would be absolutely mortifying, and, it would be totally rude.

Johnny backs out of his spot, pulling on the freeway.

He's silent, and just gently taps his finger on the steering wheel as we ride in silence. A few cars pass us, and I feel at ease knowing Johnny is behind the wheel.

I'm proud of myself, knowing that I can ride in his truck without freaking out.

Looking back, the first time we were in the truck together, it's embarrassing how I acted.

I almost can't believe I had that fear.

I mean, I know I did, but it's hard to imagine being fearful of being in a truck with Johnny.

I feel the sun on my face, and the heat from the glass on my skin. It's actually, almost comforting.

My eyes start drooping, and as soon as I'm consciously aware of the fact, I snap my head up and sit up straight in the seat.

Johnny glances over, probably slightly startled by my sudden movement, but he doesn't say anything.

My eyes start drooping again, and I force myself to place my feet firmly on the floorboard, making myself uncomfortable, hoping that it will keep me awake.

Not being comfortable usually does that to me.

I stare straight ahead, and focus on the dotted lines on the road. Focusing on something other than sleep seems to be doing it, although I feel my eyes starting to lower again.

I recall last night, remembering my sleeplessness, fueled by my dreading of today.

Not necessarily dreading, but at least being stressed out about it.

It sounds crazy to say, now, seeing as I'm so relaxed that I'm almost asleep.

Ironic, isn't it?

"Are you tired?" Johnny asks quietly, not taking his eyes off of the road. I feel my face flush.

"A little. Not very much, though." I quickly reply.

Johnny smiles, and while he doesn't take his eyes away from the road, I can tell he's continuing to watch me out of the corners of his eyes.

"I'm really not." I insist, feeling the need to make sure he knows that I mean it.

Even if it's far from the truth.

Johnny just nods and makes an uh-huh sound, his smile firmly planted on his face.

A chuckle escapes him, and I fold my arms over my chest and stick out my tongue at him.

His smile deepens at this, and another chuckle escapes.

I can't even take myself seriously, and a laugh of my own escapes my lips.

Johnny flips on the radio, and changes the channel from one that has music in either Korean or Japanese playing, to an upbeat pop channel.

I nod my head to the beat, Johnny's impressive sound system shaking off my drowsiness.

Johnny exits off of the highway, and within a few minutes we're driving on the park's private road that will take us the rest of the way home.

Chapter Twenty-Five

"Do you want to wait in the parking lot for Rory, and hear our scores now? Or would you rather just go home?" Johnny asks.

"We can wait." I reply.

I don't need to be home anytime soon. And, if I'm being honest, I am a little bit curious to see who won.

Not that winning is that important, but the fact that I caught a large fish, and Johnny's was even larger than mine, does make me a little bit curious.

Johnny nods, and he takes the road towards the parking lot instead of going straight to our houses.

Within minutes we're in the near vacant parking lot, the bus nowhere in sight.

"It should be only about three or four more minutes until they get here." Johnny says after he checks the time on the truck screen.

"And you just know this?" I ask, a teasing tone in my voice, not at all expecting an answer.

"Well, I'm just guessing, but judging by the speed limit, the model of the bus, and the passengers that they have, I'm concluding that they'll be here in three to four minutes." Johnny says, looking over with a grin.

My mouth opens a little, and his smile is forming.

I'm in awe.

He can just… calculate that?

"Wow, I'm impressed." Is all I can say as I look over at him.

I must be completely overreacting, but the way he just explained his thought process, just… impresses me.

Johnny smiles, and we gaze into each other's eyes, neither of us breaking eye contact, hardly blinking, and hardly breathing.

Johnny must see or hear the bus behind us, pulling into the parking lot, because he breaks eye contact, and watches it pull in.

I look over at the clock, and notice that it's been three minutes and thirty seconds since Johnny's prediction.

We both watch and wait a few more minutes before we get out and walk over, allowing the bus driver to park, and for everyone to unload.

As we walk, the gravel crunches beneath our feet, the only noise between us.

We gather around Rory with everyone else, and Johnny and I stand next to the two brothers that had originally been at the lake before us, and beside them is Jayden and his teammate.

I inwardly shudder, and I try to discreetly move to the other side of Johnny, giving me more space between Jayden.

It's not that I'm scared of him, he just… weirds me out. I mean, the way our small conversation went earlier was completely inappropriate.

The way he just brought up wanting to spend more time with me—whatever that means—and his more than a little bit weird way of doing so… it's all a no for me.

Just no.

Another inward shudder passes through me, and Johnny

notices.

He bristles as he looks over and notices Jayden.

I'm not sure what he has against Jayden, or even if he's looking at Jayden, but it's weird for me to see him in a mood that's anything but controlled and happy.

Super weird, actually.

"Okay, I did the calculating on the drive back, and I have our winners." Rory says, waving her clipboard around, excitement in her voice.

She really enjoys this.

"For the first and largest fish, that will be team Johnny and Lelia. Congratulations."

A few claps come from almost everyone else, and I turn to Johnny, his hand raised in a high-five. I clap our hands together, both of us beaming.

"And for most fish, that will be team Ben and William. Congratulations."

I peer past a few people, and see them clap each other on their backs, some of the boys around them doing the same.

Johnny and I clap for them, and Rory waits until there's silence before speaking again.

"Since we have everyone here, I want to remind you that our first night hike is tomorrow, and we'll be meeting at the Owl's Hollow trail head. If you need or want a map, please note that they're in the main office, so feel free to grab one before tomorrow night. Side note, please make sure you have permission to be out late. I know you're all almost adults, but I would prefer if your parents aren't calling the police, completely frantic because they're not sure where you are, and it's somewhat late. That's all for today.

I hope you all had fun today, I know I did. Thank you." Rory announces, making eye contact with everyone in our half-circle.

She moves her clipboard in a dismissive gesture, and we all scatter in our own directions.

Johnny and I climb back into his truck, and he starts the short drive home.

"That was actually really fun. Not the worm part, but everything else." I say, glancing over to view Johnny's expression.

Instead of his usual smile, there's a tight look on his face.

He quickly shifts to a smile, and nods.

"I'm glad you enjoyed it. Next time you go, you'll have to buy some bait, instead of worms. Then, you'll be fishing like a pro." Johnny says in an encouraging tone.

"I don't think I'll be doing any fishing for a while, but I'll keep that in mind. Thanks." I say, noticing how he says 'you' instead of 'we'.

Ouch.

Of course, I know that our time together is almost up, but Johnny saying it so casually, hurts.

"Why not? You still have the rest of the summer to travel, right?" Johnny asks, confusion in his voice as he talks.

I'm not sure how to explain to him that our lives are so different.

That my family isn't like his.

That we don't just do things like this.

"Yeah, I guess so. What will your family be doing after this?" I ask, diverting the attention from me to him.

"I'm not really sure. Some months we have planned in advance, but sometimes we decide the day of. We'll probably slowly drive to

California to visit Julianna, but I'm not sure. We're planning to visit her the week before classes start." Johnny says, easily rolling to the new topic.

"I bet she's excited to see you." I respond, noting that he grins at this.

"I hope so." Is all he replies with, and I look over to see his smile.

We pull up in front of my home, and I quickly scramble out, not wanting Johnny to come around and open the door like he would normally do.

I'm making myself do as many of the things that Johnny would normally do—such as opening doors, and doing them myself—so that I don't become used to this, and maybe the heartbreak of our separation and just a few short weeks will be spared.

If only, just a little bit.

It's unavoidable, but maybe the small things won't be so bad. "Thank you, Johnny." I say as I shut the door, giving him a small wave as he waits for me to walk inside before he drives away.

"You're home, already? How did it go?" Mom asks as I slide off my shoes.

I look up to see her with her laptop on her legs as she works on the couch.

"It went well, thank you. Johnny and I won a few of the competitions." I say, giving her a smile.

She grins, and while I can tell she's not all that into it, I appreciate the effort.

"What are you working on?" I ask, wanting to give her a chance to talk.

"Oh, just the usual. I've been busy recently, with all these new clients and business deals." She says, waving her hand in a nonchalant gesture.

"That's good. I'm glad." Is all I can think to respond.

Mom ducks her head back down and rapidly taps away at the keys of her laptop.

I gather my clothes for a shower, and I take the walk over to the bathhouse.

To my horror, I see Jayden sitting outside a nice motorhome, only a few sites away from Johnny's house.

I keep my eyes focused on the road ahead of me, avoiding all eye contact with him.

I'm not even sure if he's seen me, but I don't want to risk it.

Sure, Jayden hasn't actually done anything, but he's really giving me weird vibes.

I'm not sure what it is, but ever since earlier on the trail, the few times I've seen him, I feel weirded out.

I feel bad for being weirded out by him, since he actually hasn't done anything, but a small part of my brain tells me to stop.

After I've showered off the smell of lake and outdoors, I towel off and dress, my loose shorts and T-shirt feeling extra comfortable after my warm shower.

A few minutes later, I walk out, my clothes and towel and a small bag, my sandals wet under my feet.

I don't feel like the bathhouse is gross, but do I trust the floor with my bare feet?

No way.

I walk back home, and start grilled cheese for dinner.

I'm in the middle of blending the tomatoes and flipping the toasted bread, when there's a knock at the door.

Both Colin and Jasper bark from their place on the couch, and since Mom, Dad, and the twins are gone on a walk, I guess it's up to me to check.

I don't have a problem with checking it, it's just, I can hardly think of a single time this summer I've had to check the door when there's been a knock.

It's... weird.

I look out the window to see an employee of the park, and quickly open the door

"Hello." I say, looking down at the middle-aged man. He has a clipboard, and looks impatient.

"Hello, ma'am. Is there anyone else home?"

I know it's a complete lie, and he is an employee, but I remember my parents saying that you never say when you're home alone.

"Yes, they're both busy, but I can help you. Is there anything you need?" I ask.

The man takes a look at his clipboard before looking back up.

"No, I'd just like to inform you that the sewer connection should be fixed tomorrow afternoon, and to expect our maintenance crew to be around here tomorrow morning." He says.

"Thank you, sir. I'll be sure to let my family know." He nods, and after wishing me a good evening, and walking away, I turn and see black smoke rising from the stove.

One of my sandwiches is burning!

I rush over and pull it off, the smell of burnt butter and bread strong.

The smoke alarm goes off, making everything ten times worse.

I'm quick to flip the burnt sandwich on a plate, and it takes me a few seconds to flick off the smoke alarm.

Why are the ceilings so high?

I open a few windows to air out the smell, but it doesn't seem to do the trick, because only a few seconds later, the smoke alarm goes off again.

No!

Our sites aren't super close to each other, but the neighbors can definitely hear this.

I turn on a few fans, and I leave the air conditioner on, hoping that it will waft the smell out the windows.

It still persists.

I turn off the stove, needing a minute to figure out what to do, now.

Maybe it's broken?

There's another knock on the door, and I almost scream in frustration.

Why can't the person out there hear that I'm struggling and just go away?

There's another knock, and I give up ignoring whoever it is, and throw open the door.

In doing so, I nearly swing the door into Johnny's outstretched hand.

He catches it with lightning-fast reflexes, and I stare at him, probably looking crazed and somewhat frustrated.

"Hi." Is all he says, peering past me, presumably trying to find the fire.

Berry is sitting expectantly at his feet, and after a second I bring my gaze back to his face.

"Hi, Johnny." I say, the alarm still blaring behind me.

"Do you need help? I heard the alarm while I was walking, and the guy next door looked… less than pleased with the noise pollution. I can leave, though." He says, noticing the horrified look that appears on my face.

"No, you don't need to leave. I accidentally seriously burned a sandwich, and this stupid alarm won't turn off." I explain sheepishly.

"Oh, I can turn it off if you'd like. These alarms are a bit different than your average alarm." Johnny offers sympathetically.

"That would be fabulous." I say, stepping back, the alarm almost making me dizzy from the sheer noise it's releasing.

"Berry, stay." Johnny says, motioning for her to stay outside. "Oh, just bring her in. I don't mind at all." I say, and Johnny motions for her to climb the stairs behind him.

"It's been a while since I've seen you guys." Johnny says in passing to Colin and Jasper, as he reaches up and pulls down the alarm. Colin and Jasper wagging their tails at his words.

I sit on the ground, giving Berry a pat as he flips a few switches on the alarm, successfully shutting it off.

"Thank you so much. I was going crazy." I say from my position on the ground.

I continue loving on Berry as he secures it back on the ceiling, the height not an issue for him.

"No worries, I don't think anyone else would have checked on you, though, rather just put in a noise complaint." Johnny says, subtly motioning at the guy in the next spot down, a scowl on his face as he eats his dinner.

I stand and start shutting windows—seeing as it's dark enough for people to be able to see inside—Johnny noticing and doing the same.

"I had these open to try and rid the place of the smell, and I thought that would shut the alarm off." I explain, gesturing at the fans directing air towards the windows.

"Good idea. These alarms are just weird. Ask me how I was able to turn it off so fast." Johnny says with a laugh, obviously having a few stories of his own.

As he shuts the last window, I turn back to the stove, flipping it back on and starting the oven.

Johnny stands awkwardly by the door, as if not wanting to just walk out and seem rude.

Do I want him to go, though?

I don't allow my rational side to argue with my impulsive one, because I end up blurting out an invitation to dinner.

Johnny stands, conflicted, and I immediately realize how this will look when my parents get back from their walk.

Those same thoughts are probably running through his head, too.

I check the clock, noting that they should be back in about ten minutes.

"I'm making grilled cheese sandwiches, tomato soup, and brownies. My parents will be back soon, so it won't be a long wait before we eat." I say, motioning at the island which is covered in flour, sugar, chocolate, bread, cheese, butter, tomatoes, and the rest of my ingredients.

"Um, sure. If you insist." Johnny says, taking another fleeting look at the door.

I wince.

Maybe he doesn't want to eat with me, and now I'm basically forcing him to stay.

I open my mouth to offer him a chance to leave, but he takes a glance at the island, and gestures at the spread.

"Is the bread homemade?" He asks, noticing my loaf of bread.

"Yes, I put it in the bread machine before we left, earlier."

Johnny nods.

"Cool. I bet our friend out there loved the noise that came from the machine." He teases, his gaze floating over to the window at the cranky man who is probably still out there.

"Then he'll just love the noise that the repair company will be making tomorrow morning." I say, laughing.

Johnny smiles and laughs, too.

The sound filling the room.

Is it bad that we're laughing at someone's misery?

Yes. Do I care right at this moment?

No.

"You can sit down anywhere." I say, gesturing at all of the seating options. Johnny sits on the couch, Berry laying down at his feet.

I notice the waves in Johnny's hair as he sits, now that his head is lower than mine, and I have to wonder if it's because he showered and his hair is naturally wavy.

"I really need to finish this up." I say, gesturing at the mess before me.

The clock is ticking on my family, and I know that everyone will be hungry.

Johnny immediately stands, washes his hands, and comes over to stand at the island.

"I can help. I'm not as skilled as you, but I can still help." He says, and for a split second, the world stills.

I'm not sure exactly where my head just went, but I snap back to reality.

"Thank you, what do you want to help with?" I ask, giving him the option instead of just instructing him.

"Anything. Whatever you think I'll be best at." Johnny says.

"Um, you can make the sandwiches. I need to finish my soup then the brownies." I say, glancing down at the complete mess and disarray of the counter.

"Yes, ma'am." Johnny says, grabbing a few pieces of bread and cheese, placing two sandwiches on the pan.

I finish my soup and add it to the pot on the stove, Johnny next to me, silently flipping the sandwiches.

I leave the soup on low heat, and quickly return to the brownies, adding my batter to the glass dish, and into the oven.

As I'm reaching into the oven, my leg knocks the door. Johnny must have been watching, because he acts fast and grabs the handle, and I narrowly escape a burn.

"Thanks." I say sheepishly.

How many times has Johnny come to my rescue today?

Too many to count, that's for sure.

I turn off the heat on the tomato soup as Johnny pulls his last sandwich off of the stove.

"All done." Johnny says, a satisfied smile playing across his face as he lands the sandwich on the plate.

"Thank you so much, I'm not sure what I would've done without your help." I say, feeling impulsive and giving him a hug.

The door opens then, Mom, Dad, and the boys walking. I jump away from Johnny, heat rising in my cheeks, and even though Johnny did literally nothing, he freezes like a deer in headlights.

"Well, hello, you two." Mom says with all I can describe as a knowing smile.

Whatever she thinks she knows is probably far from the truth, but she doesn't seem to think or realize that yet.

"Hi, Mom." I say, gesturing at the food we've placed on the island.

Just then, the oven alarm beeps, and I take that as my escape route, dashing over and opening it much faster than necessary.

I test them with a toothpick, deeming them done and removing them from the oven.

"Wow, dinner looks and smells delicious." Dad says as he leans over the counter, inspecting our meal.

"Good. That's what I hope, too." I say, plating a few plates and handing them to Mom and Dad for them to give to the boys.

Johnny notices, and starts making a plate, too, handing it to Dad with a smile.

Dad looks him up and down before accepting the plate, and I release the breath I didn't realize I was holding after he bites into his food.

I pass Mom a plate, and it's then that she notices Berry, sound asleep next to the couch where Johnny left her.

"Oh, she's just so cute." She exclaims.

Johnny smiles proudly.

"Thank you. I think she's pretty cute, too." I make another plate, offering it to Johnny, and he shakes his head telling me to eat it, saying that he'll make his own.

I slide into the seat next to Dad, allowing Johnny to sit next to Mom. We're a little bit squished at the smaller-than-average table, but no one complains.

"The food is excellent, Laelia." Mom comments, breaking the silence.

"Thank you, Johnny helped, too." I say, giving him the credit he deserves.

"Wow, good job, Johnny and Laelia." Mom says, correcting herself and giving Johnny a warm smile.

"Thank you." We say in unison, giving each other a smile before we both lower our heads to our plates.

Dinner is eaten in near-silence, everyone happily enjoying their food.

I start clearing plates after a few people are done with their food, and Johnny immediately stands, gathering the last few plates.

"Oh, thank you." I say, as he places the plates in the sink after wiping them each off with a paper towel.

I slice the brownies, and Johnny watches for a second before realizing I have a package of strawberries next to a cutting board and knife, and without me asking, he starts slicing them.

I turn back to plating the brownies, and I just can't help myself. I have to talk.

"Do you like strawberries and whipped cream on your brownies?" I ask, completely changing the words that almost came out of my mouth.

His hair is falling into his face with the way his head is angled, completely focused on the strawberries.

"Yes. How could one turn down strawberries with chocolate?" He teases.

I smile, and I feel butterflies in my stomach.

After I've added whipped cream to the tops of the brownies, Johnny adds strawberries to each plate.

While Johnny brings the plates of desserts, I set forks in front of the place settings, and notice that Mom has moved next to Dad, leaving Johnny and I to sit next to each other.

I freeze for only a second, and regain my composure. Where did my 'only be around Johnny if absolutely necessary' go?

I slide into the seat, Johnny sliding in after me, and lightly brushing my leg with his.

Everyone bites into their dessert, silence enveloping us.

The tension between Johnny and I is strong, and I'm surprised that no one says anything.

As if they can't hear and feel the electricity crackling around us.

I risk a glance at Johnny, and while his face is the definition of relaxed, the rest of his body is rigid.

This is so awkward.

If it's awkward for me, I would hate to be Johnny.

This is definitely not an ideal situation to be in.

"So, Johnny, how are your parents doing? I'm surprised they're not here tonight." Dad says, finally speaking up.

"My parents are doing well. They're actually not here right now, they made the drive to town, and are on a date." He says with an easy smile.

"Oh, that's so sweet. We should go on a date, soon." Mom says, giving Dad a wink.

I take the last bite of brownie, and make a move to stand, but realize I'm trapped.

Johnny is currently blocking my escape route.

I'm about to open my mouth and ask him to move, when he looks over, and without hesitation, stands.

I didn't even say anything.

I quickly slide out, and carry my plate to the sink, Johnny setting his plate on top of mine, brushing his hand across the back of mine.

I risk a glance at his face, and I feel like I've been hit with a train.

I stumble back at the expression he's wearing.

It's… yearning?

I can't describe it as anything other than yearning and desperation.

For what? I rip my eyes away and focus them on something else.

Anything else.

I feel Johnny's gaze burning into me even as I'm no longer looking at him.

"Laelia, why don't you walk Johnny back to his house, and we'll start cleaning up." Mom says, motioning to Dad taking the boys to change into pajamas.

I risk another glance, and Johnny is giving me a curious look.

I just nod, sliding on my shoes.

Johnny whistles so low I almost can't hear it, and Berry awakens, standing and walking over to him instantly.

I raise my eyebrows, completely impressed by her training.

Only to myself, will I ever admit that I let my dogs get away with too much.

Their training is minimal to none.

Johnny opens the door, walking out with Berry by his side, and I follow.

He gently shuts the door after I'm outside, and we stand next to each other, neither of us looking each other in the eye.

"Do you want to walk for a few minutes?" Johnny asks, breaking the silence between us.

"Yes." I answer immediately, not even considering it.

I take a few steps, Johnny next to me.

"So…" I drawl, unable to keep my mouth shut and needing there to be noise between us.

Johnny releases a chuckle, and I glance up at him, seeing amusement—and something else—playing across his face.

"What's so funny?" I ask.

We're walking in the direction completely opposite of his house, but neither of us seem to care.

Berry is wagging her tail as she walks next to Johnny, and through the low amount of orange light floating through the leaves, I see the shadows of Johnny's face.

His eyelashes are cascading long shadows down his cheeks, and I'm struck again with his beauty.

"I just think it's cute that you can't stand silence and always love when there's conversation." He says, and I'm shocked.

Partly because in my admiration, I'd forgotten I'd even asked a question, but mostly because of his answer.

Did he seriously just say that I'm cute?

I stutter for a second, completely bewildered.

"Did you just call me cute?" Is all I say, my voice coming out much steadier than I feel.

I'm shocked by my question, but even more by his answer.

"Yes." Is Johnny's response, and I feel even more unsteady than I did before.

Johnny slides his hand into mine, and I don't hesitate to wrap my fingers around his.

Tingling is rushing through my veins, and my whole body feels electrically charged.

There's butterflies swirling and fluttering through my stomach, but I still feel completely at ease.

For once, I don't need noise, and there's only the sound of our footsteps on the asphalt.

I must be completely in a daze, because I'm not really sure how it happens, but we're back in front of my house.

"Hey, wasn't I supposed to walk you to your house?" I question.

"Yeah, but do you really think I'm going to let you walk back alone? I'll be fine. Good night, Laelia." Johnny says, raising our joined hands to his mouth and gently brushing his soft lips against my knuckle.

Heat rushes from the tips of my fingers and spreads like a wildfire in my body.

I freeze, and Johnny gently lowers our hands and unclasps them, turning and walking in the direction of his house.

He turns back once as I open the door, ensuring that I go inside safely.

The picture of his receding figure with the low, almost non-existent light is the last thing that I see before I sleep.

Chapter Twenty-Six

I roll over, sunlight flooding down from the skylight and onto my face.

Squinting, I reach for my blanket and wrap it tighter around myself, wanting to taco myself even deeper into the comfort of my bed.

I smile, pressing my face into my pillow, remembering last night.

What even happened?

I replay last night a thousand times, the thrill never leaving me.

My alarm sounds, and I sigh, not wanting to get up.

I stretch out and stand, grabbing shorts and a long sleeve purple shirt.

Wrapping a few strands of hair around my fingers, I try a new braid style that I saw on social media the other day, and I'm surprised by how pretty it looks on me.

My face is a lot more round than the girl I saw in the tutorial, and I'd expected it to look strange on my face shape.

Grabbing a tube of mascara, I fluff up my lashes and smile, the new hair style and swipe of mascara look amazing together.

Carrying eggs, bacon, tortillas, peppers, and potatoes, I step into the fresh, morning air, my bare feet hitting the concrete. I start the griddle, everyone still asleep inside.

My pink toenails are a stark contrast on the gray concrete below, and I smile to myself as I slice my potatoes.

The bacon is sizzling and splattering, blending into the sound of morning birds chirping. I cook my peppers and potatoes, dousing them in seasoning.

I jump when I hear someone walking by.

"Hey, is some of that for me?" A middle aged man calls out with a chuckle as he passes.

I glare at his receding figure, his unexpected voice startling me.

I flip a few pieces of bacon, removing the cooked pieces and placing them on a tray with paper towels to absorb the excess grease.

More people are awake and going about their mornings, walking and enjoying the day.

Three more people make a joke as they walk by, asking about eating the food I'm making, and by now I'm tired of people commenting on my food.

"Can I-" A voice says from behind me, and before I even register who it is, I snap back.

"No, you can't have any of this."

I whirl, and see a slightly confused, and slightly amused, Johnny behind me.

"Rough morning?" He asks, a smile playing across his lips.

The same lips that kissed my hand last night.

I blush, feeling self-conscious over my sudden outburst. "Um, not really. I've just been out here for a bit, and it seems like everyone can't stop commenting on my cooking, and I was kind of annoyed." I say, turning my gaze back down to the eggs I'm scrambling.

"Ah, yes, the people who can't keep to themselves." Johnny says with a nod, taking a few steps closer, so he's right next to me, watching as I cook the eggs.

I reach over and use my fingers to flip a few tortillas, my arm brushing Johnny's as I do so, sending little lighting bolts up my arm.

"Wow, I'm impressed. I think you might need to teach me how to cook." Johnny says, admiration in his voice.

"Really?" I ask, surprised. He's never given me the impression that he wants to cook.

I look up when he doesn't reply immediately, and a shy smile is playing across his face.

"Really. I guess I didn't have a lot of interest in it before." Johnny says.

Before what?

I don't get the chance to ask, because just then, Archer and Arden tumble outside, their hair already tousled, though I'm sure Mom fixed it just minutes ago.

"Boys, please be careful on this concrete. Your bones aren't meant to be slammed into it." Mom says, stepping out from behind them.

"Good morning, Laelia, Johnny." She greets, taking the few steps to the table before sitting down with a book.

"Good morning." Johnny replies, and I nod, pulling the last few tortillas from the griddle off and into the warmer.

"Your dad will be out in a few minutes, and I think he's going to take the boys for a little hike or something after breakfast. I need to work, but he's free today." Mom says, her eyes never leaving her book.

"That sounds good." I reply, starting to plate food as Dad walks out, two cups of coffee in his hands, the steam rising from them and swirling in the cool morning air.

He passes a cup to Mom, and they call the twins to the table as I place food in front of them.

"Do you want to stay for breakfast?" I ask, turning to Johnny.

"Oh, no, I can't. I have to be on my way. I'll see you tonight, though. Have a good meal, Laelia." Johnny says, giving me a quick wave and a smile before walking away.

I take my plate and sit next to Mom, feeling slightly confused.

I mean, he never did say he was going to stay, but I'd just… assumed he would.

Everyone compliments my breakfast tacos, and I smile as Dad plates more food for the twins after they eat their first one within seconds.

"What did he mean by he'll see you tonight?" Mom asks, her eyebrow raised in question.

"Tonight is one of the night hikes for Teen Summer Fest." I explain, taking another bite of my potatoes.

"Oh, okay. That should be fun, right?" She replies, moving her eyes back down to her book.

"Yeah, I hope so. There should be a few of them, and I'm pretty excited."

Dad takes the boys for a walk, and Mom goes into her room, starting work for the day.

I clean up breakfast, saving the leftovers and washing the dishes.

It takes me a few minutes to put the griddle away, but after I'm done, I pull out my laptop and start typing away at the keys.

Sighing, I close my computer and put it away, sliding on tennis shoes and walking out the door.

I blink my eyes, realizing the car is gone—not that I had any plans of driving—and I start the walk on one of the footpaths that will lead me around the park.

Dad must have taken the boys into town, probably to the grocery store.

I need to clear my head.

I do something I rarely do—partly because it's difficult, partly because I don't enjoy silence—and I force my brain to clear.

As I walk I enjoy the chirping of birds and the sound of my feet crunching on the dirt path.

Every time thoughts of writing, Johnny, anything, comes to mind, I push them away.

A few bikers pass me, a woman walking her dog, and a dad with a baby strapped to his chest jog past me.

I pull my phone out of my pocket and tap the screen, in disbelief that I've been gone for over an hour.

The sign up ahead indicates the path is ending and this is my last chance to walk another path before I'm taken back into reality.

I walk into the empty road, and I realize with a start that this is where I originally almost ran right into Johnny, the day that I arrived.

It feels like years ago.

I look both ways before crossing, and I can't help it when my mind drifts.

It feels like years ago, but in reality, it was only a few weeks ago.

How did I become so comfortable with him?

I never let people know me this well, and yet, here Johnny is.

He knows just about every part of me.

Parts of me I rarely let even myself acknowledge.

Johnny knows all of the parts of me I've hidden, and all of the parts of me I don't show.

Chapter Twenty-Seven

I'm back home soon, and the car is still gone, so I'm not expecting Dad to be home.

I am surprised when I don't find Mom, but a pink sticky note is stuck on the counter, and I read the contents.

Mom is gone at the pool and is spending the rest of her afternoon there. Apparently, the internet is stronger there, and she's having trouble while working here.

I pull out my phone to see that while the service isn't terrible, it also isn't as strong as someone with an online-based job would desire.

I make myself a bowl of popcorn and settle into the couch with my book.

I read for what feels like only minutes, but must be much longer because I hear the car pull up and the sound of doors shutting outside.

I peek out the window and see Dad with the boys, loaded with groceries.

I wash my bowl and open the door for them, allowing them to place their bags on the island and table.

"Wow, you got quite the haul." I comment, opening the bags and placing items in the pantry and fridge.

"Hopefully it will last us the rest of our stay." Dad replies, helping the boys with their shoes and ushering them to the bathroom to wash their hands.

I freeze, and realize he's referring to the fact that we won't be here for much longer.

I sigh, and a new wave of emotions crashes over me.

I want to stay in this dream that these past few weeks have been.

I don't ever want it to end.

Mom is back soon enough, and everyone settles down for an afternoon nap.

Instead of laying down in bed, I sit in the recliner.

I pull open my laptop and play an episode of the television drama I'm watching, and while I'm not all-too interested— television hasn't ever really been my thing—it still captures my attention for the next two hours.

I peer into my parents' room, and see that the twins have climbed into bed with them, and they have some cartoon playing while they use their phones and read.

I pull out all of the ingredients for dinner, and start preparing them. As I slice the vegetables and cook the meat, I add everything to the glass dish I'll be using for the casserole.

After I've done everything and put it in the oven, I clean the kitchen extra well, trying to find ways to pass the time.

It's ten o-clock now, and I'm waiting outside for Johnny.

I don't admit even to myself that the reason I'm so on edge is because of my hike with Johnny, but I know deep down that it is.

It's crazy.

It's not like we'll be on a hike alone, but every time I've thought of it, I've completely ignored the fact that we'll be with everyone else.

It doesn't really matter, I only care about spending time with Johnny.

Where did my previous attempts to evade Johnny go?

I should have put my foot down and really attempted to keep Johnny at arm's reach.

Now, here I am.

Acting silly over a walk through some trees, just because Johnny will be there.

I purse my lips, trying to find it within me to scold myself for not sticking to my plan.

I can already feel the heartbreak of our separation, but I push that behind me.

I need to live in the moment.

No matter how hard that is for me, or how hard it will be down the road.

I'm deciding to let whatever happens happen, but still play it safe.

This is my last summer to really spend free.

Next summer I'll be an adult, and opportunities like the one being dangled in front of me will be gone.

I'm not sure why it's taken me this long to realize this, but I'm not ever going to have the chance to experience something as amazing as this summer, ever again.

I suck in a deep breath when I hear the crunch of asphalt and see Johnny's dark silhouette approaching.

"Hi," I say, greeting him as he nears.

"Hi, Laelia." Johnny says, and when he steps under the small light by the front of our site, I see his usual smile playing across his face.

"Are you ready? I have water, a few snacks, a first aid kit, binoculars, and bug spray in my backpack." Johnny says, a hint of pride in his voice as he lists off his items.

"Yeah, I have my water and phone." I say, motioning at my pocket, and the bottle in my hand.

Johnny reaches for my hand that's holding my bottle, and I'm confused.

"Here, I'll put it in my bag, there's no reason for you to carry it the whole time." Johnny says, and when his hand clasps around my cup, I allow him to slide it into the side pocket of his pack.

"We probably won't need anything besides our water, but Mom and I agreed that having these other things is smart." Johnny says, straightening the straps that don't need to be straightened on his backpack.

I take this as a chance to do as I promised myself earlier and live in the moment, and I reach out, wrapping my small hand around Johnny's large one.

Johnny sucks in a breath, but doesn't hesitate to clasp his fingers around mine.

My hand tingles, and my heart thumps in my chest.

The butterflies in my stomach fluttering and flapping wildly.

"Lead the way." I say, squeezing Johnny's hand lightly, breathless from my boldness, and the fact that I'm really allowing this.

Allowing myself to feel breathless and excited about tonight.

We approach the group that Rory and Janelle are leading at the head of the trail, and there's a buzz in the air.

Maybe I'm the only one that feels it, but tonight feels electrified.

"Please stay near your partner. Yes, you're allowed to walk with your new friends, but remember that you are responsible for your partner and vice versa. Talking is allowed, but please don't be exceedingly loud. We are in animal territory, and I know you kids don't like being woken up, so imagine the animals out here." Rory says, before clicking on her light and walking.

Johnny and I hang at the back of the group, and there's no way we'll be losing each other in the dark.

"You know, when we first met I never dreamed I'd be able to spend all of this time with you." Johnny says in a low voice, close enough to my ear that the hair on my neck prickles and goosebumps rush over my neck and shoulders.

"Me either." Is all I can reply, my brain short-circuiting.

"I also never imagined that I'd ever be this close to you. You know, besides this." Johnny says, lifting our joined hands slightly.

I know what he means even if he isn't really saying it.

He's talking about how much we've opened up to each other, and how much we know about the other.

"Same. I really wanted to know you then, you know? I immediately felt like I could trust you, which is a little silly, when you think about it." I say, thankful for the darkness that hides the blush creeping up on my cheeks.

"Really?" Johnny questions.

"Really." I breathe, feeling both glad and worried at the thought of how open I'm becoming.

There's well over an hour of hiking, and I'm already being way too open about my feelings.

"Do you want to play a game?" Johnny asks, and I trip over a small rock in the path, caught off-guard by his question.

My sock has been slipping below the ankle of my shoe, and it's starting to chafe.

"Sure. What do you have in mind?" I question, knowing I'll agree no matter what the game is.

"I just made it up, so don't laugh, but what if every time we see a constellation or other interesting part of nature out here, the other one has to find something that connects to the original object." Johnny explains.

"Or we could just ask each other questions or something. I'm not that knowledgeable when it comes to nature stuff." I reply.

"Hey, I need to show off my astrology knowledge to someone." Johnny teases, and I burst out in giggles.

"True, true. Be warned, though, I do have a few astrology facts hidden away somewhere." I tease.

"Really? I always find it so interesting how-"

"Hey! I was joking! I have basic knowledge on astrology, I made that up." I blurt out when I realize he's actually about to start talking factually.

Johnny laughs out loud, and I clearly surprised him with me not actually knowing all that much about the stars.

"Sorry, sorry. I can teach you about some of these constellations, if you'd like. It's actually quite fascinating, really." Johnny says, and I realize I'm bringing out the nerdy side to him.

I love that part of him.

How he's effortlessly funny, cool, exciting, smart, kind, everything.

I love how he never fails to amaze me.

"I'd love that." I say, and Johnny starts rattling off stories about the stars, and their patterns throughout the sky, and after ten minutes or so, I can't help myself from interrupting him.

"Wait, you just need to know that I can listen to you talk about this stuff forever. Go on." I say, and Johnny doesn't say anything immediately, but I'm sure he's smiling.

It's true, listening to him talk is so entertaining.

"Thank you." He says before continuing.

He trips over his words when he picks back up, and I can't help but imagine that I'm the cause of it.

I hope I'm the cause.

When Johnny takes a break to sip his water, I listen to Rory up ahead, rattling off facts.

The chafing on my ankle has become exceedingly more painful.

"Do you think Rory will notice if we stop for a second?" I ask Johnny, hoping he says it'll be fine.

I don't want to get in trouble, but I also want to adjust my sock.

"I didn't take you for a delinquent, Laelia." Johnny teases as he stops.

"Hey!" I say before he continues talking.

"Yeah, I mean the worst she'll do is send us back, which, makes us even further from her. We'll be fine. Besides, how will she know that we're gone unless she has reason to believe we're gone? Which, she won't, because we haven't been walking with anyone, meaning no one is missing us."

"Perfect." I respond, dropping his hand and reaching down to my foot.

"Are you okay?" Johnny asks, his playfulness stripped and replaced with a serious tone.

"Yeah, my sock is just slipping and I need to fix it." I say, trying to fix it without taking off my shoe, which proves worthless.

"Here, let's walk over here so you can take off your shoe and lean on a tree." Johnny says, noticing my struggle.

He points to the edge of the path and the trees that surround us.

"Thanks, that'll be a lot easier." I respond, and within a few seconds I've pulled my shoe off and I'm readjusting my sock.

"Do you want a small bandage to cover the spot it rubbed?" Johnny asks, reaching for the straps of his backpack.

"No, it should be good. I'll let you know if I need one later. I think I was just careless when I pulled it on earlier." I say, looking up, realizing how close we are.

Johnny had been leaning down with a small light, and now that our heads aren't bent, our faces are close.

So close.

I suck in a breath and meet Johnny's gaze.

My back is pressed pretty closely to the large tree behind me, and it sinks in that we really are alone out here.

Johnny's eyes never leave mine, but he reaches a hand out and gently brushes a few stray hairs that have fallen from the braid behind my ears.

I feel his speeding pulse when his wrist brushes my neck, and I'm sure he can feel mine.

Shivers travel from my neck to my whole body as his hand

moves back and cups my face.

Johnny brings his free hand to the other side of my face, and I realize what's about to happen.

Johnny is about to kiss me.

In that instant, he brings his soft lips to mine, brushing them ever so softly.

I gasp, and electricity shocks through my body.

Johnny brings his lips back to mine, and it's like there's a thousand fireflies flashing behind my eyes.

I bring my hands to the back of his head, wrapping strands of his hair around my fingers, drawing us closer.

Johnny's breath quickens, and I'm sure mine is doing the same.

The flood of emotion that washes over me is incomparable, and I want more.

Electricity rushes through me, sending every nerve through my body on fire.

I can almost hear the crackling of sparks and lighting that surround us, enveloping our bodies in our own storm.

My pulse is pounding so hard in my throat, that even if Johnny's hands weren't in the prime position to feel it, he can surely hear it.

It's drowning out the sounds of anything else.

Johnny's hair tangles around my fingers as I use them to pull us closer.

Johnny and I freeze as something on the path sends small rocks skittering across the ground, alerting us to someone's presence.

Chapter Twenty-Eight

"Ah, that's where they are. Our two cheaters are playing make-out session." A voice says, a flashlight flicking on and blinding me.

What?

I'm too confused to even pull away from Johnny, but he straightens and turns to face the voice I now recognize as Jayden.

His teammate is next to him, and while he looks uncomfortable, he still looks confrontational.

"What are you talking about?" Johnny asks, shifting so he's now standing next to me.

"Oh, don't act like you don't know. The fishing was just the icing on the cake. You're bribing Rory into giving you a good score on all of these events. And really, did you think no one would notice when you had the largest fish out there? *Both* of you?" He says, frustration and anger seeping into his voice.

"Hey, we haven't cheated or bribed anyone." Johnny says, his voice only slightly defensive.

I'm sure the only reason he's not being completely defensive is because Jayden is being irrational, and we're out here alone in the dark.

"Lies." He says, taking a step closer to us.

Another two steps and he'll be close enough to reach out and touch us.

"We haven't cheated, and don't plan on it. Ever. Is Rory looking for us?" Johnny asks, obviously wanting to know why they were looking for us.

"That's not important." Jayden says, taking another step forward, completely within arm's reach, now.

"What's important is-" He breaks off, as Johnny interrupts him. "Stop coming closer." He says firmly.

"Or what? Are you going to stop me?" Jayden says, trying to tempt Johnny. When Johnny doesn't reply, I suck in a breath, realizing what's happening.

Johnny is not going to be the first person to cause any more conflict, unless it's necessary.

"Jayden, let's just head back. They aren't worth our time." Jayden's teammate says, sounding like he doesn't want to betray Jayden, but also doesn't agree with what he's doing.

"Maybe not, Quinn, but I'm not done."

Johnny breathes deeply, picking up my hand.

"We're leaving."

Jayden reaches out and tries to grab my arm, and I jerk it back with a yelp like he tried to burn me.

I blink, and I almost don't see Johnny's fist land square on Jayden's jaw.

Jayden cries out and stumbles back, his teammate reaching out and grabbing him.

"Oh, you're going to re-"

He's once again cut off when his teammate talks over him, trying to sound threatening, but sounding tired of this whole altercation.

"Jayden, let's get home and fix this up before you start bruising."
He must be the older of the two, because I'm surprised when
Jayden doesn't directly ignore him, and tries to act like leaving is his
idea.

They walk down the trail, and I can almost hear the
teammate—Quinn—scolding him in a raised whisper.

"Are you okay?" Johnny asks, looking down at me once their
flashlight disappears down the trail.

"Me? Are *you* okay?" I ask, knowing that his hand must be
bruising.

"I'm fine. Are *you* okay? Did he touch you?" Johnny asks, a
hardness to his voice that I'm not sure I've ever heard before.

"No. I'm fine, really. I was just freaked out when he tried to grab
me, or whatever he was trying to do. Your hand must be bruising,
do you have an ice pack or something?" I reply, brushing away his
concerns.

"Laelia, really, I'll handle it when I get home later. I'm sorry he
tried that. I should have known that he'd try something like that."
Johnny says, running his uninjured hand through his hair.

"What do you mean? You couldn't have known." I insist, hating
that he's somehow blaming himself.

"Yeah, I kind of did, though. Jayden said something in passing
a few days ago, and after the fishing, he was acting super sour. I
assumed there was hard feelings, or something. I really didn't think
it would come to this, though." Johnny says.

"Whatever, nothing is going to come from you blaming
yourself. It's over now. We'll just report Jayden to Rory, and if he
tries anything else, it'll just make him look worse." I reply, crossing
my arms.

We stand awkwardly for a few seconds, both of us unsure of what to say or do next.

The crickets chirping around us harmonize with the calls of owls, and the rustling of the trees in the night breeze.

I look up and meet Johnny's eyes, and I pursed my lips when I realize there's not that many options on what we're going to do now.

"Do you want to catch up to the group or just start back?" Johnny asks, looking over his shoulder when a rabbit runs across the path.

I don't respond, and I act on impulse, reaching forward and placing my hands on either side of his face, bringing my lips to his.

Johnny immediately wraps his hands around my middle, his strong arms pulling me close.

All of my thoughts slip away, and it could be seconds or hours slipping away.

Either way, I don't care.

I should, but I can't find it within me to give it a second thought.

We both hear the approach of footsteps, presumably Rory's group on their way back.

Johnny laughs against my lips, and I press mine against his harder, signaling for him to be quiet.

"Do you really want us to be caught?" I whisper, leaning back far enough to see the sparkle in his eyes.

"I mean…" Johnny teases.

"Okay, what are we going to do? I would prefer to not be on the delinquent list." I say, giving Johnny an urgent look.

"We can either walk back ahead of them, or just wait here on the edge of the path and resume our spot in the back, as though we never left."

"Option two. Definitely option two." I quickly reply.

"Yes, ma'am." Johnny says, wrapping his arm around me and leading me into the trees bordering the path.

I stifle a giggle at the absurdity of our predicament.

"What's so funny?" Johnny says, a small laugh escaping him.

"Just… us. How did we end up here?" I say, clamping my hand over my mouth as Rory walks by, the rest of the group talking. Completely oblivious to us just a few feet away from them.

"I would say-" Johnny says, gripping my hand and falling into step about ten feet behind the last team. "-that your sock slipping was the catalyst to this."

I press my lips together, feeling like hours have gone by since then.

Which is pretty close to the truth.

"True. Lesson learned, though. Never wear socks that will allow your shoes to rub your ankles." I say with a laugh.

Maybe I'm extremely tired, or just on a high from our kiss, because I'm almost never this silly.

"I think you're tired." Johnny says, gripping my hand tighter when I stumble over the world's smallest pebble.

"Maybe."

"Definitely."

We're quiet the rest of the walk home, and Johnny makes sure I've walked inside my house before he walks home.

Chapter Twenty-Nine

Spinning the muffin tray in the oven for the last five minutes, I catch my reflection in the glass.

In it, I have a full smile, my eyes crinkling at their corners.

I check the time as I reset the timer, and blush.

It's eleven, and I only woke up thirty minutes ago.

Everyone else is at the pool, so it's just me and my muffins for the rest of the morning and afternoon.

I could walk over to the pool, but I want to revel in last night a little bit longer.

I feel… different.

I guess maybe I had thought that there was a chance Johnny might like me in the way that I like him, but I didn't expect *that* to happen last night.

The way he'd kissed me.

The way he'd protected me.

Everything feels like the pieces of a puzzle, and the pieces are slowly falling together.

My phone buzzes on the counter next to me, and I jump.

Startled, I pick it up to find an email from the Teen Summer Fest address.

The email reads out a request for me to visit the main office at eleven-thirty.

Weird.

I suck in a few breaths, and pull out my muffins, buttering two of them and adding them to my plate with an omelet.

After eating, I wash my plate and dry off my hands, before changing into a knee length dress and sandals, my hair falling in waves down my shoulder and back, courtesy of my braids.

Breathing deeply as my steps thud against the pavement, I try a few of my breathing tactics to relieve anxiety.

It only soothes so much, and my breath quickens as I open the main doors to the office, stepping into the air conditioning to see Rory, Johnny right next to her.

"Thank you for coming on such short notice. I'm so sorry for having to bring you all the way down here, but I'm hoping you'll spare me a few minutes of your time." Rory says as I approach.

"Um, sure. No problem." I reply, glancing over towards Johnny, his eyes more relaxed than stressed, but a fair amount of stress lingering.

"Thank you. I've been advised by your partner, Johnny, that you two were… harassed last night on our walk. Is that correct? He mentioned that you needed to adjust your shoe, and as you were, Jayden and Quinn hung back and began creating a… scene." Rory finishes, and I wonder just how much Johnny told her.

She's been spot on about everything except for the part where I technically wasn't still fixing my shoe.

Not that I'm going to mention that we'd been kissing.

I wonder if Johnny told her that part and she preferred to leave that part out, or if he left it out all together.

"Yes, that's all true." I state, unsure if she wants me to offer more information. "

Thank you. I would like as much detail as possible concerning the events when things became physical. Do you remember what all went down?" Her formal tone and grammar alerts me to the fact that this is a serious matter for her, and while I appreciate it, it does stress me out more than a little bit.

I speak clearly, not hinting at the fact that this is becoming more and more stressful, and I give the details as accurately as possible.

"Jayden had been confronting us, and as things started to escalate, Johnny and I tried to walk away, then he reached out like he was going to grab me. It freaked me out, and that's when Johnny…" I try to find a more gentle word rather than punch, but end up with "hit," which isn't all that gentle anyways. "That's when Johnny hit him. His teammate—which, by the way, didn't really get involved and was trying to tell Jayden off—pulled him away, preventing anything else from happening. They left down the path, and Johnny and I joined back up with your group."

Rory nods.

"I see. Your stories are just about identical. Thank you for alerting us to this, and please be assured that this won't happen again. Jayden has been on a… probation of sorts with us here after a different—very minor—incident a few days ago. I have to speak with a few other people, but I believe I'm going to remove him from our Fest. If he makes any more threatening advances, I want to know." Rory says, looking down at her clipboard, dismissing us. Johnny wishes her a nice afternoon, and I do the same.

Johnny opens the door for me, and the warm sun hits me, warming me up from the chill of the building.

"So you reported him?" I ask, squinting up at Johnny, barely fast enough to catch a strange expression cross his face.

"Yes, I did. It needed to be done. I've… heard things about him that made me feel obligated to be the one to stand up to him." Johnny says, not elaborating, only leaving me with more questions.

"What do you mean?" I question, not being able to restrain my curiosity.

"I… I don't think we should talk about that right now. Oh, by the way, I didn't think Rory would drag you down here. Sorry about that." Johnny apologizes, giving me a regretful smile.

"Oh, no worries. I bet she just needed to check her bases before she booted someone for a claim someone made. It's not a problem."

We've reached the spot where Johnny should walk the few steps to his site, and leave me to walk the short distance to mine, but he just keeps walking with me until we reach my house.

"I hope last night wasn't ruined because of Jayden." Johnny says with a smile, turning and walking back towards his home.

I watch as his figure recedes, and after he disappears around the small curve and the trees, I walk inside, picking up another muffin before curling up on the couch with my book.

Mom and Dad come back after another hour and a half, and I promise myself that I'll fill them in about last night before the end of the day.

They *do* deserve to know, and I wouldn't be surprised if Rory or someone else informed them of the situation.

It sounds strange to admit to myself, but this morning I'd almost completely forgotten about the Jayden situation.

I guess I'd felt confident that Johnny nearly breaking his jaw was enough to deter him from now on, but now that I'm dwelling on the topic, it almost makes more sense that he'll be out for blood.

Maybe not literally out for blood from me, but definitely Johnny.

Wouldn't most teenage boys want to avenge themselves or something?

I suck in a few deep breaths as my thoughts spiral, and now I'm completely and totally in a panic.

What if he tries to attack Johnny and he doesn't know he's coming?

What did Johnny know about him that made him report him?

Is he dangerous?

Well, obviously, he's somewhat unpredictable whenever he's upset.

I stand, walking into my parents' room, and they're both cleaning. Mom washing the mirror above the dresser, and Dad sweeping the floor.

"Do you have a minute to talk? Both of you?" I ask, sitting down on their bed and tucking my legs up underneath me.

Dad looks up confused, and Mom sets her supplies down, walking over and sitting next to me.

I suck in another deep breath, feeling strange.

"What's going on, kid?" Dad asks, sitting down and patting my arm.

I relay the events of last night—at least, all of the important parts—and leave off with my concern about Jayden.

I'm not overly worried about myself, but he will definitely have hard feelings towards Johnny.

"Oh, well, honey, you should have told us sooner. That boy needs to be removed from the premises if all of that is true. I think we need to discuss this with someone who has more power in this sort of thing. At least Johnny's parents. Do you know if he's told them?" Mom says, standing and brushing her hands against her long skirt, her hair swishing over her shoulder as she spins.

"Come on, honey, we need to get this handled. My daughter was harassed and almost attacked. I'm not okay with this." She strides out of the room, and I give Dad a look, wondering just who she was talking to.

We both follow Mom outside, Dad giving instructions to the boys, allowing them to watch television, and no food or candy while we're gone.

"Honey, let's visit the Sawyer's, then the main office. Do you know if they're home right now?" Mom calls out as she strides in the direction of the Sawyer's home.

"Maybe we don't need to-" I start, suggesting—well, trying— that we don't need to make a big deal out of this, but Mom cuts me off with a "Hush, please" and I snap my mouth shut and follow her.

Hanging more than a few steps behind her and Dad, the crunch of my shoes mixes softly with theirs, and I suck in a breath as we pass the bend and approach the Sawyer's place.

Johnny and his parents are sitting outside, eating a fruit assortment and talking.

Oh, great.

We're about to completely ruin their meal.

"Hello, Lucia, Christopher, how lovely to see you. Oh, Laelia, sorry, I didn't see you, lovely to see you, too." Katherine says, standing and greeting us.

Johnny stands, but Mom and Dad don't even look at him before they launch into their reason for being here.

Standing next to Johnny, I risk a glance over at him, and instead of seeing his—rather impressive—side profile, I'm looking right into his chocolate eyes.

I can't help myself, and a smile forms on my lips, and I feel it reach my eyes.

Johnny's lips turn up, and for a moment, we're smiling at each other like lovestruck teenagers.

Johnny lifts his eyes from mine, and turns to our parents.

They all simultaneously turn and face the two of us, and I feel the heat on my cheeks rising.

Not like when Johnny does something that I find cute or attractive, but more along the lines of "Oh, everyone is staring at me and I'm not one-hundred percent sure why" kind of way.

"Johnny, your parents told us that you explained the whole story, but we would love to hear it from your point of view, too. Laelia told us of the events, but I just want to make sure I have the story correct." Mom says rather demandingly.

Looking up at Johnny's expression noting how calm he looks under the pressure Mom is laying on him, I admire his ability to stay cool under pressure.

He relays the events of last night, leaving out the kiss part, and I wonder if he's let it slip to either of his parents when he surely discussed this with them.

I mean, besides the fact that Mom just said he already told his parents, I'm sure they must have suspected something was afoot when he was randomly visiting the main office earlier this morning.

As he finishes repeating the turn last night took, and takes a breath, both sets of parents eye us over before resuming their conversation.

"I wonder what they plan to do. I mean, Rory is kicking Jayden out of Teen Summer Fest, right?" I quietly question, looking over at Johnny as he shrugs.

"I'm not really sure. Yeah, small things have happened over the years here, but I think physical contact like last night was the furthest it's ever gone. I believe they want to make a statement about screening the people that participate, but I don't really know."

Physical contact.

For half a second I thought he was referring to our kiss, and I immediately feel so stupid and embarrassed when I realize he's talking about the physical contact between his fist, and Jayden's jaw.

"I can see that. I'm not really sure what will come of this, but I guess the only thing I'm slightly worried about is… you." I reply, say, looking him in the eye as I finish my statement.

"Me?" He asks, stunned.

"Yes, you. Think about how angry Jayden is right now. You literally punched him and he was practically drug away by his teammate, Quinn. He probably feels humiliated or something. Isn't that how guys feel after losing a fight?" I question.

"I wouldn't really call it a fight, but maybe. I haven't ever lost a fight, though, so I wouldn't know." Johnny replies, a cocky smile playing across his lips.

"Oh my gosh I can't even deal with you. I'm literally concerned about your safety, and you're making jokes?"

"Hey, it's not a joke, I haven't ever lost a fight before." Johnny says with a wink.

I succumb to his charms and drop the topic, but I know Mom and Dad are enraged enough to take things a step further, so I drop the topic with Johnny.

"Will you two please stay here? We're going to make a quick trip over to the office. Laelia, please make sure your phone is on, so if we need to call you and have you come down, we can reach you." Mom says before she and the rest of the adults leave. I turn to Johnny, a questioning expression in my gaze. "I guess we're to stay here until further notice." I say, looking up at Johnny, my expression changing from confused to mock-serious.

He gives me a serious look in return before bursting into laughter. "I guess so. Do you want fruit?" He asks, gesturing down at the fruit assortment he and his parents had been enjoying before we'd showed up.

"Um, sure. So I'm guessing you told your parents about last night?" I question, picking up an unused set of chopsticks, and setting a slice of watermelon in my mouth.

"Yeah, I was going to anyway, but when I got back I was rinsing off my hand and my dad saw…" Johnny says trailing off before finishing the story. "And he saw my hand, and asked what happened. I told him the major details, but he just said we'd discuss it today, which we were doing when you arrived. Mom wasn't too happy about the whole thing—neither was Dad—but they were glad that nothing bad had happened, either." Johnny replies.

"How much of last night did you tell them?" I ask shyly, looking down at the table, my hands resting next to the plate of fruit.

Johnny slides his hand over mine, and gently squeezes it.

"If you're referring to us kissing, they don't know. I didn't think it was right to share that without you knowing." Johnny says.

I look up from our hands and into his eyes, his gaze unwavering.

Taking a deep breath, I swipe my tongue over my dry lips and try to form words.

"I- you- thank you. Do you not want anyone to know, then?" I ask, self-consciousness seeping through me at the thought of Johnny not wanting to be seen with me.

"What? No. Not at all. I just felt like everything happened so fast, and it wasn't really fair to… I don't know, tell people without you knowing, you know?" Johnny quickly replies.

Most of the anxiety that had been flooding through me vaporizes, but a small part of me screams that he doesn't want people to find out that we're together.

"I guess so. I don't really care if people know, but maybe we can… launch this softly or something. I feel like it would be so weird if we just kissed or something in public, right? Wouldn't it be weird?" I ask, my cheeks flushing at the words tumbling out of my mouth.

Johnny nods, deep in thought.

He gazes into my eyes as thoughts flash behind his.

"We can do whatever you want, Laelia."

We sit in silence as thoughts race between us, and suddenly I'm hit with the reminder that the summer is almost over and we don't live near each other.

Thoughts like those have been swirling in my head for weeks, but now it's worse.

Now I've kissed Johnny. I can't turn back and just leave our short past behind.

I squeeze Johnny's hand, and his gaze stills, silently questioning what is crossing through my head.

Pretty soon the silence has engulfed us, and I've taken to

talking Johnny's ears off about random topics, my aversion to the previous topic evident.

He listens earnestly as I explain what I do for writing, and nods at all the right places.

He shifts his eyes for a split second, and in turn, I do, too.

Our parents arrive with chatter flowing between them as they walk, and I purse my lips, realizing how much I've been talking.

"Oh, dear, I almost forgot that we left you both here. Well, we've brought up the issue, and seeing as we're paying for a safe experience here, the directors are taking further action to make sure this doesn't happen again. I'm not really sure what that means, but if either of you have any more run-ins with that Jayden boy, I want to know. You shouldn't be harassed like this at all, especially on vacation of all places." Mom says, "tsking" her tongue as she finishes.

It takes all of three seconds once they're closer for everyone to notice our hands, and I suppress the urge to pull my hand away.

It's not like I'm embarrassed, rather just shy.

I've never considered myself shy, but in this moment, I feel it seeping through my veins.

"Johnny, will you start slicing the vegetables for dinner? I think Lucia and I are going to take a moment to chat." Katherine asks.

I notice Dad walking in the direction of our place, presumably to check on the boys.

"Sure."

Katherine lists off the ingredients Johnny needs to prepare, and Mom interjects, saying I can help him.

I don't mind, and within a few seconds, we're inside and Johnny is collecting the ingredients. Setting onions, tomatoes, mushrooms, and a few other items on the island.

"Do you actually want to help? I know your Mom offered, but you really don't have to. I've got it." Johnny says, sliding a chopping board across the island and setting a large knife on the board.

"No, I can help. Pass me a knife and board." I say, washing my hands and taking the original board and knife.

"What are we making?"

Johnny smiles, grabbing a tomato and tossing it up, catching it and placing it on his board.

"Spaghetti, but Mom has a special recipe and makes her own sauce. Kind of like yours the other night for soup. We'll need all of these ingredients, and I'll show you how she prefers her vegetables sliced, then you can go wild." Johnny says with a chuckle, slicing the tomato into quarters, the mushrooms in small slices, and the onion diced.

His hands move rhythmically as he demonstrates, and I feel a blush creep up my cheeks as I watch him.

It's freeing to be able to watch him and not feel like I shouldn't be.

Johnny's eye lashes flutter as he looks up at me, and instead of shifting my gaze, I allow his to meet mine.

He doesn't say anything, he just rolls a tomato on my board and walks around to my side.

His hand slides from the board and on to the edge of the counter, inches from my torso.

I suck in a breath as he gazes into my eyes, and I swear he can hear my heart pounding.

The butterflies in my stomach flutter, and I feel my pulse throughout my entire body.

I raise my hand and brush it across his jaw, the feeling sending tingles through my fingers and down my arm.

Johnny's breath hitches as I do so, and his ears redden.

His Adam's apple bobs as he swallows, and I can almost feel the pumping of his heart rate beneath my fingers.

I trace my fingers lower on his neck, sending goosebumps across his skin, scattering from my fingertips.

Johnny's eyes lower to my lips, and that's the only indication of what's to come, before he wraps his hands around the back of my head, crashing our lips together.

Chapter Thirty

I gasp before wrapping my arms around his neck, pulling him closer as I do so.

Johnny turns and presses my back into the edge of the counter.

Time flows freely as I run my fingers through his soft hair, our lips moving against each other.

Johnny's hands wrap around the back of my neck, his large hands allowing his thumbs to brush my cheeks.

I pull back, the realization that we're supposed to be making dinner and anyone could walk in at any time.

"We- we should stop." I say breathlessly, Johnny's hands continuing to rest on my face and neck, no doubt flushed and warm.

It takes him a few seconds to process what I've said, but once he realizes what we've just done, he nods.

"Yeah, you're right. I… I got carried away."

I giggle, pressing my hands against his—extremely well defined—chest, and gently push him away from me.

"I'm serious. You're…" Johnny trails off as he starts slicing vegetables, and curiosity bubbles throughout me as I wait in anticipation for the rest of sentence.

"I'm what?" I finally ask, unable to resist my curiosity.

"You're so… I don't even know. Amazing? That's not it—I mean, you *are* amazing—but it's more than that. You're… I'm going to have to find a word to describe you. Give me time and I'll find the perfect word to define you." Johnny says, looking up with a bashful smile.

"I'm going to hold you to that, Johnny. I want to know what you think describes or defines me." I say, and Johnny smiles before nodding.

"Don't worry, I'll be sure to let you know."

Within a few minutes of our conversation ending, Katherine walks in the door. She looks expectant, then… disappointed?

I can't place the look of emotion as it washes over her face, and I don't have a chance to before she begins speaking.

"Wow, you're almost done. I'll start the stove, and we can cook this all."

She pauses before turning to me.

"Laelia, I hope you'll stay for dinner. Your mom went home, but she said you're more than allowed to spend the meal with us."

My eyes scrunch in confusion, the actions of Mom unlike her. I decide to dwell on that later, and nod my head in agreement.

"I would love to stay. Thank you for offering." I say, dipping my head in thanks.

"Ah, lovely. I'm so glad. Why don't you and Johnny set the table and converse while I boil the pasta and make this sauce? I seasoned the bread this morning, so all I need to do is pop it in the oven. You've both made it so easy to finish up, now that everything is sliced." She says, shooing Johnny and I out of the kitchen, gesturing at the cabinet which probably houses their plates, a drawer below it surely storing the cutlery.

"I'll grab these, don't worry." Johnny says, reaching inside the cabinet and drawer, simultaneously pulling out plates and forks. I reach out to take some of the load off of him, but he pulls his arms back, not allowing me to help. "I've got it, you can relax. You're the guest." He says, a small laugh at the edge of his words.

"Okay, then. If you insist." I reply, sliding into the booth and resting my hands on my lap.

Johnny sets the table and sits next to me.

Close enough that if we were strangers, it would be uncomfortable, but far enough that it wouldn't be obvious that we're maybe more than friends.

What are we?

My fingers drum against my leg as thoughts swirl around my head.

Johnny must notice, because he slides his hand over mine.

I stifle a gasp.

Johnny's hand is literally on my thigh.

Well, it's more my knee that his hand is touching, but the action is still the same.

Risking a glance over at his face, I'm surprised to see him mouthing something to his dad, behind his Mom's back.

James either isn't interested in the fact that Johnny and I are much closer than we usually are, or he can't see his son's hand on my knee.

James replies, and to my—wrongful—dismay, it's in Japanese.

It's almost impossible to hear any sound from either of them.

Their conversation only lasts for a few more seconds, and within a few more minutes, Katherine has the food set on the table.

Johnny reaches for a plate from her, setting it on the trivet, his hand leaving my knee.

After the food is plated and everyone is seated, with Katherine across from me, and James across from Johnny.

"Laelia, it's so nice that you stayed for dinner. James and I are thrilled to be able to spend more time with you. Are you enjoying your summer? I think I remember you saying you're in private school?" Katherine gushes, taking a bite of her pasta, allowing me the chance to speak.

"Thank you for inviting me, this is lovely." I take a pause before continuing. "I've been having a great time this summer. I really like it here. I do go to private school back home, yes. I'm excited for the new school year, but I'll be sad when summer is over." I say, taking another bite of food after answering her questions.

James and Katherine nod, and out of the corner of my eye, I see Johnny not-so-subtly gazing at me with a smile.

A blush creeps up my cheeks, and I focus my eyes on my plate in front of me.

"Oh, we always miss our summers here. I'm not sure if Johnny has mentioned it, but we visit here every summer. Julianna—Johnny's older sister—is his teammate every year. They always have so much fun, so I'm absolutely pleased that you two have become such good friends, and are in this together."

Good friends.

I smile inwardly at the words, knowing that we're more than that, now.

I feel a pang of guilt for keeping our families just about in the dark over our... progressed relationship.

"Me, too. I can really say that this has been one of the best summers ever."

Johnny's hand that has been resting on the booth between us has moved ever so slightly towards mine, and as the conversation continues, Johnny's hand moves closer and closer, eventually on top of mine.

My whole hand is tingling and shooting little lightning bolts through my veins, up my arms and throughout my body.

Johnny's thumb gently strokes the top of my hand as we all talk, and with every small movement, a gentle reassurance rushes through me.

After dinner, and after our goodbyes are said, Johnny announces to his parents that he's going to walk me home.

Our pace is slow and relaxed, with our hands linked and my free hand wrapped around his arm.

"I'm glad that you stayed for dinner. I know my parents—Mom especially—liked spending time with you. I did, too." Johnny says, a smile in his voice.

"Thank you. You know, I really like your parents. They're both so… kind." I reply, squeezing his hand softly.

Johnny takes a breath before speaking, the sound blending with the sound of the breeze in the leaves, and the distant crackling of campfires.

"They are. I'm pretty lucky." He pauses before speaking again. "I was wondering if you wanted to do something before the bonfire tomorrow. We could get ice cream, or go on a walk or something. We could do something else, too, if you don't want to do something like that." Johnny says, rushing his last sentence.

"Really?" I ask, stopping to gaze up at Johnny's eyes.

They're illuminated, the moon working its magic and making his eyes even more beautiful.

"Yes." Johnny says immediately.

"I'd love to do something with you, Johnny. Anything you

decide will be fun." I say, standing on my toes and giving him a soft kiss on his cheek before I walk the few steps to my door.

"Goodnight, Johnny." I call out, turning and giving him a small wave, before closing the door softly behind me.

Chapter Thirty-One

Swiping a light layer of sparkling lip gloss over my lips, I flip my hair behind my shoulders for the last time before walking out the door.

I suck in a breath, my hair already annoying me.

I rarely have it down, and I'm reminded of why when it falls into my eyes for the tenth time in the last five minutes.

Johnny is waiting a few feet from my doorstep, and without permission, a smile creeps up my cheeks, reaching my eyes, as Johnny's eyes do the same.

"Hi, Johnny." I say, stretching out the "Hi" much longer than necessary.

Johnny doesn't reply, instead, he takes my hand and brings it to his lips.

His lips brush lightly across the back of my hand, sending goosebumps down my arm.

I'm vaguely aware of the fact that we're in broad daylight, and literally anyone could be watching us, but the thoughts vaporize after a few seconds.

I don't care.

Johnny takes my hand, and starts talking about our plans, but I'm hardly listening.

I don't care.

I don't care that people could be watching us.

Maybe it's because I've matured, or maybe it's just because I don't feel like anyone judging me will have any affect on us.

Our linked hands swish gently between us the whole walk to the cafe, and the feeling of contentment washes over me.

Johnny insists on me waiting outside, under one of the umbrellas, and saving us a table while he orders a "surprise" dessert for us.

The setting sun casts an orange haze over the atmosphere, and I bask in it while I wait.

Johnny sits across from me a few minutes later, a cute box of strawberries and two partially melted brownies on small plates in his hands.

"Strawberries with chocolate?" Johnny offers, opening the package of strawberries, and placing them in between us, and setting a plate with one of the brownies and a spoon in front of me.

"Oh my gosh, this is such a fun idea." I exclaim a few minutes later.

Johnny gives me a smile, and I can't help but notice how he does this when he's proud but doesn't want to seem conceited.

"I'm glad you think so. I know people usually use chocolate bars when they have these picnics, but I figured this might taste better."

"It does. This was really thoughtful, Johnny." I reply, taking another bite of strawberry and brownie.

"Your turn." I say, squeezing Johnny's hand lightly as we walk behind most of our group.

We've taken another trail tonight, Rory at the head of the group and Janelle at the back.

The incident from the other night causing there to be more… security when it comes to Teen Summer Fest.

"Would you rather live in Alaska or Hawaii for a year?"

"Hawaii. For sure Hawaii. Think about how cold Alaska is during winter." I reply.

We've been playing "Would You Rather?" for the last thirty minutes as we walk, and our questions are becoming less and less interesting.

"True, true. I guess I would choose Hawaii over Alaska for a year, but I would love to spend at least a summer in Alaska. The sun basically never sets, there's the northern lights, and there's all of the wildlife and scenery. I think next year we might visit Alaska. Mom wants to photograph some birds up there." Johnny replies.

Neither of us ask any more questions, and for a moment, I wallow in the fact that we have all of these plans—him with travel and finishing school, and I with school and going back home—and none of these plans include each other.

They could include each other, but we haven't talked about it.

We seem to talk about everything *but* what our futures look like.

We have to at some point, and I hope it will be soon.

"Mom let me know that we're leaving in a week." I say easily, as if he already knows, and Johnny stops for a split second before continuing walking.

"Oh. Do you know what you'll be doing afterwards?" He asks cautiously.

"Yeah, we're going to Florida for a little bit, before starting the drive home. My school starts a little bit earlier than most so we want to be home a little bit early." I say, rambling more than just a little bit.

"That's exciting. You'll have to send me pictures of your travels. I'll send you some from California, and wherever else we end up."

"You'll have to do that. I'll make sure to send a bunch of pictures. Maybe one will be from the hospital after a shark attack." I tease, trying to brighten the mood I've brought down so low.

"You do that." Johnny teases back.

Chapter Thirty-Two

"Mom, the dance is tonight, do you want to help me do my hair?" I ask, laying out the sundress that I plan to wear.

It's nicer than most of my other sundresses, but still fits the outdoorsy vibe that the dance will most likely have.

"What are you wanting to do with it? You know your hair skills are so much better than mine. I'll still help, of course." She replies.

"I'm thinking that we can do a crown braid or something, and just give more definition to my waves. So just a small part is braided, and the rest will kind of flow down my back, you know?" I reply, leaning into the bathroom and plugging in my hair curler.

"Ah, yes, I can do that. Let's do your outfit and makeup first."

We hurry through my makeup, and while it's a natural look I'm going for, I still add small flecks of glitter in the corners of my eyes, as well as a light layer under them and across the small freckles on my cheekbones.

"Oh you're just adorable. You braid your hair how you want it done, and I'll do the curling. Back when you were little, I hardly braided your hair, but looking back, I could have done so many adorable styles. I'm so glad you do so many braids now. They're always so cute." Mom says before adding a small amount of heat protecting product to my hair, and wrapping the first small section around the curling iron.

Thirty minutes go by before we're done, but the finished product is *so* worth it. My hair, makeup, and outfit look amazing together.

"Oh, you're so beautiful. You're really going to shock Johnny when he sees you."

I give her a look of both confusion and curiosity, wondering just how much she knows about us.

"If you're wondering about how I know about you two, just know that moms really do know a lot. I started piecing it together recently, but to be honest, I kind of assumed that you two would have something between you before the summer is over much earlier. Like, the first indicator was when you pulled your head out of your writing, and opened your eyes up to the world around you. Then, when you were being a teammate with him for this Fest thing, then, the biggest of all. You rode in a vehicle with him. I'm always a little bit skeptical when it comes to people, and while I couldn't find anything to dislike with Johnny, I was still cautious. I felt completely safe with you being gone with him all of the time after I saw you with him, in his truck."

I nod, and Mom reaches out.

Without messing up my hair, she pulls me into a hug.

"Have fun, Laelia. I've seen you change so much this summer, and I want you to know that I'm so proud of you. Seeing you be this adventurous has been beautiful, and has made me want to do the same. I've seen so much growth in you—your father has, too— and we want you to know. Let's go outside and show your dad and brothers how beautiful you are."

Mom rushes ahead of me, and a small tear pricks at the corner of my eye. I brush it away and smile, walking out the door to see my family and Johnny, all waiting.

I feel slightly awkward with so many eyes on me, but instead of focusing on that, I focus on how much I care for everyone here.

Johnny's eyes have a special twinkle to them, and his full smile is one that I've memorized by now.

The next ten minutes is a blur, with Mom taking pictures of Johnny and I, his arm wrapped around my waist.

Dad and the twins telling me I look beautiful, and Mom's peck on the cheek before we make the extra-short drive to Johnny's house.

"My mom would like to take some pictures of us together." He explains, opening my door for me and helping me down.

"Sounds good." I say.

Within a few more minutes, we're making the drive to the dance.

Rory and all of the staff have converted the area designated for picnics into a dance floor, with hundreds of small lights twinkling in the large trees, and a few tables for snacks and drinks.

There's even a booth for a DJ, and I have to say I'm more than impressed.

Already, there's music playing, and a few couples and friend groups are dancing.

The evening is late enough that a few stars are visible, and the temperature has cooled enough that there's small chills running up my exposed arms.

Johnny and I hang near the edge of the crowds for the first part of the dance, but after a few more songs, Johnny asks if I want to dance.

It's fun, but most of the music is party music, and less *dance* music, which a lot of other people seem to enjoy.

One slow song comes on, and under the twinkling stars— which are out and shining brightly—and the soft lights that the trees are housing, Johnny and I dance.

Johnny lowers his head far enough that his lips can press against the bare skin between my shoulder and neck, sending goosebumps across my neck.

The song ends, and another upbeat one replaces it.

Without hesitation, I turn my head, whispering in Johnny's ear.

"Do you want to watch the stars?" I ask, knowing he'll say yes.

"Sure. Where do you want to go?"

I pull him off of the dance floor, feeling both spontaneous and brave.

"Hey! Before you two leave, can I talk to you for a moment?" Janelle calls from behind us as we walk back to Johnny's truck.

We both turn, and Janelle takes a few more steps before stopping.

Her short hair is curled, and her outfit consists of jean shorts and a sleeveless top.

"Hi, my grandma—Rory—wanted me to let y'all know that you're the winners of our Teen Summer Fest. She saw you leaving, but didn't want you to miss the announcement. We'll have your TSF sweatshirts for you tomorrow in the gift shop, as well as your coupons for your next visit. Thank you both so much for enjoying these games and for being one of the best teams. Have a good night, and please don't forget to pick up your prizes tomorrow." I glance up at Johnny's smile, seeing that it mirrors mine.

"Thank you, Janelle. Please let Rory know that we're so

appreciative of all that she—and you—has done this summer." I say, squeezing Johnny's hand and giving a small wave to Janelle as she nods and turns back to help monitor the dance.

"Wow." Is all Johnny says before leaning down and pressing a light kiss on my lips. Once we're inside Johnny's truck, I realize I have no clue where we're going to watch the stars.

"Do you you know of any good places to stargaze?" I ask, turning to Johnny.

"We can drive to one of the lookout points. It's maybe ten miles down the road. It's kind of near the edge of the mountain, but we'll be fine." He says.

"Take us there." I say.

We drive in silence, but it's not uncomfortable.

Johnny drives slowly, and as we slow and pull into the gravel, makeshift parking lot, I gasp.

"Oh my gosh, this is so pretty." I say, opening the door and stepping out as soon as the truck is parked. "It is. I've only been here a handful of times, but it never disappoints me." Johnny replies from a few feet behind me.

We sit on one of the benches, overlooking the edge of the somewhat terrifying edge.

Johnny wraps his arm around my shoulder, and we talk about minor things and watch the stars.

"Hey, there's a shooting star!" I exclaim, pointing at the now-passed star. It may be childish, but I make a wish on the fallen star.

"Did you make a wish?" Johnny whispers in my ear, causing the hair on my neck to stand and goosebumps to raise.

"Yes. Do you think that's silly?" I ask, turning to face him.

He shakes his head no.

"Not at all. I *do* think it would be silly if you didn't tell me what it was, though." Johnny says with a soft chuckle.

"But then it won't come true." I chide, tapping his nose as though he's a child.

"Maybe you're right." He agrees.

Ten more minutes pass by, neither of us speaking, just simply enjoying each other's company.

More and more clouds roll in, and soon enough the stars are invisible.

"This could be bad." Johnny mentions, standing to do a three-sixty of the sky, seeing not a star in sight.

We should be getting back." Johnny says, just before a downpour starts.

I giggle, grabbing his hand and pulling him far away from the edge.

He's confused for only a second before he dances with me.

We're both drenched before we decide to find shelter, also known as his truck.

Johnny passes me a blanket from the back seat, and I wrap it around myself before I sit, pulling my knees to my chest.

"Can you drive in this?" I ask, not pulling my eyes from the windshield that allows me to see the lightning that flashes over the valley ahead of us.

"Yes. I wouldn't say it's ideal, but I can."

"Why don't we just wait, then? We can watch the lightning and wait until the storm calms a little bit. That way it's just a little bit safer." I reply, glancing over at his features that are illuminated from the lightning ahead.

It's essentially pitch black outside, and the rain is pattering on the roof.

"If you're okay with it, I don't mind." Johnny replies, wrapping himself tighter in his blanket.

"We haven't talked about what we will be after we leave here." Johnny says, and I can hear him shift, facing me.

"We haven't." I reply, taking a deep breath in.

"I want you to know that I *really* like you, Laelia. A lot. I don't want to lose you just because of some distance. I think we would be crazy to lose our relationship over that." Johnny says, sincerity in his voice.

"I really like you, too, Johnny. A lot. In fact I would say that it's scary how much I like you. I just don't know how far liking each other goes. Will that be strong enough?" I ask, taking another breath.

"I don't think it's about liking anymore. I think we just have to choose to make it work. Just like we've chosen to stay teammates throughout all of this. We can think of each other as teammates from now on. Only we're not against other people, just ourselves. We can choose to stay together and work together until we reach the finish line. Whatever that is."

A small tear slides down my cheek, and I brush it away.

"Are you sure? Do you *want* to be tied to someone that is usually across the country from you? Am I worth that much to you?"

"Absolutely." He answers with no hesitation, and I smile.

"What if I'm in New York and you're in California? Or I'm in Florida and you're in Alaska?" I ask, fear creeping into my voice.

"Laelia, I'll follow you anywhere."

"Anywhere?"

"Everywhere."

Epilogue

"Are you sure this is the right way?" I ask, slipping on a stone as we cross the small river.

The Montana sky reaches for miles above us, and the birds in the trees around us sing.

"Of course. Last time we were here, you asked me that same question." Johnny teases, reaching back and allowing me to grab his hand.

I take it, stepping on dry ground on the other side of the river.

I smile at the memory, it flashing through my mind. Even though it's been more than five years since we've been here, the memory is still fresh.

We'd spent one more summer doing TSF, but both of us had aged out, and our parents wanted to explore a more northern region for the summer.

I'd been eighteen at the time, Johnny twenty, as we'd explored the mountains. We'd hiked all of the way to the end of the trail, landing us at some cliff, near the top.

Now, here we are five years later, trying to find the same place.

A few more hours of hiking continue before we stop at the bluff, it looking almost identical to our previous visit.

The cool air blows across my face as I step close to the edge, peering at the river and trees below us.

"Hey, look at that eagle!" I say, turning to point Johnny in the direction of it.

Only, instead of seeing him looking over my shoulder, he's on one knee.

I gasp, and stumble slightly.

"Please don't fall off the cliff before I can ask you to marry me." Johnny teases, looking more than a little bit concerned at the near proximity between me and the edge.

"Yes." I say, answering his question before he can even ask.

"Yes? I didn't even get to ask the question." Johnny says, his wide smile reaching his eyes. The corners of them crinkle, and I feel my own smile stretching across my face.

"You don't need to. I already know my answer." I say, taking a step closer to him, reaching down and cupping his face.

I bring my lips to his, bringing them together.

He stands, sliding the ring on my finger, our lips never breaking contact.

Review!

*If you enjoyed Anywhere, Everywhere, let others know!
I would love it if you shared a review or your thoughts on the
platform(s) where you purchased Anywhere, Everywhere, social media, or even with your friends and family!*

Stay Connected!

*I hope you enjoyed Anywhere, Everywhere!
If you haven't already, follow me on social media and sign up for my
newsletter, ensuring you never miss an update on my books.*

Author Jenevieve Hernandez

Acknowledgements

I've had so much love and support during the writing and publication of this book, and I can't thank my family enough.
My parents listened to me as I discussed plot, publishing, and everything in between, and it genuinely made such an impact on the shaping of this book.
They've supported me every step of the way, and I'm eternally grateful for them during this process.

I've received so much excitement for Anywhere, Everywhere (much more than I expected!), and it truly means so much. This is my first published book, and it feels so unreal that it's actually in your (reader) hands. Thank you for taking a chance and picking up my book. I'm so thankful for you!

Last, and most definitely not least, I thank God for gifting me with the talent of storytelling, and being able to craft these books. He has blessed me beyond measure, and never fails me.

About the Author

Jenevieve Hernandez is the author of sweet and swoony romances, filled to the brim with the feeling of falling in love. She loves portraying character growth, unique plots, and, of course, romance in her books. Her books will never contain any explicit content, and are always guaranteed happily ever afters.
She enjoys spending her time in the pages of books, traveling from one story to the next, or outdoors, exploring the world around her.